Margareta Osborn is a fifth-generation farmer who has lived and worked on the land all her life. She also writes about it in the *Gippsland County Life* magazine.

Home is the beautiful Macalister Valley of East Gippsland in Victoria, where, along with her husband and three children, she spends many hours in the mountains that form the backdrop of her novels.

Bella's Run, her first novel, was a bestseller on its first release in March 2012. Her new novel, *Hope's Road*, is available now, as is her hilarious festive novella, *A Bush Christmas* (available as ebook only).

Visit www.margaretaosborn.com

Praise for *Bella's Run*

'A real tonic' *Country Style*

'An intoxicating outback romance' *Border Mail*

'A fun read' *Australian Bookseller & Publisher*

'Osborn's characters and dialogue stand out for their realism …
most enjoyable' *The Age*

'A delightful romantic novel sprinkled with our Australian sense
of humour. It is just the thing to curl up with on the weekend'
Toowoomba Chronicle

'Fun, love, adventure and tragedy are woven into this Aussie
rural romance . . . Amid a spate of rural romances, this stands
out from the pack. The characters are true to life and the
storyline engaging' *Take 5*

Bella's Run

MARGARETA OSBORN

BANTAM BOOKS
SYDNEY • AUCKLAND • TORONTO • NEW YORK • LONDON

A Bantam book
Published by Random House Australia Pty Ltd
Level 3, 100 Pacific Highway, North Sydney NSW 2060
www.randomhouse.com.au

First published by Bantam in 2012
This edition published by Bantam in 2013

Addresses for companies within the Random House Group can be found at
www.randomhouse.com.au/offices

National Library of Australia
Cataloguing-in-Publication entry

Osborn, Margareta.
Bella's run/Margareta Osborn.

ISBN 978 1 74275 896 1 (pbk.)

A823.4

Cover photographs: cowgirl © Stockbyte/Getty Images; cowboy © Henry Arden/Getty
Images
Cover design by Christabella Designs
Internal design by Midland Typesetters, Australia
Typeset in Adobe Garamond 13/17pt by Midland Typesetters, Australia
Printed in Australia by Griffin Press, an accredited ISO AS/NZS 14001:2004
Environmental Management System printer

Random House Australia uses papers that are natural, renewable and recyclable products
and made from wood grown in sustainable forests. The logging and manufacturing
processes are expected to conform to the environmental regulations of the country of
origin.

In loving memory of the three women
who have helped shape my life:

my mother, Ellen Osborn (1939–98),
who always encouraged me to throw my hat into the ring;

my grandmother, Margareta Osborn (1910–2006),
our refuge and safe harbour;

my aunt, Elizabeth Shepard (1941–2011),
for showing me what guts and determination are all about;

and

for my dearly loved father, John Osborn,
who believes in me.

Prologue

Every ounce of the thirty-tonne semi-trailer bore down on the ute, caught like a startled rabbit in the fog lights of the B-Double.

On impact the ute disintegrated, the shriek of tearing metal, breaking glass and screeching air brakes shattering the peace of the surrounding valley. One sound cut through the rest, reverberating across the wide, open paddocks sprawled beyond the mist.

The piercing screams of the dying.

Filled to the brim with grain, the semi rested against the broken boundary fence, its driver slumped over the steering wheel. His shocked gaze took in the devastation ahead of him.

On the far side of the bitumen road lay two bodies. The first, splayed at an unnatural angle, and unrecognisable as either man or woman, did not move from the white line on which it lay.

The other, some 5 yards on, was female. Her chest moved spasmodically underneath a shirt patterned with splashes of brilliant red. The woman's denim jeans were already black with blood, and only one of her feet was visible, clad in a brown leather elastic-sided riding boot, surprisingly intact.

White-gold, curly hair lay tangled across her blood-smeared face, which minutes before had been wreathed in smiles of happiness, laughter and love.

PART ONE

Ainsley Station
Outback Central Queensland

Chapter 1

Sunlight shone through the glistening soap bubbles in the sink, turning the suds a rainbow of colours. They were far too pretty to be found in spartan stockmen's quarters on a remote and rugged cattle station in Central Queensland.

Peering through the grimy aluminium window, Isabella Vermaelon sighed at the glorious scene outside. It was so hard to stay in this dreary 1970s Formica kitchen cooking. She wanted to be out there in the sun, galloping across the open plains with the stockmen or mustering cattle hidden in the Brigalow and Blackbutt scrub.

The stock camp had been short of a ringer this morning, and someone would've loaned Bella a spare plant horse. After all, she could ride and muster stock. The only thing she couldn't get a grip on, here on Ainsley Station, was lacing rather than buckling a damned girth. Her best mate Patty, on the other hand, was a natural, so *she* was the one now out mustering cattle for the feedlot, the breeze riffling through her auburn hair and sunlight streaming onto her tanned face.

She was right where Bella wanted to be, ducking and weaving her horse across this remote landscape with its miles and miles of red soil scattered with stands of yapunyah trees and sally wattle bowing and twisting under a sweltering sun. Bella could almost smell the earthy stench of hot cattle, the eucalyptus scent of the scrub; feel the flying insects dive-bombing her face.

'Can you thread this up for me?'

Bella jumped, startled by a broad-shouldered, ruddy-faced stockman who was peering around the kitchen door. Wearing tiny half-moon spectacles, he looked fifty rather than twenty-eight.

'Jeez, Rodney! Didn't anyone teach you to knock? You scared the crap out of me.'

Rodney ignored her, focusing instead on what he held in his big hands. 'I can't see the damned eye in this needle for looking at it.'

Bella moved to the door and glanced over Rodney's shoulder into the stockmen's dining room. A torn chambray work shirt lay on the table, sporting a rip that looked terminal. 'Do you really want to have a go at mending that? There's a bin in the corner.'

'Nope, it'll be right. Just use those pretty green eyes of yours to thread this needle, ay.'

Bella's eyes were blue. A brilliant lapis-blue actually. And her halo of long, white-gold curls, a legacy from her mother, made the colour of her eyes stand out like the sun appearing on a foggy day. She smiled to herself as she took the needle, threaded it and shooed Rodney out the door. Bloody Queensland blokes were as stubborn as the men back home in Victoria.

Bella heaved a sigh and returned to what she was supposed to be doing.

Trying to make a sixteen-egg pavlova using one Mixmaster probably wasn't the cleverest thing she had ever done. Then again, browning eight kilos of beef mince using two small frypans was pretty silly too; but the frypans were all she'd been able to find, and they were making the cooking of her mother's famous spaghetti bolognaise excruciating.

She had missed her family dreadfully this past year, especially her mother. They'd all been supportive when she had taken twelve months' leave from her job at the Department of Agriculture and convinced Patty to put her nursing career on hold to head off on this road trip. After drinking and partying their first few weeks up the Kidman Way and over the border into Queensland, they'd scored a couple of jobs on Johanna Downs, a small cattle station by Queensland standards, owned by an elderly couple, Stan and Betty Johnson. There, under the tutelage of Stan and his old stockman, Harry Bailey, they'd learned all about being a ringer – mustering cattle day after day, working horses, helping with fencing, fixing windmills and pumps. They'd loved every minute of it.

Unfortunately, after only six months the Johnsons had sold their property to the owners of neighbouring Ainsley Station, which had absorbed the smaller place. Stan had negotiated for them to be taken on by the new owners, but there had been only one ringer's position and Bella had lucked out. So now her regular job on Ainsley was to mow the acres of lawns, and care for the island gardens scattered around the buildings on the cattle property.

But not a cook. *Never* a cook.

This whole kitchen job stank of her boss, Siobhan Davidson's petty mindedness. The station manager's wife had taken a dislike to Bella soon after they arrived. Patty reckoned Siobhan had Bella pegged as trouble, which was weird since Patty usually held *that* title. What sort of trouble Bella had no idea, but if she'd known she would definitely have caused it. She couldn't stand people stomping on her for no good reason.

This weekend, Siobhan had worked it so Bella was the relief cook, which meant she exchanged her Akubra hat, sunshine and mower for an oven, Mixmaster and an apron with pink tits on it. Jimbo, the usual cook, had a lot to answer for in his choice of kitchen attire. What was Siobhan – who was supposed to relieve her own staff – doing?

Shopping, that's what.

All in all, life on Ainsley sucked for Bella. The question was, what to do about it. Maybe it was time to ditch this job and head down south, back home to the blue-grey mountains of Victoria. Or find another joint like Johanna Downs. A station on which she could ride a horse, muster cattle – be a jillaroo again. A place where she *didn't have to cook.*

Cursing, Bella stomped into the cool room to hunt up some more ingredients. A door on the far insulated wall was suddenly reefed open and a voice bellowed from the butchering space beyond. 'Come out, you little brats. I know you're hiding in there somewhere!' Knackers Anderson, Ainsley Station's head stockman, shoved aside a hanging beef carcass and walked into the cool room, coming face to face with Bella.

'Only me here, Knackers.' Bella blushed, her gaze straying to his groin. She wished the man wouldn't wear his beige cowboy jeans so tight. They gave a whole new meaning to a snug fit. Bella forced her eyes back up to his florid face. He was breathing hard and fast, and she could hear the air whistling through the holes in his teeth.

'Those kids of mine have disappeared. Supposed to be loading the sausage skins but they've pissed off.'

A rumble on the roof caused both Knackers and Bella to look skywards. The rumble turned into skittering, the sounds of sliding bums and scrabbling feet on burning corrugated iron, raucous laughter then a thud and a yell came from outside the butcher-room door.

The boys had landed.

'There they are, the little bastards.' Knackers smacked the beef carcass aside and stormed out. A steer's tail swung haphazardly catching Bella across the nose and mouth. She spluttered and snorted. The coarse hairs tasted vile. The stink of cow shit was rank.

Bloody Knackers. The man caused mayhem wherever he went. The stumpy, barrel-chested head stockman was outgoing and loud. His wife Wendy, a big woman who worked in the office at the feedlot, was quiet. Limp. Like the marrow had been sucked from her bones, her muscles sapped by the harsh outback surroundings in which she lived.

The Andersons' marriage was a mystery to Bella. There were no obvious signs of love between the couple. Not a peck on the cheek, a cuddle or a caring hand. Last week Wendy had told an incredulous Bella that in all their fifteen years of marriage, Knackers had never taken her and their sons home to see her family in New South Wales.

'But why don't *you* just go?' Bella had asked. 'Pack up the kids and head down to Parkes on your own.' Biting her tongue, she stopped. Two days in the car with those four little ferals would be enough to get anyone committed to an asylum. 'On second thoughts, leave the kids with Knackers and go by yourself.'

'I haven't been past Rockhampton since we married. Don't think I could manage going to Parkes on my own. I've lost me confidence, you know, with the kids and all.'

Bella was dumbfounded. Kids did that to you? How could you lose your confidence *that* much? Rockhampton was only a few hours away, and a woman had to have a life. After all, that's what she and Patty were doing – they'd loaded Patty's ute and set off on this adventure up north for a year, just for something to do! Two thousand kilometres and eight months later, here they were.

'Hells Bells! Where are you?' called a light-hearted female voice.

Bella turned and walked back into the kitchen.

Patricia O'Hara swung from the sink grinning, a glass of water in hand. Her toffee-coloured eyes peered at Bella through multiple layers of dirt. 'I'm bloody starving. Is there anything to eat, chef?'

'I'll give you bloody starving. Siobhan can stick her kitchen right where it fits. Look at that glorious day out there. You can cook next time. *I'm* going mustering!' Bella stopped and studied her mate. 'What on earth happened to your hair?' Dried mud hung in clumps from Patty's head like badly made Christmas decorations.

Patty tried to run her fingers through her short hair and failed. 'Came off my horse. Bloody thing bucked me into the river when a weaner went straight under its belly. Boys thought it was a hell of a joke. Me wallowing in mud, the weaner sticking its head out from under the horse's tail looking for a hairy escape.' Patty grinned and deep-set dimples, one on either side of her mouth, winked. She went to jump up onto the kitchen bench, and Bella caught her grimace of pain.

'Are you okay? Did you hurt anything?'

'Nah, just my pride. And a few bruises.' Patty smiled as she stretched out sideways to drag a cake tin along the bench, but to Bella, her mate's usual rude aura of earthy vitality seemed slightly dented.

Patty tugged impatiently at the stubborn lid of the cake tin. 'At least you can cook. I'd be crap 'cause I'd burn everything. Is there anything to eat in here, cookie?'

Patty was still winding her up, so things couldn't be too crook. But then again Bella knew her best mate couldn't help herself. Being a relentless tease was one of the reasons why Patty was so much fun to hang out with. Many times over the years Bella had wished she could be like Patty, the life of every party, reeling in the boys with all the dexterity of a fly fisherman. Bella gave a rueful smile. Wishes were for dreamers. And Bella really didn't do too badly with the boys, just by being herself.

Having finally prised the stubborn lid off the cake tin, Patty pulled out a chocolate lamington and set about demolishing it. Her dirty face relaxed into soft lines and she let out a gentle sigh of contentment as she chewed.

Finishing her last mouthful, Patty reached back into the tin to grab the remaining cake. 'Maybe Siobhan hates you for talking those feedlot boys into moving your mulch with the front-end loader the other week.'

'I had to get the job done!' Bella was indignant. So what if she'd wiggled her arse, undone a few press studs on her well-stacked shirt and sweet-talked the boys into helping her? 'The loader got the job done a hell of a lot quicker than the damned shovel Siobhan wanted me to use.'

Unfortunately, she'd mistimed her little plan. The feedlot manager, Jack McLaverty, decided to do a snap site inspection and found the two blokes and a loader missing; a loader that was supposed to be pushing up piles of grain for the feedlot. Twenty tonnes of machinery wasn't hard to find. The tongue-lashing Bella got from Siobhan later in the afternoon hadn't been pleasant. Siobhan took great delight in ticking her off and Bella had walked right into her manipulative hands.

'No. Taking off with the loader just added to it. She hated me before that. I just don't know why.'

She leaned forward and snatched the lamington from Patty's hand, leaving her friend blinking in dismay. Bella sank her teeth into the cake, allowing her tastebuds to savour the comforting chocolate. She sighed with pleasure. Siobhan's doughy, spiteful face disappeared and visions of her family farm at Narree flitted into her mind – the delicious aromas of her mother's kitchen, her father's tawny port, the smell of the mountains heavy with rain.

Bella looked sideways at Patty, who was staring hard at her, considering. 'What?' she asked smiling, thinking she was about to get a razz for snatching the lamington.

Patty didn't say anything, just dragged over a fruit basket and grabbed an apple. Looking at it in disgust, she took a bite before moving her eyes back to her friend. 'Bella,' she said with her mouth full, 'you really should take a look in the mirror. I reckon it's not what you've *done* to Ms Davidson that's the problem.'

Bella blushed. Patty turned her attention back to eating her apple, while sneaking out a hand to crank up the Mixmaster to maximum speed. She grinned wickedly at Bella as blobs of egg white were flung from the mixing bowl, sailing up to hang off the ceiling. Bella swore at her friend as she lunged to turn down the beaters. Now she'd have to clean that mess up too, damn it.

Swinging around, Patty aimed her apple at the garbage bin, 'I wouldn't worry about it, Hells Bells.' The core hit the back of the bin like a basketball on a backboard before dropping down. Patty grunted in satisfaction. 'After all, the worst thing she can do is sack us.'

She sounded almost cheerful about it, which surprised Bella. She'd thought her mate was happy here on Ainsley, but the look on Patty's freckled face suggested otherwise. The toffee-brown O'Hara eyes seemed to lose focus for a minute, seeing something far removed from this austere kitchen in the remote Queensland outback, which led Bella to wonder if maybe she wasn't the only one filled with a quiet longing for home.

Chapter 2

The two-way radio, sitting on a shelf near the dining-room door, crackled to life.

'Anyone on Ainsley Station? Ainsley Station! Are you there? This is Red Eye. Over.'

'Red Eye?' said Bella, looking at Patty.

'He's one of the grain-truck drivers, supplying the feedlot. You know the dude with the red glass eye and the bung leg?'

Bella looked puzzled.

'The one with the fake leg from the station party last Friday night?' prompted Patty.

Bella vaguely recalled a nuggety bloke doing a boozy rendition of 'Jake the Peg' as he swung his fake leg from his crotch; a glass eye sloshing around in a pannikin of rum and coke.

The call on the radio came again, this time more urgent.

'Anyone on Ainsley Station? Come in, damn you, this is Red Eye! Over.'

There was a pause then 'For cripe's sake . . . SOMEONE COME IN!'

The radio was a party-line, with all the houses, vehicles and most buildings on the station having a UHF. No-one else was answering today.

Bella leaped towards the Mixmaster to shut it off, as Patty strode across the kitchen and reached for the handset. 'Yeah, Red Eye, this is Patty at the stockmen's quarters. What's up? Over.'

'Thank Christ!' Red Eye responded. 'Call a bloody ambulance. I've run two kids on a four-wheel motorbike off the road. They're in a big empty irrigation channel and I can't see anyone moving.' The voice quavered among the transmission crackle. 'I didn't see the little sods coming round the corner! Oh, hang on!' The radio went silent for a minute. 'One's climbing out now. No-one else's coming up the bank and there were two kids on the bike. Bloody hell! Call the ambo!'

Bella already had hold of the phone. She dialled 000, filled them in on the details and agreed that if they could move the child they'd meet the ambulance halfway to town.

Meanwhile, Knackers appeared at the cool-room door. 'Did Red Eye just say kids?'

'Yeah,' said Patty as she swung to turn off the stove.

'Oh fuck!' Knackers' florid face drained to white. 'They're probably mine. A couple of them took off on the motorbike.'

Two remaining little dark heads appeared from the side of his blood-stained arms. 'We didn't do it, Dad! Whatever it was, we didn't do it!' But Knackers was already following Bella and Patty as they ran outside, Patty snatching a small first-aid kit as she went. Rodney followed from the dining room, leaving the two little boys staring at each other in confusion.

Bella flung herself into the driver's seat of a spare Land-Cruiser ute sitting idle outside the ring-lock fence surrounding the quarters. As she gunned the diesel engine, Knackers jumped into the passenger seat. Patty, Rodney and the first-aid kit went up onto the tray in the back.

Bella grabbed the UHF mike as she spun the vehicle out and away from the tight cluster of weatherboard buildings. 'Red Eye, this is Bella. We've called the ambo, and are now on our way to you. Where on the station are you? Over.' With Ainsley covering over forty thousand hectares, Bella needed some idea where the child was and she was approaching a T-intersection up ahead on the gravel track.

Knackers roared from the passenger seat. 'Go right, RIGHT!'

Bella swung the steering wheel, careering around the corner on two wheels, the back of the ute fishtailing on the stones.

'They'll be somewhere in the cropping area. That's where the irrigation channels are,' yelled Knackers, clutching the Jesus bar – a grab rail – on the dash in front of him. 'He'll be tangled up in some of those fuckin' siphon hoses, I'll bet. Bloody farmers, should know better than putting fuckin' channels in the way of me kids' motorbike.'

Bella held her tongue. She'd come to understand that up here in northern Australia farmers worked the dirt and stockmen worked the cattle, with plenty of rivalry between the two. At the moment, however, the siphon hoses and farmers were the least of their worries.

The radio crackled again. 'Red Eye to Bella. We're ten metres from the northern machinery shed – on a track running east–west. The kid's not moving. His colour's not good.'

Bella peered intently through the ute's windscreen. She could just make out the machinery shed towering in the haze out to her left. A sudden thump on the roof had her winding her window down, and Patty shoved a finger out in front of her. 'I can see the truck over there. Turn left here and then head straight down past that sorghum crop to the next intersecting channel and I reckon we'll be right on them.'

Bella swung the steering wheel left, and drove on until she saw a truck pulled up some twenty metres down the track, angled across the road, which was laced with skid marks. Slamming on the brakes, she brought the ute to a stop right beside a main delivery channel.

Amid a cloud of flying dust, a HiLux pulled up from the opposite direction. Wendy Anderson spilled from the passenger door. Running towards the channel where the motorbike's skid marks disappeared over the side, she went sliding down on her bum, to a man huddled over a little body at the bottom. Her cries of horror echoed up the channel walls.

Knackers sped past Bella, the next to skid down the bank after his wife.

Sheila McLaverty, the feedlot manager's wife, got out of the driver's side of Wendy's HiLux. Dragging an impressive-looking first-aid case and a spinal board from the tray of the ute, she yelled, 'Heard the call over the radio. Wendy and I were having a cuppa.'

Sheila, just like Patty, was a trained nurse. One-time registered, Sheila was retired now, and was designated station medic. Patty dropped her smaller first-aid kit into the dust and went with Rodney to help Sheila manoevre the case into the channel. Bella hesitated on the bank, and looked down at the scene in front of her.

The child lay face up; near a motorbike that was on its side partially buried in the red dirt. Except it wasn't buried at all.

The right side of the bike had actually been pushed in on itself by the force of the fall. The kids must have been fairly flying to cause that kind of damage.

Her gaze swung to Red Eye, kneeling in the dust a little way from the small, inert body. The poor man was a mess. A Vietnam veteran, she remembered. Holding his head in his hands, shoulders shaking, she could hear him talking to himself as he rocked to and fro. 'I didn't see them. They were going so fast. I've killed the poor little sod.'

Wendy started to wail, 'Max, oh my Max.'

Bella stirred herself, sliding down the bank and in beside Wendy. The woman was leaning over trying to pick her unconscious son up around the shoulders and draw him to her breast.

Grabbing Wendy's hands, Bella said, 'No, stop! He might have spinal injuries. We can't move him yet.'

Wendy ignored her. 'My boy. Oh my boy.'

Bella forcefully jostled her backwards out of the way of the two nurses. A glance at the boy and the other women had told Bella enough. Although there was no obvious blood, he was breathing quickly, lips slightly blue, and Sheila and Patty were unable to raise a response. Both nurses looked worried.

In her peripheral vision, Bella could see Knackers watching stunned. The only part of him moving was his hands as they pulled and worried the felt hat he was holding. She wished to hell he'd come over and comfort his wife, but he just stood staring. Rodney was beside him, awkwardly patting his shoulder.

Sheila spoke up. 'Bella, jump on the radio, honey, and find out where that ambulance is. Rodney, Knackers, come here and let's put the little bloke onto the spinal board.' Sheila's steady voice galvanised everyone into action.

Bella left Wendy and scrambled up the bank of the channel to use the radio. 'Ambulance travelling to Ainsley Station, this is Ainsley Station, do you copy? Over.'

'Ainsley Station, this is the ambulance responding to your emergency call. We are approximately half an hour from your front gate. Is the patient conscious and able to be moved? Over.'

Bella called down the bank to Sheila. 'They're about half an hour away from the main gate. They want to know if he's conscious and if we can move him?'

'Yes, we can move him. Tell them he's unconscious, not breathing too well and on a spinal board. We'll meet them somewhere on the road. Tell them to look out for the HiLux.'

While Bella lay across the ute seat relaying the message to the ambulance, a little dark head pushed into her crotch. When she finished on the radio, a husky voice said, 'Me brother, miss, Max . . . is . . . is . . . is he gunna be or . . . orright?' A grubby hand came up to wipe snot from a face with beseeching hazel eyes. Bella was at a loss at what to say. She wiggled her way upright, hauled the kid out of her lap and onto the ute floor beside her.

'Rohan, isn't it?' The dark head nodded. 'Well, mate, I'm not sure, but I *can* tell you everyone's doing all they can to get Max to hospital and get him fixed.' Bella crossed her toes inside her work boots, hoping she wasn't lying. Max sure didn't look good.

Rohan brought an arm up to swipe at more snot running from his nose. 'We were riding flat-out, didn't want Dad to get us. We didn't look before we turned the corner. We saw the truck. Maxy headed for the drain. I told him to jump off; I told 'im, miss. But he didn't jump when I did. Me little brother, he didn't bloody jump.'

With a hiccup he hung his head and cried. Loud, gasping, little-boy sobs.

Bella put her arm around him, cuddled him into her side and blinked really hard. She was supposed to be the grown-up here. She would *not* cry.

At the sound of scrabbling rocks Bella shifted Rohan to one side and jumped to her feet. Knackers hit the top of the bank; little Max was laid out on the board behind him.

'Go easy, ya bastard!' Knackers roared at poor Rodney, who was jostling the other end, trying to fumble his way up the gravel and over the edge.

Sheila, coming up on the outside of Knackers, placed a soothing hand on Knackers' arm. 'Easy, big fella.'

Knackers just shook his head, a run of tears falling from his face, and strode towards the HiLux, towing his son and Rodney along behind. Gently placing the spinal board on the back of the ute, he jumped up and moved forward beside his son's head while Rodney slid the rest of the board onto the tray.

'Rodney, you drive; I'll sit in the back with Knackers and Max.' Sheila pushed Wendy towards the passenger door. 'Wendy, you jump in with Rodney.'

'But . . . but . . . Max needs me,' Wendy quavered.

'No buts, Wendy,' Sheila instructed. 'If he needs you, I'll bang on the roof. We can stop. Now get *in*. We have to go.' Sheila then turned to Bella and Patty. 'Can you head back to the quarters, girls, and I'll radio you if we need a relay to the ambo? The aerial on this ute looks like it's taken a few pot shots while the boys have been out pig- shooting.' They all turned towards the aerial. It dangled at half-mast.

Sheila went on, 'Take Rohan with you and ring Mrs Cunningham, the school-teacher's wife. She'll take care of the other Anderson kids until we get back. Okay?'

Bella and Patty nodded.

Rohan just stared up at them, dazed. Sheila took in the expression on the child's face and stooped to peer intently into his round eyes. 'On second thoughts, mister, you'd better come with us too.' She pushed him towards the cab door. 'He's probably got concussion, looking at those dilated pupils.'

A door slammed behind Rohan as he hustled into the ute.

'Righto, we're off. I'll radio or ring you. Thanks for your help, girls.'

Sheila jumped up beside Max and banged on the roof. Rodney slowly took off. Bella and Patty, hands to their brows, watched the vehicle's progress through the maze of tracks that cross-sectioned the Ainsley River flats, until the ute finally turned onto the main track leading to the station's front gate.

A noise behind reminded them there was one more casualty in this accident. Red Eye had arrived at the top of the channel bank, both eyes now living up to his nickname. Bella jogged towards him. 'Hey, Red Eye, you probably should have gone to the hospital and got checked out too. Are you okay?'

'Yeah, mate, I guess so. Just can't stop seeing it all happen again and again before me eyes. Think I'll just drive me truck home and have a lie down.'

Patty spoke up. 'You sure you should be driving the truck in your state? I can have a go at it for you. Me or Bella . . .?'

Red Eye pulled himself up to his full five-foot-five and pointed a hairy finger in Patty's direction. 'You don't think I'm letting a *Victorian* behind the wheel of my baby.' The girls laughed tentatively, not sure if he was joking. Somehow Bella didn't think so.

'You think he'll be all right?' she asked as Red Eye stomped away.

Patty shrugged a shoulder. 'Don't know. Just adds another nightmare to those he's got from Vietnam.'

Both girls watched the man shuffle to his baby, a cab over Kenworth. The door slammed and the big rig rumbled to a start. As it moved off, an arm appeared from the window in a half-hearted wave. An arm still visibly shaking.

Bella and Patty picked up the abandoned first-aid kits, loaded them onto the LandCruiser tray and then jumped into the ute, Bella taking the wheel. Slowly they meandered the vehicle through the sorghum and onto the main station track.

Patty spoke up first. 'You *did* ask what else was going to go wrong this arvie. You tempted fate, girl.'

Bella didn't answer. She was still reeling from the afternoon's events, replaying them in her mind. That poor kid. She hoped he was going to be all right. And what about Knackers and Wendy? What was this going to do to them?

'So, what's for tea now, cookie?' Patty stirred again.

Before Bella could think of a smart reply, the radio crackled on the dash between them.

'Bella? Patty? Come in, it's Rodney.'

'Oh hell, what's happened now?' Patty grabbed the mike. 'Yeah, Rodney, we're here.'

Rodney's panicked voice came from the radio. 'Turn around and head back to us, will you? The kid's having some sort of turn and we need . . . what was it, Sheila?' They could hear Sheila yell something before he said, 'Yeah . . . we need a can . . . a cana . . . a *what*?'

More yelling.

Sheila to Rodney.

Rodney to Sheila.

20

'A cannula, an IV cannula from the first-aid case you've got – and we need Patty.'

More asides to Sheila then Rodney spoke again. 'A cannula or a biro, Sheila's saying. I can't bloody find one.' Rodney's voice was rising. Desperate.

The girls could hear Wendy in the background screaming, and that was enough for Bella. Without checking the rear-vision mirror or bracing herself, she reefed on the handbrake. Patty threw the radio mike to the floor and grabbed the Jesus bar as the ute did an immediate 180-degree turn, front tyres pegged, back wheels sliding in an arc, throwing dust and stones in all directions.

It was a doughie that Bella knew her brother Justin would have been proud to see.

The ute came to a halt, now facing the way they'd come. Dust obscured everything in front of them. Patty expelled the breath she had been holding. Letting go of the grab bar, she slapped Bella on the arm. 'Woo hoo! Go, *girlfriend*!'

And so Bella did.

Right into the path of an oncoming ute.

Chapter 3

'Holy SHIT!'

Slamming on the brakes, Will O'Hara spun the steering wheel of his four-wheel drive to the left. His passenger, Drew 'Macca' McDonald, threw his arm across his face; a fat lot of good that was going to do, but Macca knew he didn't want to see what would happen next.

Will wrestled with the steering wheel and finally managed to bring the vehicle to a halt twenty yards from the track, thanking God he got off the gas early because he'd seen all the dust up ahead.

The other ute had already stopped.

A head covered with a bird's nest of blonde curls was thrust through the open driver's-side window glaring at the boys, gesticulating with her middle finger and swearing.

'You stupid bastards! You could have fucking killed us!' yelled Bella, forgetting *she* was the one who'd been stationary in the middle of the track. 'What the hell do you think you were—'

Bella stopped shouting mid-sentence, staring at the male honey of a face that was looking at her with amazement. A face she had known all her life but seemed to be seeing clearly for the first time. 'Oh my God . . . Patty . . . is that *Will* under that hat?'

'Yep. Sure is. I'd know my brother's dimples anywhere.' Patty leaned across Bella and yelled, 'Hey, bro. What the fuck are you doing here? Is that you, Macca? Bella, it's Macca.' Patty smacked Bella on the leg as Bella glanced at the passenger and realised it was her cousin. 'Sorry, fellas,' Patty continued. 'Love to chat but we've gotta go. An emergency.'

The radio beside the girls came to life again with Rodney's voice, hysteria threatening: 'For Christ's sake, girls, where are you? We really need that flaming cannula thing and we need it NOW!'

Bella snapped to attention, tearing her eyes away from the gorgeous features of the man she had run off the road. She needed to drive. And fast.

Patty called out to her brother as she pulled herself upright, 'Make yourselves useful, boys. Get in behind us.'

And with that, Bella took off in a hail of stones and fury. Again.

'Well,' said Macca when the air cleared, 'better do what the sweet lady asked and *make yourself useful, bro*.' The toothpick poking from the corner of Macca's mouth lifted as he smirked at his best mate.

'Yeah well, I suppose so,' replied Will. 'There's bound to be something worth seeing.' He spun the steering wheel, bumped the ute back onto the track and set off in the direction of the flying dust.

Bella and Patty could hear the commotion even before they saw the stationary ute. Wendy, standing in the middle of the road, was screaming at Knackers, who was trying to calm her down, his arms waving in futile placatory gestures.

'You selfish bastard!' Wendy slammed Knackers in the chest with her hands. 'How could you let this happen?'

Smack!

'How *could* you? He's not even five years old.'

Smack!

'It's your fault. ALL YOUR FAULT!'

Smack!

'I wanted to leave this God-forsaken place. Head home to civilisation. Bring the kids up proper. But no, you had to stay. You and your cattle. This bloody station miles from flaming nowhere. Our kids are ferals, Arthur, FERALS!'

The last came out as a wail as Wendy slid to the ground face-first.

Bella, who'd brought their vehicle to a halt, watched through the windscreen, transfixed by the scene of a marriage shattering before her eyes. And Knackers' real name was *Arthur?*

Out on the track, Knackers dropped to his knees and threw his arms around his wife, who'd curled herself almost into the foetal position. The man's expressions flitted from bewilderment to misery. Then desolation. The couple huddled in the dirt while their son fought for life on the back of the ute.

Patty whacked Bella's arm. 'Come on.'

Grabbing their hats, the girls jumped out of the ute. Patty raced towards Sheila and Rodney, who were up with Max.

'The cannula from the case, swabs . . . and gloves. Quickly!' Sheila yelled to Bella, who was still distracted by Knackers and Wendy.

Bella moved to the first-aid case, flung it open and grabbed what she guessed to be an IV cannula from its resting place snug against the lid. She snagged a few sterile swabs, stuffed rubber gloves into her pocket and then ran over to the group on the ute tray. Handing over her supplies to Patty, Bella saw first-hand the shocking deterioration of Max's condition. The child was turning blue, his breathing shallow and extraordinarily fast.

Patty slapped the cannula into Sheila's outstretched, shaking palm and then grabbed the boy's wrist. 'His pulse is weak and rapid, Sheila.'

'He's got a deviation of his trachea to the right side, so he's punctured his left lung. If we don't relieve the pressure he's going to die.' Sheila spoke quickly, hands moving to the middle of the boy's left clavicle and then down two intercostal spaces. She tapped a spot in between the second and third rib and held the cannula ready to insert. 'We need to pray like hell we hit the pleural cavity we need. And miss the heart.' She took a deep breath and pushed the cannula into the boy's side.

A small spurt of blood then air gushed from the needle end. 'We need a valve of some sort,' said Sheila, panicking.

Patty hesitated a moment, then grabbed her multi-purpose pocket knife from a pouch on her ringer's belt. She thumbed the scissors-release button, snatched up a rubber glove and cut off a finger. Snipping off the tip, Patty made a rubber sheath, which she then slipped over the end of the cannula. The rubber acted like a valve, air blowing out but not back in. The women looked at each other and then at the child. His colour was improving dramatically. Patty felt for his pulse.

It was slowing, but the boy wasn't showing any signs of regaining consciousness.

Patty and Sheila were doing what they could. Realising things were going pear-shaped, Bella moved out of their way to let them work, and headed back towards her ute. Rodney had jumped off the tray and was watching helplessly.

She swung her attention to the couple in the middle of the road. Knackers lay curled over his wife, shielding her, whispering into her ear. It was the first time Bella had ever seen them touch. Initially there appeared to be no response from Wendy, but then she heard a thin voice murmuring back.

They seemed to be communicating at least. Bella wondered why it took a disaster like this to get a couple talking, touching, loving. Things couldn't ever get that bad, could they? Would the Andersons be able to get through this, a couple who'd weathered fifteen years and borne four sons? Surely?

Surely.

There was movement in the dust, as Knackers picked Wendy up and turned her around. He lifted his wife's chin and stared into her eyes. And it was then that Bella saw it. She'd been looking in all the wrong places for evidence of the love Knackers had for his woman.

It was in his eyes.

They blazed down on his wife with such love and compassion, it moved Bella to tears. With sudden clarity she realised there was another language in life far beyond what she'd ever known. And she couldn't help but wonder if she would ever be lucky enough to experience it; to be looked upon as if she were the epicentre of the universe, to have all that love from a man, so pure and devout.

Bella heard the roar of double exhaust stacks and quickly wiped away the tears. Will and Macca pulled in behind her and came from their vehicle at a run.

'What's going on, Isabella?' Will asked, grabbing her elbow to catch her attention. His touch seemed to blast an electrical shock through her veins. Bella jerked her arm away, stung. Will looked discomforted, annoyed even.

Her skin tingled and her elbow burned where Will's fingers had touched. She looked up past the brim of her hat to where he was looking down at her and she suddenly forgot how to breathe.

He was totally gorgeous.

A loud curse came from the girls on the back of the ute.

Bella forced her mind back to Will's question. 'There was an accident. Motorbike went into a drain with two little boys on it. One's not too good. The girls are working on him. Those two are the parents. I don't think there's much we can do. The ambulance is coming. I didn't want to get in the way.'

A distant whisper of sound from a screaming siren made them all look in the direction of the station gateway, still miles off to the south.

'There it is,' said Will, eyes far-seeing, laughter lines creased with concentration. Dust clouds billowed as the back end of a white-and-red vehicle bumped through a creek wash-out, a flicker of red, blue and a glinting sunlit flash. The muted wail of the siren came again, carried by the slight afternoon breeze.

Bella moved.

Sliding around the ute door, she strode over to Knackers and Wendy slouched in the dirt. Wendy was once again burrowed into the bulldust, her back the only thing Bella could see. She reminded Bella of an echidna trying to dig its way from harm, or maybe a freshwater tortoise seeking refuge inside its shell. Knackers was looking across at the ute where Sheila and Patty were still working over Max. He was trying to force Wendy to get up.

Crouching down beside him, Bella murmured, 'Knackers, mate, I'll help you with Wends. You need to get to Max. The ambo's here. It's going to be okay.' She nodded towards the ambulance still in the distance, crossing her toes in her boots for the second time that day.

Knackers grunted and jumped to his feet. Together they lifted his wife. Wendy had lost use of her lower limbs and was keening to herself. Staggering under the woman's weight, Bella heaved her into her husband's embrace and Wendy buried her face into Knackers' wide chest. Holding his wife under one arm, Knackers turned and half-carried her towards their son.

He leaned over the ute's tailgate, tears pouring from his eyes as he grasped hold of Max's grubby little hand and squeezed it murmuring, 'Hang on, you little bastard, hang on, me boy . . . Christ, I love you, you little villain.' He snorted back tears and phlegm.

The big man's arms around his wife were shaking. Bella put her hand on Knackers' shoulder and gave a squeeze, trying to force into the gesture all the comfort she could.

'The ambulance is coming, girls,' she called.

'Thank God!' Sheila was puffing with exertion and stress, sweat dripping off her face. 'His heart's still beating and he's breathing a lot better now, but we need to get his right side up a bit. We don't want him to obstruct, and we have to look after his head injury.'

'What head injury?' Knackers' voice was hoarse.

'He's still unconscious. We think he may have a serious head injury. Possibly a fractured skull,' said Sheila before glancing at her hands, checking the cannula.

'Sheila, would you like me to take over?' Bella asked, shocked at the older woman's state.

'No, the ambulance will be here in a minute, they can have him. Don't want to hand over now. Silly too.'

Bella threw a quick glance at Patty, who was shifting the child slightly onto his side. Patty gave a small shake of her head. So Bella just stood with her hand on Knackers' shaking shoulder, and watched.

She became aware of quiet murmuring behind her; the sound of a few backslaps and subdued male voices. Before she could turn and see what was going on, the siren wasn't a whisper on the breeze anymore; the bright lights weren't glints of the sun. Clad in its white-and-red armour, the ambulance was right on top of them and Bella thanked almighty God.

Chapter 4

The ambulance drove off slowly. The paramedics had stabilised Max, sedated Wendy and loaded Knackers on board along with a woebegone Rohan, who'd been hiding in the back seat of the ute. Standing in the middle of the track, the two girls and Sheila watched the vehicle until the swirling ochre dust obscured it.

'I hope he can hang on until they reach the hospital,' said Sheila, slumping forward with exhaustion. She stood back up, stretching.

Bella threw her arms around the older woman, giving her a hug. 'You did good, Sheila. Without you and Patty, he wouldn't have lasted this long.' Bella drew Patty into the little circle for a group hug.

Sheila was the first to break away. 'One of us best follow them in the HiLux and be there for Knackers and Wendy.'

Patty put her arm around her. 'How about I go, Sheila? You're exhausted, and if you head home you can help Bella sort out the other boys.'

Sheila nodded, too tired and wrung out to disagree.

Macca appeared from behind, where the boys had been quietly talking. Chewing on his toothpick, he threw an arm around Patty's shoulders. 'I'll go with you, Patty, make sure you behave yourself with those dashing doctors at the hospital.'

Patty whacked Macca across the chest and flashed a tired grin. 'Didn't recognise you for a minute back there on the track, Macca. It's that ten-gallon hat you're wearing. Obviously when you cross the Victorian border you toss your Cattleman Akubra in the Murray River and buy a Queensland Bronco instead. It suits your ugly mug, you big boofhead.'

Macca smiled, his big face lighting up. 'You like it?' He doffed his hat and sketched a bow.

'You behave yourself with those nurses, Macca – and with Patty. We all know what you're like with the ladies, ay.' Rodney sounded cynical.

The familiarity of his tone caught Bella's attention. 'You lot know each other?' Six degrees of separation was alive and well in the outback. Someone always knew someone else – everywhere.

Rodney was shuffling his feet. 'Yeah, me, Macca and Willy boy here studied together at ag college in Geelong.'

'Mmm. Right. I reckon there'd be more partying than studying with you lot,' said Bella with a wry smile. 'We'd best get moving. Sheila looks all done in.' She clapped her hands together. 'I'll jump in with you, Will. Rodney, can you give Sheila a lift home?'

As everyone started to move in the direction of their ride, Bella gave Patty a quick hug. 'You take care, okay? Macca, you'd better drive, and make sure she has a rest on the way into town. I reckon she's going to need it so she can deal with what's going to be waiting at that hospital.'

Macca moved up beside Patty, slung his arm around her and led her off, whispering something which sent Patty into whoops of tired laughter.

Bella heard Patty say, 'Bossy? You call *that* bossy? You haven't seen nothin', mate. You should try and live with her.' Bella lost Macca's reply as the pair jumped into the girls' borrowed ute. Pulling away, they headed towards the station gateway and town.

Rodney and Sheila were already in their vehicle and moving off back towards Sheila's house. Sheila yelled to Bella from the open passenger-side window, 'I'll sort out the other two boys. If they're still at the quarters kitchen give us a yell. I'll send someone over to pick them up.'

'Righto.'

And with that, Bella and Will were left standing, silent and alone, looking anywhere but at each other.

'So . . .' said Bella at last, chancing a look Will's way. 'What are you blokes doing here anyway?' She could see the beginnings of a grin, and his dimples made her catch her breath again. She was a sucker for dimples on a bloke, and these were rippers: gorgeous, deep-set, one on either side of his mouth.

She took in his tanned and rugged face, his molasses eyes so liquid she just wanted to roll in the sweetness of them. Standing a few inches above her five-foot-seven, he wasn't overly tall, but the muscled breadth of his shoulders within his chambray shirt and the curl of sun-bleached hair peeping from above the blue singlet spoke of a man used to working outdoors.

Bella's heart was thumping so loudly she was sure the whole world could hear it –and she was certain it wasn't just leftover adrenaline from dealing with the accident.

Where had she been *living* for the past twenty-two years? William O'Hara was Patty's brother. He was pretty much a neighbour. Why hadn't she noticed him before? The answer came to mind instantly: he'd always been so much *older*. A blurry figure in the background, off doing 'big brother' stuff, at ag college and hanging out with older mates. Sure, sometimes he'd been working at Tindarra while she and Patty had been tearing around having fun, but she'd seen him as a grown-up. He'd never registered on her radar. He was far too old for her. Heck, at twenty-eight he was ancient, gorgeous or not.

'So,' she repeated. 'What are you and Macca doing here?'

She knew she sounded belligerent but couldn't help herself. First she had missed out on mustering and had to cook. Then there was the accident. And now this. Her body was instinctively responding to Will, leaning like a drunken fence post seeking firmer ground. Where the hell had her free will departed to in the last half-hour? HE. WAS. TOO. OLD. Plus she didn't need serious man complications. And a bloke like this would mean *serious*.

'We've been up around Mount Isa for a bit, checking out some trucking work for Macca's old man, your Uncle Bryce. I'm surprised your mum didn't tell you.'

Bella was surprised too, mentally cursing her mother for forgetting to share *that* piece of information. Forewarned was forearmed, or something like that anyway.

'The drought is pretty bad at home and there wasn't much doing. I've sold most of my stock and the lucerne isn't ready to cut yet. Dad's irrigating my place as well as his own while I'm away. He's growing a bit of lucerne now too.' Will paused and raised an eyebrow. 'You knew that when my Uncle Bill died, I took over his property next door to Dad's place at Tindarra?'

Bella nodded. She'd heard that from Aunty Maggie, who also lived at Tindarra, next door to Will and Patty's parents.

Bella might've grown up on her family's dairy farm at Narree a couple of hours away but her aunt always kept her informed of the goings on up in those mountains. A lifetime of weekends and school holidays staying with Aunty Maggie, and roaming the surrounding hills with Patty, had given Bella a sense of place and home at both Tindarra and Narree.

Will went on: 'Macca and I wanted to have a look at a few properties up around Isa while we were there, to see something different. Was good to get away for a bit. We're on our way home now and thought we'd look you two up.'

Come to think of it, Bella vaguely remembered Patty saying something about her brother being away for a while. She'd thought he was in the Territory, though, and hadn't realised her cousin was with him.

'It was quicker coming home through Charters Towers, rather than going down the coast. So here we are. Scenery's a whole lot better too.' His grin was wicked. His eyes caressing her body without touching, burning without flame, making her flush with heat.

Will wasn't sure when or how that pigtailed, skinny runt of a kid had turned into this luscious, sexy creature standing before him. Tumbling ringlets of white-gold peeked from beneath the broad-brimmed hat. A cleavage so well rounded, sweaty and sweet, a man would have to be a priest not to want to bury his head in it. Legs so long, slim and well formed, they could have wrapped around his waist two times over – well, nearly.

And the face.

Tanned snubby nose, high-boned lightly freckled cheeks and blue eyes that flicked and fluttered with so much wantonness. He was in meltdown. And that was just her appearance.

Watching the confident and compassionate way she handled herself with that poor couple in the middle of the road. Will was sure glad it wasn't him trying to help in that situation. He wouldn't have known what to do or say.

If anyone had told him ten minutes ago it was possible to be suddenly and utterly bewitched by a woman, he'd have said they were an idiot. Now *he* felt like the idiot – a besotted idiot.

But then there was her friendship with his sister to consider. In fact, the Vermaelon and O'Hara families had been friends for three generations. They even had a mutual relative in Aunty Maggie, Bella's aunt who'd married Will's uncle, if anyone could work out that convoluted connection. And getting on the wrong side of Maggie wasn't an option. Not to Will's mind anyway. Maybe he should just turn and walk away.

So many thoughts swirled through his brain as he took in the girl in front of him. His senses were aroused. His blood was stirred. Testosterone was pumping and Will was smitten with lust.

'So are you coming or are you going to stand there all afternoon?' Bella was getting into the boys' four-wheel drive.

'Oh yeah. Coming.'

Bella watched as Will moved to the driver's side and jumped in, dragging his cream felt hat from his head and tossing it behind the seat.

Turning, she looked out the passenger-side window. She was exhausted.

Maybe it was the drama of the afternoon. By profession she was an agricultural officer who advised people on landcare. She certainly wasn't a medical guru who was used to keeping people alive.

Maybe it was meeting the man beside her – someone she'd known all her life without really knowing him at all.

Perhaps. But she wasn't going to admit that to anyone, least of all herself. Fun, fun, fun in the sun was her motto for this year. She didn't need emotional complications. Unfortunately her body had other ideas. Every nerve ending was buzzing. She breathed in his scent, felt his warmth. The transparent thread of attraction between them seemed to have somehow metamorphosed into a solid rope. Sharing the same airspace in the ute made her feelings seem so much stronger, louder, clearer. Again Bella mentally shook herself. Too old, too serious, too close, too much. Think of something else, she told herself firmly.

She trained her eyes out the window. A lonely ribbon of dirt unravelled across the plains in front of them. As the ute followed the track back towards the stockmen's quarters, she could see billowing clouds of red dust in the distance; a mob of startled horses, moving, pounding their hooves in the late-afternoon light. As both ute and horses drew closer, Bella could see a multitude of colours: strawberry roan, bay, chestnut, palomino, dappled grey and even skewbald, their four-legged shadows silhouetted through particles of dust as the leaders swung the mob in flight at sight of the vehicle.

Then the horses were past.

The ute drove on.

Dropping her head back against the seat-rest, Bella allowed her surroundings to become the sole focus of her consciousness, her only frame of reference the bush outside. The scrub rolled out over hill and down gully; lancewood, bendee and rosewood, tragic-looking yapunyah and ironbark trees with limbs spread in supplication to the burning heat. Black speargrass, purple pigeon and bambatsi all clung to the ochre-coloured soil.

It seemed to Bella that the bush up here was wild with hostility for man's intrusion but at the same time it sucked you in, made you become a part of it, like a parasite feasting on your soul. Before you knew it, it had you utterly bewitched and you felt like you could never live anywhere else in the world. It reminded Bella of Tindarra, the beguiling valley hidden amid the massive mountains of the Great Dividing Range at home in Gippsland, where her Aunty Maggie and the O'Haras lived.

On the opposite side of the ute, Will was thinking hard. He wanted to say something to the girl sitting quietly beside him chewing her red and luscious bottom lip.

But Will knew whatever he said would come out wrong. She made him feel like a fumbling seventeen-year-old on his first date. Her body language spoke volumes anyway, head and shoulders turned away. All he could see was a tumbling mass of curly hair, spilling down under the back of her hat.

Better not to say anything, he decided. Just shut up and drive.

Like a lazy Sunday afternoon spin on a sunny outback day.

'Oh no!' Bella sat up straight, and thumped the Jesus bar with frustration as they approached a hand-drawn sign indicating the turn-off to the stockmen's quarters.

'What's up?' asked Will, glad for something to talk about.

'See that green Toyota wagon over there?' Bella waved her hand in the direction of a group of dongas to their left. 'That's the boss from hell, and I've left a humungous mess in the bloody kitchen. Damn it!' The Jesus bar copped another couple of thumps. 'She was supposed to be in Rockhampton.'

'Surely she can't be that bad? Who is she anyway?'

'*She* is Siobhan, the station manager's wife. And *she* is my boss. I'll be out on my butt over this one.'

'Surely she can't carpet you over a messy kitchen. You've just been saving a little boy's life, for goodness sake. She'd have heard it all on the two-way radio anyway.'

Bella sighed. 'Siobhan doesn't keep the radio on. Got more important things to do than listen to station chitchat, she says.'

'Just tell her then. She'll understand.'

'No, it's you who doesn't understand, Will. Siobhan hates my guts, has done since we arrived. I've been in awful trouble lately. You'll see what I mean.'

Will swung the LandCruiser into the parking area and brought it to a halt in front of the ring-lock fence surrounding the group of buildings the stockmen and women called home. Bella jumped out of the ute and slammed the door. Jamming her hat further down on her head, she strode off towards the kitchen.

Following more sedately, Will admired the way Bella's butt moved from side to side, her long legs eating the distance across the lawn. He increased his stride to try to catch up as she strode onto the kitchen verandah.

He could hear the shrill female voice even before he saw its owner. Through the huge side windows on the walk up to the sliding door, he glimpsed one scary sight. Standing adrift in the doorway between the kitchen and dining room, she was wrapped in a copious pomegranate sheath that screamed expensive but looked hideous on a dumpy, pear-shaped body. Her painted face reminded him of a circus clown he'd once seen as a little kid – white with scarlet and black slashes. From memory, he'd been terrified. This creature tapped a pointy-toed, high-heeled, devil-red shoe against the laminate floor as her voice rose and fell, twisting with scorn like a striking snake.

'Isabella? Isabella! What is the meaning of this *disgusting* mess? When I made you fill in for the weekend, I assumed you could actually *cook*. This is *not* what I would call cooking, young lady. *And* to just walk out and leave our supplies to the blowflies is simply *unacceptable!* You STUPID IDIOT!' The pomegranate sheath whirled, doughy neck rolls quivered and white manicured hands flew through the air, punctuating the screeches. '*Where* have you been and *what* are you going to do about this MESS?'

Bella stood at the dining-room door spellbound, but not by the woman tearing the very fabric of her character to bits. No. Bella was focused on the globule of egg white hanging precariously above Siobhan's coiffured head. A head on which every strand of hair was blow-waved and slicked into savage submission. How the heck that bit of goo hadn't already succumbed to gravity, Bella didn't know. But it was about to . . .

The globule wavered in the breeze from the opened sliding door. Swinging lazily, the gooey strands securing it to the ceiling slowly but surely drooped downwards, slipping and sliding with malicious intent.

And then the gluey muck was on its way.

Phlat!

Chapter 5

It was chiming ten on the kitchen clock as Bella flipped over the cheese sandwiches lined up like soldiers in the frypan. Over the orchestral voices of insects and frogs abroad on a typical outback night, she could hear roars of laughter coming from the dining room in the stockmen's quarters.

Chairs thumped on the worn vinyl floor as both Rodney and Macca rocked back and forth, doubled up with laughter over the vision of an egg-white-daubed Siobhan. Bella could hear Will's deep voice rumble on through the laughter as he described the pomegranate she-devil from hell.

Despite the dire outcome, Bella couldn't help but grin to herself at the picture that came to mind: a speechless Siobhan, mouth wide open to the flies, swiping at a slick blob of slime that had first hit her lacquered hair and then slowly slid south to adhere itself to her mascara-encrusted eyelashes.

Siobhan had immediately flung her hand to the mess in her eyes, which only made matters worse; a flick of her wrist split the now blackened mess in two, sending it downwards to stain the folds of the outlandish sheath.

Bella and Will had watched in silence.

The fallout from the disaster hadn't been instant termination of employment as Bella predicted.

It was worse.

She now had to clean every inch of the guest quarters – *on her own* – for the company VIPs who were arriving next week. Six bedrooms, six bathrooms, six toilets, kitchen, dining room, two lounges, and built-in verandahs, all thickly coated with red bulldust. There were all manner of creatures to be evicted too – frogs, cockroaches, snakes. *Yuck!*

What's more, she had to clean up after they'd gone, and do it every time VIPs came and went until the end of the year. And that was on top of gardening. Her job description was starting to weigh so heavily it was likely to drown her in the nearest turkey nest dam.

If Bella hadn't needed the money she'd have tossed the job in right there and then. But she and Patty wanted a holiday on their way home at the end of the year, so she bit her tongue and wore it, although that didn't stop her from bursting into tears once the bitch had gone. Will had opened his strong arms and she'd walked into them blindly, crying like a baby.

'You don't *have* to stay, Bella. Both of you can come home with Macca and me,' he suggested.

But Bella wasn't walking away with her tail between her legs. She'd be buggered if Siobhan was going to win that easily. And she didn't need any bloke to carry her home either. Throwing back her shoulders and drawing in resolve, she moved away from

Will – away from temptation. 'Patty and I made a commitment we'd stick it out for a year and that's what we're going to do. That bag isn't going to get the better of me this easily!'

'So, I ended up introducing myself,' Bella could hear Will finishing the story as she walked into the dining room with her tray of toasted sandwiches. 'Siobhan didn't really seem that interested, though. Might have had something to do with the mess she was in.' Glimpsing Bella, he then went on, 'And now here we are, with what I am sure is the most delicious-looking meal ever to grace these stockmen's quarters.'

He looked straight at Bella. The heat of his gaze suggested it wasn't *just* the cheese sandwiches that looked delicious. She could feel herself blushing as she placed the tray on the table. Crikey, she hated that. She usually left all that red and randy stuff up to Patty. Speaking of which . . .

'How's the famous spaghetti bolognaise and sumptuous pavlova coming along, cookie?' Patty arrived at her friend's side as if beckoned, smelling like Pears soap. 'Beats me why you were going to the trouble of cooking all that stuff. Not many here to eat it anyway.'

Bella gritted her teeth. 'It was a challenge, and the food was to last the whole weekend so I didn't have to cook *again*.' Lifting the plate of sandwiches she pushed them into Patty's chest. 'There, smart alec. And before you ask, it's tinned two-fruits and cream for sweets.'

Patty opened her mouth.

'Don't say a word!' Bella held up her spare hand signalling STOP in capital letters. 'Not unless you want to wear the two-fruits over that head of yours.'

Patty took the plate of sandwiches in one hand and zipped her lips with two fingers of the other, at the same time winking at Macca.

⁂

It was a quiet Friday night at the quarters. Most of the other ringers had taken off for Gundolin, a small town a few hundred kilometres away. The rest had already had their tea and departed to bed.

All those involved in the day's traumatic events sat around the table munching their food as Patty and Macca filled everyone in on Max's medical evacuation to Brisbane. He was still critically ill but had stabilised which was a relief. The conversation then moved to lighter matters.

'Are you two blokes in for tomorrow night's rodeo at Gundolin?' Rodney spluttered around a mouthful of toast and cheese.

Bella swiped at the wet crumbs that had landed on her hands. 'Jeez, Rodney. Didn't your mother ever teach you some manners? Or at least that fancy boarding school you went to?' Rodney ignored her, focusing instead on Will and Macca. 'Gundolin rodeo, boys . . . bucking bulls, Bundy, beer, band and boobs. You both in?'

Will and Macca looked at each other, then across at the girls.

'Yeah, too right,' said Will as he gazed at Bella.

The dimples flickered. The man who owned them had no right to look so damned good. The 'too old, too serious, too close' mantra Bella had been reciting in her head for the past few hours wasn't cutting it anymore. Her libido was in goddamn overdrive. She really *was* in deep shit.

Chapter 6

The day of the Gundolin rodeo dawned hot and heavy. The air was filled with moisture and there were clouds hanging low to the north-west.

'Better pack our Driza-bones, Patty, it's going to rain before the day's out,' Bella yelled through the kitchen door across to the accommodation dongas where her friend was packing an overnight bag for them both. Bella flipped the eggs she had frying in the pan and glanced up at the station clock ticking loudly on the wall. 'And can you dash out to the verandah and ring the bell to bring the boys in? Lunch is nearly ready.'

She could see Will, Macca and Rodney out in the horse paddock, arms elbow-deep in mud trying to find the leaking pipe that was supposed to be supplying water to the stock trough. 'And tell them to bogey on up before they think of crossing the doorway. I've just mopped the dining-room floor.' Bella paused. She looked out the window at the amount of mud

44

wallowing around the boys. 'On second thoughts, tell them to just have a wash and I'll serve lunch on the verandah. I haven't spent all morning cleaning this kitchen for them to dirty it again.'

Patty appeared in the doorway. 'So, do you want them to have a shower or not?'

'Well it doesn't look like they're anywhere near fixing that leak because water's still spraying out everywhere. We'll be lucky to get to Gundolin before dark, the rate they're going.'

'Fair go, mate. They've been at it all morning. Their swags were rolled up near the ute when I got up at six-thirty for a pee, so they haven't exactly been standing still pissing into the wind, you know.'

'Yeah, I know.' Bella looked repentant. 'I don't know what's wrong with me today. Just grumpy, I guess.'

'Wouldn't be a case of a little *luvvve* sickness, now would it?' Patty's grin was as wicked as her brother's. It just lacked the carnal edge.

'Love? Now who in the heck would I *luvvve* out here?'

'How about just plain old *luuust* then?' Patty sang, until she saw the glare on Bella's face and thought better of it. 'I'll just go and ring the bell to call them in, shall I?' she said.

'Yeah, you do that!' Bella slammed some bacon into the frypan on the stove. She tried to work out why she was so out of sorts. It didn't take long. In her heart of hearts she knew this was the way she reacted to fear, nerves or anger: flight, fright or fight.

What did she have to fear?

Your feelings for Will, whispered her subconscious.

What was making her nervous?

Your feelings for Will. This time the whisper was a little louder.

What was making her angry?

Your feelings for Will. The whisper became a shout.

'Crap!' she bellowed, as the bacon spat fat into her eyes. 'Oh damn!' she yelled again as she blindly stuck her hands out searching for the sink.

'What's the matter?' a deep voice rumbled at her side.

'Oh!' she jumped, slamming a hand down on the tap.

'Bella, what have you done?' Will's voice rumbled again.

'You know, you really shouldn't be let loose in a kitchen,' Patty's voice joined in.

'Shit, the bacon's burning to a crisp,' said Macca.

'Just as well I like my pork well done.' Rodney had the last say.

'For crap's sake!' Bella could hear herself yelling. 'I've got hot fat in my eyes, so if one of you would be *kind* enough to turn some water on I might be able to rinse them so I can *see again*!'

'All right, all right, keep your shirt on.' Patty's voice was all businesslike and brisk. She took Bella's hands and guided them to the now-running water. 'Wash out your eyes with this.' A soft cloth was put in her hands. As Bella gently wiped, her blurred vision slowly cleared . . . to see three mud-covered men standing in her spotless kitchen.

'Argh!' she screeched again, causing them all to jump.

'Jeez, Hells Bells, you've always been jumpy, but you don't have to share it around,' Patty laughed.

'What the hell do you think you're all doing in my kitchen looking like *that*?' Bella swung around to Patty. 'Didn't you tell them to bogey on up, or at least sit on the verandah?'

'Settle, petal,' a droll Patty replied. 'They haven't finished the pipe patch-up session yet, so it's no use having a shower. And then you yelled . . .'

'. . . so we thought we'd see what was going on. We were worried it must have been a snake or something,' finished Will, as he placed a hand on her shoulder.

Bella peeled back like she was stung, and found herself hard up against the island bench.

'Christ,' said Rodney as he viewed the blackened bacon resting in the pan. 'The Springsure roadhouse is looking pretty darn good for lunch. Let's put a temporary patch on that pipe leak that'll do till Monday, and piss off out of here before Bella decides to cook again, ay?'

Bella threw what she had in her hands. It was lucky it was only a soft cloth, because Rodney wore it smack in the middle of his forehead.

Chapter 7

The gates had been open since late Friday afternoon, so when their vehicles rocked into the recreation reserve grounds at Gundolin, hundreds of utes and four-wheel drives were already there. Swags were rolled out in all directions, as people set up camp with others from their own properties.

'Crikey!' said Bella. 'Half of western Queensland must be here.'

'Yeah, it's a great rodeo. You always have a good time at Gundolin,' said Rodney as he looked for where the Ainsley Station mob had camped down.

Straddling the gearstick in the LandCruiser, Bella was jammed in between two men. On her right sat a stocky Rodney, whose body just felt warm against her thigh, like a good mate. To her left sat Will, a hard body pressed up against her left side; a side that had been on fire for the last couple of hours as it rubbed and pushed against him on the gravel roads.

'There they are over at the horse stables,' said Rodney. 'I'd know that ute of Sandy's anywhere with all those flamin' aerials giving a finger to all and sundry. They must've made it here pretty early to get the stables. Might need the shelter too,' he said, looking up at the heavy sky.

Rodney directed his ute to the left of the main recreation reserve pavilion. Bella looked around for the stables, grateful they would have four walls for shelter, warmth and privacy. The ute pulled up in front of a long and simple corrugated-iron roof held up by upright steel poles; under the roof were basic steel-railed pens with gates fronting the gravel track that ran along in front.

'Here we are.' Rodney turned off his ute.

'*This* is the stables?' said Bella, unable to keep the incredulity from her voice.

'Yep,' said Rodney looking perplexed. 'What'd you expect? The Hilton?'

'Nope,' replied Bella, as she baled out of the ute behind Will. 'In Victoria, Rodney, stables generally mean four closed walls and a neat little half-and-half door. I guess the dawn dash is a bit more laidback and public in Queensland.'

'You reckon?' said a puzzled Rodney, not sure if the piss was being taken out of him or not. He glanced at a smiling Bella and decided he might be safe to go on. 'Anyways, the loos are over there, the bar's over there and . . .' He looked pointedly at Will and winked, '. . . the girls are everywhere. I'm going to find the station blokes. Catch you later.' He walked off in the direction of the bar.

The twin stacks on Macca's ute made a deep growl as they halted behind Rodney's four-wheel drive. Jumping from the driver's seat, the black-hatted, big-framed Macca strode around the front of the vehicle and made it to the passenger door before Patty had a chance to jump down. Thrusting out his big hands, he grabbed her under the arms and knees and carried her from the ute.

'Here we are, darlin'. Welcome to your new home. Shall I carry you over the threshold?' Macca made his way through the steel gate and into the little pen, where he proceeded to dump his 'bride' on a pile of old hay left by the previous inhabitant.

Obviously they hadn't wasted any time on their ride to Gundolin; Bella could practically see chemistry zinging above their heads. She'd never thought of these two getting together before. She probably should have, though – they complemented each other perfectly.

'When you two have finished horsing around you might like to come with us to hit the bar?' said Will, already primed with two rums downed on the trip from Ainsley. Grabbing Bella's hand he walked off towards the main pavilion, pulling her with him.

Bella's smile quickly disappeared as she tried to extract her hand from his grasp, but he held on – real tight. In fact he hauled her in close, hard up against his side, his arm coming up around her shoulders, pinning her there. She felt his breath on her face and then his seductive lips were moving the sweet rum-laden air near her ear. He half-whispered, 'You are one mean little mountain woman. Poor old Rodney didn't know if you were yanking his chain or not. But I tell you what, hold on tight, cowgirl. You and I are going to find some Bundy, a band and a rodeo, and . . .'

Bella tried to pull away. Will nipped her ear, stilling her before he went on, 'The trip here beside you was akin to grievous bodily harm. Get ready for a wild time, Isabella Vermaelon!'

❧

'What do you mean, a bet's a bet?' Will asked incredulously, a couple of hours later as they lay looking for satellites among the stars overhead. It had bucketed down with rain earlier and then the sky had cleared, giving them an unobscured view of the diamond-filled night sky.

'I've made a bet with your sister and I'm not going to lose. There's a lot at stake,' said Bella.

Knowing his sister, Will was sure the high stakes could be anything from a cattle station to a damned Cadbury chocolate bar. 'So what's the bet *exactly*?'

'You don't want to know the details, but it means I can't sleep with you for at least six weeks.'

Inwardly Bella cursed. Her mind flicked back to the event that caused the wager to be made in the first place.

'Pat Me Tuffet, you can't sleep with *every* bloke you find attractive!' yelled a worried Bella, as Patty blearily staggered in the door one Saturday morning a few weeks before, after spending the night in a passing stock-buyer's swag.

'Who says I can't?'

'*I* do!'

'Since when have you become my mother?' asked an unruffled Patty, as she stifled a yawn and stretched her arms to the ceiling like a satisfied cat. 'Anyway, last time I saw you, you were dirty dancing with that government bloke working in tick control.'

'I wasn't dirty dancing – *and* I left him at the party. I don't sleep with blokes I don't know.'

'Yeah, since when?' asked Patty with a smirk. 'What about that truckie—'

'I was drunk!'

'My point exactly. I *too* am usually drunk at station parties and I can't help it if lonely, hunky men succumb to my charms. How can I say no?'

Bella stood and considered Patty. She was worried about her friend. She didn't want her to become known as the Ainsley Station bike. How could she get Patty to say no? There was really only one way.

'Let's have a bet.'

Patty quirked an eyebrow, looking interested. 'What sort of bet?'

'No sleeping with anyone until six weeks after you meet them.'

'Mmm . . . tricky . . . And the stakes?'

'A slab of rum.'

'Nup, not good enough. Those stock agents are hot.' Patty turned and walked into her bedroom and collapsed on the bed. Bella could see her through the door, spread-eagled, eyes closed.

Bella sighed. 'A slab of rum . . . and fifty bucks.'

Patty struggled to a half-sit and smiled.

'Done.'

It had sounded good at the time. And it was all for Patty's benefit, but Bella wasn't going to tell *that* to her best friend's brother.

'She won't know, Bella,' said Will in a low, inviting voice.

'Of course she'll flaming well know! She only has to look at my face and she could tell you the story of my last twenty-four hours.' Okay, that was a slight exaggeration, but it was close to the truth. She and Patty knew each other better than two sisters ever would.

'All right . . . all right,' said Will, disappointed that a wild night between the sheets, or swag in this case, had disappeared.

'Look,' said Bella, grabbing his arm. 'A satellite. It's humping along, east to west.'

'Don't talk about humping anymore,' said Will with a mock grumpy face.

Bella gave the satellite one last look before lifting her upper body to lean on her elbow and rest her head in her hand. Looking down into Will's face, she put out a tentative finger to trace the strong, square jawline. They'd spent most of the night laughing, flirting, talking. And she'd never had anyone focus on her words, her thoughts and ideas like this man. Most blokes her age were focused on themselves. But not Will O'Hara. His interest in what counted to her was absolute.

His eyes crinkled with laughter. He tried one last time. 'Don't you females always reserve the right to change your mind?'

Bella smiled and shook her head.

Will sighed. 'Well, I reckon I'll just work on getting you into my swag and leave it at that for now. If I can't have the cup full, I'll have to settle for half.'

'Huh?'

Will's body shook as laughter rumbled through him. He sat up and downed the remains of the can of Bundy rum sitting at his side. 'If I can't bonk you senseless, I'll just have to cuddle you instead. Want another drink, cowgirl?'

Bella nodded and watched as he jumped to his feet and strode his tightly muscled Wrangler-covered butt towards the bar.

'Bella!' Wrenching her eyes from the view of Will's backside, Bella looked towards the bull-riding ring where the rodeo was in full swing.

Patty's arms were waving in the air, trying to get her attention.

'Want to dance?' Patty yelled from her place at the top of the viewing stands. Bella could see Macca beside her, head bent in a solid conversation with Rodney and his mate Sandy.

'It's Sara Storer!' Patty yelled again, trying to be heard over the loudspeaker calling the bull ride.

All Bella heard was the word 'Storer', but it was enough for her to tune into the music coming from the stage.

'Cry don't cry
Better things are in store and I just can't explain it yet
High up high
Oh I see you both dancing through tumbleweeds'

Sara Storer in Gundolin – Bella whooped with joy, punching the air as she jumped to her feet.

'C'mon, let's go dance through tumbleweeds!' she yelled to Patty.

At that moment Will arrived back clutching two cans of Bundy-and-coke. Grabbing one from his hand, she spluttered, 'Sara Storer. Here. Gundolin. Gotta go dance. You go to Macca,' and she pushed him in her cousin's direction.

Patty pulled up beside them and snatched the other rum from Will's grasp, leaving him empty-handed. 'Thanks, bro. Didn't know you cared.' Grabbing Bella's hand, she took off at a run, heading towards the music, both girls dancing as they went.

Will heard shrieking, as they spilt the full cans down their shirts. He closed his eyes imagining that black, sticky liquid dripping through Bella's full cleavage. He could still hear their high whoops of delight as he made his way back to the bar.

Now he *really* needed a rum.

It wasn't until the sun was reflecting her first yellow-orange glow in the sky that Bella found herself stumbling back towards the stables with Will. Patty and Macca had long since disappeared. As they reached the pair of utes, Bella could see Patty's swag still sitting up beside her own, whereas Macca's had disappeared.

So much for Pat Me Tuffet keeping her side of the bet! But then again, Bella couldn't be sure . . .

Will hauled his swag down from the ute tray and grabbed Bella by the hand.

'But—'

'I know, I know . . . a bet's a bet, but there's nothing to say I can't just cuddle you.' Will pulled both swag and Bella into a pen under the stables' skillion roof.

'Are you sure you can keep your hands to yourself?'

'No, I'm not sure, but I can try.' He dumped the swag on the ground, unsnapped the ockey strap holding it together and gave the roll a kick so it unravelled itself.

Bella looked at the long, skinny length of canvas.

'Are two of us going to fit in there?'

'You betcha, cowgirl.' Will dragged his cobalt-blue stockman's shirt over his head.

Bella just managed to stifle a gasp at the sight of his naked chest. Reddish-gold sun-kissed hair curled and then ran in a straight line down before fanning out and disappearing below his R.M. Williams belt buckle. Thinking of the bush girl's yardstick 'the bigger the buckle the smaller the equipment', she saw that Will's buckle was a nice average size.

She shook her head.

A bet's a bet, she reminded herself, and dragged her eyes away from the muscular chest in front of her. Flustered and embarrassed, she watched as he kicked off his boots, stripped off his Wranglers and slid into the blankets inside the swag.

'You coming in or am I coming back out to get you?' Will's wicked grin flashed.

Bella turned and slowly removed her bra from under her shirt, feeding it out through her shirt-sleeve. Boots and jeans followed, unintentionally giving Will a good view of her bum. Bella turned around to see a look of agony on his face. 'Will, are you okay?' She dropped to the swag beside him. 'What have you done? Are you hurt?' Her breasts swung full and free inside her shirt as she leaned over to touch his face with concern.

'No . . . no, not hurt . . . I just . . . um . . . bit my tongue.'

Bella wasn't convinced. 'Maybe I should just roll my own swag out for a while, hey?' She moved to get back up.

'*No!*' said Will as he grabbed her hand. 'It'll be fine, Bella, jump in. We'll just cuddle. That's it. I promise.'

'Well . . . okay. If you're sure.' Bella knew if an O'Hara made a promise it was one set in gold. 'But one wrong move and I'm out of here.'

Leaving her shirt and undies on, Bella squeezed her way into the swag beside him, sliding her body down past his long, nearly naked length, her nerve-ends tingling at his touch. She thought she heard him groan once or twice, but other than stealing a kiss – his warm, firm lips on her mouth nearly proving to be her undoing – he settled her into the crook of his shoulder and just cuddled her in tight.

As Bella felt weariness spread through her limbs, her mind rewound back over the night. She'd had the best time. Will was wonderful. He made her feel witty, appreciated, desired. A bloke so totally in sync with her own beliefs and ideals, she felt as though she'd found a new best friend.

He'd shared his plans for the family property, ideas on how he wanted his future to pan out. Then he'd listened to her thoughts – aspirations for her job, love of the land and family. Teasing one minute, serious the next, here was a man who engaged both her body *and* mind. Passionate without being too intense, gentle but by no means a wimp. Strong, but not over-bearing. And him being older had ceased to matter hours ago.

For now she was just happy and content to be held securely in his arms. She snuggled in closer and felt a kiss lightly brush across her hair. Closing her eyes she let the night's rum and the warmth of Will's body send her to sleep.

Will lay quietly and felt the golden head in his arms become heavy with sleep. He smiled to himself as soft snores came from the girl at his side. Gently he adjusted Bella's body so it tucked into his more comfortably, making sure the blankets covered her so she stayed warm.

Sleep was a long time coming. He lay watching the sunrise as he gently twirled a blonde ringlet around his finger and wondered at his luck at having such a gorgeous creature in his arms.

Chapter 8

'I'm on my way, Siobhan,' Bella called into the microphone, silently cursing. She hung the mike back on the side of the radio, which was attached to the front carryall of her four-wheel motorbike.

It had been a couple of weeks since the boys had left.

A couple of *very* long weeks, and Bella could see the next few months before they were due to head home, dragging like a reluctant child. Siobhan was on Bella's back to clean the guest quarters, a crowd of VIPs having recently been and gone.

Bella missed Will. She hadn't expected that. He'd awakened in her feelings that left her confused, scared even. Life had been so free and easy up till now. She didn't need or want this complication.

Or did she? Will made her feel so good about herself, attractive, interesting. And when he focused on her, Bella felt like she was the only person in the world. He seemed to really care, about her, about the things she believed were important – family, friends and country life.

Patty was struggling too, dragging her feet out of bed where a few weeks before she had been bounding out before the alarm. Macca was to blame for that.

Bloody Will and Macca.

They'd also brought to Ainsley Station in northern outback Queensland the sweet calls and smells of the southern mountains and home. Station life out here had lost its shine, and Bella knew her uncertainty about what to do next in life was resolved. They were going home. And Bella couldn't wait.

But now, she needed to move her butt.

She slung her gardening tools onto the back of the motorbike, pulled on her helmet and set off in the direction of the stockmen's quarters.

The sky was bright; the warm wind whistled around the collar of her long-sleeve chambray shirt and the sun kissed her cheeks as she rode. The day was improving rapidly. You couldn't stay disgruntled on such a beautiful, Queensland morning.

She felt her mobile phone vibrate in her back pocket. Surprised, she reached around with one hand to retrieve it while using her other hand to bring the bike to a halt. She hauled off her helmet and could hear her mother's voice even before she got the phone to her ear.

'Bella? Are you there? Hello?'

'Yes, Mum. I'm here. Sorry I missed your call on Sunday night. How are you?' she said to the woman who was the anchor in her young life.

'Good, thank you, darling. I wasn't sure I would get you.' The relief of reaching her daughter was obvious in Francine Vermaelon's voice. 'And you?'

'Yeah, I'm good. We just had a visit from cousin Macca and Patty's brother Will. We had a good time.' Bella just managed to keep her voice level. 'Why didn't you tell me they were up this way?'

'I don't know. Must have just slipped my mind.'

'They've gone now. They should be just about home.'

'Oh good,' said Francine. 'Rhonda will be so pleased to see that rascal back again. He didn't lead you or Patty into any trouble, did he?' Her laugh tinkled down the phone.

'No, Mummy dear, he was as good as gold.' As good as tarnished gold anyway. Quickly Bella changed the subject. 'How are Justin, Melanie and the kids?'

'Good, sweetheart. Mel's five months' gone now. She's already counting down to her due date.'

'What about Beccy and Joel?' asked Bella.

'Beccy just won Champion Rider for her age group at the gymkhana on Sunday, and Joel's decided he wants to be a dairy farmer because you get to go home to have lunch with your family.' Her mother laughed again.

Bella giggled. Joel was a card, a steady, placid little boy who loved helping his dad and Bella's brother Justin on the farm. Beccy, on the other hand, was a dare devil. Anything that moved quickly and she was on it, in it or doing it. Bella reincarnated, said Francine, although Bella didn't see herself like that at all.

'Anyway, darling, I've got to go. Mobile calls cost the earth. Just wanted to remind you it's your father's birthday tomorrow. Justin and Mel are putting on tea for him at their place, so give us a call there, okay?'

'Okay, Mum. Thanks for reminding me. You lose track of the date up here. And give Beccy my congratulations. I'll check out her winning ribbons when I get home. I've bought them a nursery rhymes CD as a present but I'll have to get something else instead. I forget how quickly they're growing up.'

'Yes, they are, my darling, just like someone else I know,' her mother added. 'Miss you. We'll talk to you tomorrow night. Don't forget to ring. Your father will be counting on it.'

'Okay, Mum. Love you. Bye.' Bella clicked her phone shut and shoved it back into her pocket, amazed there'd been mobile reception. She'd had to rely on a Sunday-night call from the stockmen's quarters phone and email to stay in touch. Even her brother, who was five years older, had sent her a couple of emails over the year.

She knew they missed her at home. Twenty-two years before, her parents had almost given up hope of having another baby – then surprise, surprise, she'd come along. And life had been Hells Bells ever since, her father was fond of saying. Bella smiled at the thought of home. Cranking up the motorbike, she shook her hair in the breeze, pulled on her helmet and rode on, a grin as wide as the horizon spreading across her face.

As she drove up to the quarters, she could see Patty letting one of her plant horses go in the paddock. 'What's going on?' yelled Bella as she reefed off her helmet.

'Finished mustering.'

'This early in the day?'

'Yeah. Truck was due early arvie, so we pulled out all stops and had the mob in by lunchtime. Have you eaten?'

'Nope, and I haven't got time. Siobhan's on my case and I've got to clean the guest quarters . . . now!'

'What's her hurry?'

'I don't know,' said Bella. 'But I'd better move. I just hope those toffy company VIPS weren't too messy. The last lot were ferals.'

'I'll come help you if you like, though it'll cost you.'

'Like what?'

'Mmm . . . let me see. How about lending me your new Ariat boots for the Burrindal B&S at home in December?'

Bella had to weigh that one up. It was big. She'd only bought the prized boots a few months earlier, shelling out a couple of hundred dollars of her hard-earned cash. It was just her luck to have a best friend with the same size feet. Then again, those guest quarters were mighty big and she really hated cleaning.

'It's a deal but, girl, you are going to *work*.'

The guest quarters stood alone on a rise looking down over the sweeping alluvial flats of the Ainsley River. They were in an impressive long, low brick building with broad verandahs shading all sides, and had been built primarily to house pastoral company visitors, Ainsley being only one of a group of stations held by the owners.

Bella and Patty entered through the laundry door. The cleaning products were in a neatly packed box above the laundry wash trough, the vacuum placed in the doorway where, Bella assumed, Siobhan wanted her to trip over it.

Avoiding the vacuum, they made their way into the main hallway of the house and came to a halt in front of the formal lounge bar, which, sadly, was empty. 'A drink would've helped us get through this. Wonder if they left any liquor in any of those little bottles Siobhan puts in each bedroom,' said Bella.

'The toffs probably drank it all,' said Patty as she collapsed into a soft leather chair. 'Jeez, the décor's a bit flash.'

'Yeah, the visitors are mainly from Brisbane and overseas.

They like the finer things in life. I'll have a snoop around,' Bella said as she walked off down the hall towards the bedrooms. 'See if I can find us something to tipple.'

'Fat chance,' called Patty, bouncing up and down in the chair. 'They would've taken it home. Like the cute little bottles of shampoo you flog when you stay at a motel.'

'Oh ye of little faith!' Bella waltzed back into the lounge holding an armful of clinking bottles. 'I reckon there's at least half left in each one. And there are six bedrooms, which means . . .'

'. . . there should be plenty!' Patty grinned. 'This'll help that vacuum go faster.'

'And I reckon we deserve a reward for working so hard this year.' Bella placed the bottles on top of the bar.

'You betcha, girlie!' Snatching a Bundy rum, Patty ripped off the top. 'Here's cheers, big ears!'

It was dusk when Siobhan walked in the laundry door of the guest house. Jimbo down at the stockmen's quarters had been calling Bella and Patty over the radio for the last hour to no avail. He was wondering if they wanted their tea. Worried, he had rung his boss, and the boss – Siobhan – had responded.

Clad in a tight black miniskirt, topped with a deep V-neck top and tottering on killer heels that made her bunions hurt, Siobhan was on her way to Jack and Sheila McLaverty's for dinner – a monthly get-together for all the station bosses. She'd left Robert out in the wagon taking a call on his satellite phone, while she checked on the whereabouts of the pain-in-the-arse Victorian floosies.

Thinking of the beautiful and buxom girl she was about to confront, she adjusted her tight skirt, wiggling it a little higher. She then pulled down her V-neck to show more of her meagre cleavage, pushed her arms into her sides to make the most of her push-up bra and tottered through the laundry door . . .

. . . face-planting over the vacuum cleaner she'd left there a few hours before. A vacuum that obviously had not been moved or used.

'Shit! What was that?' said Bella as she sat upright in the cane easy chair in the lounge.

'What was what?' asked Patty, who was sprawled in her favourite place when drunk – on the floor.

'That noise!'

'What noise?'

'That noise I heard?'

'What noise?' repeated Patty.

'Oh no, it was *that* noise!' cried Bella as she tried to jump to her feet, overbalancing and crashing down across Patty instead.

'The two Victorians were drunk,' Siobhan told her dinner companions later on that evening. 'Not just tipsy. Blind drunk. So drunk they were sprawled on top of each other on the floor. Disgusting.'

Indignant and self-righteous, she'd held forth over dinner with her opinions on the two girls and their behaviour until a wearied Sheila McLaverty had forcefully changed the subject. Privately Sheila cheered the two girls, knowing what a bitch Rob Davidson's wife was. Sheila had her own thoughts on Bella and Patty, seeing first-hand the fun – and, yes, compassion –

the two girls had brought to this far-flung outpost. Helping when Max had his accident and then ringing the Andersons in Brisbane every couple of days to see how they were all going; it was more than Siobhan had done. Thanks to Bella the gardens on the station had never looked so good, a cool green refuge for the stockmen after a long and hot day in the saddle. And then there was the previously high rate of sick leave from the stockmen's camp. It was down to nil lately, thanks to Patty.

Sheila sighed. Having adult children herself, she knew it had been about time for the two girls to break out – young ones these days could only be good for *so* long – but it was just unfortunate they chose to do so on Siobhan's time and turf.

'So I told them they were *fired*!' said Siobhan, satisfaction in her voice. 'Didn't I, Robert? They leave tomorrow. I will *not* tolerate such behaviour. It's a bad influence on the rest of the staff.'

Jack stifled a laugh, and Sheila knew her husband was thinking that half the station hands would have been long gone if Siobhan had her way. Most of their best stockmen had a love affair with the bottle. It was just the way it was in this lonely part of the world.

Sheila made a mental note to go down to the stockmen's quarters in the morning and bid the girls goodbye. She'd also ring the old stockman from Johanna Downs, Harry Bailey. He was really fond of the girls, which was saying something; not much crept under that crusty bushman's veneer. He was better with horses than people. Harry could take the most recalcitrant, wild-eyed steed and in a couple of hours have that same animal lying on the ground with Harry sitting on its belly whispering sweet nothings in its ears. He was known throughout Queensland and the Territory for his horse whispering.

Looking across the table, Sheila could see Rob's uncomfortable expression. No doubt he was thinking he was now down a ringer, a gardener *and* a fill-in cook. It served him right. If he couldn't keep his wife's spitefulness in hand, he deserved all the trouble he got.

There was quite a crowd to see them off, something the girls hadn't expected. Sheila and Jack, having got over his missing loader by now. Rodney along with Jimbo the cook.

Harry Bailey turned up at the last minute to give both girls a handmade leather wallet, each engraved with their name; a souvenir from their time in outback Queensland. Tears came to both girls' eyes as old Harry handed over his presents. 'I've been making them for a while, but finished them off last night after I heard you were leaving. Now don't you go forgetting, Bella me girl.' Harry leaned in and gave her a rough hug.

'Don't forget what, Harry?'

'How to lace that bloody girth.'

Bella burst out laughing, making everyone turn in their direction, while Harry ducked his head in embarrassment.

'We use *real* stock saddles in Victoria, Harry. With proper girths that have buckles. You come on down one day and I'll show you how we do it in the mountains.'

'Now, Bella,' cut in an amused Patty, 'don't you think he's a bit old for you? Plus I think a certain brother of mine might get jealous.'

The whole crowd around Patty's red Holden ute roared and Harry didn't know which way to look. 'Just kidding, Harry, just kidding,' said Patty as she gave the old man a hug. 'And

I promise, if I win the whip-cracking championship at the Nunkeri Muster again this year, I'll give you a ring.'

'You do that, girlie. Be nice to hear all those Sunday-morning practice sessions didn't go to waste.'

'What's this, Harry? You haven't been giving her lessons, have you?' Bella pouted at the old man. 'Patty was impossible to beat last year, without having a master like you to help her.'

Sheila stepped forward next to offer a hug. 'By the way, girls, Knackers rang this morning. Looks like Max will be let out of hospital tomorrow. They're all going on a holiday in the Whitsundays. Knackers sounded so excited. Just like a big kid himself really.'

Patty laughed. 'Knackers in shorts? I'd like to see that! His legs have never seen the sun. Ever. Oh God, those white chicken legs.'

Bella tried to swallow her giggles but the vision of a red-faced Knackers, broad-brimmed hat on his head, big barrel chest clad in a striped cowboy shirt sauntering down the sand with psychedelic board shorts on was too much. Unfortunately the Queenslanders standing around them couldn't see the joke.

'Well, *something's* funny,' said Rodney, looking puzzled.

Sheila smiled. These two girls really had brought a ray of sunshine to Ainsley Station, even if she couldn't understand some of their jokes. They would be missed. 'Good luck, you two. Stay in touch.'

Piling into the fully laden ute, the girls flung kisses from the windows as they spun the wheels on the track for the last time.

'Well, that's it,' said Patty, as she nosed her ute through the gateway of Ainsley Station. She pulled up beside the forty-four gallon drum mailbox. 'Which way do we go? We're running a couple of months early.'

'Well, I've been thinking . . .' said Bella, and Patty buried her face in her hands.

'Last time you *thought*, Hells Bells, we got fired.'

'Yeah well, we had a good time doing it, didn't we?'

'Too right we did. That liquor was top-shelf stuff.'

'As I was saying, I was thinking we could pool our bucks and still have a little holiday on the way home.'

'A *little* holiday? Neither of us is due back to work until January, although I wouldn't mind getting home earlier.' Patty's dark eyes turned dreamy and Bella knew she was thinking of Macca.

'I wouldn't mind getting home either, so how about we check out the coast and make it home in time for the Burrindal B&S and Christmas – what do you reckon? If we're careful with our money we might be able to do it.'

'It sounds like a plan,' said Patty. 'But . . .'

'But what?'

'Maybe we should try and be a little bit responsible here. Go west and get another job?'

'Responsible? Since when have *you* been responsible?'

'C'mon. I've been very responsible since we made our last bet.'

'Bullshit! You slept with Macca!'

'And you should have slept with Will. Maybe you wouldn't be so bloody cranky if you had. Although why anyone would want to get down and dirty with my brother . . . Yuck!'

'The bet was no sleeping with anyone until six weeks after you met them.' Bella was indignant. 'You just gave in, Patty. How could you? We were trying to save *your* soul, after all.'

'I've known Macca for years, so he doesn't count.'

'You're splitting hairs, Pat Me Tuffet.'

'You're just dirty you didn't work out the loophole first.'

Yep, she was. Totally. 'You owe me a slab of rum-and-coke and fifty dollars, girl.'

Patty ignored her and pulled a coin from the ashtray. 'Heads we go left to the coast and a holiday; tails we go right and inland to find a job out west for a while. We'll head home in time for the B&S, though; I can feel those Ariat boots on my feet already.'

'No way, sunshine. You didn't *clean* the guest quarters.'

'I did so. I helped you clean up the grog. Doesn't that count?'

'No.'

Patty looked momentarily disappointed.

'Heads for the holiday.' Bella wanted a decision.

Patty spun the coin in the air and slammed it down on the back of her fist.

They both held their breath as Patty lifted her hand.

'Heads,' she said, a grin lighting up her face. 'Who needs to be responsible?'

'Yee ha!' yelled Bella. 'Watch out, coast, here we come.'

Chapter 9

It was five weeks later, on a sunny Friday afternoon. They'd just left Tamworth, having decided no trip for two country girls was complete without a visit to the Australian capital of country music. They'd swung in from the coast on their way home.

It was Bella's turn to drive, and she was struck by the sight of hundreds of umbrella-like grass seed heads rolling across the ground, piling up against fence posts, chasing each other over the paddocks and along the roadsides, looking for all the world like tumbleweed.

Sara Storer's tumbleweed.

'Tumbleweeds!' she yelled.

Slouched in the passenger seat, hat pulled over her eyes, Patty roused from a doze.

'Look at them go,' said Bella. She jabbed at the ute's accelerator in an attempt to outrun one that was rolling in the grassy long paddock beside her.

'That's flaming windmill grass, you dill, not tumbleweed, and it's got a tailwind, so unless you want a speeding ticket I suggest you give up the chase now.'

'It looks close enough to tumbleweed to me. Where's that CD?'

'What CD?'

'Sara Storer. *Silver Skies*. With the tumbleweed song she played in Gundolin. Where did we put it? . . . Oh here it is.' Bella found the CD right where it should be, in the CD holder. One-handed, she shook it free from its cover, then went to jam it into the CD player.

'Hang on a minute.' Patty stopped Bella from killing the radio. Jacking up the volume, the Americanised country twang of the radio announcer filled the cabin of the ute.

'For anyone interested in crossing the border, the Nunkeri Muster will now be held this weekend. Usually held in February or March, the organisers have moved the event forward because of concerns about bushfires later on in summer due to the drought.

'But regardless of the time of year, they've got the Stockmen's Challenge, a demanding and hotly contested horse race, which will test out the best horsemen in the land. There's some hay-stacking, round-bale-rolling, whip-cracking and bush poetry. On Friday night a country-music DJ will hit the stage. He'll be followed by a cover band on Saturday night . . .'

Bella looked at Patty.

Patty looked at Bella.

No-one knew they were on their way home. They'd decided the news they'd been sacked was better told to their parents in person. And they'd wanted to surprise Will and Macca. All phone calls home had been brief, text messages vague. What better way to end a year of fun and freedom than with the Nunkeri Muster?

And Will and Macca were sure to be there.

'You in?' said Patty, looking across the ute at her best mate. 'Boy, oh boy, I'm in!' yelled Bella, dropping the CD and shoving her left hand in the air.

'Let's do it then!' cried Patty, slamming a high five.

'You realise we won't get there tonight,' said Bella, a little while later.

Patty grunted, again nestled under her hat against the seatrest.

'If we start out early in the morning, we'll get there in plenty of time for tomorrow night, though.'

Another grunt from the passenger seat.

That was enough encouragement for Bella. She notched up her speed and firmly pointed the ute's bonnet south while the radio announcer voiced the local rural news. With nothing to do but drive, Bella snagged her Sara Storer CD from the floor where it had fallen, shoved it into the player and cranked up the volume.

She felt the music transport her to another time, another place.

She was in Gundolin.

Back with Will.

Dancing with Will.

Man, she'd missed him. Never before had she been so struck on a bloke. Will had somehow broken through the rules she and Patty had lived by: all fun; no pain or gain, especially when it came to men.

At unexpected moments over the last couple of weeks when

she was riding the motorbike, or just mowing the lawn, she'd found herself yearning to see him, to hear his deep voice and laughter, to smell and feel his warmth.

The few mobile phone calls and text messages they'd shared had only accentuated the hundreds of miles of distance between them and made her yearn for him all the more.

She wanted to taste him. Make love to him.

Six weeks was up.

She'd won the bet. All wagers were now off. The booty was hers; Patty owed her a slab of rum and fifty bucks.

Her eyes slid across the ute to Will's sister. Bella had been worried about Patty too, since the boys left. Patty had been quiet – almost reflective – and that wasn't like her at all. Strangest of all was that Patty hadn't been forthcoming with information after the night in Gundolin. When Bella asked how things had gone, Patty just smiled. With dreamy eyes she'd responded, 'Good, *really good*.'

That was it. Not a skerrick more.

Although, Bella hadn't exactly bared her soul to Patty about Will either, other than to complain about a certain bet.

More roaming windmill grass caught Bella's eye in the paddock out to the right, tumbling wildly like her thoughts and her unexpected feelings for Will. Her whole body suddenly seemed as light as air at the thought of what was waiting in those mountains. Bella pulled the ute to a halt by the side of the three-chain wide road. Unsnapped her seatbelt.

'What are you doing?' asked Patty, the sudden stop making her pull the hat from over her eyes. 'Where are you going?' she said again, jolting upright.

Bella jumped from the driver's seat, grabbed her hat and slammed the door.

Through the open window she called, 'Out to dance through tumbleweeds!'

'They're not tumbleweeds, they're just bloody grass heads! You're an idiot.'

'So are you. Come *on*!' Twirling, Bella threw her hat into the air. 'We've lived one of our dreams, Patty. Our outback road trip is done. Now we're free and ready for our next adventure. I love my life!'

And she ran.

'I can't fucking believe I'm doing this,' said Patty as she unsnapped her belt and got out of the ute.

'Come on, grumble-guts. Have you ever seen anything like it?' called Bella as she threw her hands in the direction of the hundreds of tumbling weeds scooting down the road. 'They look so wild. So free. Just like us.'

'If you say so, girl,' said Patty, parking her bum on the bonnet. 'So free in fact, in the US, North Dakota I think, they considered erecting a fence all the way around the *whole state* to stop the tumbleweed taking over. See, I'm not just a dumb-arse nurse.'

'I never said you were.'

'No, but you've thought it plenty of times.' Patty lifted herself off the ute and slung an arm around her friend. 'I agree. We're as free-spirited as tumbleweed – but we're not half as prickly!'

'Speak for yourself.'

Patty went for a full arm-lock around Bella's neck. Bella jammed a pair of hands into Patty's sensitive ribs and tickled for all she was worth.

Patty roared and let her go, laughing.

Gasping for breath, Patty took a few moments to compose herself. 'We need a photo. So we have proof for our grandkids that we actually did this.'

'Grandkids? Whoa back. I can't even contemplate the idea of kids.'

'Okay. How about so we've got proof we're legends in our own lunchboxes?'

Bella raised an eyebrow, then grinned and nodded. 'You're just so full of yourself.'

'You reckon?'

'Yep.'

Patty looked contemplative. 'You're probably right.'

Then she ducked into the ute to grab her camera, and set the self-timer.

'So are you coming?' asked Bella.

'Where to?'

'To dance, my friend . . . To dance with Sara. Let's pretend all this blow-away grass is tumbleweed and dance like lunatics. We've got the Nunkeri Muster and two boys waiting in those mountains of ours on the other side of the border. What's not to be happy about?'

The driver in the four-wheel drive coming in the opposite direction was mystified. Two young girls – one a long-ringleted blonde, the other a shorter, claret auburn – looked like they were dancing by the side of the road on a Friday afternoon. From the camera perched precariously atop a felt Akubra hat on the roof of the ute, they also appeared to be trying to pose for a photo.

Figuring they were half-cut from an early finish shearing a mob or maybe they were starting early for a B&S weekend, he kept them in his rear-vision mirror long after he'd passed by.

They were easy on the eye, that was for sure. And at his age the talent had all but dried up. Maybe he should have offered to take the photo for them.

A bit late now. They were on the move again, twirling, laughing. They reminded him of the yearlings he had at home, playful young horses full of the thrill of life. Arms swinging, heads bopping, elastic-sided boots flying through the air, their features slowly became blurred until they were just a pair of shadows dancing in the breeze.

Chapter 10

Will O'Hara shouldn't have been at the Stockmen's Muster on the Nunkeri Plains. He should have stayed at home, baling his paddock of lucerne before the cool change hit. Downing a gulp of rum-and-coke, he slumped his shoulders forward over the can in his hand and tried not to think about the green crop languishing in neat rows on his river flats, waiting to be baled into squares.

His thoughts shifted to his broken-down ute, sitting in the workshop back home on Tindarra Station. He'd inherited the ute along with the hundreds of acres which made up the station from his late Uncle Bill. He could have had the new water pump fitted to the old girl by now and she would've been running real sweet. He needed her going so he could start repairing the boundary fence between his place and his father Rory's property next door.

He let out an audible sigh that floated into the night air above his tousled russet hair, heard by no-one who really counted. He *had* to get the place through this drought. So far he was doing okay; he'd de-stocked as much as he could afford to and was now only running a few steers he'd picked up cheaply. He had his new cropping regime sorted, and Bill had been able to see the first crop of lucerne cut before he died a couple of years ago. A stab to his guts reminded him how much he missed the old man. No, he shouldn't be sitting in front of a huge bonfire on this grassy plain in the middle of nowhere drinking rum.

Two hours before, Macca's LandCruiser had poked its nose into the wide doorway of Will's tumbledown workshop. Built by Will's Uncle Bill, the workshop was a lean-to add-on to a machinery shed that had seen better days. Head down, butt up, Will was trying to extricate a buggered water pump from his ute's engine bay. The vehicle was so old it really should have been replaced, the odometer already well into its second round. But there was no money for that kind of luxury up here in the mountains at the moment, with the drought clinching farms and lives within its deadly grip. The ute had finally died yesterday, a few kilometres from home, and had to be towed back with the tractor.

'Comin' to the Muster, O'Hara?' Macca's big voice had boomed out from inside the LandCruiser. Through the ute's open windows Lee Kernaghan's music was pouring out to thump around the old workshop walls and compete with Macca's voice.

'Nope.' Will had pulled his head out from under the bonnet of his buggered vehicle. 'I've got to get this water pump in and the old girl going by the end of the weekend. Got stuff to do, places to go, namely shopping in Burrindal before I run out of tucker.'

Inside his ute, Macca reached across and turned down the CD player so he could be heard more easily. 'Bugger the bloody old girl. And I'll ferry you out some food. Come on, mate. Climb aboard. We've got some rum to drink. Girls to woo. Not to mention a bloody good horse race to watch, although if you want my view, the butts and boobs strutting around that plain are far better entertainment.'

Will shook his head and bent back down under the bonnet.

Sensing he'd need to be more persuasive, Macca opened his door and got out, all six-foot-three of him uncurling into a mountain of a man. With a head of thick, curly black hair, Bob Hawke-style eyebrows topping dark, brooding eyes and florid cheeks where blue-red veins ran amok just under the surface, Macca didn't need much effort to look intimidating.

'Don't make me pick you up and stuff you into the passenger seat, Will. For crying out loud, you need a break. What better way to get away from this flaming drought than to hit the Nunkeri Muster for the weekend? I promise I'll have you back here safe and sound tomorrow. You can spend the night with the water pump and the ute then. If you're up to it, that is.'

'That's what I'm worried about, mate, the bloody up-to-it bit.' Will poked his head out again, grinned and then grappled one-handed for another tool off the workbench beside him. 'We're too long in the tooth for getting hard on the piss, and I've got lucerne down waiting to be baled.'

'Fuck the lucerne, O'Hara. And are you calling twenty-eight *old*? This drought's got you by the balls and quite frankly it's about time something – or someone – took its place.'

Macca paused for a cheeky wink and waggled his eyebrows up and down. 'That's unless you want to saddle up a horse for a ride instead?'

Will dived back under the bonnet.

Macca fished into his pocket for the ever-present tooth-pick to jam into the side of his mouth. Chewing, he leaned up against the hoist, which was standing at right angles to the grainy cement floor. 'Maybe you *should* have another go at riding in the Stockmen's Challenge. Your ego should just about be over the bashing it got ten years ago.'

'One ride in The Challenge was enough for me. I'm good, but not that good,' came from under the bonnet. There was a crash and a rattle as something dropped to the ground under the ute. 'Bugger it.' Will stood up and stepped away from the ute to stretch his back. Moving across to the workbench, he dropped the spanner he'd been using among the piles of tools lying jumbled together on the slab of red gum stained black with sump oil.

'Mate, that was a hellish ride,' he recalled. 'I was only eighteen and I was bloody lucky to stay on the horse.'

'Yeah, I remember.' Macca rumbled with laughter, the toothpick bobbing up and down in time with his shaking body. 'When you galloped across the finish line, you were clinging to that saddle like a drowning man hugging a lifesaver.' Macca wiped tears from his eyes.

'Yeah, well, you should try it, you big wuss.' Will got down on his belly and crawled under the ute to grab the fallen nut off the floor. 'At least I know when I'm outclassed.' He wiggled back out and stood up, the tiny offending nut glistening in his hands. 'The Challenge's a feat of bloody good horsemanship. Once was enough for this bloke.'

Since then Will had left all the riding of four-legged animals at the Muster to the experts, and instead concentrated on attracting the interests of the two-legged fillies who pranced around the plains. The lure of a ride on one of those had kept him – and Macca – going back year after year.

He walked to the bench, grabbed the spanner and dived into the engine bay to replace the recalcitrant nut, thinking as he went. Macca spread his charms far and wide, making himself a legend of the 'dawn dash', that sunrise bolt from a girl's swag clasping boots and trousers in hand after a hot and heavy night.

Will was different. Not caring for a one-night stand, waking up the next morning staring at a sheila who looked nothing like you remembered from the night before.

And as Will tightened the nut on the ute, in his tumble-down workshop on that searing Saturday afternoon, there was only one girl who came to mind as he weighed up whether to go or not. He wondered if she would be there. He should have asked his mum exactly when they were due home.

Communication with the girls had been intermittent and unsatisfactory. No-one was really certain *where* they were. But there was one thing he did know for sure: a dawn dash would be the furthest thing from his mind if he finally managed to snare Bella Vermaelon.

'Come on, mate . . .' Macca wheedled as he spat the mangled toothpick from his mouth. 'We can grab some cans from the Burrindal pub and we'll be there in less than two hours. What do you say, big fella? Am I gunna have to stuff you into me ute or what?' Will straightened and threw the spanner back on the old bench. Wiping his greasy hands on a rag, he stood considering his mate, the bloke with whom he'd played merry hell since they were small boys.

Should he go? His neighbour, Wes, was probably already there spruiking poetry, and Will loved listening to the old man when he was on a roll. The other inhabitant of the valley, his Aunty Maggie, would be there in the morning, or so she'd said earlier in the week when he'd called in for a quick cup of tea. His mum and dad were away in Melbourne for a few days.

If he didn't go, it would just be him in this big, lonesome valley feeling sorry for himself. He'd miss out on all the fun. He could just go easy on the grog then he'd be right to fix the old ute tomorrow night, and maybe he could bale the lucerne on Monday. It would probably just be another dry storm tonight. Again those white-gold tumbling curls flashed past his eyes. Maybe . . . just maybe? Would they be there? He wouldn't put it past those two, an outside chance for sure. But all the same . . .

'Oh bugger it, why the hell not?' he finally said. 'Let me grab a quick shower and I'll be with you.' Slamming down the bonnet on the ute, he set off across the yard, throwing words over his shoulder. 'Grab my swag out from beside that old lathe, will you, and there's an esky on the verandah. There might be a can left in the beer fridge, if you're thirsty.' One final yell came across the yard before the screen door slammed. 'I'll be back.'

'No problemo,' called Macca grinning, as he watched Will practically run across to the house. 'Plenty of time, old mate. We'll be there before dark.'

Chapter 11

Bella tried to focus on the tiny glasses swimming in front of her eyes. A bunch of Akubra hats worn by the cattlemen clustered around the bar kept distracting her. Was Will here? What would he think of her down on her knees, swilling like a pig?

Damn Patty and her bloody bets. Her mind flicked back to half an hour before when she was considering the best spot in the river for a swim. The water was packed with people, swimming or sitting waist-deep on deckchairs drinking and yarning. There were dogs splashing about, barking, plus a few horses trying to stay cool – it was standing-room only. Patty ran up and tackled Bella from behind.

'Hey, Hells Bells! C'mon, Jonesy and me have organised a drinking competition. And have I got a bet for you this time, girlfriend! Seeing as I haven't paid out the other wager we had yet, how about double or nothing? *Two* slabs of rum-and-coke and a hundred bucks, I beat you. What do you reckon?'

'No.' Bella shook her head. 'You know I can't hold my grog as well as you can. You owe me, girl. I'm going for a swim.' She tried to extricate herself from Patty's hot and sweaty arms. 'Plus, you can't organise a competition and be a competitor.'

'Where's your sense of adventure? In Queensland still?' Patty let go, stood back and planted her hands on her hips. 'And pig's arse I can't compete. That's why I've organised the bloody thing. Jonesy here's going to adjudicate.'

For the first time, Bella noticed a middle-aged bloke slouching against a nearby four-wheel drive, a green can of VB in hand. Jonesy lifted his arm in salute. It looked like he was drunk. And dribbling. Oh boy, thought Bella.

'Excuse *me*, but you're leaning against my vehicle.'

The hoity-toity voice belonged to Prudence Vincent-Prowse, the girl who since childhood had loved to make life hell for Bella and Patty. Bella couldn't believe she'd managed to forget Prudence Vincent-Prowse for a whole year.

'Yeah. So?' Jonesy sprawled himself out some more and scratched his balls.

'You're scratching it, you idiot!' Prudence's face – which normally looked like it had been lifted from a Covergirl advertisement – was screwed up and turning slightly crimson.

'You gunna do somethin' about it?' Jonesy looked delighted.

'It's *my* fucking four-wheel drive. *Now get off it!*'

'Okay, okay – no need to get tetchy.' A disappointed Jonesy lifted himself off the vehicle, leaving dusty scuffmarks on the shiny duco. 'You need to kick back a bit, love. How 'bout a drinkin' competition to loosen those bra straps and G-string?'

'How did you know I was wearing a G—' Prowsy stopped and then scowled at a laughing Jonesy, who was prancing

around, bum tucked in, wrists limp, doing a good impersona-
tion of a stuck-up poodle.

'C'mon, Prowsy, how about a few drinks?' Patty dropped
herself neatly into the conversation, turning the focus away
from Jonesy's drunken antics. 'I need some contestants for a
drinking comp I've set up and we haven't seen you for *so* long.
Nothing like a welcome-back drink with some *mates*.'

Prowsy swung round and took in her female observers. 'Well,
well, well . . . what do we have here?' she said, while looking
like she had dog shit on her boots. 'The two stooges are back
from Queensland. I was hoping we'd gotten rid of you both for
good. Obviously Gippsland's luck didn't hold.'

'Cor-r-ection!' Patty rolled her r's in jubilation. 'Gippsland's
luck is bloody marvellous. And to celebrate, I've organised a
welcome-home treat for us all. So are you in? I betcha Bella and
me can drink you under the table. We've been practising real
hard up north.' Patty looked almost jocular, which surprised
Bella because Patty *hated* Prowsy. Then again maybe it was a
look of pure cunning; Patty could drink almost everyone under
the table.

'I bet you, you can't. I'm rather good at games,' said Prowsy,
narrowing her baby-blue eyes. 'What's the prize?'

Patty looked stumped for a minute . . . then her face cleared.
'What do you say about a night out with any single man here?
You choose.'

Bella, Prowsy and Jonesy's voices competed with each other:

'Patty, you can't do that!'

'Your brother?'

'Me! Me! Choose me, girls!'

Bella didn't hear Patty's response. She was focused on Prowsy.
Did she just say 'your brother'? Patty only had one. Will. And

there was no way a double-barrelled bully was getting a night with him; not if Bella could help it. She could just imagine those long French-manicured fingertips of Prowsy's moving sinuously across his hunky, muscled chest. The thought of it made her want to puke.

Ever since Prowsy had shoved Patty's head into a bucket of cow and horse shit twelve years ago at the Narree Agricultural Show, to stop her from entering the Miss Junior Showgirl competition, there had been battlelines drawn in the dirt between the three girls. Bella had used her fledgling stockwhip skills to belt the crap out of the older bully, who'd cowered in the corner clutching a bleeding cheek.

Later that day Bella – wearing a pink-and-white chequered shirt, hair tied into matching gingham ribbons and denim jeans with shiny riding boots – had been crowned Miss Narree Junior Showgirl. Prudence had flounced past, a poor loser in second place in her white chiffon party dress and silver-buckled high-heeled sandals, shooting dagger looks. Bella could just make out the slash marks down her left cheek, under the liberally applied make-up.

Prudence's mother, Mildred Vincent-Prowse, hadn't wasted any time honing in on the girls' mothers in the cooking-and-crafts pavilion. 'Your two girls are wild cats, heathens the pair of them,' she'd hissed at a startled Francine Vermaelon and Helen O'Hara as they'd walked the pavilion aisles to see how their cooking and quilting had faired. 'We'll sue you both if there is a permanent mark on my little girl's face,' she'd threatened, before spinning on a spiked heel and prancing off.

Francine and Helen had looked at each other in horror and fled the pavilion in search of the two wild cats, who were finally found brushing down their horses ready for the early-evening novelty events.

'But, Mum,' said Bella, 'she pushed Patty's head into a bucket of poop.'

'It doesn't matter, Bella,' reprimanded an exasperated Francine. 'You can't go cutting up people's faces with your stockwhip, for heaven's sake. I'm confiscating it for a month.'

'But it's all I had in my hand at the time . . . and she deserved it.'

'Not another word, young lady, not another word.'

Meanwhile, Helen O'Hara had been picking pieces of horse shit out of her daughter's matted hair.

'That little bitch,' Helen said to Francine later, out of hearing of the two girls. 'She should know better than to bully other kids. She's a couple of years older too!'

'Like mother, like daughter,' said a grim Francine. 'Prudence probably deserved the beating she got, but I can't condone Bella using that damned stockwhip to cut people up.'

'No, I suppose not,' Helen had agreed. 'But I have to say I like her style. And my daughter *stinks*.'

'Yes, well . . . have you ever known our girls to go down without a fight? You tussle with one, you tussle with two. God help Prudence, is what I say.'

❧

Some things never changed. Here they were again, Bella and Patty, tussling with Prudence – alongside a truckload of other girls.

Bella's vision was blurring at the edges; the air around her head spinning like crystallised sugar in a fairy-floss machine. She couldn't see Patty anymore or any of the other competitors in the Cock-Sucking Cowboy Shot-Shooting Competition.

She could, however, hear the packed crowd in the large green canvas tent whistling and cheering and stomping their feet, chanting, 'Skol! Skol! Skol!' Fifteen young women were lined up on their knees as if in homage to the liquor set out on the makeshift bar, a battered wooden tabletop sitting unevenly on two A-frame trestles; young women whose drunkenness could be ascertained by the ratio of empty to full glasses.

'Skol! Skol! Skol!'

The roars got louder.

Bella knew she was slowing down. She lunged for another shot – and missed, hands flailing in empty air rather than landing on glass. She had another go.

Got it. Lifting her hand to shoot the shot, she gasped as dizziness suddenly kicked in. Stopping mid-toss, she waited until her head stopped whirling like flotsam adrift in wild seas.

Images of Will flirted with her mind – dizzying reality duelled with the arousingly erotic. Her awareness took flight to another realm, far beyond its usual self. Unbidden, her tongue lapped, savouring the taste of the drink in her hand. It tasted *so* good. With growing abandon she lapped again, her mind flickering through images as vivid as the sun on a burning hot day.

A naked torso with tanned skin moulded over muscle patterned with russet down, snaking below a belly button into illicit depths.

She had to have it.

Tight bum cheeks wrapped in denim, a tattered brown leather belt tail hanging unrestrained, drawing attention to the nicely rounded bulge snuggling into the front zip.

Bella slid her tongue around inside her soft cheeks, touching the searing heat of the decadent liqueur. It was all too much. She couldn't stop.

Brown eyes dripping like molasses – syrupy and sweet. Dimples that dived into cheeks of wickedness . . . and then there was the wink.

Succumbing, she swallowed.

Oh. My. God. It was good.

The smooth slide down her throat . . . velvet softness, the smoothness of cream, a slow burn and throb.

The taste of the lover yet to be hers.

Throwing all caution aside, Bella grabbed the next shot and then another, her desire to win driving her on.

Maybe tonight?

She sucked and gulped, again and again, until the very last drop of creamy liqueur was gone. The roar from the crowd ramped up an octave.

Bella smiled like a sated she-devil.

Tonight – if he was here.

The PA system crackled and gave a long squeal. Jeers erupted from the crowd, directed at the man holding the microphone standing atop a chair near the makeshift bar.

'Sorry about that, folks.' He cleared his throat.

'Just get on with it, Jonesy,' a voice yelled from the crowd.

Jonesy hitched up his strides, sniffed back hard.

'Um, well . . . Here in front of you tonight is the Sheilas Only Cock-Sucking Cowboy Shot-Shooting Competition.' Jonesy paused for a swig on his beer. 'What a mouthful!' He snivelled back hard again and shifted his weight so his hips pointed out towards the crowd.

'And my, oh my, folks, wouldn't we boys just love to experience the endurance of these cock-sucking sheilas tonight.' Jonesy thrust his hips backwards and forwards to yells of approval and laughter.

'Oh yes, siree, it's quite a sight, ladies and gentlemen. If you're not taking in the show, then wiggle those Wrangler butts up here and take a gander, before the cocks . . . or should I say shots, run out.'

The crowd roared. 'Skol! Skol! Skol!'

For Bella, Jonesy's voice and the crowd's roar were just a loud buzz in an otherwise insular world. The erotic images of Will had long since departed. The only shot glasses left were the ones empty of temptation, held in her hands.

The butterscotch schnapps kicked in; the Irish cream remained a memory.

Her knees started to go.

Eyes closed, she began to sway.

She was going down.

Bella slid sideways, taking little time to hit the ground. The shot glasses – those tiny, incongruous shells of glass responsible for her current state – followed, sliding from the clutch of her slack hands to the dirt, smashing together with a tinkle. Oblivious to the uproar around her, Bella lay in a drunken stupor, a tumble of limbs resting on mother earth.

'Jeez, Hells Bells, don't pass out on me now!'

Patty had flung herself sideways, trying to halt her mate's slide into oblivion. Missing her only by inches, Patty cursed as Bella hit the dirt. Bella's breasts started to slide from their position perched inside her scarlet push-up bra, her Wrangler singlet doing nothing to help contain the boobs so intent on escape. Patty gave her best mate a shove with the heel of her hand.

No movement.

Not even a flicker.

She softly kicked Bella's boots. Bella stirred in response.

Patty nudged again. Bella grunted.

A cursing Patty shoved and kicked together.

Bella moved to a half-sit. Realising she was semi-naked, she frantically helped Patty, who was trying to stuff her boobs back inside the gravity-defying bra.

'Bloody hell. Why'd you have to be so well stacked?' Patty frowned as her hands warred with Bella's.

Laughter and cries of disappointment reigned equal among the watching crowd.

'Let her go, Patty, you spoilsport!'

'Let 'em rip, Vermaelon!' mingled with roars of encouragement directed at the remaining drinkers still downing their shot glasses of cowboys.

'Skol! Skol! Skol!'

Bella sat upright, startling Patty into letting her go.

Flinging her hands into the air, she screamed at the top of her voice, 'I won! I bloody well DID IT!'

She turned and started pummelling Patty. 'You owe me, sunshine. It was double or nothing. I *won*.'

'You bloody well didn't, you bag. I did.' Patty launched herself at Bella, punching and roaring back. 'You passed out. I didn't. That means I won.'

Baring her teeth, Bella pushed Patty down on her arse. Throwing out an arm, Patty hooked Bella around the knees. The two girls tumbled together, wrestling their way across the ground, rolling through spilt rum and beer, cigarette butts and cow shit.

Some of the crowd moved with them, eager to see more female flesh. The rest stayed behind, eyes trained on the other contestants.

Gaining the advantage, Bella perched on Patty's belly, hovering just above her friend's prized crystal-encrusted belt buckle, the buckle awarded to Patricia Maree O'Hara as winner of the Nunkeri Muster Ladies Whip-Cracking Championship last year.

'Give way, O'Hara!' She started to move her hips backwards and forwards, riding Patty like a cowboy on a bucking rodeo bull. Hips thrusting, one hand in the air to keep her balance, Bella whooped with joy. 'I won the bet. *Yee ha!*'

Patty gasped and spluttered.

'Give her over to me, Bella; I'll do a better job than that.'

The voice sounded familiar. Bella looked for the owner.

It was Macca, the man who no doubt had his heart set on getting Patty into his swag later that night. 'It's great to see you here, Hells Bells, but you ain't got the right equipment, girlie!' Wearing a belt buckle with bullock horns on a bright silver disk, Macca rocked his hips.

Bella laughed and punched the air with her fist. 'I won! Say it!'

Patty reached out and grabbed Bella's legs. 'Stop! I think I'm going to puke.'

Bella wasn't listening. If Macca was here, Will probably was too. And s*he* didn't need some silly drinking competition to get him in the sack for the night. But two slabs of rum-and-coke plus a hundred bucks? That was a different story. She wasn't giving way until Patty conceded defeat.

'I won! Say it, girl!' Bella yelled again, throwing a hand into the air.

So Patty did the only thing she could do: she stuck up her palm for Bella to slam a high five. 'Okay. You won.'

'YES!'

'Now . . . get the fuck *off me!*'

Chapter 12

Will stretched his long legs out towards the flames, more as a reflex than to gain warmth from the bonfire in front of him. With temperatures reaching the thirties during the day, the fire wasn't really needed, but it was as much a part of the Muster as the Stockmen's Challenge.

A massive construction, with whole trees placed side by side and then on top, the bonfire took all night and half the next day to burn itself down. A CFA truck stood on standby, although Nunkeri had had more rain this season than Tindarra and there was at least a tinge of green left up on this plain. Even so, the tanker was good insurance in case a spark got away. With his butt planted on an old gnarled gum tree log set a strategic distance from the leaping flames, Will tuned into the poem being recited by an elderly man on the other side of the fire.

It wasn't hard to see that Wesley Ogilvie – cattleman, bush poet, legendary stockwhip-maker and Will's neighbour at

Tindarra – adored every minute of his annual Nunkeri Muster performances. For as long as Will could remember, Wes had regaled them with poems, bringing to life Banjo Paterson's ballads and adding a few of his own. Every tale he told was played out on the grazing properties in the high country mountain ranges and valleys of Tindarra, Burrindal and Ben Bullen. Probably to some townies it smacked of a long-winded whine session but, unfortunately, Will knew otherwise. The droughts, fires and floods Wes wove into ballads – they'd had them all in the space of a few years, here in the towering blue mountains of the Great Dividing Range.

'He loves it, doesn't he?' a soft, cultured voice came from the darkness behind Will.

He swung around. Dressed in a faded pink-and-black chequered woollen bushman's shirt, under which there appeared to be at least two more layers, a small rotund figure stood watching old Wes.

'Aunty Maggie! Aren't you hot in that get-up? I didn't think you were coming until the morning.'

'Neither did I.' Disgust was evident in Maggie O'Hara's voice. 'And no, I'm not hot. It's colder when you're older, sober and away from the fire.'

'What changed your plans? It must have been good to get you swagging it. You haven't been too keen on the idea since Uncle Hughie died.'

'Yes, well I'm *not* happy. I love my own bed these days. Getting old and set in my ways. But the woman we've brought in to judge the bush poetry competition tomorrow decided she wanted to try "this camping-out business" as she called it. She's from Melbourne. As I organised the competition, I felt obligated to keep an eye out for her.'

'She'd have no better mate than you, Aunty Maggie. Did you give her your famous camp-oven rabbito for tea?'

'How could I do that when my favourite nephew wasn't there to shoot, skin and de-bone it?' Maggie's voice was teasing and accusatorial at the same time. How did she manage to do that? She made him feel like a naughty school boy caught out by the Catholic Brothers all over again.

'I'm sure you would have managed it. My guess is the lady poetry judge wouldn't have managed watching you do it, though?'

Maggie grinned then affected rounded vowels. 'Yars, I really could not stomach any bush cuisine tonight, thank you, Margaret. Surely you have some smoked salmon and basil pesto? Oh, and a little sour cream with some sun dried tomarrr-toes on top would be simply scrumptious.'

Will laughed. 'That bad, is she?'

'Yes, that bad.'

'So what did you feed her?'

Maggie giggled, eyes crinkling in the corners. 'I served up baked bean and cheese jaffles straight from the fire and she loved it. Asked me for the recipe and where she could buy one of those "contraptions" to cook them in.'

'You really can pick them, Aunty.'

Maggie looked sad. 'Yes, I know, love. My Hughie, God bless his soul, always said I was a dreadful judge of character. But she sounded okay on the phone. A bit up herself, but she seemed to know her stuff.'

'You still miss Uncle Hughie, don't you?' said Will, a gentle but concerned note in his voice. 'Even after twenty years.'

Maggie nodded and blinked hard before turning her attention to Wes and the fire. The silence floating around them stretched out. Will adored his spirited and fiercely independent aunt but he barely remembered her husband Hugh.

A vague image came to him of a large but stooped man sitting near the honey-coloured stone fireplace at the homestead at Tindarra, cleaning his pipe. As a boy Will had been fascinated by the brightly coloured, fluffy pipe cleaners the old bloke used to poke and prod at the tobacco encrusted in the pipe's stem. Hughie had a knack of turning those pipe cleaners into twisted wire animals, in varying shades of blue, green and red, delighting the child at his knee. Will was sure he still had one at home somewhere, probably tucked away in an obsolete corner of the kitchen dresser. It was a shame the couple hadn't been able to have kids.

Maggie still ran Hughie's place down the road from his own, and Will understood why she had stayed in the valley after her husband died despite having no children to raise and keep her company. Tindarra had a tendril-like spirit that twined itself through your body and buried runners deep within the very marrow of your bones.

For Will, the valley, which wove a pattern into the landscape with its golden pastures, lush river flats and soaring hills of grey-blue trees, lifted his soul into the very heart of the rugged mountains and held him hostage with a yearning to be there.

On his trip up north with Macca he hadn't been gone three weeks before he found himself desperately longing for home; yearning to feel the sweet rush of mountain air hitting his face as he stepped outside at sunrise, hungering for the deep-scented tangy smells of the bush that were normally only a breath away.

The loud crack of a tree limb falling onto glowing coals and Maggie's soft voice murmuring at his shoulder brought his thoughts back to the Nunkeri Plains. The smell and feel of Tindarra receded from Will's mind, leaving a sense of loss in their wake.

'Yes, I still miss Hugh. Especially on nights like this. Hughie used to love the Stockmen's Muster. He used to say, there was nowhere else you could find such a mix of generations – grand-parents, parents, teenagers and kids – having so much fun. There's something here for everyone.' She frowned. 'This was one of the few places he could come and really enjoy himself with his mates, after he came back from that damned war. These mountains were his saviour, you know.' Maggie sounded wistful rather than angry. She looked over at old Wes as a roar of laughter came from the other side of the fire. 'Wes misses Catherine too.'

They both stopped and looked across at the diminutive man, standing with his back to them, his body reflected in the fire's light. Will could just make out the red baling twine trailing from the belt loops holding up Wes's 'best' work trousers, a stained and torn pair of khaki drill pants that had seen better days.

When Wesley's wife Catherine had been alive the Ogilvies had lived on their big station at Ben Bullen Hills, two hours by sealed road from Tindarra via Burrindal. Then Catherine had been diagnosed with breast cancer. It had been too far from help on that Ben Bullen mountaintop for an old woman battling for her life, so the couple had moved down to Tindarra, buying a disused school block with its small miner's cottage in dire need of a spruce-up. Across the rough mountain bush tracks, it only took Wes about an hour to travel to Ben Bullen Hills from the Tindarra Valley, every second day.

'Yeah, his place looks so sad and rundown now, since Catherine died,' said Will quietly. 'Remember how happy she was when you painted the old verandah yellow? I didn't know they made paint that bright.'

Maggie chuckled and Will could see her eyes twinkling with the memory of her old and dearest friend. 'Yes, I remember. I got the bloke in Narree to mix it specially. She wanted the same colour as the daffodils you and Wes planted under the old crab-apple trees. Said it would brighten her days whether it was summer, winter or when she was just plain sick and tired.' Maggie's eyes glistened with unshed tears. 'I'm glad they came to us at Tindarra, Will. It was a good compromise. They would have been so alone up at Ben Bullen Hills, and Tindarra was closer to the doctor.'

'Yeah. I have to say I really enjoy having another bloke in the valley too, someone to yarn with and crack a beer. I've learned a lot from old Wes, he's a real man of the bush.'

Maggie nodded and shrugged her chequered shirt in closer to her body, swiping at her eyes surreptitiously with the rough edge. Will pretended he didn't see, choosing to look towards the fire instead.

'Well, William, I'll be going. I was just taking myself off to bed. Needed to use the loos but they're closed. I had to squat next to a log instead. Far too much information for a young bloke like you, I know.' Maggie was grinning again now. 'I heard Wes as I was on the way back to camp. Just wanted to come over and check he was okay.'

Will had once wondered if Aunty Maggie and old Wes would ever get their shit together and marry each other. They spent so much time arguing over this and that during their daily cuppa ritual, they were practically hitched already. Perhaps they still felt married to their late partners.

Maggie was talking, but Will only caught the end of it.

'. . . I have to look after my neighbours, you know,' she finished.

'What about me? I'm your neighbour too.'

'I reckon you're capable of doing that yourself. And if you aren't, I'm sure a certain niece of mine might be able to help you out.' It was Maggie's turn for a stir.

Will could feel heat suffusing his face.

Maggie went on, oblivious. 'That's if she's here, of course. I forgot to ask Frank and Francine if Bella was home yet. She's with Patty, isn't she?' She stopped. 'Why, William, I do believe you're blushing.' Maggie smiled, a smug look patterned on her sweetheart face, her grey bun of hair flopping sideways as she leaned forward and patted him on the shoulder. 'Goodnight, William. You take care.' She waggled her fingers and strode off, a cuddly bear decked out in a lady's chequered bush coat.

Will shook his head. What had he told her when he came home from up north that gave that one away? How much did Maggie *know*? No, he corrected himself. How much had Maggie *guessed*?

Will took a look at his watch. It was a good hour since Macca had gone to find the beer tent and get some more rum. Suddenly a bloke he didn't know appeared at his side.

'Where's your can, mate? Your drinking hand's empty.'

'A mate's gone to get me one, but I don't know where he's bloody well disappeared to.'

'Here, have this one on me.' The bloke raised a matching black can in salute. 'Here's cheers, mate, the next round's on you.' He wandered off to the other side of the fire before Will could thank him.

Will could hear snatches of conversation about some girlie drinking match going on in a tent somewhere. Patty would have enjoyed that, he thought with a rueful grin. He wondered again when she and her mate were due home from Queensland. He'd really hoped they'd be here but he hadn't seen Patty's ute around. It stood out like a neon light – bright fire-engine red with the 'Pat Me Tuffet' bug deflector sitting in pride of place on the bonnet; the bullbar, back window and tailgate plastered with stickers from every B&S around.

Thinking of Patty brought that other girl to mind. Isabella Francine Vermaelon, Auntie Maggie's niece from the verdant irrigated, dairy country in the valleys of Narree. She was the reason he slammed down the bonnet on the old girl with her buggered water pump and climbed into Macca's ute, the reason why he hadn't been able to think straight since coming home from up north.

Yep, if those girls were here, Will was sure he'd know about it. He wouldn't have been able to stay away from Bella even if he tried.

Chapter 13

Bella and Patty slammed a high five, as a nasal and slightly high-pitched voice came from the centre of the watching crowd. 'Let's throw a bit of water around and get some mud happening here. Always love seeing anything with good tits have a wrestle. Roll on, girls, let it rip. Where's the water, guys?' Eddie Murray was panting with desire.

He'd seen the write-up on the Nunkeri Muster in a city newspaper during the week. Ever since, his nights had been filled with wet dreams straight from *Penthouse*; mobs of curvaceous country girls spilling creamy bosoms, romping with him in piles of hay. And by God he was getting his money's worth. No hay but plenty of bosoms.

A merchant banker by day and connoisseur of anything sinful at night, Eddie was on the hunt for sex. During the week he'd visited R.M. Williams and kitted himself out in what the sales lady assured him was the *right* gear. Preening himself in front of the dressing-room mirror, he'd reckoned he cut a fine figure in his bush clobber. His black Italian Fiorelli suit lay scrunched on the dressing-room floor and the soft leather moccasins, which had minutes before been wrapped around his knobbly feet, had been kicked into a corner while their country cousins took centre stage. He admired the way the two-inch Cuban heels on the tooled cowboy boots made his stocky legs look much longer.

The five-hour drive up from Melbourne to this arse end of the world had been worth it. The show was even better than he'd imagined. He *so* wanted to bury his head in those heaving knockers being thrown around on the ground. The redhead wasn't bad, but the blonde was hot.

He jumped up to try to see over the broad set of shoulders, emblazoned with the word 'Wrangler', moving across in front of his eyes.

Still on the ground, Bella could feel the sudden hostility rolling through the air. The crowd parted like Moses cleaving the Red Sea and the man who'd spoken now stood on his own, grinning, trying to catch the eye of one of the blokes he called 'guys' – blokes who thought a 'guy' was a pansy, a poofter, someone who batted for the other side.

Bella rolled off Patty and moved to her feet in one fluid movement, then stuck out a hand to haul her mate up beside her. She didn't recognise the bloke who'd spoken, clearly visible now that Macca had moved out of the way. In his brand-new moleskins that still wore the creases of their packaging, he stood apart from the well-worn, rumpled-looking people around him. She took in the new R.M.'s and the pristine hat that needed a good dousing of sweat, dirt, blood and grease. He stood out like a cheap neon sign blinking, 'Can I be a country boy too?'

And man, was he short! He must've had the moleskins custom made, or they were three-quarter pants faking it long.

Eddie Murray had always prided himself on his quick mind and innate ability to read a situation before an actual event occurred. It was what had made him a very wealthy man, a mover and shaker in the finance industry. When he noticed the hum of conversation from the crowd had gone silent he looked around and realised he was standing alone. With belated clarity Eddie knew he'd read *this* situation wrong. What he'd been watching was in fact country *fun*, not erotic bawdiness.

He'd buggered up big-time here, and some of the guys were *fucking huge*. Particularly the bloke who'd moved out to face him.

He shrunk back into his new clothes, making his five-foot-five frame look even smaller, and set his mind to self-preservation; namely, finding a fast-track way to the exit in one piece. Before he could even begin to formulate a plan, the silence erupted into jeers.

Macca planted himself in front of the girls, shoulders hunched over in his cobalt-blue work shirt, farmer's fists clenched. The veins in his hands stood out like knotted cords looking for something close by to throttle. With his feet planted firmly hip-width apart and his face a boiling red, Macca resembled a protective bull set to charge.

Bella saw flickers of fear in Eddie's eyes.

'Listen, you pimple-dick little tosser. Piss off to your big-city bars and clubs. Leave good country girls like me cousin and Patty here alone.'

'Onya, Macca.'

'Yeah, piss off!' Voices from the crowd joined in.

With little steps, Eddie backed up. 'Ah sorry, old fellow. I didn't mean to upset anyone. Calm down a bit. I just thought . . .' Eddie's rush of words stopped abruptly as Macca raised a bushy eyebrow.

'You thought what?' Macca ground the words like a pestle.

Eddie rushed on, words spilling from his mouth like vomit. 'Ah well . . . never mind. I'll . . . um . . . go, shall I?' He started to wiggle his way backwards through the throng of people now crowding around him. Strangers pressured him from all sides, pushing him, forcing his retreat, silently daring him to stay.

When he'd reversed himself clear of the main crowd, Eddie spun on his high heels and bolted for the tent doorway. Never being one for knowing when to keep his mouth shut, he turned for a last retort before he ran out of the tent to disappear into the night.

'You're all just a bunch of hick cowboys anyway!'

Everyone erupted into loud, raucous laughter.

'Never a truer word spoken, hey fellas, and we're bloody proud of it too!' roared Macca.

The crowd moved back to the bar, where the rest of the girls were swaying on their knees in the shot-shooting competition. Ignoring the action still taking place, Macca spun to face an unkempt Bella and Patty. Both girls had plunked back down on the ground. 'If you see or hear of that wanker again tonight, any time this weekend for that matter, you just find me or one of the boys here and we'll deal with him. Right?'

Bella could see his gaze was filled with the ferocious protectiveness that came with love. The remaining few men who'd stayed at Macca's side, blokes who'd known the girls and their families all their lives, added their voices to Macca's.

'Yeah!'

'Hear, hear!'

'Thanks, fellas.' Bella could feel a blooming flush of heat on her face. The whole incident had sobered her as quickly as a dousing of ice-cold mountain water. She knew they'd almost caused a fight and she wasn't proud of it. Visions of what they must have looked like rolling around, riding each other, flooded her mind and she shuddered as she thought about the trouble they might have caused. What would her parents say if they heard?

'I just hope that toffy little shit gets in the fancy four-wheel drive he's most likely driving and bales out of the valley pronto.' Macca hunkered down beside the girls. Looking from one to the other and waving a warning finger in front of their noses he went on. 'But I tell you what, you two. I don't trust bastards like that one. No more flaunting yourselves, ya hear me?'

Bella heard him and bit back a retort. Beneath his usual easygoing personality, Macca had an autocratic attitude that could piss her right off.

But not this time.

She knew they deserved what he dished out. And she was glad he'd been there to protect them, even though it irked the crap out of her they'd needed him. Instead, she shut her mouth and looked at Patty to check what she thought. Seeing the glint in her friend's eye and the pout on her lips, Bella could tell that Patty was thinking the same.

'Girls?' Macca laced his voice with warning.

As they reluctantly started to nod, Macca raised an eyebrow. Bella knew he'd guard them all night if they didn't agree. Where was the fun in that? So she nodded energetically until it felt like her eyeballs were spinning.

'What are you two doing here so soon anyway?' Macca sat back on his haunches and settled in to roll a smoke. 'I thought you were still up north enjoying station life for another month or so?' He pulled out his baccy and paper from a top pocket. 'Well, that's what you said when we last saw you anyway.'

'Well . . .'

'Um . . .'

Both girls stopped and looked at each other.

'I sense a story here,' mumbled Macca, a tobacco paper on his lip, a plug of baccy now in his hand. 'What did you do, the pair of you? Light a fire under a couple of ringers so they didn't know which way was up? Flash a brown eye at the grader-driver while the boss was driving past?'

Conspicuous silence.

Eyes alight with laughter, Macca allowed the girls to guiltily squirm while he deftly rolled his smoke. Cupping his hands and leaning forward, he lit the rollie, then sat back on his heels. 'Come on. Give it up. What'd you pair of minxes do?' With his free hand he ruffled Patty's hair then slid his fingers along her freckled nose to tap at its pert end.

Patty blushed. Watching closely, Bella was shocked to see that beyond the teasing humour in her larrikin cousin's eyes there was possibly something else. And in return, Patty was staring up at Macca like he was God himself.

'Now I don't think I've ever seen *that* before.' Macca was set to do what he did so well. Tease. 'Pat Me Tuffet, blushing? That's a new one on me.'

Patty reddened all the more.

Watching fascinated, Bella took pity on her best mate and rushed to Patty's rescue. 'Thought we'd drop into the Muster on our way back. Didn't think we'd be home this early either, but, well . . . a few things happened . . . and, well . . . here we are.'

'Huh?' said Macca, eyes still on the red-haired girl by his side.

'You wanted to know why we were here.'

Macca pulled his attention back to Bella. 'Mmm, that definitely smells to me. You were enjoying yourselves *so* much; all those rodeos, race days and parties. What happened? Did that bitch, the station manager's wife, finally find a reason to be rid of you?'

Patty looked at Bella; Bella looked back at Patty. Both girls laughed.

'Mmm, well you could say that.' Bella didn't want to recount the drunken escapade that had led to their expulsion from Ainsley Station. Not after what had just happened. 'Anyway, we thought we'd hoon down the east coast for a bit of a look-see. Heard about the Muster on the radio near Tamworth, so we decided to come straight here. A last piss-up before arriving home early to surprise everyone.' She didn't add that they'd been hoping the boys would be there.

Macca nodded, naïve to the female mind. 'Must have been a bit of an eye-opener hitting the mountains after that flat, scrubby country up north.'

'You can say that again.' The first sight of the massive, blue-grey Great Dividing Range after a year away had been breathtaking. And their first glimpse of the final road to home, that ribbon of black tar that ran up, into and then through the mountains, had moved Bella to tears.

Patty finally found her voice. Touching Macca's muscled arm to get his attention, she asked, 'So, what have you been up to since I saw you last?'

Bella saw her cousin soften as he looked down into Patty's dark eyes.

'Macca?' said Patty.

He sure was in trouble. Bella had never seen her cousin so lost for words. Macca stubbed out his cigarette butt and cleared his throat, then only managed a grunt before a commotion behind them saved him from answering.

It was Caroline Handley, an old school mate of Bella and Patty's, and a contestant in the forgotten shot-shooting competition. Toppling from her spot at the makeshift bar, she'd accidentally shoved Prudence Vincent-Prowse as she went down, which started a domino effect along the line of still-kneeling drunken girls.

High-pitched squeals rang out.

Tinkling and chinking of smashing shot glasses followed.

The girls started to fall in a tumble of splayed limbs.

Forward momentum from the weight of all the lurching girls pushed against the A-frame trestle holding the tabletop in place.

The bar went down.

Dozens of discarded shot glasses still sitting on the bar started to freefall to the ground. Any contestants left kneeling and using the table as a prop finally toppled like a row of skittles one on top of the other, as the copious shots of Cock-Sucking Cowboys hit home.

The crowd went wild.

Chapter 14

Macca had wandered off in search of rum, so the girls crawled on hands and knees through the wreckage to an esky they'd hidden in the shadows of the tent walls. Grabbing a cruiser each, Bella slammed the esky lid shut, the effort causing her tummy to protest loudly to her brain.

'Jeez, Irish cream and butterscotch schnapps is a lethal brew,' she muttered as she tried mentally to force her insides to settle. She really wanted to spew.

'Yeah, too right, totally lethal. Just like a real cowboy, a dick or a gun, hey – it's much the same: one fatal shot and you're out.' Patty made the shape of a pregnant belly with weaving hands. This sent the pair into peals of hiccuping laughter. The seething crowd of drunks in the beer tent started drifting their way, ignoring the scrunching of glass underfoot. A hobnailed boot stomped down near Bella's hand. 'I reckon we should get out of here, Pat Me Tuffet, before we get trampled.'

'Okay, but you'll have to help me get up.'

'What makes you think I'm in any better state than you?'

'You owe me, girlfriend, big time. If I hadn't stuffed those boobs of yours into that singlet, you could've had dirty male paws all over you by now.'

Bella shuddered. 'Okay, so I owe you, but I'm going to grab my vest before we go. I always feel cold when I've had too much grog.' Helping Patty to her feet, Bella grabbed an oilskin vest from beside the esky and started to make her way through the crowd towards the tent doorway. In the distance a band started strumming the first few bars of the classic 'Khe Sanh'.

She loved that song.

Halfway to the exit Bella stopped and bent over. 'Shit, I shouldn't have stood up.' A pinch to her butt cheek had her back upright. Turning her head all she could see was a big black hat and a very male Wrangler butt. 'Whoa, mate. Don't touch what you can't afford.'

Patty grabbed hold of her hand and tried to tow her towards the doorway.

'Jeez, I feel crook,' said Bella. Burning bile was rising in her throat and her body started the pre-vomit sweats. 'Let me outta here.' Shaking away Patty's hand, she took off in a shambling run, making it to the canvas tent opening in record time.

Eddie Murray was mightily uncomfortable. The tumbledown wattle-and-daub walls of the old hut where he was hiding were full of ants; inch-long, black, angry jumping jacks pissed off their hiding place had been usurped. Hidden from the beer tent's view by crumbling clay, rotting wattle and a thicket of blackberries, Eddie lay face up on the hard, packed ground contemplating his options.

To stay or not to stay.

The most sensible idea would be to get the hell out of Dodge, or Nunkeri in this case, while he was still in one piece. Those blokes in there had looked very pissed off, and Eddie was happy with his face the way God had given it to him, although his height always caused a bit of concern.

He was damned sure that if he was spotted again the bushmen's reception wouldn't be so restrained. But Eddie had never been known for doing the sensible thing. That's why he was so successful in high-powered finance. Living on the edge was what he did.

He slapped at an ant on his moleskin-clad haunch, once again marvelling that the little black buggers could bite through such thick material. He rolled onto his front and peered over the crumbling clay wall. Surely there had to be an easier way of getting a *Penthouse* romp with lusty, hay-covered sheilas.

A retching sound drew his attention back to the tent he'd recently exited. A girl staggered from the tent's opening, her body listing from side to side. Peering hard through the blackberry bush and surrounding gloom, he couldn't believe his luck. It was the blonde.

Under the floodlights he could see sweat glistening across the top of her heaving cleavage. A tumble of ringlets covered most of her face as she was obviously trying hard not to vomit. She halted in the reflected glow of the generator-driven lights and pushed the sun-bleached curls from her face with the back of her hand. Eddie caught the upward movement of those glorious breasts as they threatened to topple from their restricting cradle once again. He felt his dick harden in an instant and he knew he couldn't and wouldn't 'get the hell out of Dodge'.

Not just yet anyway.

Through slit eyes Bella glimpsed a long, low stock trough. Drawn to the cool moonlit water, she moved in its direction, willing her legs to scramble the last ten metres. Ignoring the icy cold, Bella thrust her face into the water hoping to cool the heated sweats trembling through her body. A couple of seconds later, she had to admit it wasn't going to work. Again swallowing down burning bile, she dragged her head and arms from the trough. Spotting Patty fifty metres away, near the entrance to the port-a-loo semi-trailer, Bella lurched towards her and grabbed Patty around the shoulders. 'I think I'm gunna puke, Pat Me Tuffet.'

'Yeah, me too. Best head for the loo, mate.'

Patty had a pale, milky sheen of perspiration smeared across her face, the telltale sign of a queasy stomach about to let rip. The pair clambered their way up the steep port-a-loo steps using handrails to haul their bodies into the dimly lit semi-trailer.

Caroline Handley was already there, leaning her diminutive frame against the wall. Bella hadn't seen Caro since she'd left Burrindal to train as a teacher in Melbourne. Caro had always preferred bright lights over the bush.

'Hey, girls! I haven't seen you for *so* long and the minute I see you again, you're back up Prudence Vincent-Prowse's toffy nose,' said Caro, smiling. 'She *really* wanted to win that drinking competition. Had her sights set on a night out with Will. She's real keen on him, you know.'

'But Will's with m—' Bella bit off her sentence. Caro had no idea what happened in Queensland six weeks ago.

'He's with who?' Caro moved forward eagerly, eyes blinking with interest.

'Sorry, I was thinking of someone else.' Bella shut her gob in case she revealed anything more.

Caro went on, 'Prowsy's really pissed off. You know what she's like, always wanting to win – and what *she* wants *she* gets. The blokes have no idea that underneath all that honeyed exterior is a high-maintenance bitch. She was threatening to use those Paspaley pearls of hers to choke you two.'

Bella grinned. Bring it on, she silently vowed.

'And Prowsy's never been able to hold her liquor, not like you guys. She's passed out over at her parents' camp. That girl's as thick as a brick shithouse . . .'

Bella zoned out from Caro. Where *was* Will? She should've asked Macca if he was here. What if he hadn't wanted to leave the station so soon after being away up north? Disappointment seeped into her heart. Then, it was probably just as well he wasn't here; his view on the Bella and Patty shot-shooting show wouldn't have been pretty. And then there was the ruckus with that city slicker. Bella shook her head. Nothing she could do about it now. At least if he only *heard* about it, she could say it was all wildly exaggerated. Besides, it didn't matter what Will thought. Did it?

Bella tuned back into Caro just in time to see her face go white and her body start to wilt against the wall. She whispered so softly, Bella and Patty had to crane their necks to hear. 'I'll let you two in on a secret. If I move from here, this wall is going to tumble.'

Bella peered at her. She knew who was going to tumble and it certainly wasn't going to be the wall.

'I swear I'll never to do this again. I feel awful, and I'm going to have to leave this poor wall to its own fate now 'cause . . .' Caro bent over double and started to retch. Long, silky, straight hair fell into the puddles of muck on the floor. And watching Caro wilt brought the bile back into Bella's mouth. Her vision started closing in. Perspiration erupted from her pores. She shot a glance towards Patty; saw she was the same.

A couple of toilet doors behind them simultaneously swung back on their hinges as the occupants tumbled out. In unspoken collusion the three girls flung themselves at the open doorways. Toilet paper covered a floor floating in water, pee and mud. The girls couldn't have cared less, as they threw themselves down in front of the loos and vomited – all that good liquor wasted as it washed into the toilet bowls.

Eventually they staggered out to wipe their faces with wet paper towels. Bella looked around at the little group and her quivering body erupted into shaky laughter. 'Sheesh, those cock-suckers don't taste nearly so good second time round.'

Chapter 15

'So, what shenanigans did you two get up to in the wide open spaces of the outback?' Caro asked a long time later as they rested on the grass.

The vomit session, followed by another dousing of cold water, had sobered Bella up. Leaning against one of the forty-four gallon drums serving as rubbish bins that rimmed the area outside the port-a-loos, she struggled to reply.

How best to succinctly describe their year away? Idly listening to the country music from the distant stage, Bella tried to form into a one tangible thought the most important lesson she'd learned from the University of the Outback; one she hoped would stay with her for life.

A person didn't need a university degree, loads of money and material possessions to have a wonderful life. Whether it was way out west or up in the mountains, nature ruled the beast, two legged and four. The bush was your university, money equalled enough to get by and materialism was non-existent. The essence of life wasn't about 'stuff'; it was about living.

How could she explain something she felt so deeply within her being, so deeply inside her soul? She couldn't. And Caro looked like she had fallen asleep anyway.

A huge burst of sparks and embers spat into the air as a burned log abruptly shifted on the bonfire. Crashing down into the centre of the fire, it split and splayed before settling. Will shifted his body into a more comfortable position. The bloke who'd given him the can of rum was now standing beside old Wes, an arm around his shoulders, whispering in his ear.

Will could see a similarity in the two faces, one smoothly shaven, the other wrinkled and stubbled with grey wire bristles. The same long aquiline nose, maybe? Or was it the double set of arctic blue eyes that glinted in the leaping flames in front of them? The younger man slapped the older one on the back, the air around them filling with guffaws.

The younger bloke, noticing Will's interest, left the octogenarian and came back around the fire, planting his butt beside Will on the stringy-bark log. 'It's a good night.'

Will nodded in agreement while raising his can. 'Thanks for the rum.'

'That's all right. As I said, the next round's on you. Cheers.' The man's private-school accent spat plummy vowels from his mouth as fast as machine-gun bullets.

'You're on,' said Will, laughing. He stuck out his right hand. 'I'm Will O'Hara.'

'Trinity Eggleton.'

Will tried hard to keep a straight face as his hand was pumped up and down.

'Yes, I know. What were my parents thinking? Trinity. I was definitely standing at the back of the line when God handed out parents, or names at least.' Trinity shrugged. 'I'm over it. Hellish at school, though. Everyone calls me Trin now. Except my parents, that is. They reckon at the grandiose age of twenty-seven I *am* the Trinity; the divine all-in-one, *the* only child, holder of the Eggleton family expectations, all your eggs, pardon the pun, in one basket.'

'Right,' said Will, a little baffled. 'That must be a bit difficult.'

'You could say that. That's my grandfather there.' Trin pointed to old Wes, who was about to sit on a hard wooden chair someone had dragged from goodness knows where.

'Wes is your *grandfather*?' Shock caused Will's voice to rise to choirboy levels.

'Yes. He's my mother's father. I didn't know about him until a while ago.'

Will stared at old Wes, remembering now that Maggie had once told him the couple had a daughter somewhere. The old fellow looked like he was starting to recite a new poem, sitting backwards on the chair, rocking it like he was riding a horse.

'"The Geebung Polo Club"?' guessed Will to his new friend.

'I'd reckon so.' Trin sighed and then went on, 'The old man's great. No expectations beyond where his next beer or rum's coming from. It's bloody marvellous.'

Will noticed the plummy voice was slightly slurred.

'Shit. There I go again. What am I saying; you don't want to hear about my worries. Where are you from? What's your story?'

Will looked out across the fire towards the mountains rimming the valley, where the twinkling lights from hundreds of small campfires set the whole plain aglow. A couple of thousand people were camped here tonight. He guessed they all had families with secrets of their own.

'I'm from Tindarra,' said Will, waving his hand out to the south-east. 'Over that-a-way. I live near old Wes. Run a few cattle and grow lucerne. How 'bout yourself?'

'I'm a tooth-puller. From Melbourne. Over that way.' Trin grinned and waved to the west.

Trin moved up a notch in Will's estimation. He might be a city boy but he knew how to take the piss. 'So what are you doing here?' Will was intrigued. Why had old Wes never mentioned he had a daughter and a grandson?

'I've been staying up at Ben Bullen Hills on and off. Fixing up the homestead there with Wes. The whole family's a secretive bunch, so I'm not surprised he hasn't told you. I was really pissed off my mother didn't tell me about my grandparents. I'd assumed all these years they were dead, and she never disabused me of the notion. Apparently Wes and my grandmother didn't like my father. They had a falling-out with Mum and never made up. Pride runs deep in my family.'

'So, how'd you find out about them?'

'I found a letter Wes sent to my mother after my grandmother died. They hadn't seen or spoken to each other since my mother eloped with my father.' Trinity then seemed to struggle, like he was trying to work out how much to say. 'I decided after that little effort, I was done with fulfilling my parents' dreams in dentistry. I'm now going to pursue a few dreams of my own.'

'What sort of dreams?'

Trinity hesitated before going on. Then it came out in a rush. 'Head bush, become a farmer and get to know my grandfather before he kicks on.'

'So, what are you doing about it?'

'What do you mean?'

'If you want something bad enough you'll do something about getting it. Do you really want to move to the sticks and become a farmer up here? Not much money in it.'

'Yes, I surely do and I don't care about the money. Not anymore.' Trin's gaze drifted to his grandfather still rocking his 'pony' on the other side of the fire.

'So, what are you doing about it?' Will wasn't going to let him off the hook.

Trin honed back in on Will. 'You sound like you know what you're talking about.'

'Oh believe me, I do. I certainly do,' said Will. Sudden visions of Isabella Francine Vermaelon danced before his eyelids . . .

'Earth to O'Hara, earth to O'Hara . . .' Trin's voice permeated Will's erotic dream.

'What was that?' Will was mildly pissed off at the interruption.

'You were asking what I was doing about becoming a farmer.'

'Yeah, I was.' Will tried to look contrite. 'Sorry about that.'

'It's a girl, is it?'

'What's a girl?'

'This thing *you* want really badly.'

Will looked at Trinity Eggleton and now *he* pondered how much to say. The eyebrow rose once again. Will shrugged. Better told to a stranger than someone who really counted. 'Yeah, it's a girl. Not just any girl. It's *the* girl.'

'Mmm,' said Trin. 'Quite a statement. *The* girl, huh? So I guess it's a bit tricky if it's causing a problem?'

'Yeah,' sighed Will, 'you could say that. She's a flighty young filly. Six years younger than me, my sister's best mate.'

'Right. You'd better point her out to me; otherwise I might try and crack onto her myself.'

'Oh, she's not here – at least I don't think so. But if you see her I reckon you'd know her. She's a hot-looking blonde.' Will sketched a curvy figure in the air with his hands.

'There's a few of them around tonight. I've just seen the most gorgeous-looking creature over near the loos. Long, straight, blonde hair. She's a bit worse for wear but her willowy body certainly did it for me. I wouldn't mind knowing who she is.'

Will let out the breath he'd been holding – Trin's description didn't match Bella. A long-haired blonde with a willowy body in no way described Bella's tumbling white gold curls and buxom figure. 'Well, mate, just point her out to me, I'm sure I could tell you. My family have lived around here for a while and we know a few people.'

'I just might take you up on that one, old fellow. She was pretty hot.' Trin looked across at his grandfather, who was bringing his poetry recitation to an end. 'I think the old man over there might need his grandson's help to get off the chair.'

Trin stuck out his right arm and shook Will's hand. 'Great to meet you, mate.' Coming from Trin, the word 'mate' sounded foreign and strangled.

'Yeah, good to meet you too, Trin. Sounds like we'll see you around?'

'For sure, Will. You can count on it.'

As Trin moved off towards his grandfather, Will swigged the last of his can and pondered on the surprise revelation that old Wes had a grandson. And just how did a city dentist turn himself into a high-country cattleman?

As he observed the striking paradox of long, lanky Trinity Eggleton gently helping little, gnarled Wes Ogilvie from his hard wooden seat, he couldn't help putting voice to the thought. 'If anyone can manage such a culture shock, I reckon it could be him.'

'You reckon who could be what?' Macca plunked himself down beside Will, rum in hand. Extra rum appeared from his back pocket, and quickly replaced Will's now-empty can.

'About bloody time you appeared, mate. Glad a man's not dying of thirst. Where've you been?'

'Not sure you want to know the answer to that. Then again, if you plan on staying warm in that swag of yours tonight, maybe you do.' Macca sounded like he was considering another angle.

'What's going on? What don't I want to know?' Will took a deep suck on his can to ready himself.

'Well . . .' Macca sounded pensive. 'To tell or not to tell, that remains the question, old boy. Just how much do you need to know, is what I'm asking myself right now. Let's just say a certain curly-haired blonde has appeared on the radar . . .'

'Bella? Here at the Muster?' Will felt his spirits lift in an instant.

'Your sister too.'

'Well, now there's a surprise. Where there's one, there are usually two.' The twist on Will's lips was wry. 'What exactly have they been up to? I overheard a conversation about someone organising a women's drinking competition. Those girls haven't been at it, have they?'

Macca hunched over his rum. 'Mmm . . .' He relived the events in the marquee in his head, two girls riding each other like a cowboy and his bull.

'Macca? Oh no. What have they done?'

'Well . . . they haven't been complete idiots, but they haven't exactly been angels either. You know those two, Will. They're either in or they're out. No in-between. Let's just say they've been wallowing in Bailey's and butterscotch schnapps up to their pretty little necks.'

'Fuck!' Will half-rose but Macca pulled him back down on the log.

'It's okay, mate, they're okay. They're a pair of pissheads but they're still walking. They're fine. We'll catch up with them in a bit.'

Will made a mental note to carpet his little sister. He wouldn't have her making a spectacle of herself, and then being talked about across the mountains. It was a small community and everyone knew everyone else's business. Patty had a good nursing job to come home to, which required a certain amount of respect from the patients she treated. That's not what she would get by carrying on like a drunken idiot on the Nunkeri Plains.

'You were saying someone was going to do something?' Macca prompted Will.

'Huh?'

'Who was going to do something?'

'Oh. Trin. Trinity Eggleton. Old Wes Ogilvie's grandson. He's a dentist in the city and he wants to work up with Wes on Ben Bullen Hills.'

Macca looked morose. 'I can understand that. I know I'd rather be working on the station at home than driving a bloody truck for me old man.'

Will looked across at his mate, sympathetically. Macca's father Bryce had both a high-country station outside Burrindal and a successful interstate cattle-trucking business. With the meanness of the drought, Bryce had all but shut down the farm and was concentrating on the trucks. With the dry, cattle were being trucked up north to feedlots and temporary agistment.

Will clapped Macca across the shoulders. 'The drought's got to end sometime. At least you got a trip to Mount Isa scouting for business. If the drought hadn't been so tough, I couldn't have come with you. Would've been too much work at home. So at least we got a bit of a holiday out of it.'

'Yeah,' Macca's eyes glinted. 'And what a trip that was.'

Will gave Macca a steady look. 'If you go out with her and sleep with her, then you stay with her, old man. You hurt my sister and I'll nail that bloody big ugly mug of yours to a gum tree. And I'll add that black hat just for decoration.'

'Twenty-six years of friendship wouldn't come into it?'

'Not when it comes to my own, mate,' replied Will. 'Or Bella,' Will added under his breath.

'Speaking of sisters,' Macca said as he stood up and stretched, 'how about we jump in my ute and move on down to the band? I reckon that's where we'll find those two cowgirls, that's if they haven't passed out under a tree somewhere. We need rum anyway, and I should move my ute before I'm over the limit.'

'You okay to drive a few hundred metres? How about we walk?'

'Nuh, I want to dump off your swag somewhere cosy, so I can have my ute to myself tonight – and that stand of old gums over there looks a pretty good spot for you.' Macca pointed to a cluster of eucalypts down the paddock a little way. 'I reckon you'll be wanting some privacy yourself, seeing my cousin's here too,' he added. He peered at Will from under his black hat.

'Okay.' Will's dimples danced. 'You're an ideas man, that's for sure.'

Together they walked in the direction of Macca's ute. Trin and Old Wes had disappeared, and Will could see the crowd was slowly moving from the bonfire towards the band playing on the back of the semi-trailer, down the valley.

Looking up into the sky, he could see swirling cumulous clouds overtaking millions of stars lighting up the heavens with their brilliance. On the backs of the ridges, in the mountains above the Nunkeri Plains, lightning flashed and forked, causing the whole sky to come alight. The cool change was on its way.

But it was all nothing compared to the brilliance of his Bella. He already thought of her as his. Her vibrant spirit, keen mind and gorgeous body coupled with a wilful temperament – determined but kind. Nothing could compare with her sheer delight in living or the way she danced through her life. Into his.

A life together? His subconscious tried the thought. To Will's surprise he didn't feel the need to bolt in the opposite direction. As lighting flashed around him, he moved with a determined step, his heart and soul on fire.

Anticipation.

Yearning.

Forward towards love.

Chapter 16

Bella came to, lying on the grass. Cold shivers snaked through her body from her damp singlet pressing against her chest, underneath her oilskin vest. Looking around, she saw that Patty and Caro had disappeared, leaving two areas of squashed grass on either side of her. Hauling herself slowly to her feet, Bella realised the spew session had cleared her head but had left a spearing headache in its wake.

Cupping her right temple where it felt like a knife blade was on the prowl, she looked around for Patty but saw only swathes of swaying backs as the crowd moved to the music from the band on the flat-bed tray of the semi-trailer.

She glimpsed an auburn head passing through the gaping doorway of the beer tent. Another shiver ran through her body, and Bella realised she needed to get her wet singlet off or she'd be coming down with something worse than a flaming headache. Looking at her vest, she contemplated what body parts it covered. Enough. The vest alone should do. She headed towards the loos to take off her wet clobber, but when she got there she found someone had hung a sign up on the port-a-loo's closed door: 'Loos buggered. Use other toilet block.'

Just great. She shivered once more.

The other loo trailer was halfway up the valley, and she'd be blowed if she was going to stagger all that way in complete darkness, just to take her singlet off. She glanced around.

Beyond the glare of the overhead lights, she spotted the tumbledown walls of the old Nunkeri Plains homestead. Smothered in blackberries, the homestead had been the hard-won creation of the original settlers; a house full of dreams of a summer settling family who hoped their farm would be prosperous on a lush, open plain high up in the mountains. But after a few years of battling with variable seasons, along with snow for up to six months of the year, the original settlers had obviously given in and moved on. Time had wrought its destruction on the house that was not much more than a rough shanty really. The clay in the walls had been mined from the nearby creek bed, the timber cut on site. Amazingly for something which looked so fragile, sections of the house still stood over a hundred years later. For now, though, all Bella wanted was a little privacy, and it would do the job. Trying to ignore the pain in her head, she moved towards the relative shelter of the dark and crumbling wattle-and-daub walls.

Eddie Murray had always been a patient man. He was used to sitting quietly and waiting for his chance. Now he couldn't believe his luck. He wouldn't have to go anywhere, or do anything, because she was coming to him.

'There is a God after all,' he whispered to himself as the glorious riot of ringlets moved in his direction. Her rounded hips swayed, and her luscious breasts swung with the momentum of the loping gait of her long legs. Her left arm moved up once again to push those curls from her stunning face and at the upward lift of a tanned, smooth arm, her breasts seemed to thrust their way towards him with welcoming glee.

Manna was coming to him and he hadn't moved a muscle.

Bella reached the blackberry-covered walls of the old hut and made to push her way through the opening that had once been a doorway.

A blackberry bramble slapped against her bare skin.

'Youch.' She grabbed at the spike-laden branch with its thorny barbs now stuck in her flesh. 'Bloody blackberries.'

Her arm came free only to have the thorns snag her shoulder, drawing blood. She flung away the offending brambles.

Closing her eyes to protect them, she blindly moved past the remaining leafy canes, through the doorway to open ground, and into the waiting, sweaty arms of Eddie Murray.

'Holy crap!' Bella yelled as she slammed into a solid mass. Opening her eyes, she found herself staring at a perspiring, white forehead and the top of a balding male head. She tried to spring backwards but found herself held within an iron grasp, two hands clamped on her bum cheeks, squeezing with a grip that made her yell again.

'Youch! What the—'

Mid-sentence, Bella's reflexes kicked in and with them the basic human instinct – flight or fight.

Bella fought.

She struggled hard to move out of the lecherous arms.

Eddie grunted as elbows smashed into his chest, and he responded with a thrust of his hips pushing Bella away from him, bending her waist to an impossible angle. Bella felt a set of hips grind into the tops of her legs and a very male bulge try to mount her thigh, like a lusting dog on the make.

She lifted her leg to ram her knee into his groin but he was too quick, whipping his stocky leg around and through Bella's feet, tripping her over and slamming her onto the ground.

'Whoommff.' Bella's breath dived deep into her body. The pain of her back hitting the dirt drilled into her tail bone.

And then he was on top of her.

Fat and pudgy fingers mauled at her body, grasping at her waist buckle and pulling at the press-studs on her vest. Hot, fetid, sloppy lips mashed against her mouth, her cheeks, her neck, slobbering saliva.

The crack of the stockwhip rang through the night air.

Once.

Twice.

The man on top of Bella reared.

Once.

Twice.

Baying like a dingo, Eddie frantically rolled away from the biting sting that was crashing around his arse, leaving a stunned Bella alone on the ground. He could feel blood rising, steamy and hot as the cuts through his moleskins were laid bare to the night air. Only a flicker of his brain wondered at the origin of the welts. He'd felt them so often before in the bordellos of his city, an anonymous sweetener to his carnal entertainment, it just added to his sexual excitement, his lust-filled brain failing to register a warning bleep.

He scuttled to slam his body down on a stunned Bella, his throbbing dick now threatening to explode.

'No you don't, arsehole. Get the fuck OFF HER!'

The whip came down again.

Across his back. His shoulders.

A volley of cracks, unrelenting in their attack.

Eddie staggered up onto his feet and spun, lurching, confused, reaching out for his attacker.

He grabbed at the leather that was coiling like a snake out in front of him and succeeded in taking hold of the thong, reefing it from the hands of his assailant. Stepping away with his prize, he tripped over Bella's now kicking legs and fell hard, losing hold on the whip. Bella flung herself sideways, snagging the handle with her outstretched hand and throwing it in the direction of her saviour. Eddie jumped to his feet, grabbing at space, just missing the flying whip by inches.

The shape in the darkness caught the whip and quickly moved it back and forth inscribing a figure of eight into the night air. To Eddie's horror, there were two whips in motion.

With the pair of stockwhips clasped firmly in her hands, Patty deftly flipped into a Queensland Crossover and thrashed the bloke in front of her across his face, not caring if she blinded him.

In fact, she *wanted* to blind him, to flog him to within an inch of his hairy white butt, for what he had been trying to do to Bella.

'Move, Bella, MOVE!' Patty roared at her friend, not losing her beat as she pelted Eddie with her whips.

Bella rolled over and lurched to her knees. All she could see was Patty's flying arms at one with her whips, pulling all the moves that had made her the Nunkeri Muster Ladies' Whip-Cracking Champion for the last five years.

The wooden stock of the whip rose as one with Patty's hand, the plaited thong flicking the Fall – a single strip of leather near the whip's end – hard at the man in front of her. The cracker at the end wreaked its relentless damage on the soft facial features of Eddie Murray.

Eddie was screeching as he tried to grab at the woman causing him so much agony.

But she was unassailable.

A bevy of stockwhipping moves learned at her father's knee and finetuned under the tutelage of a master in outback Queensland: a Sidney Flash followed by the Victorian Cutback. And then just as Eddie, in pain-driven terror, decided it was time to cut and run, Patty threw her red kangaroo whips into The Train.

A formidable movement of dual whips cracking out a sound like a train bearing down on an unending set of tracks. A movement that drove Eddie away from a swaying Bella and into the old hut's remaining walled corner, in an effort to stay clear of the menacing leather.

Eddie was pinned down. His face and hands a bloodied mess, he cowered in the corner like a wounded dog.

Bella finally made it to Patty's side, steering clear of the flashing leather, and wincing with pain as her bruised vertebrae shot into place down her racked spine.

'Oh. My. God. He was trying to—' Bella couldn't finish the sentence, didn't want to formulate the thought.

'I know.' Patty threw one of the whips to her friend, runner-up champion of the same stock-whipping challenge.

In perfect concerto the two girls finished the whipping display with an original and impressive Cattleman's Crack, drawing the plaited thongs around over their heads and allowing the whips to fall with a dual crisp *thwack* at Eddie's feet.

As one, they flicked both stockwhips to rest across their shoulders.

'But he's leaving now, aren't you, *city slicker*!' Patty ground the last two words out through clenched teeth.

Eddie Murray didn't reply.

He couldn't.

His bloodied mouth wouldn't cooperate and he couldn't see his own hand in front of his face. His eyes were swollen, blood-filled slits and his only thought was of escape – from these crazed mountain women, back to the city, where at least *his* kind of women knew their place.

Bella and Patty watched as he disappeared into the night, crashing through the blackberries like they weren't even there.

'I suppose we should've reported him.' Patty said.

'Nah, mate,' mumbled Bella. 'Don't really want anyone knowing what just went on.'

'But what if he tries it on someone else? What then?'

'I don't reckon we'll see him again, Patty. Not after the hiding you just gave him. You were pretty impressive, you know.'

'You didn't do too bad yourself. Besides, he deserved every bit of it and more. Wish I could've got a go at his *bare* bum and then he'd have *really* known what pain was.'

'You did good, Patty. Thanks.' Bella shook her head. 'Jeez, if you hadn't come along just then, I'd have been in trouble. How'd you know I was here?'

'I saw you when you were caught in the blackberries. I was just getting us another drink.'

'Thank God you did.' Bella's voice trembled. With the adrenaline of the fight now seeping from her veins, she could feel the aftershocks of horror shuddering through her body. It had been close. Too close.

Violation and revulsion was all she could feel now. She found herself reliving the touch of those creepy, clammy sausage-like fingers pawing across her body.

'It's over now, mate, with no harm done, ay?' Patty slung an arm over Bella's shoulders and grasped her into a sideways hug. Bella ducked her head onto Patty's shoulder, feeling the warmth of her friend's body reach out to the coldness of her own.

'Bella?' Patty brought them both to a halt and spun her friend around to face her. 'You're okay, aren't you, mate?'

'Yeah, I suppose so. It's just . . . I don't know. He was so creepy, and I couldn't protect myself.' Refusing to look at Patty, she dug a booted toe into the ground, digging divots from the dirt.

'Listen to me, girl.' Patty forced Bella's chin up and let her brown eyes bore into the opposite blue ones. 'It's finished, it's over. He didn't get you. We fought him off together. He couldn't get his shiny white arse out of here quick enough. We *can* defend ourselves. It just takes a little country creativity, that's all.' Patty tried a smile. She leaned forward and grabbed hold of the stock of the whip resting across Bella's shoulder.

'For a runner-up, you didn't do too bad a job yourself. I'd better watch myself in the championships this year.'

'Yeah, right.' The sarcasm was back in Bella's voice. 'Where'd you get the whips from anyway? I haven't seen these two before. You been stashing some secret arsenal? Are you *that* worried I'll whip your arse?'

'For your information, old Wes Ogilvie made them for me, ready for tomorrow's big competition. I went to grab us some more grog from the esky and ran into him on my way back. He's pretty tanked and pissing poetry for conversation but he'd been looking for me to give me these.' Patty proudly held up the whip. 'Beautiful, aren't they? Genuine Wesley Ogilvie 12 plait kangaroo hide whips. They cost me over five hundred bucks, but they'll be worth it. I'm lining up for my sixth title, you know.'

Bella whistled. 'Wes Ogilvie *made* you a pair of whips? Crikey, that's impressive. I've got no flaming hope now. What is it with you and these old blokes? You just wind them round your little finger. I didn't think he was making them anymore, not since Catherine got sick. Didn't think he had the time, or maybe his heart wasn't in it.' Bella lifted the whip from her own shoulder, took in the skilful weaving of the rawhide and then reverently returned it to its proud new owner.

'He's got a grandson. A city slicker who's helping him out a bit, he said, so old Wes's making a few whips again.'

Bella shuddered. 'Oh no, not another city boy.'

'Nah, this one's all right. Seems like a nice bloke. He's a dentist or something toffy like that. I met him just before with Wes. Got a heck of a plum in his mouth but he turns out well in a pair of Wranglers.' Patty waggled her eyebrows. 'Come on, mate. Let's put these whips with our esky and go find a party.'

Sometime later Patty disappeared again. Probably gone for a wee, thought Bella as she swigged on a bottle of water and idly listened to the new band on stage. Over the music she heard the distinctive, low-pitched rumble of the twin stacks mounted on her cousin's ute. Bella honed in on the sound of the approaching vehicle. Her heart accelerated, pumping at double-pace. All senses went on high alert, nerve ends tingling in the deepest regions of her body.

She could sense it was him.

Hoped it was him.

It had to be him.

The stacks grumbled to a halt, somewhere near the cattle yards over to her left, so she swung around trying to pinpoint the LandCruiser's final place of rest. As her eyes raked across the undulating grassy paddock, she eventually spotted the bug deflector emblazoned with 'Tearin' Down the Mountain' reflected by the lights set up on the back of the makeshift stage.

Macca exited the driver's side of the ute, pulling his huge black, high-topped Akubra down onto his tousled head as he went. But she was more interested in seeing if there was a passenger. Craning her neck, she saw there was.

He revealed himself more slowly, a large cream Akubra already sitting snugly on his head. He was smaller in height than Macca but as broad across the shoulders. Bella knew she would recognise this man in her sleep.

Her dreams were full of him. Her whole being soaked in his scent.

Flashes of another night in faraway outback Queensland flitted before her eyes and red-hot heat slowly started to consume her body. She saw his far-seeing gaze sweep across the paddock, and she knew with certainty when his eyes alighted on her and stayed fixed. Even standing some hundred metres apart, she knew that he knew too. They would end up together in one swag tonight.

A dance as old as time, started in earnest six weeks before, was mid-step – and the outcome was as certain as tomorrow's dawn.

They would be together, as one, finally tonight.

Her mind knew it as well as her body; a body already yearning for his embrace, his touch, his sweet kiss. She moved towards him intent to savour it all, eager to start that final waltz, to consummate what had started but not ended at a Queensland rodeo in the far, dusty north.

She didn't see the sprawled, dozing body of Patty . . . and tripped arse over tit into a cast-iron bath full of water and empty beer cans.

Chapter 17

'The wet T-shirt competition is scheduled for tomorrow, cowgirl.'

Bella could hear Will's muffled voice through the gallons of water pouring off her head. The water was warm from the day's heat, but the breeze wafting around her was cold, making her nipples snap to attention. Or was it the voice causing that? She should be resigned now to the fact she was just supposed to spend the night wet.

'Jeez, Bella, did you have to wake me up?' Sitting beside the tub, Patty was soaked, hit by the wave of water erupting from the bath as Bella fell in.

'You could've found a better place to pass out, you stupid nong,' Bella said as she clambered out of the tub.

'Hey, wait on a minute,' said Will. 'I was just thinking of joining you in there, Hells Bells. Looked mighty comfortable, not to mention wet and wild.'

Patty whistled as she got to her feet. 'Go, bro.'

Macca walked up beside Will. 'What's the joke?' His eyes alighted on a dripping Bella. 'Ah, Miss Vermaelon, bit late for a bath, isn't it? Or are you getting in before the morning rush?'

Bella inhaled, counted to three, then spun on her heels and stormed off towards the beer tent.

'What's wrong with her?' Macca asked no-one in particular.

'Where are you going?' Will and Patty yelled together.

'To get a bloody rum, beer, cruiser . . . anything to get away from you lot . . . and to find a flaming shirt that's dry!'

'Hang on, cowgirl, I'll come and give you a hand.' Will took off after her.

'I guess that's the last we'll see of them tonight.' Patty turned to Macca.

'How's that? She looks ready to kill someone, not get laid.'

Patty leaned into the big man beside her, put her tanned and freckled arm inside his own and gave him a pitying smile. 'You boys really don't get it, do you?'

❧

Will stood beside Bella, surveying the scene before them. 'My swag's that way. I threw it out of Macca's ute on our way over; it's there under those gum trees.'

Bella didn't reply. She was cold and probably still drunk. Judging by the pick-up of the wind and the increased lightning on the hills, the cool change was about to hit. She just wanted her bed. Flickering small lights covered the valley floor guiding the way to the hundreds of tents, utes, horse floats and trucks parked in camps around the plain. The problem was that every light looked the same, and Bella couldn't find Patty's fire-engine-red ute, which contained her swag, her doona and a nice warm, dry, fluffy flannelette shirt. She knew because she'd looked everywhere, Will following along behind.

Was this some sort of sign? Her sense of direction was usually impeccable; her sense of humour was usually impossible to smother – but now she was disorientated, pissed and disgruntled. The attempted rape by that wanker had unsettled her more than she had let on to Patty. And now there was *this* man at her side. She threw him a sideways glare. Uncharitable, she knew.

She'd been so looking forward to seeing him again; the man in her dreams these past few weeks to finally materialise into hunky, male flesh. But now it had happened, a multitude of feelings she hadn't anticipated flooded her mind.

This was a man who was her best mate's brother; a man who'd known her since she was in nappies.

This wasn't going to be a one-night stand followed by a sunrise bolt into the bush. The feelings this man drew from inside her were intense. Complex even. Did she want this so early in her life? Did she want to dive head-first into a relationship that could lead to marriage, kids and slippers by the fire?

But . . .

She couldn't hold back the feelings swamping her. She couldn't deny her heart, which was full to the brim with Will's scent, his touch and a more-than-was-decent amount of lust. It felt so right.

And she couldn't find that bloody ute, no matter how hard she tried.

Looking up into the dark eyes staring down at her, she heard thunder rumble out to the west. She felt the squall of wind arrive with the change. Her spirit slammed its virtual cards of chance on the table; the house full of hearts won the game. Her hand placed itself in Will's warm and comforting clasp, pure instinct dictating her moves. As a bolt of lightning cracked hard above their heads, she looked down at their hands snug together in an intimate hold and wondered just how her body knew.

Will was burning. He was so hot for this woman it was a wonder he didn't internally combust. The touch of her hand in his, finally. It wasn't enough. Not nearly enough. He didn't give Bella a chance to change her mind. Gathering her to him, he took off towards the trees where he'd left his swag. It was going to rain like hell in a minute, and he wanted to get them both under some sort of shelter, before he ravished her.

Half-carrying her across the rough ground to the gum trees, he snagged the bed roll and then kept walking.

'Where are we going, Will?' Bella stumbled, trying to keep up.

'Over towards the old homestead. There's a humpy we can shelter in out the back. It's going to piss down with rain in a minute.'

Bella tried to suppress a shudder at Will's mention of the site where she was nearly raped. He'd said a humpy out the back, not the homestead, she reassured herself.

They came up on the humpy from behind, so Bella was near the doorway before she knew she'd even arrived. Lightning strikes cracked in the hills all around, and the thunder had gone from a low rumble to an all-out crash. Will swung her into his arms and she forgot about Eddie Murray and the storm raging all around. She only had room for one tempest in her heart.

Will slammed his woman hard against his body, enclosing her in strong arms and shutting out all else but him. Her body moulded into his like it was cast only to fit his shape. Hip to hip, breast to breast, mouth to mouth. As the summer storm sent its load of much-needed rain down onto the Nunkeri Plains, Will felt full to the brim with all-consuming passion and love.

He slipped his hands under her oilskin vest, rummaging under her wet singlet until he clasped the giving, warm flesh of the woman who'd been in his heart and mind since Gundolin. His hands moved slowly up the sides of her body, slippery smooth in the rain, relishing the feel of her shivers as she responded to his touch.

He couldn't contain himself.

Ripping at the press-studs of her vest, he wrenched it from her body in one tug. She raised her arms so he could drag her wet singlet over her head, and with a snap her red bra followed, swirling on the wind. And then he stepped back and drank in the sight he had dreamed of. Isabella Vermaelon unwrapped. For him. Only for him. He wanted to claim this woman as his own. Forever.

Reaching for those creamy, succulent breasts, he touched his mouth to her firm nipples, sending his tongue on a voyage. As his groin throbbed and strained against the restriction of his jeans, it took all his self-control to taste rather than claim, to seek rather than find. Then she moved, whimpering, spreading her legs, allowing him to press his erection hard against the core of her being.

Bella couldn't contain her shivers. She wasn't cold. Oh no. She was in meltdown for this man. As Will had stood back looking at her like she was a Christmas present from God, it made her feel like the most gorgeous woman in the world, sexy, empowered, alive and adored.

As his hands had moved forward and his head followed, her breasts had sprung to meet his touch. The warmth of his breath soft against her skin, the slither of his velvet tongue, followed by the gentle lapping and suckling of her nipples caused her knees to weaken as a torrent of pleasure flooded her body and mind.

Now she knew what had been missing from the two sexual encounters of the past, why she'd walked away from those one-night stands with an empty heart. Will was different. Her body melted into submission, following the hard planes of the man who held her in his arms.

She wanted him. Inside her. Now.

Will's hands moved further south. Tantalising, teasing, drawing it out. She closed her eyes and drank in his touch. Ripping at her own fly, she sent her hands into battle with his. Will firmly pushed her fingers away and then slowly, bit by bit, eased the zipper, gently pulling her Wranglers down over her hips, nuzzling her belly and then further down. He tugged the suffocating jeans from her body until she was free. He stepped back, leaving her bereft. Eyes snapping open, Bella cried out.

Will was tugging at his own shirt, pulling it over his head.

He was beautiful. She moved forward instinctively, nuzzling his chest, sending feather-light kisses down, and down, glorying in her own nakedness as she went. Loving the pleasure her womanhood was giving him, seducing with her lips, the tickle of her breasts and hair, the need to devour driving her desire.

She tugged at his leather belt and pulled it free. Snagging his jeans down over his hips, she smiled at what was revealed. Nuzzled at what had lain hidden.

Too quickly Will pulled her to her feet. With great tender-ness, his hands brought her face up to meet his. His whisper floated between them, on the wind, on the rain, sweet against her lips. 'I won't be able to hold on, if you do that, cowgirl.'

Bella smiled into his deep gaze and was then swept away, the tides of passion urging them both on. Sweeping rain poured down from overhead. Reckless and wild, they pushed each other to the brink, until Will leaned back against the lean-to wall and picked her up, cupping her bottom in his work-roughened hands, drawing her in and over him. Bella wiggled and snuggled until she felt him move hard and deep inside her. She clamped her muscles around him, and started to ride him up and down. Her breasts moved fluidly across their rain-slicked bodies as she thrust herself onto him, driving him insane. He lost any control he had left. Slamming his body up into hers, he met her stroke for stroke until they both tipped over the edge. Together they exploded.

Thunder cracked and lightning zapped around the old lean hut. Bella and Will were oblivious to anything but each other.

And it wasn't until much, much later that they dried each other off with a sheet dragged from Will's swag and lay under the corrugated-tin humpy curled into a warm woollen blanket and listened to the rain. Sated. Complete. In each other's arms.

Chapter 18

A dim glow pierced the holes in the tin roof above her head, scattering pinpoints of light on the old, weathered swag. Bella snuggled into the blanket, backing herself further into Will's chest. He mumbled something in his sleep and tightened his arms around her.

Outside the sheltering humpy, there was a slight early-morning breeze; just enough to move the silvery leaves of the eucalypt tree crowding the sky outside the doorway. The moon still shone, an incandescent light peering through thick branches of a huge red gum, giving the old tree a haloed glow.

Just like the glow Bella knew was blossoming within her, filling her whole being with its warmth. Ignoring the dull ache of a hangover, she rolled over to face the man spooning her. The strong planes of his face, the chiselled jaw and its harsh lines were softened in sleep. The eyes were closed, the dimples gone from his tanned cheeks.

With her fingertip she softly traced the creases from the laughter lines rimming his temples. Feeling his breath gently warm her hand, she ran her fingers along the side of his face and was rewarded when an arm snaked its way across her bum cheeks, pulling her closer into his warm chest.

'Not planning on a dawn dash, cowgirl?' His soft voice startled an early-morning currawong from its perch outside the doorway.

Bella laughed. 'Not bloody likely.' She snuggled into the furry down of hair smattered across Will's chest. 'Anyway, isn't that usually a bloke's prerogative?'

'Not this bloke. And definitely not this morning.' Will's arm reached for the canvas above their heads and the top flap of the swag descended, hiding them from view. The peals of laughter soon coming from inside sent the currawong flying once again.

It was ten o'clock on Sunday morning before a weary but happy Bella and Will finally made their way back into the main entertainment arena at Nunkeri Plains.

'Feel like an egg-and-bacon sandwich?' asked Will as they walked across the grass towards a tent, which was serving breakfast.

Bella smiled up at the man loping along beside her, his warm hand firmly holding onto hers. 'Sounds great. Nothing like a bit of bacon fat to soothe a booze-soaked tummy and a pounding head. Not to mention the fair bit of physical activity in between.' Bella felt rather than heard Will's laughter rumble through his body. He grasped her hand a little tighter, as a female voice broke into their conversation from behind.

'Will O'Hara. *There* you are.' Prudence Vincent-Prowse sidled up to him and cuddled into his free side. Her left hand snaked out and sinuously moved across his blue chambray shirt, her long red-painted fingertips applying light pressure on Will's muscled chest. 'I missed seeing you last night.'

'Hi there, Prue, nice to see you too. Macca and I didn't get here until late. Would you like an egg-and-bacon sandwich? I was just heading over to grab one for Bella and me.'

For the first time Prowsy looked at Bella.

And Bella watched as the other girl registered the fact that Will was holding onto her hand. Prowsy's eyes hardened as she took in her adversary and the tender look Will was throwing Bella's way.

Prowsy stepped in front of Will, her body moving fluidly and in such a way as to effectively shut Bella out of the conversation.

'I'd just *love* a sandwich, thanks, Will. It's so sweet of you to offer.' Prowsy's voice was oozing honey, while a hand fleetingly touched at Will's chest and her eyes devoured the man.

'Righto. I'll be back shortly.' Will squeezed Bella's hand, smiled at Prowsy and strode off. Bella watched him go, admiring his bum, his back, his whole body – crap, she had it bad.

Prowsy didn't waste any time swinging into attack. 'So, you didn't have any success up there in Queensland pulling a root, so you're back here spreading yourself around as per usual? I saw you and Patricia riding each other last night. Tell me, can't you find a man willing to get it up? Or perhaps you have to pay them? I heard you raving on about a bet.'

Bella was speechless.

'Will O'Hara needs a *real* woman in his bed. Someone from the mountains to help him run that big high-country station of his . . .'

145

A real woman? Someone from the mountains? Bella tried not to smirk. Prowsy worked for her father, *a fucking real estate agent in Burrindal.*

'. . . not some scummy, good-for-nothing dairy-farmer's daughter – a wannabe cattleman.'

Her father Frank, scummy? Good-for-*nothing*? A red haze descended in front of Bella's eyes. Prowsy could throw all the shit she liked at her and Patty, but Bella would not let her besmirch the name of a wonderful man like her father.

Acting rather than thinking, Bella slammed her fist into Prudence's face.

Prowsy went down.

Bella watched the woman in front of her topple and slide into the dirt at her feet. She looked down, horrified at what she'd done.

She was in trouble.

A voice assailed her from the food tent up ahead.

'Shit, Bella, what have you done now?' Patty walked over. 'For crap's sake, is Prowsy all right?'

Prudence was gasping and rubbing her mouth. 'You bitch,' she spluttered, spitting blood from where her front teeth had bitten into her lips. 'You fucking bitch!'

The look of pure hatred coming from her nemesis abruptly reminded Bella of what Prowsy had said to provoke such a response. 'I know who the bitch is and it's certainly not me. Shelve it, Prue. You got what you deserved and you know it,' she said before she spun around and walked off, shaking.

Looking back over her shoulder, Bella saw Patty putting out a hand to help Prowsy to her feet. Spurning it, Prudence staggered upright on her own, still wiping blood from her lips.

'I'll get you,' she yelled at Bella. 'This isn't the end of it, Vermaelon!' Spinning on her tooled cowgirl boots, Prowsy staggered off.

Bella flipped her the bird, then shuddered. She could hear her mother's voice in her head, 'a goose walking over your grave, my darling, that's all'.

'She's a first-class bitch, that's for sure,' said Patty, as Bella filled her in on the conversation that led to the altercation. 'Low country scum, my arse. Your father's one of the most respected men in the district! And besides, you've spent half your life up in the mountains at Maggie's. What's she bloody talking about?'

Bella didn't have an answer; she was still shocked by Prowsy's attack and her own response. Where the hell had that punch come from? She'd never punched anyone like that in her life. What *was* it with that bloody girl? What was it with her feelings for Will that made everything seem so much more important? Why did she feel things so strongly all of the sudden when up until now life had been all fluff and fun?

Will slid in beside her and handed over two sandwiches. 'Here you go, cowgirl. Sink your teeth into this. Where's Prue? I got her a couple too.'

'Well, since she's not here, we'll take them,' said Macca, holding out his big paws as he joined the circle. 'All this extra-curricular activity . . .' he waggled his eyebrows at Patty '. . . has made me downright starving.'

'I'd highly recommend the egg-and-bacon sandwiches to you all.' A new voice, spitting plums, joined them. Trinity Eggleton walked up beside Bella and Will. 'Oh! You're already onto it.'

He then turned to Bella. 'And you would be the ravishing young lady Will was warning me off last night, I'd say? Trinity Eggleton, at your service.' Trin blushed, looking at Will. 'Well, actually *not* at your service, because . . . but anyway . . . um . . . it's nice to meet you.' Trin bumbled to a stop and stuck out his hand.

Bella looked up and smiled, choosing to ignore his embarrassment. 'And it's nice to meet you too.' She returned the shake and silently marvelled at the feel of his smooth, cool hand, so different to the rough, calloused ones that had lovingly handled her last night. And this morning. Bella couldn't stop the grin sliding onto her face.

'Bella! Patty?' Caro rushed up beside her friend, long blonde hair flying around her face. 'What happened to Prowsy? She's in the first-aid tent, swearing vengeance and death on you both and everyone associated with you.' Bella shot a look towards Will, who had an eyebrow quirked in question. She shrugged, feigning ignorance and turned back to Caro.

'Man, is she wild! She's going to pack up her camp and head home, before the whip-cracking championships and the Stockman's Challenge . . .' Caro's voice died as she realised there was a stranger in the midst of the group.

Will shoved a dumbstruck Trin none too gently in the ribs. 'Caro, meet Trin – Trinity Eggleton. He's Wes Ogilvie's grandson. Trin, this is Caro – Caroline Handley. Was she the one you mentioned last night?'

'Mmm . . .' Trin's eyes were glazing.

'You're going to have to do better than that, mate,' said Macca, with a smirk.

Meanwhile Caro, completely ignoring Macca, had moved around and wiggled her way in between Bella and the still-dumb Trin. 'How *are* you?' said Caro as she took a closer look at the new talent.

'I'm well . . . thank you . . . and . . . you?' Trin spluttered.

Looking fresher and brighter than anyone who had been so drunk the previous night had a right to look, Caro launched into a conversation intent on finding out exactly who, what and how much potential Mr Trinity Eggleton had.

The Nunkeri Muster's Ladies Whip-Cracking Competition came down to a battle between Bella and Patty. Not surprisingly, with her new whips and Harry Bailey's tutorage, Patty beat Bella to the honour of being the champion – again.

The weekend's finale had been the race they were all supposed to be there for, the Stockman's Challenge; the race that tested the skills and endurance of the best horsemen in the district. The winner, however, was a bloke from New South Wales. He'd heard about the weekend on the radio too and had trucked down his horse and dogs to do battle with the riders in the mountains to the south.

Bella said goodbye to Will on the Monday morning; he had to head back to Tindarra, but not before promising to phone, and their next meeting arranged for the Burrindal B&S Ball. Long, lingering kisses went on and on at the ute's passenger-side door, until Patty had threatened to leave Bella behind on the swiftly emptying Nunkeri Plains.

Bella wouldn't have minded. In fact, nights curled up with Will in the rustic cattlemen's hut would have been her idea of heaven. And the passion of Will's farewell assured her that he agreed.

Chapter 19

'That's number one-twenty-seven, with one to go.' Bella notched another stroke in her little Elders notebook as Patty swung the ute into the gateway of Merinda and over the cattle grid. 'That's a bloody lot of cattle grids between Ainsley Station and home.'

'Home for you, mate, not me. I'll have another couple to add to the tally.' Patty sighed. 'Feels good, though, doesn't it? Seems like we've been away for years.'

Bella stretched her arms above her head and yawned. 'Yep, twelve months away is long enough for this little black duck.'

The track wound on, through towering plane trees, leading to the homestead built by Bella's great-grandfather Alfred and his wife Adeline.

Sitting upright, Bella whooped as she spotted her mother Francine appear from the side door of the grandiose old homestead which lay sprawled in the sun. 'There's Mum!' Bella started bouncing on the seat, willing the track to end and to have her mother's arms around her. 'She must've been watching for us.'

'No kidding, Sherlock. She's probably been camped at that side door for the last two hours.' Patty shook her head at her friend.

The ute rode over the last cattle grid into the house yard, clunking loudly as the tyres hit the evenly spaced railway iron laid over the concrete pit. 'And that was number one-twenty-eight. We're home!' shouted Bella as she flung open the door of the still-moving ute.

Leaping out onto the gravel, she raced up the old redbrick path to Francine, who was sprinting towards her daughter laughing, crying and calling at the top of her voice, 'Girls! Oh Bella, my darling girl!'

'Mum! MUM!'

Mother and daughter gathered each other up and danced around and around in a jig of joy. Kisses, hugs and more kisses.

Patty pulled her red ute to a halt. She slowly opened her driver's-side door, got out and leaned on the bonnet watching mother and daughter with amusement. She knew she'd get the same reception from her mum, but to reach home she still had over an hour and three cattle grids to go.

Francine untangled herself from Bella's hug. Slinging an arm around her daughter, she called across to Patty. 'Darling, you look simply gorgeous. So tanned and fit. Come on, give me a hug. Won't Helen be *so* pleased to see you too. She was only saying the other night how much she missed you.'

Patty walked over and was kissed and hugged as well. 'This calls for a cup of tea.' Francine snuggled a girl in on either side of her. 'It's just *so* good to see your smiling faces. I can't believe you're home. Come on in and tell us *all* about it.'

Patty tossed Bella a warning look.

Don't you dare tell her about Macca, the look seemed to say.

Bella imperceptibly nodded. She responded with a dark look of her own.

Don't you dare tell her about Will!

The old Vermaelon homestead had been added onto and extended with each generation. What had started out a hundred years ago as a simple square of four rooms back to back had gradually metamorphosed into a rambling farmhouse with nooks and crannies around every corner. The weatherboard exterior was painted a creamy white, the roof was corrugated iron in differing shades of gumleaf-green depending on the position of the sun.

The homestead was surrounded by towering oaks, liquidambers, golden elms and majestic native red gum trees. The flower beds bloomed with an abundance of flowers: hundreds of roses, lavenders, camellias and azaleas, all testament to Francine Vermaelon's green fingers.

Francine led the way through the French side doors, into the serene confines of the house. The ghostly presence of generations of Vermaelons seemed to watch as they walked through the side passage into the formal entrance of the main house.

As wide as it was deep, the vestibule was elegantly laid out with an antique hallstand to hang a hat or coat and a half-circular table with ornately turned legs to receive the mail.

Francine sailed on past without a backward glance, with Bella chattering nonstop beside her. Patty wandered along behind.

Suddenly a hand clamped onto her shoulder and Patty spun around.

Bella's father Frank stood there, all six-foot-two of him. His cornflower-blue eyes twinkled and he held his broad arms wide open. 'Ah, my girls. And isn't it a sight for sore eyes to see you two.'

'Dad!' cried Bella, as she twirled around at the sound of her father's voice. Flying back across the hall, she just beat Patty into his wide, welcoming arms.

Smiling over the blonde, curly head of his beautiful daughter, Frank beckoned Patty as Bella moved over to make room for her best mate. And within the clasp of that warm and all-encompassing hug, the girls felt they were finally truly home.

The afternoon wore into night, as cup after cup of strong sugar-laden tea was drunk in the warm country kitchen of Merinda. First with Frank and Francine, and then with Bella's brother Justin and his wife Melanie, who arrived from their share-farmer's house on another part of the farm for dinner and to listen to the girls' many stories.

Telephone calls and emails just couldn't convey the thousand tales of outback adventures they'd had. While tucking into Francine's beautifully cooked roast tea, Patty and Bella had their audience in hysterics with the accounts of the antics and parties from the last twelve months.

The night carried on into the wee hours of the morning until Justin pushed back his chair from the huge kitchen table. 'Enough. I've laughed more tonight than I have in the past year with this flamin' drought, but I have to go home and get my beauty sleep.'

The clock dinged two a.m., and Frank rose as well. 'Yes, son.

You've got four hundred beautiful women's backsides waiting for you at five a.m., and I don't think you're going to look your best with only three hours' sleep.'

Melanie walked over to stand by Justin's side. Looking a picture of pregnant health with a curly mop of red curls framing a little freckled face, Melanie was as feisty as her hair suggested. 'Yeah, come on, Just. Those gorgeous black-and-white numbers will be spraying poop everywhere if you keep them waiting. Plus, the babysitter's got to be up and gone by six. She does trackwork at the racecourse,' she explained as Bella's eyebrows rose. 'I want a little shut-eye too before those two heathens you call our kids land on our bed.'

Bella jumped up to kiss her brother and Melanie goodbye. Justin chucked his little sister under the chin and grinned down into her smiling eyes. 'It's good to have you home, sis.'

'It's good to be here. I loved it all up there in Queensland, but it was time to come back.'

Justin grabbed Melanie's coat and helped her into it. 'What's on now for you two?'

'Well, my leave of absence from the hospital is nearly finished so I'm going back to taking temps and washing body parts,' said Patty, looking resigned.

'Whinger. You love it!' said Bella, giving her mate a shove. 'It's a captive audience, what more could you want?'

Justin laughed as Patty rolled her eyes. He turned to his sister, 'What about you, Hells Bells?'

'My twelve months' leave is over about then too. I'm due back at the Department of Agriculture after Christmas.'

Francine interrupted them. 'Yes, Bella, darling, David Neille rang wondering if you could meet with him next Monday.

He wants you to take on a new job within Landcare when you go back.'

'You *really are* in demand with the fellas at the moment, Hells Bells!' Patty's singsong voice was laced with innuendo as she moved off to find the spare bedroom.

Bella poked her tongue out at her friend, too tired to come up with a smart-arse reply.

Patty's laughter echoed down the hall.

It was early morning when Bella finally curled up in her own bed at Merinda. The antique Queen Anne bed, which had been her mother's and was now hers, was cool and comfortable. The lavender scent Bella always associated with home wafted across her nostrils as she snuggled into the sheets. The chiffon curtains hanging across the open window were awhirl as a cool breeze puffed gently into the room.

It was wonderful to be back, Bella thought as she soaked in the feel and smells of Merinda. It was like the grand-dame house was welcoming the prodigal daughter home into the loving and welcoming shelter of its walls.

It was so good to see her parents, particularly her mum. She'd missed that Chanel No. 5 scented hug, those sweet endearments. She was reminded of just how much her mother was the rock on which she centred her life; the one person who would unreservedly and unconditionally love her and support her, no matter what scrapes she got herself into. There weren't many parents who'd be happy to let their young daughter head into the wilds of outback Queensland with no job, no prospects and no idea of what she was doing, let alone where she was going.

But her parents had.

And Bella, wise to her father's reticent ways, knew it was her mother who'd waged the argument on her behalf. It was her mother who, along with Helen O'Hara, had supported the girls' quest to fulfil their dreams. Both women must have remembered what it was like to be young with mountains to conquer. They also knew the two girls would look after each other while they were away.

Amid all the parties and fun of the past year, Bella had come to truly appreciate just how much her home and family meant to her.

Chapter 20

The Holden ute was rocking. Patty had the volume up as high as it would go, and Bella could see Francine's good-natured grimace as the Dixie Chicks belted out 'Wide Open Spaces'. Somewhere beyond the windows of the ute was their wide open space, but they couldn't see it through the thick fog.

Out there were open paddocks, rolling on and on until somewhere near the horizon they led to Merinda, where her father Frank would be making his way into the house after locking up the last of the milking cows.

Past those paddocks and Merinda were the mountains of the Great Divide, which hid the other place, and the man so close to Bella's heart: Tindarra and Will O'Hara.

They were on their way home after a day shopping in Bairnsdale.

The dense fog had hit just after they left the truck stop fifty kilometres back. Over the washbasin of the loo, Bella and her mother had had a good-humoured argument over whose turn it was to squash in the middle and straddle the gearstick of Patty's ute.

Francine had lost and now, in the last fifteen minutes to home, Bella could see her mother's eyes closing, lulled by the music, the heated air spilling from the vents and the exhaustion of a big day out in town.

It had been two weeks since they'd arrived home. With the Nunkeri Muster crossed off the Tindarra and Narree social calendars, all thoughts turned towards the Burrindal B&S Ball, and Bella had convinced her mother to come dress-shopping with her and Patty.

And thus the 'Quest for the Dress' had begun.

The day had started at six-thirty with a cuppa and a piece of toast. Patty had driven down from Tindarra the night before so they could be on the road to Bairnsdale in time to hit the shops by nine. It was only a fortnight until Christmas and the ball was planned for Saturday night. It was now Thursday, so the quest was skidding in sideways, a last-minute sprint to make them belles of the ball. Or, as far as the girls were concerned, at least to look a hell of a lot better than that dolled-up bitch Prudence Vincent-Prowse.

Bella wondered if Prowsy still had a bruise from the right hook she'd delivered at Nunkeri. She stared out through the ute passenger-side window, not really seeing the fog enclosing them in its grey grasp. She was back at the Muster looking down at Prowsy prostrate on the grass, clutching her bleeding mouth.

Bella shook away that disquieting memory, determined it wouldn't wreck what had been a fabulous day shopping with her mum and best mate. She checked the side rear-vision mirror, and caught a glimpse of the bright pink dress bags poking out of the tool box in the back. *Burrindal B&S Ball, here we come!* She let out a whoop and threw a clenched fist into the air.

'We are going to look like hot chicky babes in these numbers, Pat Me Tuffet. Those Marlboro mountain men of ours better watch out, because we're comin' to town.' A chuckle came from Francine as she sat with eyes shut, listening to her girls.

The Dixie Chicks wound to a close and the CD spun to a stop.

'What'll we play now?' Bella looked at the depleted bundle of CDs in her hand. 'We've played them all twice. Why'd you leave your CD holder at home, Patty? What were you thinking?'

'Of getting to your place before it got dark. I didn't want to come up close and personal with a flaming kangaroo on that shitty road down the mountain.'

Francine lifted her head from where it had dropped to Bella's shoulder. 'Patty, honey, I think you should pop your lights on. That fog's getting thicker out there.' She went quiet for a minute. 'What about the CD you bought for Beccy and Joel, Bella? Have you still got it in the ute, sweetheart? You didn't give it to them in the end, did you?'

Bella leaned down to scrabble in the side pocket on the door. 'Great idea, Mum. Nope. I didn't give it to them. I should have got Hi-5 or the *Hannah Montana* soundtrack. They were a bit old for the CD I got. That's just what we need after all this country music, a blast from the past with . . . nursery rhymes!'

Patty groaned. 'Don't do it to me.'

'When you're desperate, you're really desperate,' said Bella, coming up empty-handed. 'You may be saved. I can't find it. Have you got it over there, Patty?'

'Yep, I've got it.' Patty reluctantly dragged out the CD from the driver's-side pocket. With her left hand she awkwardly tried to slide the disk into the player, jamming it on the way.

Francine opened her eyes and let out a gentle sigh. 'Patty, my love, when will you learn to slow down?'

Patty was still scrabbling with the CD, pressing the eject button repeatedly with one hand, while the other guided the steering wheel. The CD popped out of the cavity with a clatter and bounced off the gearstick onto the floor.

Francine tried to reach it, leaning forward around the gearstick. 'I can't get it with my belt on.'

'I'll have a try,' said Bella. 'Damn, it's gone under the seat.' She clicked her seatbelt open so she could lean further down. 'Nup, I can't reach it either.'

'I'll have another go.' Francine unclipped her belt and leaned over sideways to reach as far back as she could. 'Got it!' She came up triumphant, waving the silver disk. She slid the CD into the player.

'She'll be comin' round the mountain when she comes,' blasted through the speakers.

'Yee ha!' Bella leaned forward and cranked the volume to full blast.

They all joined in as Francine jiggled her knees around the gearstick in time to the beat. 'Do you remember our singsongs around the piano at Maggie's?' she yelled to the two girls. 'You all loved this one so much.'

As the chorus came round again, they sang with all their hearts. 'Singing Hi Yi Yippy Yippy Yi, Singing Hi Yi Yippy Yippy Yi . . .'

Bella grabbed her mother's hand and swung it in the air. At home they would have danced, spinning a partner around with glee.

Mid-song, Patty remembered Francine's comment about her lights. She turned them on, along with the wipers. It was now drizzling rain. Sliding her foot from the accelerator, she slowed the ute.

'What are you doing?' yelled Bella.

'The fog's getting thicker. There's an intersection with a give-way sign somewhere around here.'

They didn't hear him coming.

A 30-tonne B-Double, loaded to the max with grain destined for Atkins Fertiliser and Stock Feeds.

Bluey Atkins's right foot was touching the brakes to slow up for the intersection ahead; his left hand holding a mobile phone. His wife was on the blower wondering how far from home he was; there was a cow down with milk fever and she couldn't get it up by herself.

A pair of lights suddenly appeared to the left of his startled gaze.

He barely felt the vehicle go under the huge bullbar. The steel Mack Dog guarding his bonnet. His wife was still talking on the phone he'd hurled to the floor as he threw every ounce of his ample weight into any brake he could find with his hands and feet.

Knowing it was too late.

Knowing there was no hope.

Knowing at that moment he was killing someone.

'Bluey? Bluey? Are you there, Bluey?' The phone continued to twitter.

Trying to control the brakes, Bluey struggled to arrest the weight of his rig and its huge bins of grain from bearing down on what was underneath.

A red Holden ute.

A torrent of sound assaulted his ears; tearing metal, shattering glass, screeching tyres and, most shocking of all, terrified screams. For Bluey, everything seemed to occur in slow motion, as if he were hovering above, observing.

The massive rig out of control. Brakes locked. Leaving the road.

Punching through the wire fence like scissors through thin jute twine.

A paddock of lush green lucerne laden with water droplets, shining in the misty rain.

The 180-degree slide across the paddock of 'Montmorency Downs'; a slide, a sweep, taking only seconds to change lives.

A fire engine red ute attached to the bullbar of his truck.

Floating into his line of sight, a pair of eyes. Frozen with pure terror. Perfectly round. Lapis blue. Staring straight up and into his.

A soul in flight to death?

An angel on the way to heaven?

Images to haunt him for the rest of his life.

Bella's world exploded.

A stream of noise assailed her ears: the shrieking of crumpling metal, the shattering of imploding glass. The high-pitched screech of air brakes competed with human screams. Cassettes, CDs, boots, pliers and rolls of insulation tape became missiles inside the ute's crumpling cab.

Strapped to her driver's seat, Patty was the first to absorb the incredible force of being T boned.

Francine's unrestrained body flew forwards and out the front windscreen. Through the shower of glass Bella instinctively flung her hands towards her mother, fluking a hold on her ankle as she ploughed through the shattering window casing and out onto the bonnet.

At the same time, Bella's passenger-side door flew open.

Her mother's body thumped its way across the shiny, rain-slicked bonnet as the truck did its circular waltz across the paddock. Bella clung to the ankle that was keeping her in the cab of the ute. Her terrified and panic-stricken gaze swept across the devastation around her. Her eyes met those of a man fighting a duel with his truck.

Bella felt her mother's ankle slowly slip from her grasp. She let loose with a blood-curdling scream. Without the shackle of a human anchor, Francine flew through the air, clearing the fence and landing with a thud on the tar.

Simultaneously Bella's unrestrained body was snatched from the seat and flung out of the open passenger doorway, across the wide spaces she loved so much, rolling through a scrubby bush and somersaulting to a stop beside the road, tangled in the barbed wire that lay broken by the truck's wild ride.

It only took seconds, but it seemed like hours.

Finally both the rig and the remains of the ute ground to a halt.

The sobbing of a man and a twittering mobile phone were all that disturbed the moist, early-evening air.

Then they too were silent.

PART TWO

Eight years later

Chapter 21

Melbourne was a bright glow in the rear-vision mirror of the Mercedes.

When Bella first arrived in the city, the place had screamed bedlam to her country ears; cars, trucks, sirens and people, all fighting for attention. She'd nearly gone nuts trying to dodge the pace and aggression; had slogged it out day after day, until she realised with shock that the chaos had become normal. It was as if landscapes filled with space, trees, mountains and silence had never been a part of her life. They were conveniently locked in the dark recesses of her mind.

Until now.

Bella wove the Mercedes around a speeding semi-trailer also heading east. Her dress, a scrap of magenta silk, was rucked up around her thighs where faint scars tracked patterns on her skin. Moonbeams danced in through the back window of the car, the light frequently glancing off the large diamond solitaire ring encircling the third finger on her left hand. Pavarotti played softly through the surround-sound system. Everything around her reeked of the sleek and expensive.

Bella slammed her hand down hard on the leather steering wheel. The moonbeams seemed to pause, expectant. 'Damn him!' she yelled at the top of her voice. 'Fuck him!' The moonbeams barely wavered. Everything around her stayed the same.

Who was she? What was she?

An urbane woman in control of her life? Hardly.

A country girl playing a game of charades? Possibly.

If this was a game, she didn't want to play anymore, especially after tonight. Thank God she was out of there, away from Melbourne, away from Warren, her fiancé. *Fiancé*. The word rolled around her tongue. Funny how something that once tasted like honey, delightful and sweet, could turn into a mouthful of grit. How could things go so wrong?

Bella had met Warren at a cocktail party two years after she'd arrived in Melbourne. The public-relations firm she worked for specialised in large rural clients, and she was at the party to attract work and sponsorship from the corporate attendees.

She loved her job but she hated those nights; putting on a front, being nice to wan, spotty-faced city blokes who were more interested in looking down her shirt than listening to what she had to say. Meeting Warren had been the highlight of the evening; he'd made the other men in the room sink into the ludicrous pattern on the papered walls.

With his blond, patrician good looks and English accent, Warren had flattered and flirted and asked her out for a drink after the function. One hand held her coat, the other a large cheque. 'An investment in the future,' he'd said to her boss, while looking deep into her eyes. He was a man who knew what he wanted, where he was going and with whom. And she was sucked in.

He had about him an air of reassurance that made her feel safe and secure. After the turmoil her life had been in, she felt like she had finally reached calm waters in Warren's arms. Here was someone who truly cared. When Warren focused on *her*, it made her feel like she was the only person in the world who was important. And she had desperately needed that, to feel loved, adored and cherished.

She wasn't sure when it had all changed; couldn't put her finger on the exact moment when the adoration and cherishing had turned into suffocation. For despite all Warren's assurances that she helped him kick back and enjoy life, she slowly came to realise that wasn't true. He wanted her to focus on him and help build his career. And it had only grown worse the higher he climbed the corporate ladder. Although he maintained that their relationship was the priority in his life, Warren's career came above and before anything else. Including her.

Six years later, she could yell and curse all she wanted, but it wouldn't vent the anger she felt over Warren's betrayal. Cocking her head, she caught the faint warbling coming from the CD player. She hit the eject button and snatched Pavarotti from his cosy hole. Jabbing at the electronic buttons near her right hand, she slid the window down.

'Take that, you morbid bastard,' she yelled as she threw the disc out the window. The CD bounced once on the road and then into the thick grassy verge.

Grappling one-handed through the CDs at her side, she realised they were all Warren's. Pavarotti, Carreras, Domingo:

the operatic list went on. Bloody hell! She needed some yell-out-loud country music. And she needed it now.

It took a minute for it to come to mind. It had been so long. Swinging the car into the next truck stop, she parked and then bent to scrabble on the floor under the driver's seat.

'Got it,' Bella muttered as she drew out her find. A cheap and dog-eared CD holder. She flicked on the interior light and opened the front of the battered old relic. Inside the cover, barely legible in a flamboyant hand, was inscribed, 'Dearest Hells Bells, Yell out loud, girlfriend. You rock! Love always, Pat Me Tuffet.'

Oh dear God, could she bear it? Even after all this time? Waves of emotion fought to escape from tight confines of her heart. Bella took a deep breath; forced her feelings to stay under lock and key. She looked closely at the labels imprinted on the disks in her hands, and her walking fingers found what she needed.

She slid the CD into the slot and within seconds the Dixie Chicks bounced from the roof and plush interior. Using both hands, Bella pulled at the sleek chignon that held her hair in check. She released her tumbling ringlets, finger-combing through hairspray to send the honey-coloured locks into wild disarray.

Cranking up the stereo a few more notches, she started the car and took off, stones flying, wheels spinning, back onto Highway Number One, a road that could take you all the way around Australia if you wanted.

Singing hopelessly flat and at the top of her voice, Bella found a release for the anger that had been consuming her for most of the night. The diamond on her hand glinted again. She refused to be attracted, keeping her eyes glued to the road leading her to the Vermaelon family home, and respite.

As the car ate up the miles, the massive and brightly lit bypasses that overhung the highway became more sporadic, and finally disappeared. The luminous full moon shone white and settled itself slap-bang in the middle of the highway, lining up its radiance with the grassy verge between thoroughfares.

She hadn't been home as much as she'd have liked these last eight years. Warren was never keen to 'head bush', as he called it. He always came up with excuses not to visit her family and he sulked if she went by herself. It had been easier to just go along with him. Christmases had come and gone, and another year passed with only the odd visit to the farm, when Warren was working away.

A plane heading east slung a white hazy jet stream out behind. The fluffy residue reflected brightly under the light from the moon. She had missed seeing the night sky undimmed by blazing city lights; missed the quiet of the bush; missed her family.

Thank God she didn't feel sick anymore. The gastro bug she'd been battling seemed finally to have abated – or maybe her anger had burned it away? The fact she'd been able to attend this evening's function at all was a feat in itself. A couple of days ago, she would've vomited all over Warren's Italian leather shoes.

She knew she should have gone straight home after the rodeo rather than going onto that bloody cocktail party. But then again, she wouldn't have finally ripped off the rose-coloured glasses she'd worn these past few years. At last she had acknowledged Warren's selfishness, and the spinelessness that lurked beneath his self-assurance. Tears pricked her eyes as she sighed. There were so many choices and paths leading alternate ways.

The smaller country towns marched along the road at various intervals, and then they too grew further apart. The Dixie Chicks moved onto 'Taking the Long Way' and Bella's mood gradually slipped into the slow beat and melancholy emotions of the ballad, her anger spent. Was it something everyone went through – this search to find themselves? Her Aunty Maggie had an old birthday card on the wall at Tindarra Cottage, which read, '*Sometimes the best way to figure out who you are, is to get to that place where you don't have to be anything else.*' She wondered about that.

Was it only yesterday that her boss had handed her two free tickets to the State of Origin International Rodeo? Her job delivered some side-benefits: free tickets to a huge variety of events was one. She hit the elevator button at the lavish Docklands penthouse she shared with Warren beside the Yarra River. She couldn't wait to go, to see, feel and be a part of a country tradition from her early years, which until now she hadn't realised she missed so much. It wasn't until the elevator started its climb to the top floor that reality hit like a fisted hand.

Warren wouldn't want to go.

Her bubbles of excitement popped in mid-air.

The elevator delivered her into a sleek, minimalist living room suffering mortuary-level temperatures thanks to efficient airconditioning. Bella shivered, goose bumps rising on her arms. The intelligent lighting blinked on and she could hear the pre-programmable convection oven spinning its stuff, a couple of chicken mignons ensconced inside. Bella looked around at her sterile surroundings. What the hell was she doing here? Really?

The only part of the penthouse that was cosy was the mocha-coloured shag-pile rug on the floor and a cherry-red minky blanket she kept on the back of the leather sofa, much to

Warren's disgust. At least she'd snipped off the Target label so he could pretend it came from some fancy designer.

Slipping off her high-heeled shoes, Bella wrapped herself in the blanket and shuffled into the kitchen for something to eat. What wouldn't she have done for one of her mother's date scones with lashings of yellow butter, or even a slice of Aunty Maggie's ginger fluff sponge dripping with homemade cream freshly skimmed from the milk bucket that morning?

'We can't go.' Warren was adamant as he tapped on his Black-Berry an hour or so later. 'You did say tomorrow night, didn't you?'

Bella opened her mouth to reply but Warren kept right on talking.

'It's a definite no. You know we have that black-tie function at Crown to meet my new CEO.'

Of course, Bella should have known. Oxford, Bride and Associates always took precedence over everything else. Momentarily she wondered whether turning herself into a share portfolio or a multi-million-dollar takeover bid would give her more say over her life.

Warren moved to stand directly in front of her, BlackBerry still in hand, the downlighting casting his shadow over her. She drew the warm minky blanket closer, instinctively seeking its reassurance.

'We can give the tickets to Caroline and Trinity. It can be their last hurrah before their wedding this weekend, seeing as they're so set on moving to that God-forsaken place in the mountains. I have no comprehension as to why you people love that place.'

'Probably because you haven't been there.'

'And I have no desire to go there, but I will . . .' Warren's patrician face formed a grimace '. . . for *you*. Hopefully there'll be someone there to talk to who isn't totally preoccupied with the weather. But like I said, give the tickets to Caroline and Trinity.'

'Warren, we're *not* giving second-hand tickets to Caro and Trin as a wedding present.'

No, Bella had arranged a few nights at a luxurious retreat for Caro and Trin's honeymoon, and *that* was going to be her gift, not freebie cast-offs. And the pair deserved it after being there for her all these years, supporting her through all the grief and loneliness. Caro and Trin had slogged for the last eight years to turn old Wes's Ben Bullen Hills Station into a profit-able working property while still holding down jobs in the city to help pay for all the improvements. Now they were going to move back to the mountains and farm full-time. They deserved a few nights' honeymoon before heading bush.

In the early days of her relationship with Warren, Bella had relished the fact that he was so wonderfully different to the men she had known before. Gone were rough work clothes, elastic-sided boots, the colloquial slang of the bush. Warren was sophisticated, handsome, precise. Nobody would never call Warren a 'bloke'.

Now she wondered if she'd fallen in love with a smooth veneer – a superficial man whose cold and competitive English boarding-school upbringing was colliding fiercely with her own deep loving family, where values and principles went beyond just thinking about yourself. Their relationship hadn't started out like this, had it? In the early years, he was so loving and attentive. And surely, Warren hadn't always only done what *he* wanted to do? She pondered that. Possibly. So had she just aided and abetted him?

Warren, oblivious to all that was going on in his fiancée's head, stashed his BlackBerry back in its usual suit pocket and moved towards the bar. Relieved he wasn't standing over her anymore, Bella watched as he walked away in shiny black-tasselled leather moccasins, bum cheeks hugging fine Italian wool pants, treading a slightly mincing step.

'I'm not going.' Bella's voice was flat and even.

Warren didn't even look up from where he was mixing his drink. 'Of course you are, darling, you're expected to be there. You're my fiancée,' he said as he squeezed a lemon. 'You *need* to be there. What will the other wives think?' He picked up a bright pink swizzle stick with a laughing plastic monkey perched on its end, and continued talking as he swished his drink. 'What will the—'

Bella had heard enough.

Shrugging out of her minky, she jumped to her feet. 'What about what I need, Warren? What about *me*?'

She strode across the room, coming to a halt in front of the bar. 'When did what *I* want to do cease to count? When did what *you* need and what *the company wants* come before me? Before us?' She stopped and drew in a ragged breath. 'I want to go to the Ro-DE-o!' Bella accentuated the 'DE' in an exaggerated Queensland drawl, something she knew would offend Warren's delicate sensibilities. 'I've earned these tickets, I want these tickets, I *need* these tickets and I *am* going, with or without you! I can still come to your party, I'll just be late.'

Bella stood rigid, waiting. She had to win this battle with Warren, to try to retain a part of herself in more ways than one.

Warren set down his swizzle stick on the bar mat with precision, the pink plastic monkey staring straight up to laugh in his face. He looked up from his drink and saw in Bella's huge blue eyes something he'd never seen before.

He'd seen tears. Plenty of tears.

He'd seen laughter, love, flashes of frustration and sometimes even hints of temper. But he'd always been able to sway her, to make her see his way.

But never this.

He'd never seen absolute and utter determination.

Chapter 22

Eight years earlier Bella lay in the Alfred Hospital in Melbourne, with her father by her bedside.

Frank Vermaelon sat in a grey hospital chair, as close as he dared to the bed in which Bella lay unconscious, surrounded by machines that seemed to breathe of their own accord; the lights, hums and the beeps that helped keep his daughter alive.

After the crash, an unconscious Bella had been air-lifted by helicopter to Melbourne with head and suspected spinal injuries. A CT scan revealed cerebral oedema and spinal shock but the scan was inconclusive. The doctors told Frank they'd have to wait for his daughter to regain consciousness to ascertain her brain function and spinal-cord ability. That was the only way they'd know how much damage she had sustained.

Frank was unshaven and slack-jawed, in a light sleep that caused his limbs to jerk and twitch. His pallor was grey with suppressed fatigue, worry and grief. His eyes were heavily circled with black and he wore an obvious air of anguish and loss.

Bella's eyes blinked. The machines around her went wild in their response. She fought for consciousness.

Frank leapt forward to grab his daughter's hand, in hope. Bella, in her semi-conscious state, reached for the light, trying to open her eyes, to feel her father's hand, but she retreated when the pain became too much. The room was filled with noise, and even though the pressure of her father's warm, calloused palm was there to comfort and draw her back into the real world – it was too hard.

No, not just yet.

Soon – but not yet. It hurt too much.

She allowed the blackness to reclaim her once more. And Frank slumped back into his chair.

As the nurses rushed in to check on his daughter and quiet the whistling machines, Frank allowed himself a sliver of hope. He was sure he'd felt Bella's hand respond slightly to his gentle squeeze. And that was all he needed. It gave him strength and fuelled his belief that his determined little girl would pull through.

She wafted in and out. Sometimes she saw a fuzzy Frank, and other times she heard Will. But mostly it was just blackness with a visit from Patty from time to time.

'Bugger off sunshine,' her best mate seemed to say. 'You're not coming with me this time, girlfriend.' The voice was definitely Patty's, at her determined best. 'Much and all as it would be good to have you here.' A waft of wistfulness flickered as the words disappeared, out of sight, out of her mind, gone as silently as they had come.

When Bella finally came to, her Aunty Maggie was dozing

in the chair by her side with some sewing lying discarded on her lap.

She lay there a while just soaking in the familiar look of her aunt, her long grey hair all piled into a bun, the half-moon glasses falling from her snubbed nose, the polyester rayon 'best' dress with its bright orange psychedelic geometric print that sat awkwardly on a body more comfortable in slacks and shirt.

At the sight of Maggie, the scents and memories of Tindarra assaulted her; the call of the mountains seemed to reach out from the warm, diminutive figure sitting at her side.

'Aunty Maggie,' she whispered.

Maggie's eyes popped open and she leaned forward to grab her niece's hand.

'Bella. My love. You're back.' Maggie's face was awash with joy and tears. As her aunt fumbled to press the button for a nurse, Bella tried to make sense of her surroundings. Things must be crook if Maggie's in tears, she thought. The fuzz in her mind wasn't helping. It was all so white and the sheets on the bed felt hard, scratchy and uncomfortable, like she was lying under sandpaper rather than her mum's soft linen at home.

What was Aunty Maggie doing here? She should have been home at Tindarra. And why the hell was she crying?

'Where?' Bella croaked. It felt like she had rusty piano wire twisted around her vocal chords.

Maggie hurriedly reached for a glass of water with its angled straw.

'Only a little bit,' she warned, as she helped her niece to lift her head and sip a few drops.

Maggie waited until Bella lay back before answering. 'You're in hospital, sweetheart. In Melbourne.'

'How long?' she croaked again, a little louder this time.

Maggie put the glass back on the bedside table, picked up the discarded sewing and sat down in her chair once more. 'A couple of days.'

Bella tried to cast her muddled brain back. She could remember the trip to town with her mum and Patty. Buying their B&S dresses and then riding home in the ute, music blaring, singing at the tops of their voices . . .

'Patty?' She had been first in line to be hit by the truck.

Maggie's face drained of colour.

'Gone?' Bella whispered, as Maggie dropped her head into her hands.

A few moments passed, time that seemed like eternity. Maggie raised her head and looked into the eyes of her beloved niece. Eyes that were even bluer than usual, resting in a pallid face.

'Oh, Bella, my love. My sweet, I'm so sorry.'

Bella tried to swallow. It felt like the piano wire had eased its garrotte only to let a hangman's knot take its place. Summoning saliva to soothe the passage of speech, Bella asked again.

'Mum?'

Maggie's eyes shifted sideways as tears ran in ripples down her apple-skin cheeks. Groping for the box of tissues on the bedside table, Maggie gave a slight shake of her head.

It was enough.

Bella turned the other way and shut her eyes, closing herself off from her aunt, closing off from the world.

'No, Bella, *no!*' Maggie gasped as she realised what the girl thought.

Bella wasn't listening. She was in a bitter, dark place. Her insides felt like cold granite, her heart a frigid lump of ice.

Why was she alive when those she loved were dead?

Francine. Her warm, beautiful and loving mother.

Gone. Dead.

Fingers of terror raced through her blood.

Patty. Her vivacious, fun-loving best mate.

Gone. Dead.

Just like that.

Never again.

Why, in God's name *why*?

And why couldn't she have gone too?

Frank Vermaelon, followed by his son Justin and a nurse, ran through the doorway. As Bella turned towards her father and brother, Maggie tried again. Shaking her head so hard the glasses went flying from her nose to skitter across the laminate floor. 'No. Not your mother, Bella, not Francine. She's fighting. She's alive.'

Frank reached Bella as the nurse scurried to the other side of the bed, observing her now-conscious patient. Maggie gathered her glasses, sewing and tissues and headed for the hospital hallway to pull herself together.

Alone with the men, Bella looked up at what remained of her family, eyelids brimming with unshed tears. If she needed any confirmation of her nightmare, it was found in Frank and Justin's sorrow-filled eyes. The two men were unashamedly crying. Relieved to see their girl awake battled with the grief of the loss they may still have to endure.

They sat down to tell her quietly of the terrible injuries sustained by her mother, who was now battling for life in a cubicle down the sterile hallway.

And then they too confirmed what Bella didn't want to hear.

Patty was dead.

Harry Bailey came to the funeral, all the way from up north. So did a sun-soaked Knackers and Wendy Anderson, with four little boys standing like descending steps by their side. Max still had an arm in a sling.

Harry had rung the O'Haras to find out the outcome of the Muster's whip-cracking championship, looking to celebrate with Patty what he was sure would have been a win. He was told instead that Patty was dead.

He found it so hard to comprehend how such a vivacious, bright-eyed ray of sunshine could be snuffed. Gone. Obliterated. Just like that. Harry had finally hung up, after mumbling condolences through the tears.

Bella was determined to go to the funeral. Doctors had followed up with a second CT scan and full neurological examination, which showed the brain and spinal-cord swelling had resolved leaving no permanent injury. And because the doctors' tests said she was physically okay, Bella immediately discharged herself. Her family were horrified but she was adamant. She was going to be there to say goodbye to her best friend.

After the funeral service, Bella had turned and walked towards the only thing she felt was anchoring her to life. The one person she thought would truly understand the grief that was overwhelming her – the man she hadn't seen since waking up in her hospital bed. But Will deliberately turned away and started talking to Prudence Vincent-Prowse.

Bella halted mid-step, startled. What the hell was that all about? Why didn't he want to speak to her? To hold her? They were lovers, for heaven's sake – boyfriend and girlfriend, weren't they? He had been at the hospital while she was still unconscious, her father and Aunty Maggie told her, so *that* hadn't been a dream. But since she had started to recover, no-one had sighted him and she was at a loss to understand why. And why the cold shoulder now? What had she done? Where had he gone? And why?

Did he blame *her* for the accident?

Did he blame *her* for being alive while his sister was dead?

She looked across at the seemingly cosy twosome and felt affronted and sickened by the sight of Prowsy.

She deflected her path to her father, her brother and her very pregnant sister-in-law, who looked ready to collapse in the heat. They were standing to the side of the big, black hearse with silver trim on the duco, a stark coffin laden with carnations inside.

'You okay?' asked Frank, worry etched firmly into the creases around his eyes.

She managed a nod as she took his dry and wrinkled farmer's hand. She tried to quell her alarm over Will's behaviour, her gaze drifting to her cousin, standing nearby with her Aunty Rhonda and Uncle Bryce.

Macca's anguish was palpable; she could taste it in her mouth, feel it on her skin. She couldn't stand to look at that grief-stricken face, the bloodshot whites of his eyes competing with the florid flush of his cheeks.

He stood in his black suit, beside his parents, hollow-eyed.

As he'd linked arms with Will to carry Patty from the church, Bella had seen his body shaking violently. Without his big black Bronco Akubra atop his head, he looked a shadow of the big man he'd been at the Muster only weeks before.

Bella's gaze drifted back to the black hearse, and all thoughts of Will and Macca fled. Her whole body and mind were again consumed by absolute wretchedness. She saw Rory and Helen O'Hara barely hanging on. In her mind she could hear them thinking, *A child's not supposed to die before a parent.* She finished the sentence in her own mind, *especially this child.*

Standing silent, Bella waited with her family for her best mate to leave the churchyard on that hot and sunny day.

To depart for her final journey.

Her closing chorus, 'Singing Hi Yi Yippy Yippy Yi . . .'

Her last dance through those whirling tumbleweeds.

Chapter 23

Bella spotted the huge green-and-silver reflective sign indicating the turn-off from the Princes Highway towards Narree. As she swung left off the main road the car climbed a slight hill before hitting a plateau that in daylight allowed travellers to see the Great Dividing Range in all its glory. Even in the dark Bella knew it was there, a hulking bulk on the horizon, the looming shadow of enormous mountains. Lights occasionally dotted the sweeping irrigated plains at the foot of the hills, early-rising dairy farmers already cloistered with their cows in the milking shed.

The car's clock flashed four a.m. and Bella knew she couldn't drive for much longer, Weariness was creeping in. She'd camp at her mum and dad's for a night before heading into the mountains for Caro and Trin's wedding at the weekend. It was unfortunate her parents weren't home. They'd gone to some Young Farmers Reunion down in South Gippsland, and Bella was pleased they weren't allowing her mother's quadriplegia to get in their way of living a great life. She would see them on the drive back.

It had taken months to get Francine home after the accident, while Bella's own injuries, even though they had been serious, had resulted in no long term physical effects. She had resigned from her job and, with Frank, moved to Melbourne, taking it in turns to watch over Francine's fight to survive and be a wife and mother once again.

Caro, who was just out of teachers' college, invited Bella to share her flat in East Melbourne. 'I'm teaching all day. You can grab a tram outside the door and it'll take you straight past the hospital.' Frank meanwhile installed himself in a house catering for patients' next of kin who were from the bush.

Justin had taken over the farm, running himself ragged while Melanie started motherhood for the third time. There wasn't much else they could all do. Just sit it out and wait to see if Francine was coming back to them.

'She's very lucky to be here. I'd be grateful if I were you,' a doctor on the run had thrown across a busy shoulder.

Her mother regained consciousness with no permanent brain damage, but there was still the quadriplegia to deal with. Six months of intensive therapy followed, with Bella or Frank always by her side. After a few months, and at the urging of her father, Bella found herself a job in the public-relations firm with the help of glowing references from David Neille.

So that just left the heartache to deal with.

She felt like she'd lost everything except her mother. After Will had turned away from her at Patty's funeral, she hadn't seen him again. Aunty Maggie said he'd gone back up into the mountains, seeking solace on his station. And there he had stayed, working himself into the ground.

Bella couldn't understand it. Why didn't Will come to share in the grief they both felt so badly, so deeply? He'd sat by her bedside while she was unconscious, hadn't he? She'd tried ringing him after the funeral – at home up on the station and on his mobile. But the calls went to voicemail, and after leaving a barrage of messages that were never returned, she gave up.

She'd considered driving up to the station to confront him, or at least getting someone to drive her – the thought of getting behind the wheel was a daunting one. But then the memories of Will's grim and dispassionate face deliberately turning from her, towards Prowsy, appeared before her eyes, and she knew she couldn't deal with another rejection. He hadn't acknowledged her once at the funeral. Not at the church, nor even at the wake where, with Macca, Will had got so drunk a grim Bryce McDonald had carted them both away.

Will's parents weren't coping either, Maggie had informed her. Rory and Helen had just upped and left their station at Tindarra. Packed up and walked out, not able to face being surrounded by the memories of their beloved daughter, leaving the property for Will to manage. They bought a small house in Burrindal and only left town to travel to the larger Narree for supplies. Apparently they didn't talk with the locals much anymore, stonewalling any attempts to drag them from their safe four walls. Although, Bella knew from her father, the couple made an uncomfortable, stilted phone call to intensive care at the Alfred Hospital every Sunday night. She had to give them credit for that. Still, it was obvious to all in the district that the once-vibrant O'Haras were now a family of silence, existing within mountains of pain.

Bella tried to console herself with the thought that at least *she* was trying to live life, amid the grief. Even though she felt like a wooden marionette, at least she was trying to be normal. She just had to deal with survivor's guilt. Well, that's what her therapist called it. Post-traumatic stress and depression were the other buzz words thrown around. She'd given up on the counselling, figuring long walks beside the Yarra River would do more for her than spending hours with someone who breathed garlic fumes and asked inane questions. How the hell could she *not* feel stress and depression after losing her best mate and the man she loved, while her mother was fighting for life? How the hell could she *not* feel guilty walking away virtually scot-free from an accident in which everyone else was either maimed or killed?

Maggie had told her, time was the healer. She just had to hold on and believe in that.

As her mother got better, Bella set about rebuilding her life, brick by brick, wall by wall. It wasn't the life she'd had, the hell-raising run of the bush, but at least it was a life. So when her parents finally drove home six months later, they left their beloved daughter behind in Melbourne. There was no going back. She knew she couldn't bare the pain of the old familiar surroundings, all the reminders of the way her life had been.

It had been a dreary Friday afternoon in Melbourne, around twelve months after the accident, when Will had turned up at Caro's door. He'd hunkered down on the doorstep, hat tipped over his eyes, waiting for someone to arrive home from work.

Caro was the first to appear.

'What are you doing here?' she'd uttered, shocked to find him sitting there. 'I thought you'd buried yourself at Tindarra, never to be seen or heard of again?'

'I'm here to see Bella.'

'I don't think she'll want to see you.'

'I can try, can't I?'

'Listen, if you're here to hurt her, you can get back in that ute and piss off. She's finally getting on her feet and she doesn't need this to set her back.'

Will sighed as he stood up from the doorstep, uncurling himself slowly. 'I'm not here to hurt her. I just want to talk to her, okay?'

'Well, she won't be back for another hour. It takes her a while to get home from work on the train. You'd better come in and have a cuppa. I'll give Trin a ring and let him know you're here for the weekend.'

'Caro, don't. I'm only here to see Bella and then I'm off home. I need to be back to bale my lucerne tomorrow night. It's a quick trip, but a cuppa would be good.' He paused as she led the way through the door, grabbing at her arm to force her to stop. 'I didn't mean to hurt her, Caro.' He stood still a moment, trying to find the right words. 'I just dug myself into grief. I couldn't see a way out, can barely see it now, but I felt I owed her an explanation.'

'You bloody well do. The poor girl has been to hell and back. Granted you're not all to blame but you can stand up and take a slice of the pie. Come in and have a cuppa, but I'll warn you, I'm not sure what kind of reception you'll get from Bella.'

Bella arrived a little while later and was stunned to see the LandCruiser ute parked outside the block of flats that she and Caro called home. What did he want? Why was he here? Why now, just when things were starting to feel normal again? She battled the urge simply to turn and run away; forced her high-heeled shoes to walk down that path to the front door; forced her hand to turn the knob. The first thing she saw was the hat placed upright on a pair of well-worn and wrinkled R.M. Williams boots, polished to a shining hue. She sat down on the floor, right beside the boots and hat, quelling the rush of vomit threatening to erupt from her stomach. She could smell the musty aroma of the bush on the hat, the rich leather treatment on the boots. A slight scent of wattle was in the air.

They couldn't see her from the kitchen, but Bella could hear the slow and deep rumble of his voice. She had to do this, deal with him now he was here. Gulping down the bile in her mouth, Bella picked herself up off the floor. Straightening her skirt, she flung back her shoulders and walked head up high into the kitchen.

The first sight of him hit every nerve ending. His likeness to his sister made her stagger in the doorway. She grasped the doorframe and steadied herself before again forcing her legs to move. She walked in and sat down as far from him as she could, which wasn't very far in the tiny kitchen.

Caro mumbled something about getting in the washing and disappeared out the door.

'Bella.' Will stared in shock at the girl he thought he'd known so well. Gone was the voluptuous figure, in its place a rack of bones. The bright eyes were dulled with pain, and the bouncing ringlets were flattened and sleek, imprisoned in a rigid clasp behind her long and stiff neck.

'Will,' she managed to return.

A truck roared down the road, air brakes screeching as it changed lanes among the dodging traffic outside.

He moved his sock-covered feet uncomfortably and leaned back on his chair. Bella stared at the table. She would not look at him. She. Would. Not. But her eyes betrayed her and she felt them lift. Damn the man.

'I've come to say . . . I'm sorry. I didn't mean to hurt you. I didn't know what to do with myself. I . . .' He broke off, shifting uncomfortably. Dimples flickered as a grim smile touched his face. 'I just couldn't handle it. *Can't* handle it,' he corrected himself. 'Maggie said I needed to talk to you. I don't know what to say. How to say sorry. How to make it up to you.'

Bella sat there numb. She couldn't help him out. She felt betrayed and just so plain mad at him, she wanted to spit in his face. A face that reminded her so much of what they'd both lost – those dimples, chocolate-brown eyes, that wicked O'Hara grin.

'Just go please, Will. I can't help you. I'm barely able to help myself.' She felt tears start to well and she angrily brushed them away. She would not show weakness.

'But, Bella, I'm here to help, I want you to come—'

'Just go, damn you. Go away.' Her quiet voice sounded like a yell even to her own ears. She forced her eyes back down to the table, terrified he'd see her need for him. Terrified her eyes would betray her again.

Will stood and looked down at the girl he had loved, still loved, not knowing what to do.

'Just go, Will,' she said again quietly, staring intently at the laminex grains embedded in the tabletop. Her fingers came up to search for a pattern in the swirling plastic lines.

He turned and walked down the short hall. Bella heard him pause to pick up his hat and pull on his boots before he walked out the front door, slamming the screen as he went. The only thing that remained was the sniff of wattle floating on city air.

Bella just sat and played with the grains of the table, tracing them to and fro. She heard Will call out a goodbye to Caro and the soft murmur of their voices outside. Then came the rumble of the ute as it cranked up and slowly pulled away.

Caro walked back in and placed a hand on Bella's shoulder. 'Are you okay?' Her voice was soft.

Bella reached up and patted the fine, manicured fingers. 'Maybe.'

'You'll be right, sweetie. Like Maggie said, it just takes time,' said Caro as she swung around to sit in the next chair. 'Do you think you did the right thing, sending him away?'

'I don't know.' Bella finally looked up and her friend was shocked at the pain in her eyes, by the tears pouring down her cheeks. 'I don't know,' she repeated as her gaze moved to look out the kitchen window at the brick wall of the high-rise flats next door. 'I can't go back yet.'

And now here she was heading towards the mountains, towards her past, and it was all coming rushing back to meet her, damn it. Even though she'd driven this way plenty of times in the past eight years, they had been fleeting visits. A night here, a night there – like air kisses thrown in the direction of an acquaintance's cheek, a brief disturbance meaning little. Her life and love had been in Melbourne.

It had never felt like this.

In the early-morning light, driving across the lush irrigated plains of Narree, it felt disturbingly like Patty was sitting beside her, watching the mountains coming closer. It was almost like, together, they were being welcomed home. And with those feelings came a tumult of emotions. Tomorrow she would drive into those hills and face the memories embedded there. And the man who'd helped shape them.

Bella could feel tendrils of nervousness start to creep around inside her body. She clamped down on any thoughts straying in Will O'Hara's direction and concentrated on the road leading to her old home. She didn't *need* any more complications.

The first glimmers of dawn were spiking the sky to the east. Outside the air was still and Bella could see lights popping up across the paddocks as slowly but surely more farmers made their way to milk their cows. The CD in the car had ground to a halt and the local ABC radio had taken its place. The weatherman was spruiking of a sunny and warm weekend ahead in East Gippsland. Melbourne had been surprised by some decent showers overnight. Good. She hoped Warren had been drenched.

She'd gone to the rodeo with Caro in the end. And her friend had used the halfway interlude to tell her chief bridesmaid that she would be riding side-saddle at the wedding that weekend.

'What? Why did you wait until three days before to tell me? I've never ridden side-saddle! Hell, I'm not even sure I can ride astride anymore!'

Caroline held out her hands in a plea. 'You know me – I love anything that sounds romantic. Come on, Bella, it's my dream.'

Bella sighed. A dream. Damn it. Bella knew all about dreams – and how they could be busted, like a balloon landing on a pin. She didn't want to be the pin-head who busted someone else's dream.

'Jeez, Caro ... okay, it's *your* wedding. I suppose a girl should have what she wants on her big day. But I swear I won't be responsible for what happens!'

Bella's reward for succumbing was Brooks and Dunn roaring from the overhead speakers at the Rod Laver Arena. A cowboy dressed in a flamboyant orange-and-red chequered shirt erupted into the ring clinging with every sinew to the back of a bucking ebony horse.

The rodeo finished at ten, and after seeing Caro off, Bella ran to the toilets for a quick change from her jeans to a cocktail dress. She couldn't believe she'd opened her big mouth and offered to meet Warren afterwards. So much for taking a stand and doing what *she* wanted to do. But there was something about that hang-dog look he used when he couldn't get his own way that got to her. It made her feel annoyed but then guilty at the same time. Like, somehow it was all her fault. So she'd capitulated and offered the compromise, and now it was a bit late for regrets. He was expecting her.

She bolted from the loos, snagged a taxi and raced to the Crown Casino, where she found a disgruntled Warren waiting for her at the brilliantly lit main entrance.

'You're late!' he snapped. 'Most of the guests are already here.' He grasped her elbow and pushed her along. He was gripping the sensitive skin inside her arm so hard, she knew there'd be bruises in the morning. She tried to shake free, but Warren was having none of it.

Lined up just inside a doorway, and overseen by hulking black-clad security men, was a crowd of elegant people in a long snaking queue. Warren jostled her into line behind the rest of the wives, partners and escorts waiting to be introduced to the new CEO.

She turned to try to spy the man whom all the fuss was about. From a distance he seemed short. Very, very short. It took a while, but finally she and Warren made it to the receiving party at the main doorway. Bella said a polite hello to Warren's boss and his wife before turning towards the new bloke.

What she saw took her breath away.

Standing before her was a ghost from her past. A man she had last seen fleeing the Nunkeri Muster all those years ago – with his pants ripped to near shreds, his face a bloodied mess, his Cuban heels taking flight after she and Patty had whipped his hide.

Here he was in front of her, solicitous and saying how do you do, in a voice that still spat plums so quickly you couldn't keep up with the drivel. 'Oh Warren, what a beautiful partner you have here,' he grovelled as he leaned to kiss her hand, eyeing off the cleavage passing right in front of his nose.

She snatched her hand away so fast Eddie Murray's bulging eyes nearly popped from their sockets.

'You're not touching my hand, you lecherous prick!'

Warren stepped forward, shocked. 'Bella! You can't say that,' he stuttered, sounding like a parent chastising a wayward child. 'Now apologise to Mr Murray.'

'I will *not*. Don't you remember me, you arrogant dog turd?'

Eddie took in the ravishing creature in front of him; her stunning eyes spat luminous blue sparks, while the voluptuous breasts heaved in agitation. She was all curves and luscious lines, far too good for that weasel Warren standing indignant by her side. His quick mind flicked through his past liaisons. He was sure he would have remembered if he'd met this provocative creature.

'The Nunkeri Muster? Eight years ago?' Bella's voice rang out, causing a series of uneasy whispers to flow down the line. 'My friend Patty and I whipped your shiny white arse.'

Eddie's face turned ashen then red and his little body started to huff and puff. Seeing his distress, a hovering security guard stepped in and hustled Warren and Bella on. They found a quiet corner, where Bella sat down before her legs collapsed.

Immediately Warren swung into attack. 'What was the meaning of *that*? You've gone and shot down any chance I had of a promotion. Christ almighty, I nearly had it in the bag. I was *this* close.' He pinched his fingers together in front of her face. 'I've been working on fucking Murray for weeks. What has got into you lately? I thought you were going to *hit* that poor man!'

'Poor *man*!' screeched Bella. Warren flung a hand across her mouth.

'Christ, not so loud!' Spittle flew from his lips. 'Don't you think you've done enough damage for one night?'

Bella took a moment to calm herself. Breathe deeply. Quietly and precisely she tried to explain.

'That. Man. Tried. To. Rape Me. If it wasn't for Patty he *would* have.'

'Well, you were both probably asking for it.'

'*WHAT?*' screeched Bella again, now completely oblivious to the scene they were causing. Warren sat down beside her and clamped a hand on her shoulder.

'This Patty you were so fond of sounds like a fucking drunken idiot. It's girls like her who give men the wrong idea, then cry rape. She was a bad influence. She was probably giving him the come on and you obviously got in the way.'

Bella was speechless.

'And the damage you have just done to my career! I've spent weeks wining and dining Murray in preparation and you have just gone and . . .'

His mouth was moving up and down, forming and spitting words she no longer wished to hear. Patty a bad influence? Rape a come-on? He had to be joking, right?

Wrong.

Shaking off the hand that was still attached, lead-like, to her shoulder, she stood and smoothed her dress. She looked down at the man whom she had thought she would marry, and broke into his tirade. 'Patty was one of the best people you could *ever* meet. She stood up for what she believed in and those she loved.' Bella stopped and took a gulp of air. '*And* she put the people she loved *first*. Not like you. You shouldn't speak ill of the dead, Warren. It will come back to haunt you. *I* was the one being attacked by that *animal* over there, and Patty saved me.'

She went to walk away, to find a taxi to take her back to the penthouse, to pack a bag. But before she did she spat one more line towards the man who was sitting with his mouth open like a frog trawling for a fly.

'I'm leaving for Merinda when I get home. Tonight. Then I'm heading to the wedding. You can find your own way there – that's if you can bear to mix it with a bunch of country hicks and cattlemen, *you arrogant shit*.'

Chapter 24

After arriving at Merinda, Bella wearily collapsed into her bed and spent the rest of the morning fitfully trying to sleep. Justin saw her car in the driveway at lunchtime and called in to check on her and say hello. She blamed her groggy and bedraggled appearance on lack of sleep.

During the afternoon, the phone rang a few times and Warren's strident tones boomed through the answering machine, echoing around the old house.

'Bella, look it's Warren. You mightn't want to speak with me at the moment, darling, and maybe I said a few things I shouldn't have . . . we both did. I just want to know if you got there safely . . . Ring me, will you, darling?'

He could grovel all he liked.

'Bella, Bella! I've just rung your brother's place and Melanie said you're there. Pick up the phone, will you, darling? We need to talk . . .'

She wasn't going to talk to the bastard.

'Bella! For fuck's sake, pick up the phone! Look, I'm sorry. What else do you want me to say?'

She'd heard enough.

Pulling on her mother's old gumboots and slamming a hat on her head, she headed out the door to find Justin to see if she could help him bring the cows up to milk. Sensing all wasn't right but not wanting to pry, Justin sent her off on the motorbike to set up the paddocks for the cows that night. Bella adored being out in the fresh air, the wind streaming past her as she rode along on the bike. It was just what she needed to push Warren and their troubles far to the back of her mind.

It wasn't until the next morning when Bella headed off into the mountains, towards Ben Bullen Hills, that she started to cry again, thinking about their argument and the tumult of emotions it had wrought. Emotions that went far beyond this latest disagreement.

All the things she had been feeling about their relationship, about *herself*, but hadn't wanted to examine too closely, had come crashing in around her on the day Caro made her big announcement: after the wedding, she and Trin were leaving their jobs and lives in the city and moving to Ben Bullen Hills Station.

'What? You're moving to Burrindal? Back home? You're leaving me here by myself?' she'd responded, incredulous.

Caro had looked at her, a bemused expression on her face. 'You're hardly alone, Bella. You've got Warren.'

It was then Bella had started questioning whether Warren and their life together were enough. Why did she feel so alone and insecure? Why did she feel restless but at the same time so lacking in direction it was like magnetic north had tilted? And why, in this bustling city, didn't she have an inherent sense of place, of belonging?

She was suddenly reminded of Wendy Anderson all those years ago, up on Ainsley Station. She remembered wondering then, in the arrogance of youth, how such a woman could lose her confidence so completely. Her drive. Her motivations. Herself.

That was Bella now. It was a shocking thought.

How the hell did that happen?

And what was she going to do about it?

It was fate. The first person Bella spotted as she drove under the big metal archway proclaiming entry to Ben Bullen Hills Station was Will O'Hara. Unwanted memories came flooding back.

It had been seven years since she'd last seen him, and here he was leaning on a solid cattle-yard fence. Every nerve in Bella's body urged her to turn the car around and drive like hell away, while her eyes, heart and mind drank in the sight of him.

He looked like he belonged there, a rumpled and weathered figure blending into the background of mountain ash trees as he rested against battered, rough-sawn timber rails, yarning to a bloke on the opposite side. The other man also looked startlingly familiar. Clad in dark moleskins and a big black hat, he stood out against the blue-grey horizon, a blob of colour blotting the surrounding bush like black ink.

It couldn't be anyone else. Macca.

The toothpick shoved in the side of his mouth was wobbling up and down as he talked. Bella whooped at the sight of her cousin and pulled the purring Merc to a halt. Opening the door, she clambered out of the vehicle and yelled and waved.

Both men glanced over, a different expression crossing each face. Will frowned and dipped his head before looking back up. The O'Hara dimples weren't winking but lines like crow's feet marched in the crinkles around his eyes. Macca grinned, leaped over the high fence and came striding towards her, spitting the toothpick out onto the ground, roaring, 'Hells Bells! Gidday! What's with the Merc, you toffy little sheila! Where's your ute? Bloody hell, it's good to see you!' She was engulfed in a massive hug, and found herself breathing in stale beer, wood smoke and Brut deodorant while pressed to a bear-like chest.

'Bloody hell, I haven't seen you for ages!' Macca released her and she gasped in another breath, this time of scented eucalypts and sunshine – and the cow shit now smeared down the front of her shirt.

'Give me a look at ya,' said Macca as he moved back, thrusting a hand into his pocket, no doubt rooting for a fresh toothpick to chew into shreds. He hadn't changed, Bella thought. But she had – and so, before Macca could grab her arm and look into her face and see eyes that were swollen and bloodshot from crying, she turned and leaned into the Merc and snatched her old Akubra off the dashboard. Flipping her sunglasses down from where they were perched on top of her head, she quickly slammed on the hat to shadow her face.

As Macca slung his arm across her shoulders, she noticed that while the big man looked healthy and fit, he couldn't hide the lines of sorrow that still ringed his eyes, spreading out across his temples where the dark hair was touched with early grey.

She threw a quick glance across at Will. He hadn't moved. He was still leaning against the stockyard fence, taking in the sun. She looked at his lean body, the way his faded and weathered work clothes fell in soft creases; those wrinkles that glued the clothes to the hard planes of the man spoke of many hours' manual labour.

She raised a hand in the air in acknowledgement. The answering flick of his pointer finger against the bone-coloured felt hat sent her heart into an erratic beat. Christ, he still did it to her. She hadn't seen him in seven years and still her mind and body reacted violently against her will, instinctively leaning in his direction, pining to share the same space as him.

Would it ever stop – this chemical reaction that seemed genetically infused into her whole being, making her want this man. She knew if she lifted her feet, allowed her body to drift in his direction, any words she said to him would come out wrong. On the drive up here from Merinda, she had practised every possible conversation with him, knowing she would have to see him this weekend for the first time since she'd listened to his ute drive away. Regardless, she stood looking across at the man who still had the ability to turn her insides to mush.

Her mind stumbled. You're engaged to Warren, you're over Will, her mind whispered to her heart. In response her heart started to thump and her guts began to spin. Macca was looking at her strangely. 'Hey, are you all right?' he asked.

Forcing her eyes away from the spectre of the cattleman who caused so much confusion, she turned and concentrated on her cousin. Grabbing his big hand she said, 'Come with me to the house and tell me what you've been up to, you big boofhead. Mum said you were in Mount Isa, with a girlfriend in tow. Who is she? Is she here? Have you just come for the wedding, or are you back for good?' Words tumbled from her mouth.

'Hang on, hang on, one question at a time. I'll come up to the house and have a beer with ya.'

'But it's only midday, you old soak!'

'I know, I know.' Macca waved both hands up and down in front of himself, a placatory gesture Bella remembered of old. 'But it's five o'clock somewhere in the world and there's a wedding goin' on. Can't expect a man to be a camel, can ya? Gotta start on the piss sometime. Come on, let's get in this fancy set of wheels of yours and you can take me for a spin. Where's wanker Warren? Do I finally get to meet him?' Bella spun to punch Macca in the arm, but the big bloke just laughed and yelled to Will, 'Just goin' to grab a beer! See ya round the fire tonight for a rum!'

And the silent man in the bone felt hat just raised his pointer finger in acknowledgement again.

Will watched the woman he'd once thought would be his wife get into her fancy all-wheel-drive Mercedes. A black sporty-looking number with shiny plates barely smudged with kamikaze bugs, the vehicle had an alloy bar angling around the front grill scarcely capable of nudging a canary, let alone a roo or wombat.

Where did she go, the girl he had once loved beyond all reason? The one who drove a Holden ute with a bullbar as big as any bloke's, mounted above a bug-splattered number plate with a deflector proclaiming the driver as 'Hells Bells'? Where had she hidden herself inside this glamorous creature who had exited the flashy car, the woman who had stared long and hard at him but with a blank expression, before flipping sunglasses over her eyes?

The woman who had jumped from the Merc had straightened, honey-coloured hair with a trendy fringe cut to accentuate a made-up face with a fake complexion. Where were those unruly, tumbling white-gold ringlets, the smattering of summer freckles that stretched across a wide-open, laughing face?

He could hear Macca yelling from inside the car, something about the speakers. It took a minute then Lee Kernaghan came blasting out, thumping country music across the paddock. Macca had obviously taken control of the stereo. The slowly moving Mercedes stopped just before it topped the hill while a pair of out-of-kilter voices joined Lee's gravely tones. There were a few moments of purring silence before suddenly the engine revved up to full throttle, the wheels started spinning and dust flew through the air, as the car took off in a hail of fine stones. A roar of approval came from the passenger side, while a high-pitched '*Yee ha!*' erupted from the driver's seat.

Will allowed himself a small smile. Maybe there was hope yet for the glamorous creature whose engagement ring had winked brilliantly at him in the sun.

When Patty died, a part inside Will had curled up and died too. His sister's death really screwed him up.

He didn't see anything but his own grief, couldn't see Bella holding out her arms to seek and give comfort. He thought she was just another person silently demanding his strength, looking for answers and deliverance from this all-consuming loss. He'd lumped her in with his parents, who were like sad dodgem cars, bumping into grief each time they turned around, searching for answers and demanding his strength to give them the will to fight on.

But he didn't have salvation wrapped up neatly in a pretty gift box, daubed with a gaudy bow. And he couldn't be their strength when he didn't have any himself. That was why he hid, up on his station at Tindarra, far beyond the reach of anything else that could hurt him. He shut himself away and then tormented himself over the rights and wrongs of what he'd done. Patty was gone; Bella he loved and had so nearly lost too. Much better to shut it all away, slam a door on any more potential pain, because he was struggling to hold himself together just dealing with this one loss.

He'd really fucked up.

It had taken Maggie to bring him to his senses. She'd sat him down in her kitchen ten months after the funeral and given him the what for. Slamming a cup of strong coffee onto the table in front of him one morning when he'd called to drop off some drench. 'You bloody idiot. Just look at yourself!' she'd said. 'I should take the bloody frying pan and bash it over your head. What will it take to make you see what you're doing to yourself?'

She'd then stomped out of the kitchen, grey bun flip-flopping in her agitation, and returned minutes later holding an old thick, round shaving mirror, which she shoved in front of his face. 'Take a long, hard look at yourself, William O'Hara, and tell me what you see.'

So he'd picked up his steaming coffee first, and then taken the mirror from her and slowly brought it up to view a face he hadn't seen for around ten months. He took a look, and then looked again. And he had to admit what he saw wasn't pretty. Then the mirror fogged up from the steam coming off his brew. To be truthful he wasn't sad his image had blurred.

But Maggie swiped the mirror real quick, so he had another clear view at what was in front of his eyes. Grimy dreadlocks were all that remained of his tousled russet hair; his eyes were sunken holes of misery buried so deeply into his skull even he couldn't see if they were brown or black. His cheeks were sunk into the lines on his face, before being covered by a mangy beard that staggered drunkenly across his jaw. It was the face of a stranger, someone he wouldn't want to know.

'I don't know how long you plan to let this nonsense go on,' said Maggie, wagging an accusing finger in his face. 'But I'm not having it. Not anymore. One niece has died, the other's moved to the bloody city, so I'm not losing you too! When are you going to wake up and see that it's not your fault. You didn't kill Patty, for Christ's sake! It was an accident. Stop blaming yourself!'

'I don't blame myself.'

'Yes you do!'

'I don't!'

'You do! God knows why, but you do!'

Will sat for a minute and thought about that. Maggie probably had a point – as usual. 'Okay, maybe I do,' he said and then he let it rip, the thing that had been hammering around his skull since he'd seen what was left of his sister in the morgue.

'You didn't see her, Maggie. Oh, they'd tried to fix her up, and you couldn't see too much – but she was icy cold, and they'd put a fucking carnation on her lapel. Patty. A fucking carnation. It should have been a can of rum-and-coke.'

Will flung himself forward in agitation and curled his hands around the edge of the table, fingertips and knuckles white with tension. 'I walk around all day in a daze, and working is the only thing that keeps me going. If I don't bugger myself out I can't sleep, and when I do sleep all I can see is her.'

The last image of his sister lying dead in that rosewood coffin would remain with him forever.

'Hell, Maggie, I should have been there to protect her, look after her. It was my job since she was born, for fuck's sake!'

Maggie stood beside him, wringing the half-apron she wore between her hands, frowning at her wild-looking nephew. Pulling out the chair next to him, she sat down with a thump. 'Will, my darling boy, you couldn't have saved her. You know that. Stop flogging yourself with something you had no control over. She was a big girl, and you couldn't have done a thing.' Maggie tried to pat his hand.

But he was having none of it.

'Yes, I could've. I should have driven them; I should have taken them to bloody town. She asked me to, you know. Knew I had stuff to do. But I said no. "What man wants to be around a bunch of women shopping for dresses?" says me. And now she's dead. Gone. Forever. I should have been there that day, Maggie.'

'But, Will – we all make choices. On any other day the choice you made to stay behind would have been a good one. A cranky bloke tapping his toes waiting would've really taken the shine off their day. And they'd had a fantastic day, Frank told me. Francine rang him at lunchtime, bubbling with happiness – a fun day in town with *her* girls, she'd said.' Maggie stopped, and Will could feel her eyes boring into his head, willing him to face her. 'It was an accident, for heaven's sake. You couldn't be every-where, and goodness knows that girl, much and all as I adored her, she wasn't a saint. It's a wonder with all her shenanigans she hadn't already done herself some damage. *She* was driving that vehicle, not you. It was Patty who didn't see that give-way sign. It was completely beyond your control!'

Will let go of the table and grabbed his coffee mug instead. Gulping at the thick black liquid he stared at his aunt's brown-spotted hands as she drummed her fingers on the table. He took a few deep breaths and tried to regain some control. Maggie always did this to him. She always got him with the truth. So much wisdom, so much compassion and strength.

Silence reigned in that cosy country kitchen, red-and-white gingham curtains fluttering in the afternoon breeze above the sink. Will listened to the regular tick of the old Ansonia clock sitting on the mantle above the slow-combustion stove. He could see a crow sitting in the crab-apple tree outside the kitchen window, black beady eyes with a dead gaze on someone or something. A dead gaze he could relate to these past ten months, a black hole inside his skull.

'And what about Bella?' Maggie asked, breaking into his thoughts.

Will turned back to her. 'What about Bella?'

'I thought you two had something going together.'

'We do. Well, we did . . .'

'And so you've let her go too, haven't you? You've turned your back on that poor girl so you could wallow around in your own self-pity.'

'Self-pity? Self-*pity*? Jeez, Aunty Maggie, I lost my *sister*, for God's sake. She *fucking well died*! AND I SHOULD HAVE BEEN THERE FOR HER!' Will was shocked to hear himself shouting. He flung himself from his chair, spilling his coffee as he went. To his surprise, he began to shake, sobs welling deep from within his throat. He sank down, his back against the kitchen wall. Grief spilled like vomit from his mouth and wracked his shoulders into a rounded ball. Water leaked from his eyes and he realised he was crying for the first time since he'd heard his sister was dead.

He wasn't aware that Maggie had moved quietly from her chair to sink down on her knees in front of him. The first he knew was when she laid her soft but firm hands upon his matted hair and gave him absolution just by sitting and letting the grief and loss finally have its head.

It had taken some time before he was able to face the world again, before he was up to venturing beyond the Tindarra Valley's eucalypt walls. He spent time with Maggie, a lot of time in fact, just talking through the grief. She helped him shave his head and sent him home with hearty meals on a plate. And then after many long chats, some of which included old Wes, who always had some new piece of advice to dredge from his bushman's well, he was finally ready to get back on with life. And one morning he decided, he needed to see Bella. To beg for her forgiveness, and to explain why she should give him a second chance.

But he fucked that up too, and he came home from Melbourne alone. Maggie took one look at his face and didn't ask why. He never went back to Melbourne. Bella obviously hated him for how he'd treated her. And he couldn't blame her. He hated himself.

A year later he did the second most stupid thing he'd done in his life: he married Prudence Vincent-Prowse.

Will watched as the Mercedes disappeared within a cloud of dust, before he stirred himself to move. Slightly favouring right leg over left, he slowly loped towards the sixteen-hand ebony horse tethered to a tree sapling nearby. Swishing its tail against the clouds of tiny black bush flies hovering over its rounded rump, Wizard patiently shifted his weight from one hoof to the next.

Will unbuckled the reins from the piece of baling twine he'd tied to the small tree, and then undid the knot connecting the twine to the sapling. Wizard had a habit of pulling back; better to break the twine than the leather reins. Stowing the piece of light twine in his jeans pocket, he walked his big horse around a bit. Stopping, he clinched up the loosened girth on his stock saddle a few notches, before finally swinging his long body over and into the seat. Glancing lingeringly once more towards the direction the black Merc had taken, he neck-reined Wizard around and steadfastly headed the opposite way.

Chapter 25

'I now pronounce you husband and wife. You may kiss your bride,' said the celebrant, looking expectantly at the couple standing before him.

The day had dawned sunny with a promise of bright blue skies for the wedding of the year at the Ben Bullen Hills Station. Never had the area of Burrindal seen anything of this ilk. Trinity had spared no expense, figuring he was only going to do it once, so he wanted to do it well.

As Bella had rolled out from her bed inside the newly renovated Ben Bullen Hills Station house, she knew from the brilliance of the day that God was on this young couple's side. Out to the north, row after row of dusty blue mountains with eucalypts snugged to their sides rolled into one another as far as the eye could see. Mountains descended into the depths of a valley where the mighty Cullen River flowed.

As she sat on her horse in the natural grassy amphitheatre

where the wedding was taking place, Bella wondered how anyone could not believe in God – the magnificent visage of nature taking the place of an altar in this outdoor church.

Everyone had gathered in a sloped opening on the side of a hill, where Trinity had rough-sawn stringy-bark logs and placed them in half-circle rows for guests to sit on. Thick bush slid down both sides of the open space and everyone faced out towards the distant rolling mountains as they witnessed this true bush wedding.

Bella looked down at her close friend's face. Caroline's eyes shone as brightly as the afternoon sun as she gazed up at her ruggedly handsome new husband. Francine would've loved to have seen this wedding; loved to have seen Caroline looking so happy and beautiful in her layers of pearl chiffon.

The strapless design of Bella's raspberry-pink bustier allowed the slight breeze blowing up the mountain to tickle her neck. As the sun beat down she was sure it was the only thing keeping her from toppling in a faint from her perch atop her mare, Aprillia.

That and the burning eyes boring into her side belonging to William O'Hara who sat mounted on his own horse only metres away. She still couldn't believe she was so attuned to *that* man. She silently recited the name of her fiancé: Warren. Warren, Warren, Warren!

Will cut a dashing figure on his ebony horse. His black suit was topped with a new black Bronco broad-brimmed hat, to match that worn by the groom.

He and Bella had spoken for the first time that morning, down at the stockyards while she was feeding and watering Aprillia. He was mucking around with his own horse.

'Morning, Will,' she called, trying to keep her voice level.

'Isabella. Didn't think we'd ever see you around these parts again.'

'Well, you were wrong. Here I am!' her voice squeaked. Shit.

'Obviously,' said Will. An uncomfortable silence followed. 'I heard you were engaged to some city bloke. He coming?'

Bella opened her mouth to reply, and then stopped. She was shocked to realise that she hoped Warren *wouldn't* make it to the wedding. 'Not sure. He's very busy.' She ducked under Aprillia's neck and took hold of the water bucket; as she walked towards the tap she realised Will was doing the same.

'Nice horse,' said Bella, throwing a hand out to pat the gelding.

'Yeah. Wizard's a good fella. Had him since he was a baby.' Bella watched as Will gently fondled the horse's mane, his tanned fingers moving in a caress across smooth black hair. Wizard blew softly into his master's shoulder. Obviously a match made in heaven.

Bella's mobile erupted into a sharp ring. She snatched it from her pocket, turning her back on Will.

'Bella! Where are you? I've been trying to get hold of you for two days! Why has your phone been switched off?'

She'd been deliberately turning him off on the mobile. She was so flaming angry with him. Still. 'Warren, when I've got something to say I'll talk to you – and not before.' Bella pressed the off button and stuck the phone back into her pocket.

'You got trouble?' A deep voice rumbled near her other ear.

She jumped and landed a little away to the right, tripping on a burgan shrub as she went. She came crashing down, all limbs and angles, her body buried among the prickly fronds of scrubby bush.

Will looked down at her, a bemused expression on his face. 'Well, at least you're still jumpy. That's a start.'

'I'm not jumpy!' Bella tried to fight her way out of the bush, her bare arms flailing in the air.

Will grabbed hold of both arms in an iron grip and yanked her out of the shrub, causing her to overbalance again and fall towards his warm, hard chest. They both went perfectly still. The early-morning bush activity seemed to halt, the world seemed to pause.

Inhaling, she breathed in the warmth of flannelette, Pears soap, Lynx Africa deodorant, wood smoke and the earthy scent of horse and eucalyptus. She could feel the strength of Will's hands as they came up to steady her. His touch incited her body into a rush of heat so strong she wasn't exactly sure where she was being held.

Why didn't she feel like this with Warren? Turned on at a slightest touch while at the same time safe, warm and protected? It was such a foreign feeling, this one of security. Bella looked up to catch a glimpse of the man doing this to her, only to find herself unceremoniously thrust away.

'I'd best get going,' mumbled Will as he quickly turned, leaving Bella standing staring at his back as he walked away.

Damn the man!

Now, sitting watching the wedding proceedings, she had a perfect excuse to check him out more closely, to see what seven years and marriage to Prudence Vincent-Prowse had done to him. At first glance it didn't look like much, maybe just a few extra lines etched into his face. But when he dismounted to hand Trinity the wedding rings, Bella could see his frame was leaner and somehow harder, tougher like a piece of Number 8 wire that was extremely difficult to bend to your will. His warm molasses gaze was now a brittle toffee.

He had the unconscious confidence of a man who was sure of his place on the earth, but there was a slight flaw, an imperceptible limp favouring his right leg over his left. Only someone who knew him – or *had* known him – well would have been able to tell, so well did he disguise it.

Bella remembered Maggie telling her over the phone about Will's fall from a grain silo a few years ago; a shattered left femur refusing to heal properly, back when he'd been married to Prowsy.

Bella's stomach did an involuntary twist and she felt sick at the thought of Will and Prue together. Maggie had told her of the union two years after she'd left for Melbourne. Bella had gently replaced the phone's receiver then spent the day curled on the couch in her pyjamas and fluffy dressing gown in tears, shattered by the news.

She had thought that the bright lights of Melbourne had snuffed the flame of yearning she had once carried for Will; that the man who had briefly become an intimate part of those hell-raising, boot-stomping years of her life could be tossed aside without a care. But Prowsy, of all people? She couldn't fathom that one. Then again, Prowsy had always been good at reeling in the fellas, saving her bitchy side for any competition.

They had divorced three years later. Apparently Prowsy had run off with a property developer from some toffy horse-breeding place in New South Wales.

'She took our Will to the cleaners. He's had to mortgage the farm to pay her out. She reckons she helped him get to where he is. Pah!' snorted Maggie. 'I've never heard such rot! How can a flower-arranging class help you build the finest herd of Herefords this valley has ever seen? She nearly sent him broke buying all that "country" decorator stuff in those flash magazines!'

A canine yawn drew Bella's attention to the dog sitting at her horse's hooves. Bindi, Trin's border collie, had flopped to the ground near Bella's right stirrup, a raspberry-pink bow slung around her shaggy neck. She was clearly bored with proceedings; proceedings, Bella suddenly realised, that had finished while she was off in another world.

The crowd was surging forward to congratulate the radiant bride and groom, milling around the logs that had been their seats. Bella felt a chuckle welling in her throat as she glimpsed Dymphna, Wes's daughter and Trin's mother, tottering on two-inch heels, as she tried to cope with knee-high pointed wallaby grass seeds, snagging at her fine denier stockings. You'd think she'd have worn something more appropriate having spent her childhood in the bush.

From her viewpoint on Aprillia's back, Bella could see numerous amateur photographers urging the bridal couple to kiss. The pair were more than happy to oblige, and as Trinity's head bent to claim Caro as his prize, Bella felt Will's eyes alight upon her face.

Glancing sideways, she was caught by the intensity of his gaze. Different expressions were flitting across his face: pensiveness, resentment and hurt, duelling with fatalistic, resigned attraction. Raw longing glimpsed then shuttered away.

Bella's guts clenched as she absorbed it all.

She hurriedly turned back to the bride and groom.

A roar was sent up from the crowd as the groom kissed his bride, almost drowning out the mournful bay of a hound whispered on a slip of wind sliding up the valley.

Bindi rose to paws growling, her hackles up, her teeth bared towards the bush out to Bella's left. Aprillia pricked her ears, flicking them restlessly back and forth. Bella gathered the loose reins to keep the horse in check, sweeping her hand up and down the mare's neck. Bella noticed Will doing the same, his unsettled horse backing away from the bridal scene in front of them.

Then, all hell broke loose.

A kangaroo bounded from the scrub out to the left of the open clearing where the wedding had taken place. Like a racehorse released from a barrier in the Melbourne Cup, the roo flew across the open natural amphitheatre, blindly aiming for the crowd of milling people. Baying hounds could be heard again, louder now, on the slither of breeze, and that was enough.

Aprillia bolted.

Bella felt a sudden whiplash to her head, neck and shoulders. She tried pulling back hard on the reins but the horse had taken the bit between its teeth and was running out of sheer fear. Then she knew nothing except grabbing for mane, saddle and reins, anything to keep her on top of the horse. In her peripheral vision she saw Trinity grab Caroline and thrust her sideways, protecting his wife with his solid body as Aprillia slammed into the crowd.

People ran in all directions screaming.

Bella saw Dymphna fall onto her backside, legs flailing in the air, shrieking as her corsets and petticoats were thrust on display. Then they were through the people and all Bella could see in front of her was massive stringy-bark trees, under-storied by thick burgan and dogwood bush.

She clung precariously to the side-saddle, lying as low as she could along the horse's neck to avoid being struck by the overhead branches that would be the biggest danger once she hit the scrub.

She had no control.

There was nothing to turn the horse into to force her to stop, not a fence or yard for kilometres either way. There was nothing she could do except hang on.

The last voice she thought she heard was Will's. '*Bella!*'

Aprillia crashed into the bush, following a path only the mare could see, and as the baying of hounds resonated clearly through the air again, a terrified Bella wondered just how long she could stay on.

Chapter 26

The ride seemed to go on for hours. Sticks cracked and snapped underfoot, branches slapped at her body and the saddle, creating divots in both skin and leather. Bella lost count of how many tree limbs she dodged.

Time came to mean nothing. Much of her life flew through her mind; snapshot images flicking past, gone as quickly as they came, almost matching the beat of Aprillia's legs crashing through the scrub.

As the mare ploughed on through the bush, eating away at the ground with her pounding hooves, Bella fleetingly wondered if anyone was coming after her. The horse seemed to be keeping to wild brumby tracks that wound through the trees. Hopefully someone would find them. She just needed to watch out for the low-hanging branches, and maybe – just maybe – she'd be able to ride this one out.

Aprillia's gait finally slowed to a plodding walk. A few more steps and then she stopped. Sides heaving, legs shuddering, the mare tossed her head into the air, spraying Bella with foam from her frothing muzzle. Then she dropped her head to the ground in a droop that betrayed her exhaustion.

Bella flung herself sideways from the saddle, her own shaking legs collapsing under the sudden weight. She dropped her head into her hands and fell backwards into the thick native grass.

Tears came easily now the danger was past. As she flicked away small branches and leaves that clung to her clothes and hair, her body convulsed into sobs.

She closed her eyes and lay inert, and allowed the hot sun to kiss her face and body, and calm her rapidly beating heart.

Will pushed his gelding hard, striving to follow the trail Aprillia had left on her flight through the bush. Damn the hunters and their hounds near Ben Bullen Hills on today of all bloody days.

He was pretty sure where Aprillia was headed, that was *if* she kept to the brumby trails laid out before him. His heart was in his mouth and he knew he was pushing his horse too hard, but he couldn't help the fear that hammered through his body, coursing adrenaline through his veins.

Bugger and blast the bloody girl. Why couldn't she have stayed where she was, in the city, well out of harm's way . . . out of *his* way.

He knew it wasn't really Bella's fault. It rarely was. Trouble just followed that girl and it always had, especially where he was concerned. And at the moment his main concern, his greatest fear, was finding a pink-covered bundle, motionless on the ground.

An image of Bella at the wedding flashed before his eyes: all tousled blonde ringlets, voluptuous curves and those amazing blue eyes. Eight years and a lifetime later, Will had been shocked to see those stunning eyes were shadowed by hurt, clouded with frustration and filled with vulnerability as she gazed at Trin and Caro. He had wanted to gather her into his arms and kiss it all away.

A branch came from nowhere and clouted him across the jaw. The pain was like a dousing of cold water. 'Bloody hell!'

To him Isabella Vermaelon was a temptress on legs, and he was sick of years of temptation studded with bouts of torment and pain. He'd loved her. He'd lost her, and it was his own goddamned fault. Now she was engaged to some rich tosser from Melbourne and he couldn't do anything about it.

Although by the sound of the phone call that morning, all was not well with wanker Warren. Maybe Will stood a chance, even after all this time? He remembered her stumbling into his arms in the stockyard; the feel of her body was so familiar.

Prue of course had been a terrible mistake. She had simply been in the right place at the wrong time, and Will was the first to admit it. She seemed to think she could make him forget Bella. Make him love her instead. But she couldn't and he didn't. He'd apologised when she threw it in his face the day she'd left.

'You don't love me, you arsehole, so why the fuck did you marry me?'

'I have no idea why I married you, Prue,' he'd said as he'd heaved her suitcases into the car, wishing to hell she'd just get in it and drive out of his life. Forever.

'You're still in love with *her*, aren't you? I'm not having three in my bed anymore. At least Leyton loves me for me!'

Will had his own thoughts on why Leyton Fowler wanted Prudence and they didn't include love. More like a fashionable accessory on his arm at race-days.

'Okay, okay, I'm sorry. I guess I *was* on the rebound when we got together. But you can't say I've treated you badly. You got your Paspaley pearls, had the race-days, the housekeeper, the pedicures and manicures, for fuck's sake! What more did you want?'

'You, Will. I just wanted you.'

But Prue could never have him because he was always somewhere else. In the memories of the past where another woman stood at his side. A time when his sister was still alive.

When he had lifted Bella from the burgan shrub that morning, the smell of her hair reached up to tantalise and his knees had nearly gone from under him. All he wanted to do was hold onto this woman and not let go. The scent of her body was the same as he remembered – fresh spring roses with a touch of earthy musk.

Will shook himself in the saddle, startling Wizard into missing a pace. They stumbled, Will riding it out easily, going with his mount. He gently stroked Wizard's neck as he regained his balance and rhythm. 'Easy boy, easy fella. Keep it going, old mate. We're nearly there.'

When he finally found them, at the end of the trail in the sunlit open grassland of Hugh's Plain, it wasn't just his horse that was breathing hard.

'What the fuck are you doing?!' his voice ground out as he took in what was before his eyes.

She lay in the grass, topless. A raspberry-pink bustier was tossed negligently to the side.

Her magnificent breasts were bared in all their voluptuous glory to the dying rays of the sun. Her skirt was rucked up to her map of Tassie as she rested, soaking up the last of the afternoon's heat.

'I was hot,' Bella said, eyes closed, lying warm, moist and contented as she wriggled sensually in the sun.

Will was speechless.

He took in her body, laid out in the grass like in his dreams; watched as those breasts moved fluidly when she wiggled her bum slowly through the feathery grass. He was shocked at his thoughts as his mind moved from fear and rage to something more raw and primitive. His eyes moved lingeringly, bewitched by her sensual movements on the ground. If Bella had been watching she would have been fascinated as his brittle-toffee eyes seemed to melt, as the ruggedly handsome face seemed to darken, and a hot thrumming madness replaced the fear in his blood.

His body moved of its own accord.

He slid from his horse silently to stand over the woman who seemed intent on making his life a living hell. His gaze taking in what he had loved and lost eight years before. His conscience wrestled between what was right and wrong, while the image in front of him remained so surreal, on this remote plain deep in the mountains where wild brumbies played – far, far away from the real world.

He watched as the hot sun kissed her body, reliving tastes of the sweetness that had been theirs so long ago. Enticing sweetness he had glimpsed, smelled and touched again that morning.

He watched as she wiggled, settling her bum into a better position among the clefts of flattened grass.

Her eyes were closed. Her legs flung wide.

Without a word he kicked at his boots until they disappeared into the thick native grass smothering the open plain, then undid his belt buckle and slowly slid the fly down on his pants.

He lay down to gently mount the woman who'd haunted his night sleep for so long.

Chapter 27

'You're still good in the sack, cowgirl.'

The deep voice curled lazily around her ears, as she lay with her eyes closed, feeling warm and completely sated. The words brought Bella back to earth with a thud. Is that all he thought this was? A good roll in the hay? What on earth was she doing, making love to Will, after all this time, while she was engaged to another man?

Bella abruptly sat up, reached for her scattered clothes and hurriedly started to pull them back on.

'Hey! Not so fast.'

A hand came up from behind to cup a breast. Her sensitive nipples hardened instantly at his touch. Inwardly she cursed her traitorous body.

'I've got a UHF radio here, I'll let them all know I've found you and we'll be back in a while. In the meantime,' Will's voice turned sensuous, 'lie down here and relax.' His other arm reached out to haul her down into the grass.

225

Bella shrugged it off and wrapped her bustier back around her chest, dislodging the hand still caressing her breast. 'We have to get back now. Everyone will be wondering . . .' Her voice was sharp, almost biting.

Will slowly sat up, a puzzled look on his face. 'I said I'd let them know. What's up, Hells Bells?'

'What's up? What's up? I'll tell you what's UP! I'm engaged, for heaven's sake. I shouldn't be doing this!' Bella struggled to do up the bustier, which wasn't cooperating. 'Oh, crap!'

'Here, let me help. If you're so hell-bent on leaving.'

A hand came up again.

'No!' she cried. 'Just leave me.' She pushed the hand away, then stopped and took a deep breath. 'I can get it on my own.' She sighed, willing herself to calm down, before adding as an afterthought, 'Thanks.' It wasn't all his fault, she reminded herself. As her mother once told her, 'It takes two to tango.' And boy, did they tango. She shook her head trying not to imagine what he must have thought of her lying in the grass so wanton and shameless, waiting for him. He was a man with needs. And that was all it was, by the sound of it: a need, an itch to be scratched, a thanks-for-the-good-times roll in the hay.

Why was she reacting like this? Will wondered. It had been so beautiful, amazing – and she was making a bolt for it. He had thought she was waiting for him, had wanted him to make love to her. Now here she was acting like his touch was repulsive. What did she think he was? A country plaything to be tossed aside after the deed was done, so she could return to her rich life and her fiancé? All he'd said was she was still good in the sack.

He'd just been stirring, saying something the old Bella would have laughed at.

He lay and watched the woman he'd just made love to struggle back into her clothes with desperate intensity. He still cared deeply for her. His sister's death, time, Prue – nothing had altered that.

But in the afterglow of lovemaking he'd forgotten that this Bella was different. She wasn't the same girl he'd known eight years ago. This was a new creature. A woman who'd moved on to bigger and better things. Someone who, he was now realising, had a chip the size of a woolley butt log on her shoulder, who probably wouldn't recognise a joke if it kicked her up the bum.

'Bella, I didn't mean—'

'I know, Will, I know.' Now fully clothed, Bella walked towards Aprillia. 'This didn't mean anything. I understand that.'

'But . . . I mean . . . the sex . . . it did—'

'Just pull up your pants, O'Hara, and let's ride the hell out of here.' Bella gathered Aprillia's reins and swung herself up onto the horse's back. 'And you'd better radio in to the others anyway. They'll be getting worried.' She kicked Aprillia forward and without looking back rode off towards the brumby track that was barely discernable among the trees.

Will slowly dressed and then mounted Wizard. He radioed in to say he had found Bella safe and well. Then he headed off after her, all the while thinking that it would be really good if, for once in her life, she'd just let him finish a bloody sentence.

But if that's the way she wanted it, that's the way she could have it.

They made it back to the marquee at Ben Bullen Hills Station as the reception party was about to start. Bella flung herself from Aprillia's back, determined not to look at the man hauling in his mount by her side.

'I'll take her if you like,' said Will, quiet and remote.

'Thanks,' was all she could manage, handing over the reins and not quite meeting his eyes.

What had felt so right, so natural and primal beneath the late-afternoon sun on Hugh's Plain had now tarnished to something tawdry, dirty and baseless. She didn't know which way to look, what to say. How to find an excuse, if there was one, for her behaviour. He took it out of her hands by turning his back to lead the horses away to the cattle yards far beyond the lights of the massive white marquee.

Bella stood for a moment and watched him go, the slight limp apparent as he walked with the two horses across the rough, open ground that passed for an airstrip on top of the Ben Bullen Hills.

She knew she should have been happy: caught up in the city, with its hectic, exciting life; engaged to a handsome, successful man. But in the last twelve months she had realised something was missing. There didn't seem to be a *point* to her life anymore.

And now?

A broadside hit in the form of a country boy. A country *man*. Would she have done what she just did if she was really happy with Warren and their life together?

Happy! Did you say HAPPY? It was Patty's voice suddenly echoing in her head. *Who are you trying to kid, Hells Bells? You haven't been happy in a long time, chickadee. Admit it and move on with your life!*

As Bella turned and walked towards the wedding marquee, she could hear the thump of the huge generators Trin had trucked in for the night. The clanging of the big camp-oven lids rang out as the caterers checked the progress of roasting vegetables, basking in their cast-iron heat, sitting on coals beside the substantial fire pits. There was also the squeaking belch of rotisseries as beef, lamb and pork turned around on mechanically driven rods.

And beyond the drone of the masses of partygoers hooking into the grog from the well-stocked bar, another sound reached out into the darkening, clear mountain sky.

Whup, whup, whup.

Bella cocked her head.

Whup, whup, whup.

A leaden feeling hit her chest and travelled down into her gut.

Whup, whup, whup.

The noise grew louder and materialised into a slick-looking blue-and-orange helicopter, its brilliant white landing light beaming from a skid. The chopper made its way with precision to the airstrip, where a landing sock hung used and slack from a tall, knobbed steel pole.

With a sickening lurch to her stomach, Bella knew who would be on board, as the livery of the chopper became apparent. The rear rotors of the chopper spun to reveal the lines of writing splashed across its tail: Oxford, Bride and Associates.

The helicopter landed in a flurry of dirt, clods of grass kicking up as the skids hit solid earth. The passenger door opened and a figure jumped out. The man, bent over at the waist under the still-moving rotors, moved away from the chopper towards where Bella stood frozen in horror. The pilot powered down the machine, obviously intending to stay for a while.

'Bella? Bella! Darling, how good to see you!' The voice hailed her as he stepped clear of the rotors, which could take an appendage off without a thought.

Why not his head?

What?

Had she just thought that?

She willed her feet to move forward, one step at a time. Left then right, slight hesitation, right then left.

'Warren . . . what a surprise! I hadn't expected you to come after everything that's happened.'

And then he was standing before her, all corporate and citified-looking in his double-breasted Italian wool suit, white hanky in a pocket to the right. Pressing a kiss to her cold mouth.

'Wozza!' Trinity bowled past Bella. 'You've come just in time to party, mate! Great to see you could make it. Love the chopper, man. Great way to fly! You're lucky it's such a clear night, no rain in sight, though that would be good. We sure need it up here, my word we do.' The ebullient groom grabbed hold of Warren's shoulders and spun him towards the marquee, to where the hundred or so people had all piled out of the party to see the helicopter land.

Bella watched the tightness surrounding Warren's eyes squeeze into a grimace as Trinity bandied around the nickname from his youth. Warren wouldn't stand that from many people, but Trin, having a similar background to Warren, was the only one of her friends that her fiancé actually liked.

'I'm fine, Trinity, and yes, I'm here for a couple of hours then it's back to the city. There's no time for rest in the investment-banking world. Not like the life you lead up here, quietly farming your life away . . .' Warren plastered a smile on his face. 'Anyway, how's married life so far, old boy? Sorry I couldn't make it to the ceremony.'

Warren was obviously determined to make an effort, but Bella couldn't help wincing at the slightly patronising twist in his words. Thank goodness it had flown right past an oblivious and tipsy Trin.

'Come on, Wozza. Come inside and have a beer . . .'

Bella watched as Trin guided Warren toward the marquee, willing herself to breathe deeply and recover some composure before she faced the crowd of guests.

'So that's the *fi-an-cé*, is it?' A deep voice, thick with contempt, came from her side.

She turned to Will and took in his state. He was already on the rum. His tie was loose and hanging free around his neck and his shirt was unfastened to the point where red-gold hair sprang gently from his muscled chest. The same shirt, which was hanging loose outside his trousers, had dirt smears and sprigs of dry vegetation clinging to various places – all signs of a rumble with a sheila in the thick native grass smothering the mountain plains.

'Yes, that's him.' She went to move away, towards the marquee into which her fiancé and Trin had disappeared.

Will's hand came out and grabbed her arm.

She looked down at his strong, brown fingers. Why did this hand feel so different to the one that had clasped her in the same spot only days ago, dragging her into the casino to meet Eddie Murray?

Chemistry, girlfriend, chemistry. Patty's voice rang clearly in her head again.

Ignoring it, she looked up at Will's face, a warning, a challenge.

He let her arm go. His move was grudging; his gaze lingering. He watched her walk away, once again.

Out of his life.

Chapter 28

Like many of the other female guests, Bella hung around in the marquee under a huge outdoor heater trying to stay warm.

She watched Warren standing with a group of men. He stood out, a shiny boy in his city clothes. The blokes around him only wore a suit to a wedding, a funeral or a B&S, and even then it was usually from the op shop or smelled of another man's BO. Their feet were clad in RM's or in some cases black work boots. Warren, on the other hand, lounged easily in his black Fiorelli suit and leather loafers.

The conversation ebbed and flowed all around. She was enjoying not having to say anything, just observing the people she'd left behind eight years ago. Most had been happy to see her, asking what she'd been doing in Melbourne with avid interest, rather than the polite distracted air she'd become used to in the city. It was a welcome change to talk to the people who'd meant so much to her so long ago.

The only ones she'd avoided were Mildred and Roger Vincent-Prowse. She'd noticed they'd been skirting her too. The girl standing next to her, also soaking up the heater's rays, spotted her interest in the Vincent-Prowse's.

'Prowsy's gone to Scone,' said the girl, a blob of cerise-in-satin-shantung. She looked surprisingly like a pink jelly bean.

'I beg your pardon?' said Bella, trying hard to remember who the girl was. She knew she'd seen her before but couldn't put a name to the round, puffy face.

'Prudence Vincent-Prowse's gone to Scone,' said the jelly bean again, pronouncing the place like the cake. Scone? Bella finally got it. 'Oh, Sc-own?'

'So *that's* how you say it! It's spelled s-c-o-n-e, like the one you bake. So it's Sc-own, right?' The jelly bean giggled. 'Suits Prowsy really, thinking she's *so* ooh-la-la! Not sure how the bump will suit her, though. Might cramp her style a bit, ay.' The girl giggled again as she tenderly rubbed her own very pregnant belly.

'Prowsy's pregnant?' asked Bella.

'Certainly is, according to old Ma Mildred over there. She's been trying to rub that one into Will's nose ever since she heard. Doesn't seem to have worked. Although . . .' she paused, considering, 'you really wouldn't know with Will, he keeps his cards pretty close to his chest, that one. See, they couldn't have babies apparently. Or one of them wanted them and the other didn't. Something like that, anyway. Not too sure on the details.'

Bella frowned, confused.

'You knew Will married Prowsy, didn't you?' asked the girl.

'Yes, I knew that,' said Bella quickly, as she finally put a name to the girl's face. Shelley Lukey. The storekeeper's daughter. Standing just over five-foot tall and very round, she was

Burrindal born and bred, a hometown kind of girl. She'd married a faller, a thickset-looking timber cutter who lived up the bush during the week and came home to play on the weekends – and play he obviously did, judging by the size of Shelley's tummy.

Shelley certainly remembered Bella. While Shelley was growing up, Bella Vermaelon and Patty O'Hara were the belles of Burrindal and Tindarra: pretty, funny and always out for a good time. Then Patty was killed and Bella disappeared, back home to Narree they said and then on to Melbourne.

Shelley had seen the size of the diamond solitaire sitting on Bella's ring finger and took in the look of the man who'd put it there, standing in a group of blokes not so far away. It was an impressive rock, that was for sure, but Shelley was wise to men, even if she wasn't to the rest of the world. And that bloke didn't look like a keeper, not to her mind.

'I didn't know Prudence was pregnant. Who's the father?' asked Bella, back to the topic at hand.

'The horse-breeder she ran off with, I suppose.'

Bella raised an eyebrow, inviting more information. Shelley was happy to oblige, leaning in closer and lowering her voice.

'A few years ago this horse-breeder from New South Wales came to town 'cause he'd heard there were a few good mares to be had around these parts. He went out to Will's place, liked what he saw and took it away with him when he left town a week or so later. He probably bought some horses too! We didn't see Will at the Burrindal store for weeks, but then I think hunger must have driven him down from the hills. He looked pretty shithouse picking up all them lawyer's letters, but then again he looked worse when he came home from Melbourne a few years before . . .' Shelley trailed off, realising she'd just contracted foot-in-mouth disease.

'Oh shit, oh shit . . . I'm sorry! My mouth runs away before my head catches up.' The puffy face blushed.

'I'm sure I looked the same, if you'd seen me in Melbourne after he left,' replied Bella softly, while trying to stop her own face from reddening.

She could see Warren was turning, an impatient expression on his face. He was looking for her. It was a chance to excuse herself from Shelley. And it was time to move back in again: talk the talk, walk the walk; participate in this charade of fun and enjoyment, while all the time wondering where her mountain lover had disappeared to in the night.

Will was outside standing at the fire drum, drowning himself in rum. He knew he was going to regret it in the morning, but at this stage he didn't give a shit. There were plenty of blokes crowded around the drum, piled high with blazing logs, and Macca was having a fine old time telling a yarn on the other side of the fire. But Will was an island of silence, not inviting anyone else to share his space.

He'd let her walk away again. He couldn't believe it had happened twice. He caught himself wondering if it was three tries and you're out. 'You're a bloody fool, O'Hara,' he muttered to himself as he took another slurp to empty his can. He threw the aluminium Bundy bear on the ground, squashed it flat with his boot heel, then picked it up and threw it on the fire.

'Whoa, bucko! I'll have to clean that bugger out in the morning. Don't want to be fishing for bloody dirty cans.' Old Wes Ogilvie hobbled up to his side. 'You pissed?' he asked, peering at Will with concern.

'Yep,' said Will.

'Mmm . . . Not like you nowadays. What's up your gander, or are you just pissin' Trin's booze into the wind 'cause you can?'

'Don't really want to talk about it, Wes. Here, have a can.' Will pulled two from an esky loaded with ice, beer, rum and bourbon.

'Ta, mate. I don't mind drinking Trin's piss. He don't give it away too often. He's as tight as those molars he used to pull, is that grandson of mine. Although, I have to say, he's been splashing it around lately with this flash weddin' and then there's that new ute he's bought. I tell you, if it has tits or wheels it'll cost ya.'

No answer.

Wes took another look at Will, who was staring sightlessly into the shooting, bright orange flames. Sparks hissed into the air as a log dropped further down the drum.

He tried again. 'If you don't want to talk about it, it must be a woman who's driving you to drink. They'll do that too.'

'Don't want to go there, Wes.'

'She must be good.'

'Yeah, she's good all right,' said Will as he remembered the passionate scenes on Hugh's Plain only hours before. Then he clamped his hand around his new can and squished it a bit, as he realised what he'd said.

'Is she worth it, mate?' asked a shrewd old Wesley, as he juggled to pull out a pipe for a smoke.

'Dunno. Probably.' Will moved his weight, agitated now. 'I'll be fucked if I know, Wes.' He took another swig and stared at the blue-and-orange helicopter sitting on the airstrip.

Wes might have been old, but he'd experienced forty years of true love with his wife Catherine before she'd passed away. He followed Will's gaze to the helicopter.

'You want something bad enough, boy, you'll fight for it. But you gotta want it bad enough first.'

Will slowly turned to the old man at his side and stared silently at the wisdom in his eyes. He tipped a pointer finger to his hat and walked away, into the dark mountain night.

After the food had been devoured and copious amounts of grog had been drunk, the bride and groom threw the bouquet and garter for the spinsters and bachelors in the crowd to catch. The bridal bouquet landed on a branch in a massive manna gum tree, a fancy beribboned appendage to a grey-white trunk, gnarled and twisted with ageless grace from wind and cold. The lace and satin pink garter spun and whirled its way through the air, to land at Warren's feet.

'Argh, Bella watch out. He'll have you married, barefoot and preggers before you know it!' yelled Macca from the back of the crowd. Bella could've killed her cousin.

Soon after, Warren took his leave, kissing the air somewhere near Bella's nose and bolting to the helicopter, where the patient pilot had sat for most of the night, his head in a newspaper.

Trin had arranged for a party-hire company in Narree to set up and then clean up after the wedding, so there wasn't much the friends and family had to do after the bride and groom left.

The flash new Toyota dual-cab ute – the groom's surprise gift to his new wife – carried Caro and Trin off to the luxurious retreat that was Bella and Warren's present to the couple.

The ute trailed soup and Milo tins in its wake. Shaving cream adorned all the windows and confetti flew from the air vents. Nothing was sacred when it came to the honeymoon car at a country wedding, as Trin discovered when he got out to carry his new wife over the threshold of their posh suite – squashed flat to his arse was a dim sim that had been placed strategically in the dark crease of his seat.

Chapter 29

Bella made it back to her parents' place at Narree by very late Sunday afternoon, having taken the long way home via the coast. She had been hoping a walk along the beach would help her sort out her rampaging thoughts and feelings. It hadn't. Just made her all the more confused.

Merinda stood beckoning in its serenity at the end of the plane-tree drive, but Bella sat in her vehicle at the front gate and surveyed the paddocks on both sides of the track. Thrown across the flats was the weak, late-afternoon light she always associated with Sundays; the death throes of a fantastic weekend before school or work the next day.

She gazed at the heifers playing around in the paddock to her left, the calves of last year halfway to maturity, having a ball in adolescence. Then to her right were a few morose choppers, cows with recurrent mastitis or low milk yields that had been consigned to be carted away in the cattle truck to the chopper market on Tuesday. They'd be on the road to the abbatoirs the following day.

She and Patty had once been like the heifers: carefree adolescents. At the grand old age of thirty, she now felt like the choppers. Thoughts of returning to Melbourne tomorrow – to Warren – caused her stomach to churn.

Bella needed to see her family, to touch her home roots. See if *anything* could stop this feeling that her life was spinning out of control; help her to decide what she *really* wanted.

She walked in the back door to witness her mother on the way to bed early, Frank helping the wheelchair along the deep but warm hall.

'Hi Mum, Dad!' she called as she moved quickly to the chair.

Her mother's tired eyes looked up at her as Bella kissed the top of her neatly coiffured head. Bella had always marvelled at her father's ability to cope with her mother's needs these last eight years. From wiping her bottom to setting her hair, Frank was a dab hand at them all. The only thing he couldn't abide was cutting Francine's toenails – so he employed a podiatrist to do that.

'Have a good time, sweetheart?' Her mother's voice still held its warmth even after the long, hard years.

'Yes, Mum, had a great time,' Bella lied. 'You would have loved Caro's dress and Trinity looked beaut.'

'And did Macca behave himself for a change?' Francine's eyes glinted in the soft old-fashioned hall lights.

'Yes, he did,' said Bella. But your daughter didn't, she added silently to herself. 'The day went off really well. I'll tell you all about it in the morning.' Most of it, anyway.

Kissing her mother goodnight, she made for the kitchen at the back of the house. She couldn't handle any more emotion today and after practically no sleep the night before, her eyes were heavy. She'd grab something to eat and hit the sack. Maybe she'd sleep tonight.

Because she'd gone to bed so early, after eating some spaghetti bolognaise she'd found in the fridge, Bella's eyes were wide open and her body was ready to rise by six the next morning. She could hear snatches of humming milking machines coming from her open bedroom window, so she jumped out of bed and riffled through her ancient wardrobe for some work clothes.

By six-fifteen she was in the dairy. Her father was whistling tunelessly as he listened to ABC radio.

'What are you laughing at, daughter of mine?' said Frank, surprised to see Bella up so early.

'I was just remembering how you and Justin used to fight over the radio, the commercial channel versus the ABC.'

Frank laughed as he swung a set of machines under a cow's udder and started to attach the cups to the teats. 'Yes, the radio would change from the ABC to 3TR depending on who was at the radio end of the pit. Do you remember when I did my block at your brother the day I wanted to listen to the interview about the O'Haras at Tindarra? Justin stormed out. He never loved going up to Maggie's as much as you did. He preferred surfing at the beach with his mates.'

Bella grabbed another set of milking machines and swung into helping her father put them on the cows' teats. The cows were lined up in front of them in a row, bums facing the pit, mouths munching on grain in the feeders at their heads.

'How *did* you two sort out the radio?'

'Justin bought himself a portable. We were both happy then.'

The commentator droned on about the latest in environmental funding as Bella and her father moved into a comfortable rhythm of putting on and then pulling off the machines. Sometimes Bella dashed out into the sunlit yard to urge the cows onto the milking platforms with the help of a trusty piece of poly pipe. 'Go on, get up. Get UP, girls!' she yelled. She'd forgotten just how much she enjoyed this, working with her father and the stock outdoors in the early-morning sun, which was already giving off heat.

Frank talked on and off throughout the milking, filling her in on all the farm news. 'We're doing really well this year. Milk prices are up for a change. I've put in a couple of paddocks of maize to silage into winter feed for the cows. It's expensive to grow but it'll save us from buying in so much extra feed. Worth a try, anyway. Oh, and I've planted some lucerne for round bale silage; being a deep-rooted crop, it should go all right on these alluvial soils. It's perennial too, so it should last about five years or so. Will O'Hara's growing it really well up at Tindarra on those rich river flats, particularly since he's put in spray irrigation.'

Bella ducked her head behind a conveniently placed cow's rump, intent on getting a cup onto a teat. She didn't want her father to see her blushing.

Milking was a monotonous but soothing job, and soon father and daughter found themselves letting the last lot of cows off the platform. Frank moved around the milk room and pit areas, cleaning the equipment while Bella manned the high-pressure hoses to wash down the concrete yard and milking platforms. As the sun warmed her back, and the water gushed from various two-inch hoses, Bella found the stresses of the last few days sliding away as easily as the bucket-loads of cow shit pouring down the effluent drains.

After finishing the washing-up, Bella followed the last of the cows along the track, intending to lock them into their day paddock. She took in the brilliant, sunny morning and whistled to her old dog Kelly, who was now more Frank's dog than her own, to round up the few stragglers who'd turned into the wrong laneway. Finally all the cows were in the right paddock, heads down, tails flicking happily, munching on the lush, green irrigated pastures. Bella swung the metal gate shut and hooked up the latch.

From what Bella could see as she walked back along the track towards her old home, the lucerne her father had planted looked fantastic. Even though Frank had only cut it the week before, a watering had the dark green plants sitting up and reaching for the sky once more.

Ambling on, a smile on her face and Kelly gambling around at her heels, she stopped at the next gate in front of the paddock of maize, opened it and walked through. She plonked her neat Wrangler-clad butt on the edge of the concrete stock trough that sat ten metres into the paddock, taking time to soak in the heat. The peace. She'd forgotten how serene and quiet it was out here, the milking machines now turned off. There was nothing to be heard other than the cry of the crows and squawks of the cockatoos as they dove in to sample the golden cobs of corn peeking from husks among the crop.

Looking out across the broad acres of maize, waving its leafy green fronds in the very slight ten o'clock breeze, she heard her father clang the gate latch open. Then shut. Wearing a faded blue, floppy terry-towelling hat, he walked into his maize crop and came out a few moments later holding a handful of rich, dark soil. Striding across, he sat down on the edge of the trough next to her, pouring soil from one hand to the other, quietly contemplating.

'Maize is going to need some water. I'd better start the bore,' he said, as he frowned at the loose, free-flowing dirt.

Bella nodded, looking at the grains of soil as they poured from hand to hand. Frank should have been able to clump the earth into a ball held together with moisture from the soil. The crop needed water urgently.

Bella could almost feel her dad's concern. But she knew it wasn't just the lack of water to the maize causing him grief.

'I'd forgotten how peaceful it was just to sit here and be,' she said. 'You can actually smell the sweetness of summer and feel the rain those thunderclouds sitting out on the hills might bring later.' Her eyes went to the massive blue hills spread out to the north, just beyond the boundary of her family's farm. The mountains of the Great Dividing Range looked close this morning, like they had picked themselves up and moved nearer to Narree. The clouds hanging around the fuzzy grey-blue hilltops of bush had been there since she'd called in on Friday, on her way to the wedding.

'What's up, Hells Bells?' asked Frank.

She'd almost forgotten he was there, sitting quietly as he watched his daughter slowly and noticeably relax.

The use of her old nickname was nearly her undoing. But she didn't want to dissolve into tears on her father's shoulder, not when she hadn't quite put her finger on what was wrong herself. Not when he had so much to deal with . . . her mother . . . the farm. It made her problems seem so inconsequential.

'I don't know, Dad, just unsettled. Not sure about stuff, I guess.'

And once again her mind flashed back to the scene at Hugh's Plain.

She'd known Will would come. She had heard his call on the wind as Aprillia bolted through the wedding crowd.

'Bella!'

Will could ride better than anyone else within cooee on that day. Bella knew he would be the first to find her as she lay in the thick native grass. She could blame what happened between them on the highly sexed emotions of the bride and groom or the adrenaline of the frightening ride. She could hold Warren responsible for being an arsehole or herself for questioning so much about her life. Maybe she could even claim temporary insanity. Or tell herself Will took advantage of her – but in her heart she knew that was a lie.

As she sat on the side of the trough, moving her hand back and forth swiping at the flies, she saw her father's eyes drawn to the ostentatious ring on her finger, which was glinting brazenly in the sun.

Bella suspected that underneath his polite reserve her father didn't really like Warren. He'd never come out and said as much; it was just a feeling she always had, something she'd steadfastly ignored. Aside from meeting her parents once, Warren had always made excuses whenever she'd suggested they visit them.

Bella's gaze moved to her father's hands, now resting peacefully on his knees. She'd always had a thing about hands, believing they could tell a tale or two. In her father's she could see strength, the protruding veins of hard work, and brown liver spots of age. All the signs of honest toil, and she felt a sudden rush of overwhelming guilt, shame for what she'd done with Will yesterday. Her father and mother were good people, who'd brought her up to be decent, trustworthy and truthful. Making love to one man while engaged to marry another didn't cut it. But hard on the heels of the shame and guilt came the insidious thought – was she being true to herself? Why feel guilt and shame over something that felt so right?

She shrugged those ideas aside. Will was obviously only after sex. Nothing more, nothing less, and she'd handed herself to him on a platter. More fool her.

Chapter 30

Four weeks later, Bella was trying to find something decent to watch on TV when the phone rang in the Melbourne penthouse. It was her father, which was strange, because Frank hated using the phone. Warren was working late, as usual.

'I've been thinking . . .' said Frank.

Bella sat back in her chair and curled her fingers around the armrest to wait for a bombshell. Her father never started a sentence with 'I've been thinking . . .' unless something major was about to be declared. 'Thought I'd take your mother on a round-the-world trip. It's been something she's always wanted to do and . . . what, with everything that's happened . . . we've never done it. The cows are going well, milk prices are the best they've been in years, so I thought now's the time.'

Bella could imagine her father sitting in the hall at Merinda. Could see him leaning back in the solid carver chair as he spooled the telephone cord around his big hand.

'Are you asking me if you should do it, Dad? Or are you telling me that's what you're doing?' asked Bella.

'Well . . . I suppose I'm telling you that's what we're doing, Hells Bells.' There was that nickname again. 'The tour leaves in a month and they've got four tickets left. A sudden cancellation, someone kicked the bucket so the other three who booked don't want to go. Aunty Maggie's going to come with us – to help me with your mother.'

'How long for?'

'Six months or so, I'd reckon,' came the reply. 'The initial world cruise goes for a hundred and four nights, stops at forty-two ports. Then the travel agents have hooked us up with another land tour that takes us on a jaunt around Europe.' Her father's voice was animated and he sounded more excited than he'd been in years. Bella listened with amazement. Why hadn't he mentioned this a month ago when she was up at Merinda?

'Justin and Melanie are right to run the farm by themselves. Maggie's in a bit more strife, but I think she'll just sell the stock and get that old codger Wes Ogilvie down the road to keep an eye on the place. Of course, Will O'Hara would be around too, but he's really busy now he's expanded his station into cropping and lucerne as well as cattle. It's a bit of a pickle, because Maggie really wants to come and I need her help with your mum . . .'

Her father paused, hesitant to air his next thought. Bella couldn't have known he was wondering at the wisdom of what he was going to suggest next. If Maggie's meddlesome plot was really going to work or if it would just complicate his daughter's life even further. But he didn't want to see his beloved daughter end up with Warren *either*. He wasn't right for her. Frank took a deep breath. 'That's unless you could see your way clear for a bit of a spell from that hectic city life you've got down there?'

And suddenly Bella knew.

The telephone call wasn't to tell her of the trip of a lifetime.

No, he was slinging her a lifeline. To come back to the bush to sort out what she really wanted to do with her life.

'I didn't mention the cruise when you were up here, love, as I wasn't sure it was going to come off. But now it has and it's all a bit of a rush. What do you think? Can you help poor old Maggie out?'

Bella didn't tell Warren about the phone call. She didn't get to tell him much these days. She'd come back from the wedding after the night at Merinda, feeling guilt-ridden and miserable, to find him buzzing with excitement and humming with energy, all memories of their fight over the CEO forgotten.

Taking her into his arms, he'd burbled, 'There's a takeover bid happening, darling. And they want *me* to head up the team! What an opportunity! It'll mean I'll need to be at the office more, but what a step for my career! I'll be up for board member before we know it. They know how good I am, what I can do – and this is my reward.' He twirled her around the floor with glee, landing a fleeting kiss on her lips before letting her go.

The lights of Melbourne were his backdrop as his arms drew pictures in the air of all the things he would do to ensure Oxford, Bride and Associates were the winning players in this corporate duel. And Bella had been so wracked with guilt over her indiscretion with Will she'd faked the enthusiasm Warren so desperately wanted. He was *so* sure she would be happy for him, *so* positive she would rejoice and back him all the way; she pushed her doubts about their future aside.

But not once did he ask for her opinion.

Not once did he ask about *her* weekend.

He didn't enquire about her mother's health or her father's farm. He obviously thought he'd done his duty just by coming to the reception.

And now, after her father's phone call, she lay alone in a cold silk-sheeted bed remembering it all. Realising she needed to make some decisions. Stop taking the easy route and drifting along. The city with its frenetic pace was an easy place to do that.

Warren loved her, in his own funny way. But she couldn't continue to be what he wanted – an accessory to his success. Deep down she admitted to herself it wasn't all his fault. Up until recently she'd been happy sitting on the sidelines living *his* dreams.

But now? Wasn't it time she took control of her life and created some dreams of her own?

Her trip back into the mountains and seeing her old way of life made her realise how, deep down, she *really* missed it. She'd never wholeheartedly committed herself to being a city chick; in fact, she had been as resistant to it as Warren had been to the country. While she liked her job with the public-relations firm, the shine of it had begun to pall. All the networking and being nice to people she really didn't like, just to get their patronage and money. She wasn't like Warren, she admitted to herself. She didn't want to make her job her life.

We work to live, girlfriend, not live to work. You've got to get the balance right, chickadee. Patty's voice rang clearly in her head.

That was another startling thing since the wedding at Ben Bullen Hills – she'd heard Patty's voice in her head, come ringing back to life. She'd even felt ghostly warm arms clasped around her shoulders. It was spooky, but comforting. Was Patty telling her something, Bella wondered, as she lay in the half-dark, reflections from the city lights casting shadows around the silent room.

Bella moved her head and stared at the small photo sitting on her bedside table. Boots and hats flying, arms swinging, she and Patty danced silently in time to Sara Storer, somewhere outside Tamworth on the way home from up north.

Maybe taking time out at Tindarra was what she needed – to sort out whether she really wanted the city to be her life. The only place she could see Warren moving was further up the corporate tree of Oxford and Bride. If she married him she would be stuck in the city forever.

Marry him? Christ, you're not still thinking of doing that, Hells Bells? Patty's voice sent shivers down her spine.

A clunking noise startled her, her heart jumping a beat. The airconditioner hummed to life and pumped its artificial breath around the stark room. Warren liked to sleep in the cold when he finally made it home. *If* he made it home, she amended to herself, as she tried to find some warmth in the freezing bed. She didn't know where the hell he'd been sleeping lately, but it wasn't in this dockside morgue.

Thoughts of Aunty Maggie's quaint old cottage flooded her mind, with its corrugated-iron roof that resonated with tinny music whenever it rained. Then there was the slow-combustion stove inside that ran hot twenty-four hours a day, making a cosy welcome. Bella remembered the day she had been shocked to see Maggie pull a sponge from the top oven while shoving a live lamb back into the bottom oven with her slippered foot.

'It's the warming oven,' she had explained to Bella, who was staying for her usual school-holiday break. 'This poor little mite got a bit cold as his mother died. I'll warm him up then we'll see if he wants some tea.' She had pointed to the hotplate on the stove where a teat-topped sauce bottle full of milk peeped from an old boiler filled with warm water. Bella smiled to herself as she remembered those days.

If she listened closely enough, above the roar of the city traffic she could hear the music of Tindarra's babbling mountain stream, on its winding journey to the lower country of Narree; could visualise the peacefulness of the rolling hills with their towering trees.

Lying in her penthouse home set beside the dirty Yarra River dreaming of a mountain valley hundreds of kilometres away, Bella made her decision.

The only problem was the other inhabitant of Tindarra, and she didn't mean old Wes. She needed a clean break from *all* the complications in her life – and that included Will O'Hara. Memories of him naked and making love to her on Hugh's Plain danced before her eyes: those tanned bicep muscles holding his body inches above hers, his head thrown back, those molasses eyes crinkled in ecstasy; her own unrestrained responses to a body and hands that just seemed to know how to please her, how to love her.

'You're still good in the sack, cowgirl.'

Overwhelming shame at his words.

He'd just have to stay out of her way. The mountains were big enough for the two of them. His property might be next door to Maggie's, but it was pretty damned big, and even though they would be in the same valley, it didn't mean she had to *see* him.

Bella sat up in bed, took the remote control from the holder above her head and depressed the switch for the aircon.

Rummpfff.

The machine rumbled as it clicked off.

She got out of bed, ran into the sitting room and dragged her red minky blanket from the couch. Back in the bedroom, she wrapped herself into the blanket's cuddly warmth and set about planning how to move home.

Three and a half weeks later she was ready to go. She'd resigned from her job, leaving a boss unhappy to see her go but moving right along to start a new girl next week. There were no flies on him, she thought wryly. Another difference of city versus country. Easy come, easy go.

She still hadn't told Warren she was leaving town. She'd barely seen him long enough to say hello. Any conversation they had inevitably revolved around the takeover bid. Lovemaking in the early hours of the morning, if and when he made it home to bed, was unsatisfying. He rolled off and was asleep in minutes, leaving her to stare at the ceiling, frustrated and alone.

She reproached herself again and again for not telling him she was going.

Procrastinator, mocked Patty, playing around in her head.

'Yeah, well *you* deal with him then!' she mentally lobbed back. 'He'll pout and sulk and probably yell a bit while he goes on and on about how I'm making *his* life difficult.'

Well, what the fuck are you doing with the self-absorbed prick, Hells Bells? came the reply.

'He's not a prick. And he loves me.'

Yes, but do you love him?

In the end she left him a note.

Dearest Warren,

I am so sorry to tell you in this way, but we never get a chance to sit down and really talk. I'm leaving. I need time to sort out what I want to do with my life. You have been so good for me these past years but it's not enough. I'm not sure what I'm looking for, but I need the time and space to find it. I'm so sorry.

 I've resigned from my job, and where I'm going doesn't matter. I don't want you to wait for me and so have left the ring in your dressing-table drawer. Forgive me, Warren. I just can't keep doing this, living your life and your dreams. I need to find my own.

Bella

❧

Her father picked her up at the Narree station mid-afternoon. He gave her a big hug and grabbed a trolley to load the luggage she'd booked into the guard's van at Melbourne's Flinders Street Station. She helped him lift cases and numerous packages into the back of the old HiLux ute, all the while trying to stop herself crying at the mess her life was in.

Getting into the passenger side, she clipped on her seatbelt and waited for her father to do the same. He clambered in beside her and then reached down into his old workpants to pull out a huge brown-and-white striped men's hanky, dropping it into her lap. 'Thought you might need this.'

In the privacy of the ute, Bella finally allowed the tears to pour down her face. 'Thanks, Dad. It's been a bit difficult. Leaving Warren and . . . well, everything.'

'I know, love, I know. Just hope I've not put you where you don't want to be?' Frank frowned as he looked at his daughter's reddened, tired eyes and tear-soaked cheeks.

'No, Dad. I wouldn't be here if it wasn't where I needed to be.'

Frank patted her hands, noting the missing diamond ring. He then cranked the ignition and slowly selected first gear.

'That's good, Hells Bells. You had me worried. For what it's worth, I think you've done the right thing. A time up at Maggie's in those hills will do you the world of good.'

'Yeah, I'm sure you're right.' At least I bloody well hope so, Bella silently added.

'I've pulled your old ute out of the shed, had it checked over, given it a wash. It's all good to go.'

So she was back to driving a ute.

A voice in her head started singing out of tune. *She'll be comin' round the mountain when she comes . . . she'll be comin' round the mountain when she comes . . . Yee ha!*

Chapter 31

The shadows flung by roadside gum trees were long. The interior of the ute flickered alternately light and dark as the vehicle made its way through the gentle rolling hills of the Burrindal Valley. Bella clutched her left hand to the back of her neck, massaging the stiffness that had gathered at its base. Lately, all she seemed to be doing was driving. She had got out of the habit, living in the heart of the city with public transport at her door. Her right hand gently steered the ute around another bend and she spied the turn-off a hundred metres up ahead.

Burrindal's former school stood sentinel on the far corner of the intersection abutting the main road. Some arty type had bought the land from the education department years ago and gone about remodelling and constructing a building that looked like it was straight from a fairytale. The three-storey rectangular structure, complete with two high turreted windows peering down from the top, lurched into the air and stayed there seemingly in defiance of gravity. Patty had often joked that the brightly painted building only needed a rounded toe piece and a chimney pot to make 'The Old Woman Who Lived In A Shoe' come to life right in the mountains of East Gippsland.

Bella sighed as she flicked on her left indicator and slowly swung her ute past the fairytale house. So many memories just waiting to jump out and eat her up.

The gravel road adjoining the tar disappeared around a sharp bend after a few hundred metres. The last twenty-five kilometres to Aunty Maggie's property at Tindarra, an hour and a half drive from Narree, were the most dangerous of the trip. It was lucky it wasn't dusk – tucker and water time for the creatures of the Australian bush. Even now she could see a wallaby bounding across the gravel right on the bend. She eased the accelerator to a comfortable speed and settled once again into her lamb's wool seat cover to enjoy the beauty and peace of the final part of her journey. Driving her old Holden ute, which her father had kept parked in the machinery shed all these years, was exhilarating – taking her back to the wild years of her youth, making her feel young and free again.

It had been a very long time since she'd ventured Tindarra way. It used to be a well-beaten track for her and Patty in years gone by. Patty's parents' property circumnavigated her Aunty Maggie's four hundred acres. Spending all her school holidays up in the high country of Tindarra, her childhood had been idyllic, full of work and fun, helping Maggie on her farm. And Patty and Bella, in particular, reaped the benefits working on both the O'Haras' place and Aunty Maggie's next door.

Wonderful summers riding horses and motorbikes, swimming in the river and playing make-believe games around the sheds. Long days mustering and moving stock, helping to ensure paddocks weren't overgrazed. As a kid it had all been such fun, with no adult worries like drought and low commodity prices to cloud the days. Or sorrow and grief to prey on the mind.

The chiming of a mobile phone interrupted Bella's thoughts. Slowing the ute to a crawl, she scrambled for the phone her father had given her before she left Merinda.

'Better take this, me girl,' he'd said as he shoved it through the open window of her ute. 'That digital citified thing of yours won't work in the hills. This one here is a new-fangled country phone.' He read from the label. 'Certified to work in all country areas.' He snorted in disgust. 'That'll be the day! There's a trick to getting it out of its holder, but you'll be right.'

Bella had taken the phone, knowing it was useless to argue. When her father had that look on his face, he meant to get his way. It was a look Bella hadn't seen in her own mirror for a while. And she did feel better on those remote and lonely roads in the hills knowing she had some method of communication should anything go wrong. And – something she hadn't told her father – she'd thrown her 'digital citified thing' into the bush somewhere around Pakenham a few days ago!

Now she knew what her father meant about the bloody holder. Placed face-in to the hip holster, the phone stopped ringing as she scrabbled to pull it loose. Finally finding the magic button on the enclosing plastic, she extracted the phone with a curse.

The ute ground to a halt just as the ringing started again. Bella was ready this time. 'Hello!' she snapped.

'Bella, darling heart, is that you?' Without stopping for an answer, the honeyed tones of Caro Handley, now Eggleton, oozed across the mobile airwaves. Marriage was obviously good for her. 'Thank goodness I got you. Listen, my love, can you do us a favour?'

Bella managed to squeeze in a yes before the honey started dripping again.

'Darling, I really need you to pick up . . .' the voice trailed off. 'What's that, Trin?' Bella could hear Trinity's voice in the background, followed by Caro's voice back in Bella's ear, interrupted by static as she spoke. 'Yes I'm getting to that, darling. Bella, sweetheart, Trin needs you to pick up a parcel from Janey at the post office. He's going across to . . . to a cattle . . . and can't . . . down there himself. It has to be picked up tomorrow so . . . release . . . straight away. What's . . . Trin?'

'Caro, I can't hear you. Say again?' said Bella.

The conversation came back on line but wasn't directed at her. 'But Trinity, I can't!' Caro sounded incredulous. 'I'll do most things on this farm of yours but not *that*!' Trin's calm voice could be heard again, followed by Caro. 'Well, okay, if they *have* to be released as soon as they get here, I'll just have to ask her to do it. Darling?' Caro was back to Bella in the ute. 'You haven't had your nails manicured or anything, have you?'

Bella looked down at her short, straight nails with half-moon cuticles a manicurist had never touched. 'No, Caro, was I supposed to?' she asked with a grin.

'No, darling, you're fine just the way you are. Would you mind driving the parcel up to Ben Bullen tomorrow? We'd just love to see you, and do you think *you* could release Trin's dung beetles into their piles of cow poo for me? I just *can't* stick my hands into gooey, slimy cow shit *on purpose*! I'll do most things, but not *that*.'

Bella grinned into the phone.

'*Please*, Hells Bells?'

There wasn't much Bella could say other than, 'Okay, but it'll cost you.'

She was back in the bush.

Spinning the ute around, she retraced her drive towards the Tindarra Road intersection and clicked down the indicator to head into Burrindal. Pulling up in front of the general store, she parked the ute and got out to stretch her cramped muscles in the sun. Taking a deep breath, she steeled herself for Shelley 'Jelly Bean' Lukey, and was surprised to see Shelley's mother Janey appear from the timber screen door instead.

'An-GUS! An-GUS!' The 'gus' was delivered at an octave higher than the rest. Bella looked around to see who Janey was hailing.

'An-GUS! Come here this minute, you naughty man!'

Bella scanned the street. Not a person to be seen. It was very quiet for a Saturday afternoon.

'Ah, there you are, you naughty little boy, Mummy's been looking for you everywhere!'

Bella swung back just in time to see Janey scoop up a fluffy rat-like creature that came running along the verandah. Two little eyes peeped out from mountains of white and tan fur, twin butterfly ears revolved like satellite dishes searching for a signal, and a tiny pink tongue came from an even tinier mouth to lick his mistress on the cheek.

'Oh Angus, you are a love.' Janey buried her face into the ball of fluff.

Bella smiled and moved forward onto the step as Janey looked up.

'Bella, how good to see you!' Janey flung her arms out wide and Bella found herself wrapped up in a tight and furry embrace, Janey's arms around her body, Angus's fluff in her face. Then she felt a wet little lick on her right cheek.

She detangled herself gently and moved back to the sanctuary of the verandah rail. 'Hi there, Janey. How've you been?'

'Marvellous, Hells Bells, bloody marvellous. Meet Angus. He's my gift to myself now all the kids have left home.'

'Janey, I thought you were supposed to get the puppy *before* the kids left not after.' Bella laughed at her old friend.

'Yeah well, going soft in me old age.'

'You didn't make Caro's wedding?'

'Nope, Tom and I had a date with one of those Winnebago van things in Queensland. We'd booked the holiday already when we found out Caro and Trin's wedding date. Thought, bugger it, we haven't had a holiday in ages and I didn't want to bail out then. I'd never get Tom to agree to it again. He had a break in his motorbike tour dates, so I decided to just book the bloody thing.'

Tom and Janey were semi-retired. For years they'd run a farm Tom inherited, then sold it and bought the store for Janey to run while Tom ran trail-bike tours. Tom knew the bush around Burrindal and Tindarra better than anyone. He was in great demand to lead trail-bike enthusiasts from all over the world into the mountains.

'You meet the rat?' A rough voice came from behind.

'Tom! How are you?' Bella swung to meet the bushman walking up with his old dog Rusty. She placed a kiss on his weather-beaten cheek and patted Rusty, who sat down and released a slow and gentle fart.

Sheesh! The smell! Bella tried to keep a straight face but failed.

'Yeah I know, he stinks, but he's a good old fella, aren't ya, Rusty?'

Bella smiled at Tom. She'd always had a soft spot for him. 'How are you?' she repeated.

'Good! How 'bout you? Hear you're comin' back to the valley for a while?'

'Yeah, back for a bit to let Maggie take her trip.'

'Do you good,' said Tom as he ruffled Angus's butterfly ears. 'The only good thing about Melbourne is seeing it in the rear-vision mirror, ay.'

Bella laughed. 'Yeah, you're probably right there, Tom.'

Turning to Janey, she got to the point of her trip. 'I've come to pick up a parcel for Caro and Trin.'

'Ah,' said Janey, a pointer finger in the air. 'That would be them shit beetles. Trin's been sweating on them coming all week. He was in yesterday but they hadn't arrived. Came in the mailbag this morning. Can't believe they send them by regular post. You'd think they'd die or something, wouldn't you? I'll grab them.' Janey moved off into the store. Bella, Tom and Rusty followed her, Bella hesitantly at first.

'Shelley not about?' she dared, glancing around as she and Tom made their way over to the far corner of the old store. A slow-combustion stove burned hot, drawing them to its warmth despite the sunny afternoon outside.

'Oh! That's my other bit of big news.' Janey swung back from the doorway of the little post office, eyes alight. 'I'm a grandmother! Shelley and Joe had a baby boy. And he's *gorgeous*, isn't he, Tom?' Janey beamed.

'Well, if you call a red, screamin' scrap of humanity gorgeous, then I suppose that's what he is,' Tom growled, although Bella noticed his smile was just as proud.

'Congratulations, guys. Are they well?'

'Fit as fiddles and bright as shiny buttons,' called Janey from the depths of the post boxes.

'Had a bit of trouble with mastitis in the boobs and stitches in the bum, but yeah they're doing just fine now, ay,' said Tom, eyes twinkling at Bella's expression. 'Feel like a cuppa?' Tom moved to the steaming kettle set on the stove-top.

Bella peered at the ceiling, the floor, anywhere else but at Tom. The last thing she wanted to think about was Shelley Lukey's boobs and bum.

'Here they are, Bella,' said Janey as she appeared from the post office with a small bag in one hand and book to sign in the other. Angus had escaped from Janey's arms to prowl the town once more. Janey noticed her husband reaching for some coffee mugs.

'A cuppa, Tom. You're a sweetie. There's a bit of homemade fruit cake there under the glass cover. How about it, Bella? Will you have one too?'

Bella took in the beaming couple in front of her: Janey with her laughing eyes and open face, Tom's thickset frame and wild, longish black hair. They were the epitome of a country couple. Financially savvy and successful, passionate about the bush where they lived and worked, they welcomed with open arms any honest friend who came their way. They were always at the forefront of the community to lend a helping hand, and Bella knew from her father just how much they'd quietly assisted his sister Maggie since Hughie had passed away.

Tom lifted a thick, bucket-like coffee cup in query, as Janey moved to uncover a massive fruit cake. Bella had to get out to

Maggie's – but how could she say no to these two, who were as much a part of her past in Burrindal as the valley at Tindarra?

'Okay, I'll have a quick one.'

It was at least half an hour later before Bella could politely take her leave. But she was amazed at how much she had enjoyed sitting down with her old friends for a chat. She was also a little surprised that they hadn't mentioned Warren. Other than Tom's quick look at her bare left hand, not a word was said about the absent fiancé.

She grabbed the postal bag containing Trin and Caro's dung beetles and signed for them in the big red postal book. 'I'll be off then,' she said. 'Thanks. It was great to see you both. Give my regards to Shelley, and call in for a cuppa when you ride past next, Tom.' Bella paused and then added, 'And Janey, any mail for me, can you just send it out to Tindarra?' She slowly moved towards the door.

'Yeah, no probs. Give us a yell if you run into any trouble out there. Although you've got hunky old Will O'Hara nearby to lend you a hand.' Janey's wink was mischievous. Bella moved quickly out the screen door. She wondered if it was an inherent trait in female Lukeys: to lull you with sweetness then slam in a gut-wrencher, just when you thought you'd got away scot-free. If so, they needed to breed it out.

Chapter 32

The road narrowed from the wide, open rolling farmlands into the enclosed stretch of trees that hid Tindarra from the rest of the world. Stringy-barks stood tall beside wallowing wattle as the Australian bush welcomed Bella to the Promised Land. Well, that's what it always seemed like to her anyway.

She imagined it was like a massive natural curtain call before the final act came on stage. Mile upon mile of scrub, winding around the southern side of the Tindarra River, which was a babbling brook at the moment but could rise to a thunderous and deadly torrent after big rains.

Then finally the curtain drew back. The trees retreated and the farmlands began once again. And what farmlands they were. Snuggled in a tight-ended valley, rich alluvial river flats were laid out in front of her eyes, a carpet of emerald-green glinting in the sun. The river lazily wound its way through the middle of the valley, water dancing and leaping over rocks, flowing over tiny waterfalls, with dark rock pools on sluggish corners hiding trout of mammoth proportions.

And above all this rich grazing land towered mountains of grey-blue bush interspersed with native pastures that provided valuable feed for stock and warmth and shelter for the cattle as the winter frost and snow crept in.

Her aunt's house appeared, settled snugly beside the gravel road. A single-storey, weatherboard farmhouse of indeterminate age, it had grown like topsy with bits added on and bits lopped off, and what remained had become a comfortable haven for Maggie in her old age. Poplars stood sentinel behind it, guarding the house from the Tindarra River as it made its way around the side of the cosy home. It was a good stone's throw to the river from the back door, which stood high above the old riverbank slope. An impressive orchard ran down along the other side of the house. The deciduous trees provided thick-leaved shade in the long hot summer while bare branches allowed the sun to warm the house during freezing cold winters.

For the first time in a very long time, Bella felt like she'd finally come to a place of sanctuary, a haven filled with peace; a space so removed from the hustle and bustle that had claimed her life for the past eight years, it looked like it had remained in a time capsule, just waiting for her to return. Tindarra held some of the best memories of her times with Patty, when fun, happiness and laughter were just a heartbeat away. Why had it taken her so long to come back?

Because you ran away. The little voice inside her head was insistent. She had buried herself in the city, thinking that running was healing. It wasn't. It just compounded the problem. She might have lost her best friend. She might have lost her lover. But then she'd done something infinitely worse. In moving to Melbourne, she'd lost herself.

And now she hoped to change all that.

Smoke puffed from the old house's chimney, a generator hummed out of sight and lights glowed softly through the windows – all beckoning a traveller home. Past experience had taught her that the towering mountains guarding the Tindarra Valley slung out an aura that could not be repelled, a spirit that captivated and never let go. As she watched the early-evening mist slowly spiral and settle to blur the edges of everything in the valley, she saw the place where the love of family and friends could work magic on her heart.

The garden gate clicked shut behind her, as Bella noticed Turbo was missing. He'd be getting on a bit now. She hadn't seen him since he was a year or two old but Maggie always talked about him. A bitsa breed of border collie, labrador and goodness knows what else, Turbo's genetic lineage was as footloose as his skulking around after the neighbours' bitches in the deep dark of the night.

'Must be out having a run with Maggie,' muttered Bella. Turbs was usually the first to greet a visitor, according to her aunt. Bella wound her way up the path, dodging the old rose bushes that threatened to grab her with their sharp thorns, and mounted the worn wooden steps.

The first thing she saw as she moved around the old verandah were boots. RM's. They sat lazily on an upturned drench drum and until recently had been well polished but now retained a thin layer of dust. The creases in the leather were well dug in, where the top joint of the foot wiggled the toes.

Not like her own. Bella looked down at her cracked footwear. She never greased, only shined – and it showed. She had splits in the leather that were making good headway into the tops of her boots, intent on sending her RM's to boot heaven. For the past eight years they had been tossed in the cupboard, neglected.

As she rounded the corner she realised the RM's were connected to a pair of well-muscled denim-clad legs. The owner raised a bottle of VB in her direction.

'Well, well, well. You're back.' The voice was hard, the tone uninviting. Eyes of brittle toffee coolly appraised her from the tips of her golden shoulder-length ringlets to the leather cracks at her feet.

The man Bella had been trying not to think about for eight weeks sat on her Aunty Maggie's verandah. Bella took in his handsome but cold face.

'Hmm . . . I wonder how long you'll last this time.'

Her hackles rose but she stood her ground. He obviously wanted a fight. Well, he wasn't going to get one. 'As long as Maggie needs me,' she replied, her rounded snub nose tilting an inch into the air. Slinging her arms tightly across her chest, she leaned against the house wall, searching for an air of indifference; trying to find coolness amid the heat of her emotions. Her heart was beating double-time and butterflies danced in her gut.

Will uncoiled his lithe, well-proportioned body from the rocking chair and, with his foot, shoved another drench drum in her direction.

'I suppose if you're here, you might as well have a beer. Take a seat. Maggie's down at the river making last-minute adjustments to the pump. So you –' he pointed his bottle in her direction '– don't have any trouble with it supplying the house and stock trough water while she's away. She has such faith. Me? I don't.'

'Faith in what?' asked Bella.

'You.' The voice was flat, the tone uncompromising.

Bella was speechless. What right had he to judge?

'Have a beer, Hells Bells.'

'I'm fine, thank you. I don't usually drink before five o'clock.' Her voice sounded prim even to her own ears.

She was rewarded with rich laughter. 'Five o'clock?' his voice was incredulous. 'Since *when*?'

Bella shrugged. 'That's just the way I do things now. I've changed.' She knew she sounded defensive but she couldn't help herself. Why did this man infuriate her so much? Why did she feel she had something to prove?

Meanwhile, Will watched her, noting the way her arms crossed defensively in front of her enhanced the voluptuous bust that weeks ago had sent him crazy. He remembered the feel of that body, the taste of those breasts, and the flaming heat of passion that burned between them on Hugh's Plain.

He didn't *want* to give in to his own need to hurt her now, to wield words that would cut her deeply – they just came tumbling from his mouth unbidden, like a toey horse not ready to be reined in. He sure as hell didn't need her here, luring him. He'd had enough of that at Ben Bullen. He couldn't get that afternoon out of his head; it had become a constant part of his dreams.

Correction – it had become his nightmare for she was engaged to marry someone else.

'Well, I do believe you *have* changed, Little Miss Chic City Girl. But I'll tell you something else, *sweetheart*. It's five o'clock somewhere in the world right now, so sit down and have a bloody drink.'

Bella caught the echo of Macca. He'd said those same words to her a few weeks earlier – twenty-four hours before she'd lain naked on a remote, thickly grassed clearing, making love to this bloke.

Will pushed hard against the drench drum with his foot and shoved a bottle at her. 'You'd better remember just how we do things in the bush,' he said, raising his beer bottle to mid-height in salute. 'Otherwise you're going to bloody well die of thirst before you hightail it back to that toffy city of yours and your *fi-an-cé*.'

She was fighting the urge to deck him with the beer bottle he'd so ungraciously thrust into her hand, when Maggie's voice rang out.

'Bella, my love, you're here!' her aunt said, lumbering up the stairs near the back door. 'How good to see you. Did Caro catch you about the dung beetles? She called here first. And Will! I'll get your bolt-cutters in a sec. You'll take those beetles up to Ben Bullen, won't you, Will, and release them for Trin? You're heading up that way tomorrow, yes? It'll save Bella from doing it, there's a boy. And thanks so much for getting Bella a drink. You must be tired and thirsty, my pet.'

Maggie bustled onto the verandah, Turbo barking excitedly at her heels. 'Isn't it good you've got such a capable man down the road to look after you while I'm away cruising the seven seas!' Maggie stopped behind Will's chair to ruffle his red-gold hair.

'Yes, she's *really* lucky, Maggie,' said Will flatly. He stood and offered her his seat.

'You're a love, thank you so much.' She patted the drench drum beside her chair, the same one Will had offered Bella earlier, and beckoned to her niece. 'Now sit down here, sweetheart, and tell me all about your drive up. Are your mum and dad excited about our trip? I haven't thought of anything else for weeks!'

While Will leaned against a verandah pole, peeling at little flakes of creamy paint, Bella sat down on the drum and tried to answer her aunt's questions politely. The whole time very aware of the brooding man listening intently to her words.

❦

'So, what did old Wozza say when you told him you were disappearing up here for six months?' Will asked as he shut the gate behind Maggie's departing Range Rover the next afternoon.

'Nothing,' muttered Bella, moving back towards the house.

'Beg your pardon?' Will jogged to catch up.

'Nothing,' she repeated.

'Nothing?' Will's voice was disbelieving. 'His fiancée tells him she's going away for six months and he says nothing?'

'I didn't tell him.' It slipped from Bella's mouth before she could stop it.

'You *what*?'

Bella swung around to face him. 'I didn't tell him, okay. Well . . . I did tell him but, not face to face. I left him a note.'

'You left him a *note*?'

'Yes. That's what I said. You know, a page with words on it.' Bella knew she was being churlish but she didn't care. 'He was busy. Work had a takeover bid on and I just didn't get a chance to talk to him. So I did the next best thing and left a letter. Plus, it's none of your business anyway!'

'No, I suppose it's not.' Will looked at her bare left hand. 'Where's your ring?'

Bella mounted the verandah steps and turned to face him, both hands on her hips. 'I left it in Melbourne, if you must know. Not much use to me out here. Look. You really must have heaps to do. I'm fine here now, but thanks for coming to see Maggie off. It meant a lot to her.' Bella's tone left no doubt, she couldn't see why herself.

'Mmm . . . I guess I know when I'm not wanted,' Will said with a grin, making the dimples on his cheeks dance.

Bella glanced away. Her body was betraying her; she couldn't look for fear of what her eyes, her face would say.

Wuss! Patty's voice echoed. *Never knew you to be a piker, Hells Bells.* Bella immediately lifted her head and looked Will dead in the eye. 'I'll be seeing you around, no doubt. Thanks for coming. Now, *goodbye.*'

Will could take a hint. He'd found out most of what he needed to know anyway. He drove away from Maggie's place, a thoughtful expression on his face, a quiet and almost cheerful whistle sliding through his teeth. She'd left the ring behind, hey? That had to mean something.

He was starting to look forward to the next few months.

Chapter 33

'Around' ended up being the next Saturday afternoon.

The week after Maggie's departure had seen Bella settle into a peaceful but busy routine. Before leaving Melbourne she had emailed her old boss from the Department of Agriculture, David Neille, with whom she'd kept in sporadic contact over the years. She'd asked him if he knew of any contract work she could do from home now she was jobless and back in the country. Maggie was supplying her utilities and meat and she had savings in the bank, but a bit of money coming in wouldn't go astray either, she'd decided.

He'd replied immediately.

'You're a flaming godsend, Bella. I've got a Landcare project which is half finished. The girl doing it has had to toss it in unexpectedly. It's something you'll be able to do no worries, in fact I think you'll love it. We're drawing up project plans for some Landcare groups in the area. You'll need to be able to travel, but only locally, and we'll provide you with a computer and mobile phone. You'll just need internet access so you can upload written reports to us back here at the office. It pays pretty well. Are you interested?'

She replied, *'Yes please!'* and was pleasantly surprised at how much she was looking forward to it. She'd loved working with farmers in the old days and hadn't realised how much she'd missed it.

By Wednesday Bella had started a pattern to her days. Farm work kept her outside and busy in the mornings. She rose around seven and was finished in the house by eight. After letting Turbo off his chain and the chooks into their run, she fed Maggie's two poddy calves with some cow's milk old Wes Ogilvie dropped off every few days.

She'd found it a stinky job because after a third day in the drum, the milk smelled disgusting and was starting to congeal into sticky, white lumps. She didn't have to heat the milk, she just poured it into a four-teated feeder, tipping it on an angle as she latched it on the gate. The Shorthorn and Hereford Cross calves could then feed from two teats rather than using four.

The calves always came running, and she laughed at their antics while they were trying to find which teats to drink from. The looks of confusion on their faces when they sucked only air at the top end of the feeder were hilarious. Sometimes she had to help them find the teat that was running with milk, and then their little tails would swing briskly to and fro in delight.

After the calves were done she usually cranked up the four-wheel motorbike, loaded Turbo onto the carryall and took off down the farm track towards the river, checking all was well in the paddocks along the way.

Maggie had sold most of her stock once she knew she was going on her trip. She normally bought in eight- to nine-month-old steers and then grew them out to eighteen- to twenty-four months. She usually tried to get them up to the four hundred kilo mark before she sold them off, she had told Bella before she left – and the year before she had even managed a five hundred kilo Murray Grey. She also had a handful of breeders, heifer calves she'd reared up herself. She hadn't been able to part with these but she assured Bella there was only one of them due to autumn calve.

'She'll be okay, it's her third calf, but just keep an eye on her all the same,' she'd noted to Bella on their drive around. 'If she looks like she's in trouble, just ring Will or old Wes, they'll come up and give you a hand to calve her down.'

There was a fair bit of feed around for this time of the year, so Maggie had wanted her to strip-graze the paddocks using a portable electric fence that needed to be moved every couple of days – otherwise the small herd of cows would have just indiscriminately trampled down a whole paddock of good feed.

So Bella checked on the cows every day, winding up, moving and resetting the electric fence when she judged fresh feed was needed. Then she and Turbo cased out the rest of the farm, enjoying their morning's drive in fresh mountain air.

Afternoons were devoted to her departmental contract work, of which she was still in the research stage. Wading through a pile of reading including Catchment strategies and previous Landcare group plans, she wanted to get a handle on everything before she met the Landcare group members face to face.

And so by Saturday afternoon, other than a barrage of emails from a cross and confused Warren (which she'd manage to ignore), there had been no hiccups to upset what was a very enjoyable week.

'Thought you might need a bit of firewood.' A deep voice spoke, causing her to bump her head on the low chook-house roof. She'd been head-in, arse-out, cleaning the nesting boxes, which had been in dire need of new straw.

'What the . . . ?' Bella cursed, rubbing her head.

'It's going to come in a bit rough next week, and I normally cut Maggie's firewood for her. You're running low, I noticed last Sunday, so I thought I'd better do something about it,' said Will, moving to lean on the chook-yard post while watching her rub her noggin.

'You? *You* do something about it? I don't think so, bucko. I'm more than capable of using a chainsaw!' Bella was indignant.

Will surveyed her faded pink drill shirt, worn Wranglers and battered Redback boots. 'I'm sure you are, Hells Bells, but seeing as the wood is in *my* paddock I reckon it's *my* right to use *my* chainsaw. Plus,' he added with a wicked grin, 'Maggie's chainsaw is in the repair shop. *My* repair shop, waiting for a new chain and bar.'

So Saturday afternoon saw Bella in a LandCruiser ute with Will, climbing up into the bush-laden mountains surrounding the Tindarra Valley.

I will not talk to him, I will not speak one little word! she childishly vowed to herself.

They drove for a while in silence, and then Will reached out and turned on the CD player. Taylor Swift came blasting through the surround-sound speaker system, singing her song 'Love Story'. She didn't dare look at Will while the song played out.

'So I'll cut the wood and you can stack it in the ute. Fair enough?' Will's voice brought Bella back to the Gippsland bush, as they both exited the vehicle.

She nodded and walked over to lean on a nearby tree while he sorted out his chainsaw. The afternoon sun beamed down hot in this protected slice of the forest, and the fallen branch Will planned to turn into firewood gleamed a ghostly white in the light.

She watched as he pulled his flanny shirt over his head. Then she quickly turned away as he inadvertently exposed a six-pack of solid muscle as his blue singlet made to go with the shirt. Grabbing at his singlet, Will yanked it back down to his waist, where red-gold hairs disappeared into his belted jeans. Bella forced her gaze to remain on the bush surrounding them, looking anywhere but at that gorgeous body she remembered so well.

Those hands, which just over two months ago had coveted her breasts and helped remove her remaining clothes, now moved to pump the fuel bulb and lift the choke on the saw, then pull the motor to life.

And then there was nothing to do but shift all the logs that Will cut, and stack them into the tray of the ute. It was monotonous enough to distract her from dangerous thoughts. She'd had the presence of mind to grab a pair of Maggie's old gardening gloves, and by halfway through the load she was happy she had; the rough-sawn timber would have made a mess of her city-softened hands.

But despite the hard work she was enjoying herself, finding muscles she hadn't worked for a very long time. She was surprised when Will finally shut off the saw, the sudden quiet startling her more than its constant roar.

'All done, Hells Bells. That should do you for a good while.'

Bella nodded and went to gather the last few logs lying on the ground.

'So are you going to speak to me *at all* today, or is this as good as it gets?' he asked as he loaded his chainsaw and fuel drum on top of the wood in the back of the ute.

'I'll talk if there is a need too,' said Bella with a snap.

'A need, ay?' repeated Will, as he moved to tie down the load.

'A need,' stated Bella as she grabbed the rope she was thrown. She tied it in a truckie's knot, her fingers only slightly hesitant as they worked to remember the moves. It was with a smile that she snapped the finished rope nice and tight across all the wood.

'I remembered after all this time,' she muttered to herself as she moved to get into the ute.

Of course you did, you goose! You can take the girl from the country, but not the country from the girl.

Since when did you become a bloody philosopher? Bella retorted mutely to Patty.

As the sun set, Will and Bella wound their way back down the mountain, the track curving around the hills as it gently took the rise and fall of the land. They drove past Will's upper bush paddocks at the end of the valley, then past Wes's old house sat tucked hard up against the river, up over the wooden bridge crossing the Tindarra River and along the gravel towards Maggie's place.

The Tindarra River moved at a sharp left-hand angle, and Bella could see Will's cream weatherboard house on the hill beyond Maggie's place, its painted shutters standing out. Down below his house was a large set of stockyards, which were bigger in expanse than his home, putting into context which was the more important. She could see the roof of the corrugated-iron shelter covering his modern cattle crush, now lit by a huge, glowing floodlight attached to a pole on a massive hayshed.

Will backed his ute up to the old water tank at Maggie's, which was lying on its side serving as a wood shed. He undid the tailgate and then moved to the cab as Bella got out. Hitting a button on the console of his ute, the tray tipped up silently on a hydraulic arm to deposit its load half-in and half-out of the drum.

'I'm impressed!' Bella couldn't help but exclaim. 'That's got to be better than having to stack it a second time round.'

Will smiled to himself and called out from the cab. 'It's nice to hear you've got a voice, Hells Bells.'

Bella frowned and kicked the ground.

'I'll be off. I don't suspect you're going to offer me a beer or a cuppa?' Will looked down at Bella's stony face. 'No, I didn't think so . . . I'll head off then.'

'Thanks, you know, for today,' Bella muttered.

'The pleasure was all mine,' came the dry reply.

Chapter 34

The days continued, without much to upset the ebb and flow. The weather did turn nasty, so Bella added collecting firewood to her list of morning chores. Mentally she thanked Will for his forethought, and she knew she should have probably got on the phone to him to verbalise it.

You've got the hots for him, came Patty's voice. *You've got the hots real bad!*

Bugger off! Bella admonished, as she reached for the phone. She rang her boss at the Department instead.

'Dave, I reckon I'm ready to go,' she told him.

'Beaudy, Hells Bells, you're a bloody ripper.' David Neille was all enthusiasm. 'Did I tell you how grateful I am for this?'

Bella laughed. 'Yes, Dave. Several times in fact.' Warmth flooded through her. It was so nice to be back among friends who knew and valued her work. It made her feel good about herself.

'I'd best email you a contact list and you can start setting up some meetings with the farmers. You'll need to liaise with the Landcare groups to organise times, venues and stuff. If you email the flyers you want sent out down here, I'll get the receptionist to print them up and send them out to the members. How's that sound?'

'Just great. I'm looking forward to it. But I've made a few changes to the format. I reckon we'll do two meetings for each group. We could do the big-picture stuff, like where are you now and where do you want to be, say, in five years, and the bridges, metaphorically speaking, we need to build to get there, on the first night. And then we'll pull it down to their specific farms and Landcare area on the second night and work out who, what, when, where and why. Is that okay? Can we afford to do that?'

'Sure, whatever you think will work best,' was the confident reply.

'I think this will be better for all concerned,' said an earnest Bella into the phone. 'Then the Department gets what it wants, but the farmers also get something to take away and plan with as well. It's a win–win situation, as Warren would say.'

'And just how is Warren?'

'He's fine. Well, at least I think he is,' said Bella. 'I haven't seen him for a couple of weeks.'

'And he's okay with you doing this? He's not worried about you being up there on your own?'

'I'm hardly on my own, Dave,' said Bella, dodging the first part of his question. 'Old Wes is just down the road. And there's Will O'Hara, of course.' She looked out the window at Will's glowing stockyard light. It came on automatically at dusk each evening and was a comforting presence during the long dark nights.

'Of course, of course. I'd forgotten about Will. Nice bloke, shame about his wife. I hear she's shacked up with some flash horse-breeder in New South Wales. Up the duff to him too, I heard.'

'Dave, you old gossip,' said Bella with a chuckle. She could just picture her boss, feet propped up on the big desk in front of him, chewing the end of his half-moon glasses.

'Anyway, I'd best get home, Bella. And I'm sure you'll need to get a fire going. It looks pretty bleak up in those mountains from down here.'

Bella looked out the window to the west. 'Yes, the rain has just started to blow in from up the valley. Can you email me that contact list tomorrow, so I can start organising meetings with some farmers?'

'Righto, I'll talk to you again soon.'

'And, Dave . . .'

'Yes?' came the fatherly voice down the phone.

'Thanks. Thanks for everything.'

'You're welcome, Hells Bells. Nightie, night.'

It was in a howling southerly wind that Bella rode out to check the farm the next morning. Even Turbo was loath to leave his kennel, the wind was so bitingly cold. Drizzle softly pattered down onto her broad-brimmed Akubra hat, which she'd pulled tight over her ears in an effort to keep it from being blown off. A Driza-bone covered the rest of her.

'C'mon, Turbs, I need the company,' Bella said to the dog as she dragged him whining to the motorbike. Lifting him up onto the carryall, she snapped on his chain and cranked over the bike's motor to get on her way. The poddy calves were huddled in their little shelter shed, piled on top of one another to keep warm. The chooks hadn't ventured from the chook house yet, and as Bella rode into the wind she didn't blame them.

She manoeuvred the bike carefully down the farm track. The rain overnight had made it a grease bowl. As they slipped and slid their way along, Turbo whined and tucked his head under her arm.

'You sook,' she said to the dog as she fondled his ears with her spare hand. 'Next thing you'll be in the house in front of the fire.' Turbo barked in agreement.

Suddenly, something caught her eye through the rain. She stopped the bike at the gate of the paddock and climbed off, leaving Turbo on the chain. He whined, wanting off, but she turned and shushed him instead. Opening and then shutting the gate latch, she quietly moved into the paddock and around the animals. Cows didn't mind the rain but they hated wind, and so were all huddled in the far corner, backs to the gale.

All except one.

The cow that had caught Bella's eye sat out on her own further down the paddock. As Bella quietly approached, the cow let out a bellow and swung her head around, ears pricked, eyes dull. Bella could see the problem straightaway. Poking from out her behind was a small sack of fluid and two tiny hoofed legs. The cow seemed to hunker down into herself and then let go with a convulsive thrust; the tiny legs barely moved. The cow had another go; this time the legs didn't move at all. And they should have, Bella knew.

'Oh shit,' she muttered into the rain. She needed to get the cow on her feet. After trying for a few minutes to no avail, she realised she had to get some help and fast or she'd lose both the cow and calf. Bella sprinted through the now-teeming rain to the bike, then gunned the engine and headed back to the house. Pounding up onto the verandah, she only took time to kick off her gumboots at the door. Striding through the cosy, fire-lit room, she ignored the water pouring off her coat and hat and grabbed Maggie's teledex from the drawer.

She tried old Wes first, but then remembered this was his day to go into Burrindal. Every third day he made the trip, during which he gathered the poddy-calf milk from a local dairy farmer for Maggie, along with any other supplies anyone along the Tindarra Road needed, plus the mail, and ended with a drink at the pub.

It would have to be Will then. Bugger it.

She tried his mobile first, knowing at this time of the morning he'd be out and about, regardless of the weather. She was rewarded on the third ring.

'Hello!' he shouted. She could hear loud bellows from a mob of cattle that were obviously milling around him. They sounded so close, she guessed he was down at his yards sorting out stock.

'Will, I need help!'

'Now there's a first.' The reply held a laugh.

Bella ignored him. 'I've got a cow down. She's trying to calve.'

Will sobered up immediately. 'Where is she?'

'Still in the paddock. I can't get her up on my own.'

'I'll just let these steers go, then I'll come straight down.'

The phone went clunk. Bella rocked back on her heels, surprised at how Will's voice made her feel: reassured, secure. It felt so nice not to have to deal with this alone.

Between the pair of them they got the cow up and moving down the track to Maggie's old tumbledown stockyards. They ran her into the simple, old-style crush and Bella heaved on the rusty bar to snap the headlock in place. While she waited for Will she'd filled a bucket with hot water and grabbed soap, lubricant and some calving chains she found on a nail in the shed, and had them waiting down by the crush.

Will stripped off to his singlet in the pouring rain, and pulled a long clear plastic glove from his pocket and drew it over his hand and arm.

'Didn't think Maggie would have any of these,' he said, nodding towards the glove. 'Right, we're all set. You hold her tail and I'm just going to see what the problem is. The little bloke's obviously stuck, so I'll try and push him back in and get him presented correctly. Then we can help her ease him back out again.'

Bella nodded, the movement causing a flood of water to gush off her hat. Will's hat lay squashed flat in the mud where he'd tossed it with his shirt.

Will squeezed some clear lubricant from the bottle at his feet and smeared it over his glove-covered arm. He gently inserted his fingers in around the little hooves and manoeuvred them back inside the birth canal. The cow let out a bellow as her body convulsed with a contraction on Will's arm.

'Christ!' he muttered, the upper part of his arm turning bright red as the contraction squeezed the shit out of his limb. Bella stood to one side, holding the tail out of the way, feeling useless.

The contraction eased, as did the agony on Will's face.

'Can I do anything?' asked Bella gently.

'Yeah, grab those chains and hook on the grips. You remember how?'

'Of course I remember, it hasn't been *that* long,' she said as she let go of the tail.

'Ouch! Shit!' gasped Will, as the cow whacked her poo-covered tail across his face.

'Sorry!' cried Bella as she quickly grabbed the tail again, trying to drag the bucket towards her with her spare hand and one foot.

'Just goes with the territory, I guess.' Will swiped at his face. Bella could see a dimple flit across a shit-daubed cheek, and felt her belly lurch.

You've really got it bad if you think he looks hot covered in cow shit and mud, girlfriend.

After a few minutes of pushing and poking around, Will drew the little feet out again. He grabbed the chains from the bucket one at a time with his spare hand, and looped them around the hooves, which were trying to make it out into the rain. He then hooked the handles to the chains.

'Now, you take one handle and I'll take the other, and when I say go, pull like hell, okay?'

Bella took the handle Will offered. As he eased his hand from the birth canal and stripped off his muck-covered glove, she finally let go of the tail again.

They both hunkered down low near the cow's arse, with Will standing behind Bella with the longer chain. He watched the cow closely until a contraction rippled her sides and then yelled, 'Now!'

Bella reefed downwards and back with all her might.

The little hooves started to move towards them.

'Again!' yelled Will, and they both pulled hard.

A muzzle appeared, followed by a pair of shoulders. Then the whole mucus and blood-covered bundle slid out frontwards, sending both Bella and Will onto their bums.

Bella fell into Will, landing in his crotch. The calf fell on the top of Bella's legs, two milk teeth protruding from the thick lips and a rubbery pink tongue flapping from the side of its mouth. The calf gave a high-pitched cry as Bella used her legs to push it off herself. The cow turned as best she could from the head-lock to look at the mess and lowed softly.

Bella lay there a moment, rain falling softly on her face, relishing the warmth of Will's lap, thinking how good it was to be touching him again.

Will was in trouble as he looked down on the ringlets of white-gold, all turned dark brown in the wet. She was lying on his knackers and his thoughts weren't living up to altar-boy standards. Laughter rumbled up from deep within his belly.

Bella flipped over onto her stomach and saw his face come into focus through her wet, tangled hair. His brown eyes oozed molasses, and the dimples danced on his mud- covered cheeks.

God, he was gorgeous. She convulsed into laughter too. Here they were, lying in a cattle race, with mud, blood, mucus and shit covering most of their bodies, and it felt so right to be here; in the stockyards, laughing with this man, in this place.

As the rain teemed around them, and Maggie's farm turned to mud and slush, they lay sodden and laughed.

The sudden, restless movements of the cow in the crush sobered them up. They untangled themselves and gently pulled the calf into a small side yard. Releasing the cow from the head-bale, they let her find and nuzzle her calf. And then in long, slow movements she started to lick the calf clean.

Will was washing his arms in the bucket with soap.

'You want a warm shower?' she asked, watching the soft back of his neck as he scrubbed.

'You going to be in it?'

She paused for a moment, then forced herself to stop considering it.

'No.' She wasn't a complete hussy, regardless of what he thought. And as far as he knew she was still engaged to Warren.

'Mmm, didn't think so.' Will fruitlessly tried to dry his arms on his wet flannie. An awkward silence fell as they both looked at anything but each other. Will was the first to break. 'I'll help you clean up here and then be on my way.'

'No, I'm right. I can do it,' said Bella as she leaned down to start piling all the things into the bucket at his feet.

'Okay.' He now seemed in a hurry to move on. 'I'll check back with you tonight, if you like. Just leave her in the yards with the little bloke for a while.'

Bella looked at him and the words came out of her mouth before she could stop them. 'Would you like to come for tea? Just tea, mind you,' she added quickly, lest he get the wrong idea. 'To say thanks . . . for helping me out.'

'What are you cooking, Hells Bells?' Will paused from gathering up his clothes; his grin was nice and slow.

Her tummy lurched again as she mentally chastised herself for being so flaming impetuous. 'Roast lamb,' she said with a tilt to her nose.

'You remember how to cook it, cowgirl?'

'Of course I can bloody cook it. Come tonight and I'll prove it!'

Chapter 35

Will arrived around five-thirty, just as it was getting dark. A soft blue-and-maroon Wrangler shirt wrapped around his broad, solid shoulders, fitting him snugly, and long muscled legs were encased in dark denim jeans.

'Bloody wet out there!' he exclaimed as he kicked off his gumboots and moved into Maggie's cosy little lounge with a brown paper bag in his hand. He offered it to Bella.

'They tell me red wine goes with lamb. I don't drink it myself, so I've also put in a rum.'

'Who told you about the red?' she asked politely as she took the bag and placed the contents on the table.

'Trin did actually.' His voice was bashful but proud all the same. 'I gave him a ring, because I wasn't sure.'

Bella looked at the label and smiled. 'How did you know this was my favourite?'

'Trin asked Caro. So I went into Burrindal, and the pub had it.' His tone was surprised but satisfied.

Bella was impressed. He'd driven all the way into town just to get her favourite wine? She was glad she'd gone to some trouble with dinner.

The table was set plainly, because she didn't want him to get any crazy ideas. She hadn't put candles out, but the lights from the generator were already dim, adding a soft-lit ambience to the room, accentuated by the country music crooning from the stereo. It was all too intimate as it was, so the candles stayed in their box.

She moved into the kitchen, busying herself with dishing up.

'I took a look down at the yards and they're empty. You put the cow and calf back in the paddock?' Will asked as he propped himself on a stool and leaned forward with a hand under his chin.

'Yep. She's taken to the calf all right. It looks like she's a good mum.' Bella smiled, remembering the thrill of watching the cow and her new baby wander out into the small house paddock. She'd helped a calf into the world. It made her feel good, like she had done something really worthwhile.

'No trouble?'

'Huh?' Bella brought herself back to Maggie's kitchen. 'Oh . . . no, they were fine. It's all good, I think.' She breezed past with two plates and motioned for Will to join her at the table.

Will moved from his stool to sit down for dinner. He poured her a glass of wine and passed it to her, then reached across the table towards her, raising his rum can. 'To the new mum and bub.' There was a pause and then he added with a grin, 'And a good morning's work.'

Bella smiled proudly as she leaned forward to chink her glass.

They had a lovely night. Steering clear of anything too personal, they reminisced and laughed over their childhoods, caught up on mutual acquaintances and friends.

'That was delicious, Bella,' Will said, as he finally pushed back his plate. 'You sure are Maggie's niece in more ways than one. She cooks a mean lamb roast too.'

He looked across at the dresser, where a picture of Hugh and Maggie sat in the centre. 'I did a bit of research. Did you know Hugh's Plain is named after Uncle Hugh? He got stuck up there one day and had to be rescued.'

Bella's face flushed with embarrassment. Just saying the name of that plain brought back memories she'd rather forget. Or would she?

'Really? How interesting.' Bella grasped for a way to change the subject. 'I love that photo of my mum and dad.'

Will walked over and picked it up. Her parents were beaming into the camera. Francine was in her wheelchair, Frank kneeling down beside her. Justin's kids, Bec, Joel and Ryder, had decorated the chair with streamers and balloons for a birthday party last year. Bella hadn't made it – Warren had a corporate function that she just *had* to attend.

'Your mother is amazing, so resilient and strong. I don't know if I could have coped and been so gracious about it, if that had happened to me.'

'I think she's just grateful she didn't die,' said Bella. 'She was expected to, you know, which is what keeps her going. She's still here for a reason. She says it's to drive Dad mad.'

Will laughed quietly. 'They're wonderful people, Bella. You should be very proud.'

Bella couldn't answer. He was right.

Will moved slowly to his left and picked up another frame.

It was the tumbleweed photo: Bella and Patty dancing crazily in the afternoon sun somewhere outside Tamworth before the world had gone so very wrong.

'I love that one. We were so happy that day, just ecstatic to be coming home.'

'I love it too,' agreed Will, looking intently at the picture, his voice wistful. 'I have a copy on my bedside table.' When he glanced up at Bella, she could see tears swimming in his dark eyes, and she knew from his expression that the tears weren't for Patty alone.

Bella smiled sadly, thinking of how their lives were so intertwined. 'I usually have one by my bed as well.'

'Dad and Mum have photos of Patty everywhere. And I mean *everywhere*.' Will pulled a frustrated face. 'They really lost the plot after she died. Just couldn't get their heads around the fact she was gone. Dad, in particular. Patty was his mate and he'd taught her everything she knew. He couldn't stand to be out here at the farm anymore, staring at reminders of the things they used to do together.'

Bella stayed silent, willing him to go on.

Will sighed and ran his hand through his hair. 'So, they left the place. Just got up one day and walked out. Bought a house in town. Dad's a broken old man. Mum's not much better.' He sounded dejected.

'They lost their only daughter, Will.'

'Yes, but they still have a son.' He shrugged, then walked back to the table and sat down. 'I'm okay about it now. But I couldn't ever be a father, seeing the pain and grief the death of a child can bring on its parents.' He frowned. 'And then there's the other siblings too. The death of a brother or sister is hard on them as well.'

Bella sat stunned as his voice dissolved into the silence of the room. Outside, down at the river, a chorus of frogs thrummed constantly, relentlessly, like the thoughts flowing through her mind. She had been so caught up in her own grief and her own life that she had no idea Patty's death had caused such ongoing devastation to the O'Hara family. The pain was clearly still raw for them all, eight years after Patty's death. She looked at Will and felt a pain in her chest. He would have made a wonderful father.

'Anyway,' said Will, 'I think Mum's starting to get out a bit now. She's joined the cemetery trust and is helping to plan some new rose garden for people who have lost children. Dad potters around his yard, and has the odd bet on a horse. They've leased the station to me and I run my place and theirs as one on my own. It's probably better without Dad there anyway. He'd be trying to tell me what to do. Just like my sister used to.'

'I remember when Mum and I would pick Patty up for kinder, on the days Narree and Burrindal kinders played together,' reminisced Bella, trying to force things onto a lighter note. At the table she slowly started to stack the used plates. 'She never wanted to go, was always running away on your mum. She was more interested in playing the fool or mucking around on the farm with your dad than being stuck inside listening to old Mrs March.'

Will watched as Bella moved the dishes to the sink. 'Yeah, could be a little shit, that's for sure. Mum couldn't handle and Dad only sometimes, when she wasn't being stubbor for some reason Patty used to listen to me. I don't know

'She knew you'd just tan her hide if she didn't.' Bella as she dumped the load onto the stainless steel drain that or take away her horse.' She opened the d slow-combustion stove.

Will looked surprised. 'What – sweets too? You really haven't forgotten how to cook, Hells Bells. I thought you might have in that big, bad city.' Will pushed back from the table and stretched out his long legs. 'I've heard they're building units down there without kitchens, just a microwave and fridge. How on earth can they do it?'

Bella smiled into the stove as she grasped hold of the hot apple pie, made by Sara Lee. 'You eat out all the time. In Warren's world, it's nothing to throw away a hundred bucks just on lunch.' She dragged the pie out and put it on the bench to cool.

'Shit!' exclaimed Will. 'That's what I spend on food for a *week*! They must have more money than sense.'

Bella nodded with a smile. As Will reached over her to grab a tea towel off a hook, she felt the brush of his arm, caught a whiff of his scent. Musky and toe-curlingly male.

You're in trou-ble! sang the voice in her head.

'Bugger off.'

'I beg your pardon?' said Will, one eyebrow raised, managing look dangerously sexy and challenging at the same time.

'. No! Not you. Something's running around inside my groaned inwardly. Even to her, it sounded a piss-poor

e to take a look?' Will moved in closer, which f her composure right outside into Turbo's

ve just forget the dishes? I'll do them ets.'

f that.' Will wasn't looking at

op and skirted wide around d bowls as she went past. She

made her way to the table, where she put four foot of wood between them. Safety. But how long would that last?

Surprisingly, Will took the hint. There was no more innuendo as he set about digging for details on her former life in the city. After a while Bella found herself relaxing, answering his questions, asking a few of her own. About the farm, his ideas for its expansion, all the while steering clear of any mention of his ex-wife.

The man engaged her on so many levels. He seemed to turn his thoughts and interests to anything and everything. His intellect was bright and broad. He could talk seriously and with authority about the precariousness of the water situation across Australia, then in the next breath be laughing and telling a tale about Janey's dog Angus and the trouble he caused in town.

Bella found herself transfixed by his face and easy manner. They hadn't had the chance to enjoy this sort of time together the first time round. And she'd forgotten that being around Will when he was relaxed was so enjoyable.

After lingering over sweets they moved to the fire, Will bringing the bottle of wine and his rum, Bella careful to sit on Maggie's old, battered and *single* leather chair. Will reached out to refill her near-empty wine glass.

'Oh no, no more.' She put her hand over the glass. 'It's lovely, thank you. But if I have more I'll be anybody's.' She immediately cursed herself. And they'd been doing so well. She flicked a look at Will.

They held each other's gaze for seconds that dragged out like minutes and Bella's heart tripped into fast beat. Flustered, she broke eye contact, jumping up to play at stoking the fire.

Will watched her move in front of the flames, wine glass in one hand, poker in the other. Tonight her ringlets floated seductively from her shoulders and her face shone from the recent doses of fresh air and sun. She wore a soft cotton shirt, her buxom bosom nestling softly within its folds. Well-washed denim clung to her long, slim legs and pink explorer socks peeped out from under her cuffs.

She seemed to glow more than usual, standing in the bright firelight. A trick of his imagination, he reasoned to himself. Isabella Vermaelon was a temptress who was possibly still engaged to another man. Hands off, bucko. He forced his body to sit alone on the hard vinyl couch. She might not be wearing the bloke's ring, but he was still out there somewhere.

Chapter 36

'What do you mean I'm pregnant? Unless things have changed, you actually have to have sex to get pregnant!'

Dr Weir waved the disk holding the pink plus sign. 'It's definitely a plus, my dear, so you must have had sex with someone.'

Bella closed her eyes, disbelief flooding her mind. Quickly she tried to calculate how many months she'd been at Maggie's. Over two. Nearly three, maybe?

'How many weeks am I?' she managed to squeak.

Dr Weir leaned back in his well-creased leather chair, pulled his half-moon glasses from his nose and started to polish them with his jumper.

'Well, I can give you an idea now by feeling your uterus and so forth but for a concrete answer you'll need to have an ultrasound down in Narree. Do you remember when your last period was?'

Bella valiantly tried to put her brain in gear to think back over the past couple of months. Her mind was a total blank. She couldn't get past the words 'You're pregnant.'

'The father can attend the ultrasound too, you know.'

'Whose father?'

Dr Weir leaned forward, placed his glasses back on his nose and peered with concern into Bella's pale face.

'The *baby's* father,' he said with gentle concern. 'Bella . . . um, forgive me for asking but, you *do* know who the father of your baby is, don't you?'

Bella attempted to pull herself together.

'Yes . . . yes, of course I do,' she said with haste. 'I'm engaged to him.' One little white lie wouldn't hurt in these circumstances. 'I'm just . . . well . . . shocked. Yes, I'm shocked. I'm on the pill, you know, and it's just . . . We weren't expecting it so soon.' Bella tried to smile brightly.

'Yes, well the pill isn't infallible, my dear. There are some instances where accidents do happen, people have been caught out, especially if you've been ill. The pill isn't reliable then and you should use another form of contraception just to be on the safe side.'

Bella thought back to the gastro bug she had suffered in Melbourne, the week before Caro's wedding, all those months ago. Alarm bells rang, adding to her dismay.

Bella slid off her chair and strode to the bed in the corner of the room. 'Well, maybe you'd better check just how far along *you* think I am. That's if you're *sure* I'm actually pregnant.' She couldn't quite choke off the slightly pleading note to her voice.

'My dear, I'm as sure of your pregnancy as I am of my wife's intention to do the flowers for Sunday-morning church.' Dr Weir's tone was wry.

Bella knew then there was no going back. Dr Weir's wife Julia had arranged the church flowers for the last twenty years. Annual holidays in the Weir family were scheduled from Monday to Saturday, returning in time for church on Sunday – without fail. This pregnancy was for real.

It was some time later that Dr Weir finally moved from the bedside to strip the latex gloves from his hands. Dropping them into the bagged rubbish bin he said, 'Well, Bella, you are in fine health and your baby seems fine too. A good strong heartbeat on the little fellow, although we'll know more once you've had the ultrasound.'

'And how far along do you think I might be?' Bella asked as she sat up, swinging her legs over the side of the bed and wincing slightly. The internal examination had been very uncomfortable.

The doctor walked to his desk, pulled a form from a document holder and started writing.

'Dr Weir, how far along do you think I might be?' Bella queried again, her voice squeaking slightly with anxiety.

Dr Weir looked up from his writing. 'How long?' he repeated back at her.

'*Yes*,' said Bella more forcefully. 'How pregnant am I?

'Oh, about twenty weeks or so, my dear. It's a wonder you hadn't noticed any changes to your body, but then again first baby and all and being so fit. You young girls of today,' he went on. 'Too busy running around enjoying life to notice a thing like pregnancy, I expect.' He kept on scribbling. 'Here you go, the form for your ultrasound, my dear. Just ring the hospital and they'll make you an appointment. I think you can take a video tape in and they'll record it for you too. Jolly good idea if the father can't get there. Melbourne chap I expect, is he?' He went on without waiting for Bella's reply. 'Best come back and see me in another four weeks and we'll set up the antenatal visits then. That's of course if you intend to continue staying out at your Aunty Maggie's.'

'Why wouldn't I?' asked Bella in surprise.

'Nothing, dear. I just thought the father might want you and the little one under a flash Melbourne doctor's watchful eyes.'

Dr Weir could tell he'd said the wrong thing from Bella's affronted face.

'Ah . . . yes . . . right,' he blustered, walking towards the door. 'Organise it all with Julia out front. That's unless there are any complications.'

'Complications?' repeated Bella faintly, wondering what else she had to worry about.

'Yes, complications. Then you'll have to go to Narree. But that's for me to worry about and I'm sure with a healthy country girl like you, it'll all be fine. I'll see you in four weeks, shall I?' Dr Weir opened the door to the waiting room. 'Be sure to pass on my congratulations to the father, won't you?' he said as Bella walked on rubbery legs to the doorway.

'Yes . . . yes, of course.'

Dr Weir's wife Julia was waiting behind the desk in the waiting room, poised like a pit bull ready to strike.

'Set up another visit for Isabella in four weeks' time, won't you, my dear,' he murmured quietly, as he passed the file over, seemingly unaware his whisper had carried across the room. A gasp of surprise arose from the other woman sitting in the waiting room. Mildred Vincent-Prowse.

Bella could feel herself blushing. Mildred's inquisitive gaze bored into her back as she turned to face the formidable Julia on the other side of the desk. She could almost feel Prudence's mother moving her chair forward to earwig at the conversation that was about to take place. The bloody old gossip.

'So, that'll be an antenatal in four weeks,' said Julia with bright interest, after perusing the note on top of the file.

'Yes,' said Bella, squaring her shoulders and mentally steeling herself for what was to come.

Julia made an impressive show of flicking through the appointment book while obviously searching for her next probing question.

'Congratulations, my dear. And your fiancé . . .?' she said.

'. . . will be very happy with the news,' finished Bella as she leaned over the desk and pointed to an empty block in the book resting between them. 'That'll do, thanks, Julia. I'll see you then.' She strode from the room quickly, trying to ignore the two pairs of eyes watching her avidly. She needed distance and space. The door slammed shut behind her and leaning against the red brick wall of the building she slowly exhaled and fought to hold back the tears.

Gradually, with a few deep breaths, she pulled herself together. Then in a mutter which she hoped was only heard by the black-and-white mudlarks swooping madly at their reflections in the surgery window: 'The whole problem is, Mrs Weir, I'm not sure if my *ex*-fiancé *is* the father!'

For the next few weeks Bella buried herself in her work, trying to put the pregnancy out of her mind. She organised Landcare meetings across the area, drew up flyers and sent them off to her boss for printing and distribution. She worried over her rusty facilitation techniques and fussed over her meeting-planning notes. But at random moments the realisation she was actually having a baby would hit her again with a jolt. She tired easily, and needed a nanna nap after lunch to get through the rest of the day. Her belly was rounding out and the butterfly movements inside her tummy were becoming stronger. They caught her unawares at the most inopportune moments, reminding her of the little person growing inside her.

She found a spare day and drove herself to Narree for the ultrasound Dr Weir had requested. And it was there that she came face to face with her future. In her belly. She was going to give birth to a new life.

She was amazed, as she sat in the ute after the scan, staring at the little black-and-white photo. The blurs and blobs, which vaguely outlined the shape of the body, showed a little baby with an arm in the air like it was waving.

'Hello, Mum!' it seemed to say.

'Hello, little one,' she whispered back as she gently put the photo in her purse. Humming quietly, she drove out the hospital gateway, her mind already on how she would manage it all.

Her first thought was that she was *not* going back to Warren. She needed more than just playing second fiddle in someone else's band. She certainly didn't desire to be the trophy wife; she wanted a life for herself.

Secondly, she didn't want to live in the city. She was a country girl. Her baby would not be brought up in a concrete jungle, with no paddocks to run, play and laugh in. Bella knew she could go home to Merinda, or Maggie would have her up here. But a better plan was to get a place of her own somewhere close to her family; she was sure they'd help her cope. Much better to be a happy single mum in the country than a miserable married one living in the big smoke.

As she pulled the ute up in front of a women's clothes shop that stocked maternity wear, her thoughts turned to how she would support herself and the baby. She could get more contract work and operate from home; she knew her qualifications were good for that. And the Landcare work she was doing was working out well, so that should stand her in excellent stead.

Yep, Bella decided, she'd cope – her and the little one. She wondered whether it was a girl or a boy.

Chapter 37

Warren appeared early one Friday evening, just as Bella was coming up from the paddocks where she'd been fixing a leaking stock trough.

'Oh shit!' she muttered to Turbo as she watched his Mercedes turn into the drive. 'Here comes trouble. Just when life was getting peaceful.' Bella parked the motorbike, unchained Turbo from the back carryall and went to meet her ex-fiancé at the garden gate.

'How did you find me?' was her opening line, as Warren slowly got out of the car.

'I just rang the shop. A young lass called Shelley told me where you were.'

At that moment an old Land Rover rumbled to a halt behind Warren's car.

Turbo went nuts with excitement and raced to piss on the leg that appeared. A boot came flying from the cab, sending Turbs rolling across the grass.

'Get out, you little bugger,' came a gruff elderly voice as Wes Ogilvie exited the cab and walked over to Bella and Warren.

Standing just over five-foot-six, he nearly met Bella eye to eye. His strides were held up with blue baling twine, and a saggy shirt strained across his protruding stomach. Stains marked the place where his belly button would have sat if you could find it. Bella could make out tomato sauce, greasy butter and Vegemite.

Warren looked the old bloke over with apparent disgust.

'Gidday, Hells Bells,' drawled Wes. 'Brought you some milk for them poddy calves. The mail's 'ere too if you want it. Gidday . . .?' He nodded to Warren, expecting to be introduced.

'Oh, Wes, this is Warren. Warren, Wes lives down the road.'

Wes went to put out his hand, but then stopped as he looked at the dirt covering his palm. He spat into it before rubbing it down the side of his strides, then had another go, thrusting it towards Warren. 'How do ya do?' He smiled a gummy grin and Bella realised with a gasp that he'd left his teeth behind . . . again.

Warren gingerly grasped the tips of the old man's fingers and then retreated. Wes looked him and then the shiny Mercedes over in disgust. 'Don't they know how to shake a man's hand properly in the city?'

'Yes, they do have some funny ways, Wes,' Bella broke in quickly before Warren had time to answer. She guided the old man to his Land Rover, grabbed the drum of milk out of the back and took the bundle of mail Wes held out to her. Turbo had slunk around her heels, and he took a last dive at Wes's leg.

'Get out, ya mongrel bastard!' The boot flew again but missed its target. Turbs moved fast when Wes was around.

'See ya, Hells Bells. I'll catch you again in a few days. There's a postcard from ya folks in the mail. Sounds like things are goin' bonza.' He revved up his old ute and slung out of the drive.

Bella walked over to Warren, who was still standing by the gate with a horrified look on his face.

'You know, he's probably the richest man in Tindarra. Probably all of Burrindal too.' Bella watched as Warren stood up straighter, a gleam coming to his eye as he tracked the Land Rover going down the road. 'Of course, it's all in land. Wes reckons you can't go wrong with land. Not like shares, debentures or global investments.' She widened her eyes in innocence.

Warren gave a very English 'Hrruph,' and walked to the back of his car. He pulled a leather suitcase from the boot.

Bella looked at the case with dismay. 'You're staying here?'

'Well, of course, Bella. You *are* my fiancée, for heaven's sake!'

'That wasn't what I said in the note I left you.'

'No,' agreed Warren, a placatory hand in the air. 'But now you've had your little fling in the bush, I thought you'd be ready to come back home with me.' He beamed.

Then, for the first time, he seemed to take in what she was wearing and the wrench she was wielding in her fist. His expression became slightly unsure.

Covering her sky-blue cotton drill shirt were fine splats of mud, and she was soaking wet from her waist to her toes. The leaking pipeline that supplied water to the trough down near the river pump hadn't wanted to play ball, but she'd persevered and won the battle. She'd cut out the section that leaked and found two joiners in the shed. It might have taken her most of the afternoon but they'd been installed and she was damned proud. She'd done it all by herself!

And now here was Warren suggesting she come back and be a decorative feature hanging from his arm.

No way, José! Not for this little black duck, said Patty's voice inside her head.

Bella turned and walked off towards the house with Warren following closely behind. She climbed the steps to the verandah and then turned back to the man on her heels. 'You can stay in Maggie's front room, but when you leave, it'll be on your own. I'm not coming back.'

'You really plan to stay *here*?' Warren said, throwing his free arm around to encompass all the space, and the mountains hunched in the night's shadow with eucalypts on their slopes. 'Out in the boondocks, going no place? I thought more of you, Bella, I really, truly did. I thought you had ambition and drive, a passion to make it big . . . with me.' He sounded incredulous.

Bella stood silent and looked at him. She wondered how on earth she could have thought herself in love with this man. He just didn't get it. And he never would. He didn't see the bush as freedom, the room to breathe and live a healthy, wholesome life. He saw it as chains and shackles, a road to nowhere, the death of all aspiration.

'I'm staying here, Warren.'

He lifted his head slightly in challenge. 'I'm not moving to the bush.' The final word was twisted in abhorrence and he took a step back.

'I'm not asking you to,' was her gentle but firm reply.

'So, what now? Are we engaged or not?'

'No. We're not. I'm sorry.'

Warren ran his hand through his hair. He lifted his face and stared hard out at the shadowed hilltops then down at the verandah boards, shoving his leather-clad toe into the worn and frayed coir mat outside the door.

'Right. Well then. I guess it's over.' Warren took a moment and then looked up. Bella was shocked to see his eyes were glassy. 'I think I'll go to bed now. Obviously I'll not stay long.'

The next day dawned clear and Bella was out of the house before breakfast. She didn't want to face Warren after the stand-off last night. He'd come to the kitchen to grab a cup of coffee, declined her offer of a meal before stating he wished to catch up with Trinity.

'I have a brilliant business proposition for him. How long will it take me to get to Ben Bullen Hills from here?'

'An hour or so through the bush, but I'm not sure you'd want to travel those rough tracks in the Merc,' said Bella, with a doubtful shake of her head. 'Trin and Caro will be down in Burrindal on Sunday for the rodeo.' She mentally slapped her forehead. Damn it! Why did she say *that*?

'Good. I'll stay until then.'

And that was the last she saw of him for the evening, although she heard the clacking of a keyboard behind the closed door for half the night.

When Bella finally made it back to the house after checking every other stock trough on the property for leaks, it was lunch-time. Warren still hadn't appeared in the warm, homey kitchen. Worried, she peeked into the front room to see him snoring peacefully on top of the fully made-up bed. The screen on his open laptop blinked blindly. She nudged the mouse sideways and an email flashed onto the screen.

Just loved our time at the Versace. When's our next opportunity for a 'takeover bid'?

Larissa xo

Warren's oh-so-capable assistant.

The worst thing was Bella didn't feel a thing. They were welcome to each other. How wonderful that freedom was. She didn't owe the bastard a jot.

The afternoon passed peacefully as Bella worked on her Landcare -facilitation notes. She was making a casserole for their tea when he finally emerged from his room. Looking cool and calm, he stood in a Lacoste shirt and pressed slacks, a picture of urbanity in an otherwise functional country kitchen.

The kettle on the old combustion stove hissed merrily.

'Would you like a cuppa?' she asked.

'That would be nice,' he replied formally as he took a seat on the kitchen stool.

Bella couldn't help but compare him to the last man who'd sat on that seat. Warren was prim, uncomfortable and unsure, whereas Will had filled in the space contentedly and looked like he belonged there.

Warren crossed one knee over the other and then, swelling his chest as he spoke, said, 'I haven't slept all day, you know. I've been working on my laptop.'

For the first time, Bella felt sorry for him, that he thought he had to justify his time spent on the weekend.

'I'm well aware of that, Warren; I could hear the keys clicking all afternoon.' Bella didn't mind lying either.

She moved around the kitchen to make his coffee as he liked it: strong, straight black with two sugars.

'I'll just go lock up the chooks and feed the dog, and then I'll serve our tea. Is casserole on toast okay?'

'Perfectly.'

And they lapsed back into an uncomfortable silence.

It wasn't until later, when they were in front of the fire, that she gathered the courage to say what she had to say. Tea was finished but the dishes were still in the sink. Warren wouldn't have known how to wash and dry anyway, so she hadn't bothered to start. He obviously presumed there was a dishwasher hidden somewhere.

'There was something else I needed to talk to you about,' Bella said as she carefully sipped her tea, aware even now of the gathering swell of her belly.

Warren was checking out Maggie's bookcase, his nose scrunched in dismay. 'I can't believe the number of trashy novels your aunt has on this shelf.'

'I'm pregnant, Warren,' Bella stated in a matter-of-fact voice. 'I'm having our baby.' She stood and waited for his reaction.

Warren went still. He replaced the book very carefully on the bookshelf and slowly turned around. His expression changed from one of shock to one of anger.

'Well . . . are you going to say anything?' she asked, uncomfortable with the silence that was stretching out across the room.

Warren moved to the couch and sank his body down into the cushions. He stretched out his legs, his face finally settling into a frown.

'I am going to say five words, Bella. It. Is. Not. My. Baby.'

'What do you mean it's not your baby?' Bella burst out, indignation and guilt warring from within. What did he know?

'I can't have children,' Warren stated, as he looked at his manicured nails.

'What?'

'I can't have children,' he said again, putting down his hand to stare directly into her face.

'I heard you the first bloody time! What do you *mean* you can't have kids?'

'I've had a vasectomy,' said Warren flatly, dragging a cushion from the end of the couch to put behind his back. 'I had it done when I was going out with my old girlfriend Diana. Before I met you.'

'Why didn't you tell me?' demanded Bella. 'We were going to get married, for heaven's sake!'

'It didn't come up.' He had the grace to look slightly discomforted.

'*It didn't come up!*' She got up in agitation and walked towards the sliding door, trying to get hold of herself. A few minutes passed, and then in a quietly controlled voice, she said: 'Just when were you planning to tell me?'

'Oh . . . I don't know,' said Warren as he stood too and started to pace the old wooden floor, his Windsor Smith leather shoes squeaking as they flexed over the boards. 'I just didn't think it was relevant.' He stopped walking and turned to explain. 'When were we going to have time to have kids? What with my career and everything, kids just didn't fit in.' His moved back towards the safety of the couch. 'I made that decision years ago.'

'*Your* career? *Your* decision?' repeated Bella, as she looked out the glass door at the Tindarra Mountains. Tears started to run down her cheeks. 'But I wanted kids, Warren,' she said.

He looked up towards the ceiling. 'I know. And that's why I didn't want to tell you. I was frightened you'd leave me.'

'But these things can be reversed, can't they?'

'Yes they can, but there's only a fifty–fifty chance of it working.' Warren sat down again and drummed his fingers on the arm of the couch. He pulled at a frayed thread for a few moments before giving up. 'But, Bella, I don't want to have it reversed. That's why I had the procedure done in the first place. I don't *want* children.'

'But . . . I do!'

'It sounds like you're getting what you want then.' His tone was wry, as he turned his head up to the ceiling again, absently counting the cracks in the plaster overhead. 'Who's the father, anyway?'

He didn't get an answer in return.

'Mmm . . . well . . . that's it, I guess.' He gave up on the cracks and yawned widely, his perfect orthodontic teeth closing with a snap. 'I'm off to bed. I'll call into that damned rodeo you're going to tomorrow afternoon.' He visibly shuddered before going on. 'I'll catch up with Trinity and then head back to Melbourne.'

He got up off the couch and faced Bella. She had swiped the tears from her face with her flannelette shirt sleeve and now stood red-eyed but proud and defiant, despite feeling like shit.

'Something's different about you, Bella, something I can't put my finger on. You've changed.'

Bella lifted her chin, lapis eyes flashing a challenge. 'I haven't changed, Warren, not at all. I'm just becoming myself.'

'Right.' Warren looked totally out of his depth. 'Anyhow, it doesn't matter anymore, does it? Goodnight, Bella.' As he walked past her, Warren hesitated before reaching out a hand.

He touched her cheek with his fingertips, regret racing across his face. She shied from his stroke and turned to the mountains, which she could see standing guard in the moonlight through the glass.

She stood there long after he had gone. Arms wrapped around her belly, cradling the new life growing inside, she tried to work out how she felt.

If Warren wasn't the baby's father, then Will was. And she knew exactly what *he* thought about fatherhood. His words the night of their dinner together came back to her loud and clear. '*But I couldn't ever be a father, seeing the pain and grief the death of a child can bring on their parents.*'

How was it that the two men who could have fathered her baby didn't want to have children?

But on the tail of that thought came another realisation: at least she didn't have to return to Warren – a man she didn't love – or to a city she couldn't abide and a life that wasn't her own.

Even if he was the father, you didn't have to go back there. You can make it on your own, Hells Bells, you and the bub alone.

I know, she whispered back to Patty. I'm just relieved it's done. It's all over with Warren and I have no ties to him. No ties at all.

Chapter 38

The 'Tearin' Down the Mountain' ute nosed its way into Maggie's yard the next morning, and Shelley Lukey piled out of the passenger seat. Macca climbed from the driver's side and then a tall, auburn-haired female slid onto the ground beside him.

'Hi, Bella!' called Shelley through the open lounge window, waving with vigour.

Bella waved meekly in return. She had been trying to get rid of Warren for the last half-hour, and Jelly Bean Lukey was *not* what she needed right now. She had been reminding Warren that he hated rodeos, but he was determined to see Trinity before he headed home. He moved to the window, taking in the rotund little figure.

'Who's that?' asked Warren. 'And that ... and that?' He pointed at the other two.

'You remember my cousin Macca, from Trin and Caro's wedding? The girl in pink is Shelley; she was at the wedding too. And the third one? I'll be buggered if I know.'

Bella left Warren alone in the house and ran down the path towards her cousin. 'Macca, how the bloody hell are you? Where did you come from?' She threw herself into his arms. 'When did you get in from Mount Isa?'

'Whoa, whoa, whoa!' Macca roared back, catching up to his cousin and trying to turn her around with equal glee. 'Shit, you've got heavy, you big heifer, what's Maggie left you to graze on? You'll turn into a fat cow!'

Bella whacked him over the arm. 'Put me down, you big oaf! And I'll have you know, I'm cooking for myself. What are you doing back?'

'Now that's no way to talk to your dearest, darling cousin, who you haven't seen for months!' Macca put Bella gently on her feet and reached back to draw in the red-headed girl at his side.

'Bella, meet my fiancée, Sarah. Sarah, this is Hells Bells. But she's not as mean as she looks, mind you, her bark's worse than her bite!'

'Who are you referring to, Sarah or me?' Bella replied cheekily, as she stuck out her hand to the girl. 'Pleased to meet you.'

Then she suddenly realised what Macca had said. 'Did you say *fiancée*?'

Shelley started to giggle.

'Yep, that's what I said,' replied Macca, as he cuddled Sarah into his side. 'That's why I've come home, for Sarah to meet the family. But I made sure I had a ring on her finger before I came anywhere near you mad bastards down here.'

'Who are you calling a mad bastard, you big, ugly shit?' asked Bella, with a wide grin.

'Probably me,' said a new voice. Will O'Hara walked into the circle, to stand next to Shelley.

'I didn't hear you pull up.' Bella was taken aback to see him standing there.

'I walked.'

And he'd obviously noted the Merc in the drive and knew Warren was here.

Bella pulled her thoughts back to her cousin standing there with his intended bride. 'Well, congratulations to you both,' she said, giving them each a hug. She took Sarah's arm to lead her away – far, far away from where Will stood still staring at her with a shuttered look on his face.

'Come with me, Sarah, and we'll grab everyone a drink before we head to the rodeo. The beer fridge is on the verandah. You can tell me how you met Macca. Are you *really* sure you want to marry that boofhead?'

A round of drinks later with no sign of Warren appearing from the house, Bella finally said a proper hello to Shelley. In all the excitement of seeing her cousin and hearing his news, she'd been rude and wanted to make up for it, so she sat on the ute tray beside the younger girl and enquired about her baby and the joys of new motherhood.

'It's hard. I never thought it would be so difficult. But then the baby smiles up at you and you forget the sore and leaking boobs, nights without sleep and a pudding baby belly you've got to somehow get rid of while being on call twenty-four-seven.

And then there's Joe. He wants his bit of you too and somehow you have to find the energy. It's hard,' she said again with a sad smile.

Bella felt for the girl. Things obviously weren't as she had expected. 'But anyway, everyone's pitching in to help.' Shelley seemed to force her tone to sound bright. 'Mum and Dad said they'd have the bub for the morning. You know, just so I could get out on my own for a while. So here I am! Macca and Sarah offered to give me a lift seeing they were coming out anyway to visit you and Will. Joe and me are heading to the rodeo this arvie too.'

Bella realised how Shelley had rolled her name in with Will's. They ran together nicely, 'Will and Bella', 'Bella and Will'. She shook her head and forced her attention back to Shelley, who had uncharacteristically lowered her voice.

'So you're expecting a baby too?' Shelley whispered.

'How did *you* find out?'

'Oh, Mildred Vincent-Prowse came in the store yesterday morning. She was telling all and sundry about your wicked ways!' Shelley quietly chuckled while shooting a furtive look in Will's direction.

He was talking to Macca and taking no notice of the girls.

Shelley grinned conspiratorially at Bella. 'I told her to put a sock in it. *She* can bloody well talk. Look at her daughter!'

'You didn't?' Bella looked at Shelley with admiration.

'Yes I did. And I told her at least you're engaged!' Shelley paused for a second and then went on. 'Not like her bloody daughter, who's just shacked up with a nob after pissing off on a *husband*, a hunky one at that!' Shelley glanced across at Will again.

'So, what happened then?' asked Bella, astounded. Mildred was a customer, for heaven's sake.

'She turned tail and ran. Bloody old bat. I'm sick of gossiping crones like her. The bush telegraph is the worst thing about living in this place. Although I guess if Joe was ever *thinking* of having an affair, I'd know about it before he did.' Shelley giggled.

Bella put her arm around the girl's shoulder. 'Thanks for sticking up for me, Shell. It really means a lot.'

'Oh, that's okay,' said Shelley, with a blush staining her apple cheeks. 'I like you, Bella. I always have . . . Well . . . I mean, I never actually knew you but I'd heard all about you . . . and I guess I liked what I heard. You and Patty O'Hara were kinda my role models. I always wished I had the gumption to be as strong, independent and free, like you two.'

Strong? Independent? Free? Good Lord, what next? Bella gave Shelley's shoulders a comforting squeeze. 'Oh, Shelley, you're doing just fine.'

In Bella's mind Patty's voice came through loud and clear. *Role models, hey? Next thing, they'll be saying I'm a bloody saint!*

'Anyways,' said Shelley, raising her voice back to its normal level. 'The Merc belong to your fiancé, does it? He rang the shop, you know, to see where you were. I told him but then after he hung up I wondered if I'd done the right thing?' Bella looked at Shelley, whose freckled features still glowed red. 'I sometimes go on a bit much, Joe tells me, you see. Mouth just runs away with me and . . . well . . . I get a bit lonely, I guess.'

Bella didn't have the heart to reproach the girl. 'No, it was fine. Just a misunderstanding between two people who should have known better.' She patted Shelley's knee. 'He's not my fiancé anymore, by the way . . . Oh, that's okay!' she rushed on at the girl's distraught face. 'We aren't suited to each other. He wants one thing, I want something else. He's going home after the rodeo.'

Will looked up from his beer. She hadn't realised he was now listening. He stared questioningly at her over Shelley's head, then glanced towards the house as the screen door banged open.

The man in question appeared from the dark confines of Maggie's home, and Bella was forced to introduce him.

'Warren, do you remember my cousin Macca? This is his fiancée Sarah, and this is Shelley, who I believe you've spoken to at the shop.' Bella congratulated herself. She did that well. Not one ounce of recrimination. She just had to get through the next bit. Forcing her voice to sound neutral, although painfully aware it came out slightly breathless, she said, 'And this is my neighbour, Will O'Hara. He lives just down the track.'

Warren dismissed the first three with a brief glance, homing in on the rugged man Bella had just introduced. He was leaning slightly to the right, his hand clasped around a green can of beer.

'Gidday,' said Will in a deep voice. His tone was clear. He didn't care either way whether he scrubbed up or not.

Macca wasn't brought up to be so reserved. 'You were at Trin's weddin', weren't ya? We weren't formally introduced. So, you from the city, are ya, mate?'

'Yes, I originally came from England ten years ago, but now I live in Melbourne.'

'Mmm, righto. I reckon I'd trade those grey Pommy skies for Aussie sunshine any day too. Whadaya do for a crust in the big smoke?'

'I'm an investment banker with Oxford, Bride and Associates. Perhaps you've heard of them?' Warren was smirking as he asked.

'Nah, can't say I have,' responded Macca, picking up on Warren's sarcasm.

'And what do *you* do, Macca, to earn *a buck* in . . . um . . . Mount Isa, wasn't it?' asked Warren.

'A buck?' said Macca, playing the drongo.

'Yes. What. Do. You. Do. For. A. Living?' Warren drew the sentence out as if Macca were a dunce.

'Oh, a *living*!' said Macca, throwing Sarah a wink. 'I'm a diesel-fitter, mate.'

Warren looked confused. 'A diesel fitter . . . And where exactly do you work?'

'In a ladies-underwear factory,' said Macca, with a poker face.

'There's a ladies-underwear factory in Mount Isa?' asked Warren in surprise.

'Yeah,' said Macca as beside him Sarah started to shake. Macca then made a movement like he was pulling something down over his ears. 'You know, "dees-'ll-fit- her!"'

Sarah exploded with laughter. 'Aw, Macca . . . you're just a pisser!'

'Yeah,' quipped Bella dryly, 'he's not real smart, but he can lift heavy things.'

Warren's face went pink. He spun and walked off, muttering something about getting his luggage.

'Well, that might get rid of him anyway,' said Macca.

Bella slid from the tray and hit her cousin over the head. 'That wasn't very nice!'

'You're not gunna marry that bloody tosser, are you, Hells Bells? What a flamin' drongo.' He mimicked Warren's voice, 'And what do you do to earn *a buck* . . . !'

Bella whacked Macca again before she stormed off.

'Good on you, Macca, you idiot,' said Shelley as she made to follow.

Will grabbed her arm. 'I'll go, Shelley.' He strode after Bella, who was disappearing down the rise to Turbo's kennel.

'He didn't mean it, you know,' Will said to the figure crying into the dog's ruffled, wiry black mane.

'Who didn't? Macca or bloody Warren? I don't even know why I'm crying; I'll be glad to be rid of the arsehole.'

'Which one's the arsehole?'

'Fuckin' Warren, of course, for being so goddamned rude. Macca's my cousin. He's allowed to say those sorts of things.'

With a mother, a sister and formerly a bitch of a wife, Will had long ago given up trying to understand the workings of the female mind. What he did know, though, was that a hug usually fixed things. Taking a big leap of faith, and not a little risk, he held out his muscled arms and beckoned to the girl on the ground.

'Want a cuddle?'

Bella looked up and saw that strong, rugged face creased with worry. The brown eyes were warm, soft.

In a daze, she slowly got up and moved into the arms of the man who tugged more than a little bit at her heart and mind.

After long, precious moments of soaking in the warmth and strength of his hug, she mumbled into his broad chest, 'And I'm pregnant.'

Pulling back, but still holding her within the safe circle of his arms, Will sought clarification. 'You're what?'

'I'm pregnant, Will. It's a bloody pisser, isn't it? I've just got rid of the wanker and now this.' She pulled herself upright, swiped a sleeve cuff across her face and slowly, reluctantly, moved from the comfort of those arms.

Will let her go. He felt like a hole had been punched into his gut.

'I'll be right. Or should I say *we'll* be all right.' Bella laughed sadly as she put her hand to her belly. 'We're fine by ourselves, me and the bub.'

She moved another step away from Will. She didn't *need* any more complications and she didn't need a bloke to make it okay. Plus, this man didn't want children either. She *could* do this on her own. 'We'd better get back to the others or they'll drink all the beer and leave for the rodeo without us.' With that, she turned and walked back up the hill towards the crowd still leaning against the ute.

Will followed slowly, trying to assimilate the news. Bella with a baby. Surprisingly, he found it wasn't hard to picture.

By the time everyone was ready to leave for the rodeo, the grog in the beer fridge had run out, the main culprits being Macca, Sarah and Will, the two other girls not able to get stuck into it on account of breastfeeding and impending motherhood. The boys and Sarah were having a piss before heading off to the rodeo. Warren was still sulking inside the house; and Shelley was telling Bella all about the new-mums' group she'd been to in town.

'Jeez Louise, bloody women can talk, can't they?' yelled Macca, who was now ready to travel. 'Are you sheilas comin' or what?'

'Keep your shirt on, big fella,' Bella called back. 'Shell, can you take these two drunken lovebirds back into town? Do you think you can drive Macca's ute?'

The young mum stood up straight and thrust her shoulders back. 'Of course I can, I've driven a flamin' logging truck, I can drive just about anything.'

'Onya, girl. Go grab that driver's seat, and Macca, you shut up, get in and cuddle your intended!'

'Yes, ma'am!' saluted Macca as he pushed Sarah into the ute first.

'And what about me? Can I bot a ride off you?' asked Will, who'd come up to stand by her side. He gave her a wary half-smile.

'Yeah. You can have a seat . . .' She threw the words over her shoulder as she walked off towards the house to give Warren directions to the rodeo ground. 'You'll just have to share it with Turbo.'

Bella could hear Will's groan as he went to grab the dog.

Chapter 39

The rodeo was in full swing by the time they all arrived, with the open steer-wrestling out in the ring. The ground was packed with locals and visitors alike, everyone set up with picnic chairs and rugs laid out in the sun. The bar was a popular place to be and the local primary school and Lions club were serving up the grub: hot roast beef, lamb or pork sandwiches washed down with water, beer, coke and rum; Bella's tummy grumbled in anticipation.

Placing a rug on the side of the hill leading down to the rodeo ring, Bella sat and prepared herself to be spellbound by the competition about to start in the arena. The steer-wrestling was one of her favourite parts and she didn't want to miss a thing. She knew it wasn't considered a team event, but the rider heavily relied on his hazer, the bloke charged with the job of keeping the steer running straight so the wrestler could get into a good position. Once the steer-wrestler took off he had to move down the right-hand side of his horse and reach for the steer's horns with his hands. After he got hold of the horns, he had to jump off his horse and dig his heels into the ground to stop the animal running. The competitor then had to throw the steer down, flat on its side with all four feet straight. It was a spectacular sport to watch, and Bella loved every bit of it.

Then came the barrel-racing, the team-roping and the open bareback ride followed by the main events of the day, the open saddle bronc and bull rides. Sitting as far from Will as possible, Warren watched the rodeo with a bored expression, ignoring everyone until Trin arrived. He then monopolised Trin, quietly talking non-stop. But Trin mustn't have been interested in the 'brilliant business proposition' because Warren suddenly hopped up and called across to Bella that he was going for a beer.

'Jeez, you would have thought he'd offer to grab us *all* a drink?' said Caro, as she sat down beside Bella.

'Don't worry about him. He's a bit pissed off.' Bella watched Warren walk off like he had a pole shoved up his bum.

'Why?' asked Caro, puzzled.

Bella waggled her empty ring finger in front of Caro's nose.

'Oh.' Caro looked up into Bella's face. 'Are you okay about that?'

Trinity glanced over, interested.

'Perfectly,' said Bella, and she realised it was the truth. Time to change the subject. 'Hey, the open bareback ride's on!'

'You don't say!' said Trinity, picking up the bait and turning his attention back to the arena.

'Yeah,' Bella replied as Caro gave her a long hard look, catching the scent of a story. Bella ignored her and focused on the event. All were soon captivated as cowboys were thrown every few minutes and pick-up riders raced in to save their hides.

Bella loved a good rodeo and didn't want to miss a buck made by either horse or bull.

It was five o'clock before the open bull ride finally finished and they all started wandering back to their cars. A bunch of partygoers still hung out at the bar. There was a dance on in town that night to follow on from the rodeo, but Bella had earlier decided to give it a miss and head home instead.

Will had asked for a lift, so she said goodbye to Shelley and her husband Joe, to Caro and Trin, and then set off towards the ute, hoping Will would get the message and follow. She could see a scrap of white paper fluttering on the windscreen of the car. She drew it out from under the wiper blade and saw it was a lavish business card with 'Oxford, Bride and Associates' emblazoned in orange-gold across a heavy blue smudge. Warren's name was printed boldly across the front in a black fancy font. She turned it over to see his flamboyant handwriting decorating the back.

Good luck with the baby, Warren

Bella gave a wry smile. He was finally gone. And all she felt was relief. 'No ties at all,' she muttered as she let the card go, to twirl in the wind.

Coming up behind her, Will stomped on the swirling card as it spun across the ground. He picked it up and turned it over to read Warren's final words. The message was shockingly clear.

He watched Bella as she wiggled her body into the driver's seat of the ute. Now he looked hard enough, he could see her usually flat belly was rounding slightly from the rest of her slim figure and gently touching the black steering wheel.

'Bastard!' he uttered as he dropped the card back onto the ground at his feet. It gave him a small measure of satisfaction to squish it to a pulp under his heel.

Macca and Sarah planned to head home to Macca's parents' place for a shower before they ventured to the dance.

'See youse!' he shouted across the paddock that served as a parking lot. 'I'll call out in a day or two, after Sarah tends to me sexual needs.'

Will could see an arm moving in the ute as Macca yelled out, 'Youch, fair go, wench! What did I do to deserve that?' He was cut off as the door banged shut.

'Righto,' muttered Will, as he got into Bella's ute and gave an indignant Turbo a gentle shove off the seat. 'That cousin of yours hasn't changed.'

'Did you ever think he would?' said Bella as she settled Turbo into the centre console and started up the ute. 'Sarah's got her work cut out training him, that's for sure, but I reckon she'll do it.'

Bella was thoughtful as she guided the ute out onto the road. 'What do you think Patty would have thought of her?'

Will smiled as he looked out the passenger-side window into the sunset. 'I think she would have liked her. She's spirited but allows Macca to have his head. As long as she reins in the worst of him, they've got half a shot.'

'Mmm.' Bella swung the ute left around the T-intersection that led to Tindarra. 'She obviously loves the dickhead.'

Chapter 40

The weeks turned into months, and Bella kept busy. She and Will formed an uneasy relationship, based on remembered friendship and a remote location. She needed his physical help as she grew bigger, but emotionally she still kept him at arm's length, determined to do as much for herself as she could.

She wasn't sure what he got from the fragile friendship, forged as they worked together but he obviously got something, because he kept turning up every few days. Sometimes it was with a few groceries he'd noticed she needed, other times a paper or the mail. Once he arrived with a tiny woollen blanket he'd bought in Narree, knowing she was slowly collecting things for the baby.

He took an interest in her work, and he talked quietly but passionately about his farm and dreams of expanding his holdings. She couldn't help but look at the way he did things; his graceful movements to get a job done, his attraction to animals and the way he seemed to caress them with gentle, caring hands. Their time together was peaceful, careful as they avoided saying too much.

The Landcare meetings were drawing to a close, and of that Bella was glad. The time had been fantastic and the farmers wonderful to work with, but she was finding she was getting very tired and all the travelling was doing her in.

'How many more to go?' asked Will one Saturday as he cut her some firewood. Bella sat on a spare chopping block enjoying watching his muscles move rhythmically as he split the wood.

'I'll be all finished this week,' she said as she arched her back, trying to stretch the kinks from between her breasts and rounded belly. 'Thank heavens, and then it's just a matter of a bit more computer work to finish off the last reports and get the final document to my boss.'

Will quietly observed Bella in her efforts to make her growing body more comfortable. To him the pregnancy had made her even more sensuous, more attractive. It didn't matter to him that the baby belonged to someone else; it didn't matter she was having a baby at all – he still felt that raw pull of attraction. He wondered if it was for some primal reason he found her more attractive than ever before – something all women developed – or if it was just because Bella meant so much to him. In the last few months he'd felt like there was a purpose in his life, for the first time in years.

'So, Warren's not going to be involved with the baby?' Will ventured, knowing full well he would catch her unawares.

There was silence for a minute while Bella adjusted to the change of direction in the conversation. 'No,' came the guarded response.

'What are you going to do?'

'Have it, look after it, love it . . . What else do you think?' Bella got up from the log she was sitting on and moved slightly away. She stretched some more, aware that Will was watching. She looked across at him, and found a pair of brown eyes fixed on her.

'I'll get a job back here, my family will help me and I'll make a life for both me and the baby in the country that I know and love.'

Silence stretched between them, until a log toppled off the wood heap, breaking the spell.

'Is your boss happy with your work so far? I mean, he should be, you've been putting in so much.' Will started stacking wood again. He'd found out what he needed to know.

Relieved the conversation was back on firmer ground, Bella responded eagerly, 'Yes, I think so. He's pretty happy now I'm finished and he can use the documents to attract State and Federal funding to our area.'

Will took particular notice as she called it 'our area' with possessiveness and passion. He smiled to himself. This was the Bella he knew and loved.

He smiled again and then took a deep breath.

'Would you like to see some brumbies tonight?'

They parked the Toyota just off the main track. Bella could make out faint traces of a path through the surrounding scrub, leading off to the right.

'We walk from here,' Will said as he paused for a moment to do up her Driza-bone coat, which now strained to reach around her belly. With a tap to her nose he then started off into the bush. Bella followed. Her heart was beating fast. She wasn't sure if it had to do with Will's closeness, that tap to her nose or the fact she might finally see a brumby mob. It had been years since she'd been brumby-running and she had missed the crazed rides through the high country scrub chasing down wild horses.

And now here she was back again. Not brumby-running this time. Just quietly observing the horses in an environment they had made their own.

They walked for what seemed like miles. They didn't say a word as Will stopped and pointed every now and again at brumby signs. Recent unshod hoof marks in the soft wet soil. Piles of fresh poop all backed up one upon the other; a stallion marking his territory. Skid marks as the brumbies had scrambled up and down rocky inclines pushing their way to feed upon the verdant, grassy plains that dotted this wild, high country area.

And then, as they skirted a boggy, open stretch of ground, they came across a pond of water, its grassy edges trampled to a muddy mess by unshod hooves. Bella knew these particular ponds weren't a natural occurrence. When it was dry, the brumbies rolled themselves around in favourite spots, like this one, scooping out the dusty earth as they flung themselves from side to side, scratching and rubbing the dust into their bodies. In wet times such as now, those depressions filled with water, making a natural waterhole for the horses to drink from. Everything happened for a reason.

Suddenly, Will stopped. Silent, his body poised to listen, he swung his head this way then that, sniffing and peering intently into the surrounding scrub.

'Do you smell them?' he whispered. Bella drew in a deep breath. Wafts from Will's freshly bathed body shot up her nostrils: velvet soap, a musky-scented deodorant, peppermint toothpaste.

Moving her head away and across the wind, she had another go. Breathing in gently, she caught a wisp of fetid manure. An earthy smell mixed with horse shit; and she knew she had it.

Brumbies.

Will slowly set off again, quietly placing his feet to make the least sound. All senses on alert, his head swung from side to side as he peered through the stringy-bark trees and scrub crowding around them. The scrub opened up and they hiked across another grassy plain, covered in knee-high tussocks with patches of billy buttons and the odd wild orchid popping up in places. Will stopped abruptly again. He motioned with one hand out to the right while the other gently pressed his lips indicating silence.

Bella froze and looked eagerly in the direction he pointed.

And there they were.

A bay-coloured brumby with a white blaze cresting his proud head moved to the left of the main mob. The stallion, she presumed. Further across and partly hidden by the huge white gum trees she could just make out another four full-grown mares, two chestnuts and two bays. A plover in the trees above suddenly started a warning cry.

Sharp and urgent, his song caused the stallion to throw his head in the air. Sniffing, senses on full alert, he poised, ready to flee. The mares also lifted their heads and moved towards the stallion. Will was silently cursing the plover when suddenly the mares, led by one of the chestnuts, swung away from the stallion and broke into a gallop, flinging themselves into the waiting bush on the other side of the plain. After one last sniff in the air, the stallion took off after them. Within seconds all that remained was the plover still peeping his warning to all around.

Will set off, moving fast. 'Come on, let's go. They won't have gone far.'

Bella followed more sedately. It was only a few hundred metres on when she spotted an anomaly through the trees. A shadow that shouldn't have been there.

She tapped Will on the shoulder and whispered, 'Over there,' pointing into the tall trees out in front.

Among the eucalypts she could just make out the flowing brown manes of a number of horses. Almost immediately both she and Will heard a snort. They'd been spotted again, but this time by the stallion. The mares took off, funnelling down the hill through a natural gap in the bush. The stallion brought himself to a stop just to one side of the gap and turned to face Will and Bella. He was still a hundred or so metres from where they were. Once his mares were through and away, the stallion flung himself towards where they were standing.

'Come on,' said Will as he started toward the horse.

'Will!' Bella urgently whispered. 'What are you doing? He'll have a go at us!'

'If he comes at you, just wave your arms around and yell really loud. He should veer off.'

Will kept walking purposely toward the gap.

The stallion wasn't moving an inch.

Then suddenly he moved. Fast. Straight at them.

Proud, angry and arrogant, he came to a screeching halt about twenty metres directly in front of them. Will stopped with Bella right on his heels. The stallion poised, aggressive in his stance.

I'm warning you, piss off, he seemed to say. The stand-off continued, neither horse nor human moving. The stallion quivered with self-righteous dignity and flung his head into the air again.

He snorted; a rasping and threatening sound.

Just when Bella wondered how long this could go on, the stallion spun gracefully around and galloped away through the gap in the bush after his mares.

'So take *that*!' said Will finally as he turned to Bella, who was standing so close to him she was nearly in his arms.

'Crap, Will, you scared the bejezus out of me!' she gasped. Released from the spell of the stallion's confrontation, she sagged onto the ground, wrapping her arms protectively around her pregnant belly. 'What if he'd gone for us, you bloody fool?'

'You were safe enough, Hells Bells. He was just letting us know he wasn't happy.'

'Not happy, all right.'

Will reached down to help her up. 'You've been living in the city too long. Where's your sense of adventure gone?'

Much later they lay on their backs staring up at the inky-black night sky. After they returned from brumby-spotting Bella had cooked them up sausages and mash washed down with mugs of hot chocolate. She'd then walked out to say goodnight to Will and been captivated by the clearest sky she'd seen since she arrived at Maggie's place, shining and twinkling its way across the mountains.

Seeing her mesmerised, Will had grabbed her hand and led her down the hill to lie beside him on the riverbank. She couldn't believe the amount of stars she could see out here – there were millions of them, blazing their little hearts out. Overhead in soft white wisps was the Milky Way; a truly amazing constellation of luminous stars mixed with swathes of misty alabaster.

The sky was stunning, way out here with not a light to dim the incredible scene.

As they lay on their backs looking upwards Will touched Bella's arm gently and pointed. 'Can you see it?'

'Can I see what?' she responded in a reverent whisper, not knowing why she was whispering other than it seemed the right thing to do.

'A satellite,' said Will. 'Up there just coming past the Saucepan's handle.'

'There it is. I can see it! I can see it!' she said again, her voice full of wonder. 'Gee, don't they move fast!' The satellite was moving at least four times the speed of a normal jet.

'There's another one,' said Will as he pointed further to the right of the Saucepan. 'And another going the other way!'

Bella let out a sigh of wonder. 'It's just beautiful. You'd never see anything like that in Melbourne. Not even at Dad's, probably. There'd be too much light.' She was quiet for a minute before going on. 'Do you remember doing this years ago at Gundolin?'

Will didn't say a word. He just reached out his strong, warm hand and gently took hold of hers, which was resting in the grass. Their fingers instinctively intertwined and nestled together.

Bella didn't pull away. She probably should have, it was just complicating things. But it was so nice to lie here and be with Will.

After a long while she spoke. 'Why did you turn away from me, after Patty died?' She needed to know the answer to a question that was eight years and a lifetime overdue.

Will looked up at the stars. How many times had he asked himself the same thing?

'I don't know . . .' he said. 'I couldn't handle it, I guess.' His eyes tracked a satellite across the sky. 'Couldn't handle the fact Patty was gone, your mum was buggered and you were only just alive. I was angry, grieving, I suppose. I shut myself off from feeling because it all hurt too much. Once I knew you were going to be okay, I threw myself into work – it was the only thing I could do to take my mind off it all, to drive it all away. My sister nearly killed you and your mother and she knocked herself off in the process. I was feeling guilty. Horribly bloody guilty. It's stupid I know, but I felt I should have been driving that day. I was helpless. I wasn't able to protect or help any of you and I wasn't able to save my sister from herself.'

Whoa! I really fucked him up, didn't I? muttered the voice in Bella's head.

Bella stared at the man next to her, trying to understand.

Will struggled on, now looking right at her. 'It wasn't until Maggie hauled me into her kitchen one day and threatened to hit me over the head with her frying pan that I came to my senses. But by then it was too late.'

'Aunty Maggie? Where does she fit into all this?'

'She told me it was okay to grieve, to be angry. She told me to throw away the guilt. It was hanging around my neck like a ball and chain, making me make stupid decisions – like I didn't need you in my life. I didn't need more people to love only to have them taken away. I sat at your hospital bedside until they knew you'd pull through and then I bolted to the mountains and buried myself so deep I didn't know how to dig myself out. Maggie gave me a shovel and a helping hand. I finally realised I'd been a fool. I loved you and wanted you back. So I jumped in my ute and drove to Melbourne. I wanted to bring you home. I wanted to marry you . . . Well, you know the rest.'

And she'd turned him away. 'What about Prowsy? Why did you marry her?'

Will sighed and looked back up to the heavens. 'I was lonely, I guess. You were gone and not coming back. I threw myself into the station, trying to build the property up. Once the drought broke and prices lifted I had the money to make a go of the place. Prue was there, persistent. I simply let it happen. I knew I'd buggered up shortly after we'd tied the knot. It wasn't me she was after, just the chance to be Mrs O'Hara of Tindarra Station, which she fancied was something. It was a shock for her when she realised being Mrs O'Hara meant isolation, bloody hard work and a grumpy, tired old man to keep her company day in, day out.'

'You're not old, Will,' said Bella gently. It could have all been so different had they both only listened to their hearts and been open with each other and talked things through. Instead they'd locked themselves away, alone, and allowed wounds to fester and become diseased. Maybe if she'd heard him out in Melbourne, instead of just cutting him off . . . She should have known he was there for a good reason. But she was too hurt, too bloody stubborn and proud to allow him back into her heart. She'd buried her head in the sand and just wanted it all to go away.

She now realised that by moving to the city, she had run away, and allowed the guilt of surviving the accident to eat at her. What Will had gone through in ten or so months was what she'd been doing for the whole eight years she was in Melbourne. No wonder her relationship with Warren hadn't worked. No wonder she hadn't fitted into his world. She didn't *let* herself belong, hadn't given her wholehearted love to Warren, preferring to detach herself from anything that might mean something. She'd let her own life and dreams drift away. Warren wasn't the only one at fault in their relationship. She needed to accept a fair dose of blame herself.

With her head swirling with revelations, Bella tuned back into the conversation to hear Will say, 'No, I suppose not, but I was old enough then to know better. I should have stayed on my own, not hooked up with some fool who thought farming was prancing around in jelly-bean-spotted gumboots while *Country Style* took photos. She'll be a lot happier in Scone. At least it's somewhere near the Southern Highlands those magazines always talk about. Not down here in the "arse end of the world" as Prue used to say.'

'It's not the arse end of the world, Will. It's God's own country. I'm just realising that. And it's only taken *me* a decade'

Will chuckled, and Bella tentatively reached out her other hand. He took it gently and tucked it inside his flannie, her fingers splaying snugly against his downy chest. Bella wriggled her way across the space between them and settled herself beside him. Her belly jutted awkwardly against his body and she used his side to prop it up. Warmth flooded between them, and Bella felt more than heard a roaring start in her ears, her head, her whole body.

The baby kicked hard against Will's side. 'Hey! Was that the . . . ?'

'It sure was. It gives me a hard time some nights, when all I want to do is sleep. I read in my baby manual that during the day when you're moving around it rocks the baby to sleep. But at night when you're resting, all the baby wants to do is play.'

'Babies come with a manual; you're having me on, right?'

Bella laughed. 'No, you have to work it all out for yourself, but there's plenty of books and people out there to give you a helping hand.' The baby kicked again, then wriggled. Then it stilled.

'What's going on now?' asked Will, his hand coming up to her belly, trying to feel something.

At Will's soft and intimate touch, Bella couldn't help but feel the competing tremors of lust and sadness. This man would make the most perfect father.

'Nothing. I think it's gone to sleep.' Bella tried unsuccessfully to hide a big yawn. 'Which is probably what I should do. I'm whacked after that walk.' And I really shouldn't be enjoying this so much, she added to herself.

'Mmm . . .' The sound made a rumble in the chest so close to her head. 'I'm heading over to Trin and Caro's tomorrow. Want to come with me?'

Bella didn't have to think twice. 'What time will you pick me up?'

Chapter 41

The fog moved in, thick and fast. It had started as a huge black storm front that seemed to hover out to the west in the late afternoon.

Bella soon realised it wasn't hovering – not one little bit – and it set her on edge. That menacing grey blanket reminded her of the night of the accident. She shivered.

It swung in insidiously, a rolling bank moving quickly, gulping metres of the open plain in huge bites until there was nothing left other than a heavy mist, which in minutes left her unable to see a hand in front of her face.

They were on their way back from the Eggletons' after a wonderful day. Will had suggested a detour to the area of loosely scattered plains where the Nunkeri Muster had been held all those years ago. When they were young, free . . . and together. It had seemed like a good idea at the time.

Bella looked at Will. His brow was creased, his body taut. Then it all just seemed to relax. 'Well, at least I know where we are,' he said. 'The Nunkeri Plains hut is just through this washout and down a short track past those trees up there.'

Bella gazed out of her window. She couldn't see any muddy washout. She couldn't see a track and she definitely couldn't see trees anywhere. The fog was all-encompassing and had swallowed any landmark she could use to designate a place.

'I'll believe you,' she said, trying to suppress a shudder. Instinctively her hands moved to her belly. Will's gaze followed her hands. He reached across and patted her knee.

'It'll be fine, Hells Bells. Trust me.' And she did. Then the baby moved slightly to the right, towards the man in the driver's seat. Bella followed the movement with her hands, laughing a little, easing the tension that was building in the cab. 'Guess Junior here is all for it. I'd better be as well.'

'Good girl.' Will clapped her knee then withdrew his hand to engage the low-range gear stick into four-wheel drive. 'We just might need a bit of help through this bog hole.'

Bella could feel her muscles tense again.

Will looked across. 'What did I say, cowgirl? Trust me. Have I ever let you down before?' Bella threw him a pointed glance, and he had the grace to look sheepish. 'Yeah, right. Okay, not the best thing to say, hey, but that was then and this is now. I'm an older and wiser version.' Another look. 'Okay, delete the wiser. This way is our only option. It's too dangerous to try and find our way across the plain to the main road in this. We'd only be asking for trouble. The plain's full of soaks and we could easily get bogged.'

'What about using the mobile?' suggested Bella. 'Call Trin and ask him to come and get us?'

'Then *he'd* get lost. He doesn't know the plain that well. Plus the only mobile reception is at Phone Rock.'

'Phone Rock?'

'The only place you get mobile reception on the whole plain is at a little rock way over on the other side.'

'Right,' said Bella, now under no illusions they weren't stuck for the night.

'Righto. I'll just get out and put in the hubs and we'll be through this hole and at the hut in no time.'

Will jumped out of the ute and moved to engage the front wheel hubs. Bella looked out the side window and tried to see his shape in the gloom surrounding the front tyre. The only bit of colour she could see was a touch of red from his shirt, which stood out like a fleck on a grey-white canvas of swirling mist.

By the time they arrived at the hut, the world had moved into darkness. The shape of the hut came upon the ute in the beam of the headlights; lights that were otherwise useless in the thick mist. Bella could see rough-sawn, dark timber walls hunkered down, pressing into the earth, trying to blend with the surroundings and succeeding. One with the bush landscape.

Bella gathered up the belongings strewn at her feet – a bottle of now-tepid water, her camera and a rain jacket. The wooden door of the hut was already open, Will had disappeared inside, only to reappear within seconds to head across to the ute.

'Need some matches. Someone's left us some dry wood in the heap beside the fire. We'll have to replace it tomorrow. Why don't you stay here a few minutes until I get it roaring? It won't take long.' He grabbed a packet of matches from the empty ashtray of the ute and hurried off.

Bella was only too happy to comply. The darkness beyond the hut door was intimidating. Visions of snakes and spiders slithered through her mind; she hoped a bright fire might encourage anything creepy-crawly to find another home for the night, or at least a dark corner well away from her.

She studied what she could see of the hut. It was constructed from wooden slabs nailed vertically to a frame. Heavy, rusty galvanised iron clad the roof and any other spot missing a slab of wood. The chimney was made from the same aged iron abutted onto the gable-roofed, rectangular hut, the roof triangulated to draw smoke from the fire inside. All in all, it was built to shelter cattlemen and wanderers from the elements, and had served its purpose well over decades.

Will came back out and headed to the tray of the ute. Bella could hear him shuffling around among his stuff as she laid her head against the seat rest and closed her eyes. They'd had a wonderful afternoon. It had been just like old times, four friends reliving the wild days of their youth. Even though they were missing Patty and Macca, the stories had been told with fond regret rather than desperate and grinding grief.

The one thing that had stopped Bella from completely relaxing was Will's leg, which he had intentionally locked hard against her own for the whole time they sat enjoying the views from Trin and Caro's verandah.

Will had moved once, to take a leak, but as soon as he'd returned he'd sat down and purposely adjusted his knee to reclaim his place. He'd turned to her once, holding her gaze deep and level, burning holes through her body with the sultry heat from his stare.

It wasn't until Caro told them proudly that all the food on the table had been home-grown that Bella was able to force her attention back to the table. She couldn't believe her ears. 'You mean to say Caroline Handley Eggleton actually killed and plucked a chook herself?'

'You've got to be kidding,' said Caro, with an obvious shudder. 'No, old Wes did it for me. He was a champion – beheading, scalding and plucking the bird so well I wouldn't have picked it from a supermarket-bought chicken.'

Bella smiled. That sounded more like the Caroline she knew.

'It's all ready for you, cowgirl.' Will's voice hunkered into her thoughts.

She opened her eyes, to find Will calling her from the hut.

'What? Oh. Right. Coming . . .' She looked towards the hut door. The inside had been transformed with a bright and welcoming glow misted at the edges with the fine rain now coming down to drench everything it touched.

Gathering her stuff once again, she got out of the ute. Her body had become a lot slower to respond these past few weeks.

The rain softly pattered down on her shoulders and arms as she quickly walked towards the light and warmth of the hut. Once inside she was taken aback by the effort Will had made to turn this small, dirty, austere space into a haven. She was sure if he'd been on his own, the single chainmesh-covered iron bed folded up against the far wall would have been enough to provide him with comfort for the night. So he'd done this for her.

He'd opened up two other beds of the same ilk and pushed them close to the fire in the front half of the hut. Over one he'd folded a tattered blue tarp, and he'd slung a well-worn canvas swag across the other. Then he'd balled up a faded oilskin coat and a bunch of clean rags to use for pillows at the head of each bed. 'Welcome to the Nunkeri Plains Hilton.' Will's dimples flashed as he twirled his hands in the air like a maestro begging for applause.

Despite her misgivings, she couldn't help but smile.

A hissing sound came from the fire, a billy set over the flames to boil. Grabbing two small cans of spaghetti from the rock hearth at the side of the fire, he pierced a hole in the lid of each with a pocketknife from the leather holder on his belt.

With his back to her as he dumped the tins partially into the boiling water, Will said, 'Emergency rations. Always carry a bit of tucker around in the back of the ute. Never know when you might be stuck up in the scrub.'

'Same with the swag, and the billy, I suppose?' Bella knew there was a faint accusatorial tone to her voice. She chastised herself; he certainly hadn't organised the thick fog.

'I'm good, but I'm not *that* good, Hells Bells. I can't order God around.' He sounded pissed off.

Bella knew she deserved that one. She gathered herself up, determined to make amends. 'This looks great, Will. Thanks for making such an effort.'

Will waved a hand in response, his movements jerky with suppressed annoyance as he swung the billy, hooked on a wire rod, back across the fire.

He hadn't meant the day to turn out like this. Well, not exactly. He'd hoped something might happen between them, but not here; not on a deserted, lonely plain in a dirty, cold cattlemen's hut with nothing but a swag to sleep on and a grungy fireplace to give light.

He didn't want to say the wrong thing, make the wrong move. He wanted to get it *right* this time. He couldn't stand the pain of her misunderstanding him and walking away again like at Hugh's Plain. Granted, she was a different woman now. Instead of being so strung-up and tetchy, she was more relaxed and could take a joke. She'd got rid of that woolley butt log on her shoulder, leaving only a few splinters in its wake. But still, he wasn't sure which way this night would go and he figured it was best to leave that up to Bella rather than get it all wrong again. He could wait for her. He'd wait forever if he had to.

'Look, I'm sorry, Will. I'm just tired, I guess.'

He turned around just in time to see her draw a hand across her eyes. He was shocked by just how black the circles under her eyes were. His gaze softened.

'How about you take a seat right over here on this log?' Will kicked a sawn-off block of wood towards her. 'But just pull that door behind you closed before we lose what warmth we've managed to create in this old place.'

Bella swung back, and went to pull the wooden door tight. But just before she did, she took one more look outside. It was completely dark, no moon to light the way. She shuddered as the milky-white mist swirled around the door, thankful for the warmth and shelter now inside.

Lying on the twin wire beds much later, after having consumed every scrap of spaghetti, Bella found herself trying to get comfortable. Despite the makeshift padding, wire dug into her sides no matter which way she turned. She was also freezing in the places the fire's warmth couldn't reach.

'What's wrong?' Will's voice came from the bed next to hers. She hadn't realised he was still awake.

'I'm cold. And I can't get comfortable.'

'If I didn't know better, I'd take that as an invitation.'

Bella mumbled something.

'What was that?' Will moved a bit, then sat up and looked down at her, his body shadowed by the dark depths of the hut at his back.

'It *is* an invitation,' said Bella, a tentative lilt in her voice.

Will raised an eyebrow, and Bella's heart sank. Who'd want to make love to a hugely pregnant woman – especially if they thought it wasn't their baby? She knew she should just tell him the baby was his, even if he didn't want children. Maybe it would make things right, and all would be well. But as she opened her mouth to say the words, her throat closed over.

What the hell? Why don't you just tell him and be done with it?

I can't, said Bella to Patty. He doesn't want children. You buggered that up. You and your bloody parents. So I have to do this myself. I'm strong enough. I don't need a man to make it all right.

Fool!

Who are you calling a fool; you're the one who's dead!

Youch! Temper, temper, Hells Bells. You always were pig-headed.

Bella forced Patty away.

'I'd love to accept,' came the quiet, deep voice at her side. 'C'mon, get up, cowgirl.'

It only took him a few minutes to stow the wire beds away. He stretched the swag out to its full width on the ground, and laid the coat and tarp out over the top. Will helped her down onto the swag and then bunched the rags so she had a pillow of sorts on which to rest her belly.

He lay down behind her and Bella marvelled as his hands moved around her waist to gently cup her belly, which was straining to hold the baby within its skin. She loved the spooned warmth of him against her back as he shared life and heat with her frozen body. Then came a tightening of his arm and hand as it moved up to secure itself on her breast. Bella backed in closer to Will and felt him respond.

Slowly, they helped each other remove their clothes and Bella marvelled at how the heat of their two bodies yearning to become one, burned away any remnant feeling of cold.

With her naked back once again tucked into Will's chest, his left hand started to explore her new shape. Gentle fingers trailed their way down over her naked breasts, his hand cupping and caressing their voluptuous fullness. His warm touch then drifted across her mounded belly, stopping to explore, tickle and sensuously tease before moving along. But as he reached the tops of her thighs, she felt him tense, his hand abruptly halting. Moments ticked by before his fingers started to slowly explore the long indentations in her skin, external scars from the accident nearly nine years before. Finally, he moved his hand back up towards her breasts, away from those reminders of tragedy and grief, allowing her to let go of a breath she hadn't realised she'd been holding.

Commencing his journey all over again, Will's hand gently worked its magic until in an agonisingly unhurried motion; he dipped his fingers into the cleft between her legs.

The passion that had been on slow burn the whole day – that had sizzled in the air between them since the Nunkeri Muster all those years ago – finally erupted. It was different this time, though. There was no thunder, no lightning. No urgent need to take and be taken. Comfort, companionship and love were at last consummated in that hut, so deep in the mountains, amid the security of the blanket of fog.

It was a long time later, when Bella was sleeping, and in the afterglow of lovemaking so beautiful he wanted to weep,

Will was reminded of another time – when he held Bella at the Gundolin rodeo, wondering at his luck at having such a gorgeous creature in his arms.

He looked down at the white-gold curly hair. What changes time had wrought them both. But fundamentally they were still the same people. This woman was still Bella, the woman he'd come to know then and love now. Forever. Warren may have fathered the baby, but that didn't mean Will couldn't learn how to be a dad. If Bella would let him. The child inside Bella was *hers* and, to Will, that was everything.

Chapter 42

Dawn on the Nunkeri Plains promised a clear, sunny day. They made it home by mid-morning, and all afternoon Bella basked in the memory of Will's lovemaking. Thoughts of his gentleness warmed her as she slowly made her way through the farm jobs. She wasn't doing all that much now she was thirty-seven weeks' pregnant, just trying to keep things ticking along until Maggie came home.

Afterwards she hit her laptop, intent on finishing up the last reports on the Landcare project. But her mind wouldn't stay with the words and figures in front of her. It kept flitting to yesterday and last night, to last week and the week before.

Bella was pretty sure Will loved her, and with that knowledge her whole body buzzed with happiness. Sure, he hadn't said as much, but his eyes told the story – all gooey molasses, loving and kind. And Will *had* just made love to a heavily pregnant woman not knowing he was the father of the baby. He had to love her, didn't he?

The thought of seeing him again sent her legs scurrying down the Tindarra Road after dark, a small torch in her hand. When he dropped her off, Will told her he would be in town for the rest of the day. He wasn't due home until late, and Bella hoped he was back by now. As she walked the moonlit gravel road, she thought about how it would be much more comfortable to make love in an actual bed . . . She hummed to herself in anticipation, already feeling his hands gently cupping her naked belly. Perhaps she should take the risk and tell him he was the father. Surely once he knew, he could love them both.

She wanted to surprise him, so she turned off the torch as she walked down the driveway. She could see the huge set of cattle yards beyond Will's little house, reflected in parts by moonlight. She looked up. Storm clouds scudded across the sky, ducking and weaving around the moon. She swung towards the back of the house, surprised but pleased that Will's dog Nala hadn't yet set up a warning bark at her approach.

Probably inside with Will, she thought. As she came around the corner she stopped, startled. There was a dark green Land Rover Discovery parked hard up against the iron gate.

Her plans for seduction bit the dust. Damn it. She wondered who it was. She realised just how little she knew of Will's life now. And she didn't want to look like an idiot rocking up at his back door at this hour of the night – it would be obvious what she was there for. Asking to borrow a cup of sugar wasn't going to cut it at eleven p.m.

Bella decided to take a look in through the lounge-room window. A massive hydrangea partially obscured the pane, so she slid in sideways between the puff-ball pink flowers and the wall of the house, inwardly cursing her round belly as she went. She couldn't believe she was doing this. Grabbing hold of the shutter to steady herself, Bella peeked through the glass.

Will sat on the end of the couch, and he wasn't alone. A woman reclined on the floor against his legs, resting her blonde head in his lap.

Bella jumped away from the window, forgetting she was tight within the hydrangea. Leaves rustled and branches snapped and cracked as she fell back among the thick bush. She could hear Nala growl inside and a high-pitched voice straight from her past say, 'Oh, don't worry about it, William, it's probably just a roo.'

She could hear the rumble of Will's voice settling Nala, before all went quiet.

Bella righted herself and tried to force feeling back into her legs, her brain, her body now numb with shock. Her mind was reeling. Should she take another look? Confirm what she thought she saw? She snuck back towards the window and peeked through the glass again.

Prudence Vincent-Prowse O'Hara, maybe Fowler, still lay with her head in Will's lap. She looked much the same as she had eight years before. A few more lines of discontent between the eyes streaking up to a furrowed brow, the same sulky blood-red painted lips, a slight thickening under the jaw – the beginnings of a double chin she would inherit from her mother.

Bella felt a slight sense of gratification. Her eyes then moved down the body reclining in a sensuous position on the floor. Prowsy wasn't wearing much. What she *was* wearing strained to cover the fact that Prowsy was well and truly pregnant.

Bella couldn't tear her eyes away. Just when she thought it was all coming together, just when she and Will had finally found their way back to each other – he did this. Could she trust *any* man with her heart, her soul, her life?

No. It didn't look like it.

Patty's voice tried to speak deep within her mind, but Bella shut it down. She didn't want to have anything to do with any bloody O'Haras, ever again.

'It's just you and me, kid,' she whispered to the babe stirring gently within her belly, just as Prowsy's fake laughter tinkled through the glass.

Bella took one last look through the window to confirm what her brain was telling her heart: Will was a dirty, double-crossing two-timer, and he was out of her life.

It was at this moment, when Bella started to turn away, that Prowsy slightly raised her head to stare straight through the window into the night, right into Bella's eyes.

Prowsy smiled.

Will had been serving up a mixed grill for himself when he heard the distant drone of a vehicle high up beyond the ridge. He stood at the kitchen window, which sat squat above the sink, and gazed across the paddocks towards Aunty Maggie's. He could just make out the crisp lines of the house against the darkening twilight, a shadow of black angles against a steel-grey and violet sky. A light twinkled from panes of glass. He wished he'd been able to get back earlier so he could have made definite plans to see Bella.

In his mind he could see her at work at the kitchen table, head bent over her laptop, concentrating. He knew she was working hard to finish the final project report for her boss. His imagination wove images of those lapis eyes intent on the task. His heart lurched slightly as he remembered those eyes intent on him.

He wondered just how late was *too late* to go wandering up the road. The bunch of flowers he'd picked up from the Burrindal store, delivered fresh just this morning, sat in water at the sink. He smiled to himself and hummed along to the country CD playing quietly in the background.

The rumble of a diesel engine drowned the music out. The vehicle stopped outside his gate. A visitor. Damn it. He cast a longing glance towards Bella's beckoning light. He hoped they wouldn't stay long.

Whoever it was, was obviously opening the gate and the rumble started again, louder this time as the vehicle swung down his drive. He frowned. The driver hadn't stopped to close the gate. There was only one person he knew who didn't follow that country law; only one person who thought that unwritten rule was far beneath them.

Prudence.

'So, William, how's things? Still playing with cows?' Prue's forced laughter still rankled. 'Got enough in that pan for me? You always did do a mean fry-up.'

Will leaned against the sink, his arms crossed. He didn't move to greet his former wife. He just stood, watching her enter his house and his life once again. He didn't say a thing; he'd said it all years ago when she left.

'My oh my, the cat got your tongue? Or maybe something else?' Her eyes flicked quickly towards the window, the light and Maggie's, so quickly he might have imagined it.

She padded towards him. 'And what's this?' she said, moving right into his personal space. 'Flowers for me? Oh William, you shouldn't have. I guess Shelley told you I was in town visiting Mummy and Daddy.' Prue picked up the bunch of gerberas and roses, contaminating the flowers with her presence, stifling their sweet scent.

Will decided then and there he was throwing them in the bin. Bella wouldn't be tainted by this girl ever again. He'd take something else to her tonight. Maybe the bowl of blackberries he'd picked from up in Blind Man's Gully, or the multicoloured feather he'd found from a crimson rosella. He'd find another way to woo his girl. He caressed those words in his mind. *His girl.* Finally.

Prowsy interrupted his thoughts. 'I heard Bella Vermaelon was back in the valley. Knocked up, too.'

'You can't talk.'

Prue looked down. Shrugged. 'True. Leyton's promised me a nanny.'

'What do you want, Prue? We were about to have our tea and there's only enough for Nala and me.'

'Of course, I should have remembered. The dog comes before your wife.'

'*Ex*-wife,' clarified Will. By Prue's piqued expression, he could see she was wishing she could suck those nasty words she'd uttered right back in. Interesting. What *did* she want?

Prue smoothed her face and shrugged again. 'Let's head into the lounge and make ourselves more comfortable.' At Will's raised eyebrow, she went on irritably, 'Oh don't worry, I won't be staying long. Leyton's playing darts with Daddy at the hotel and I want to be back before he gets home.'

Prue walked into the lounge and waited until Will had sat down on the single chair, before sinking to her knees in front of him, setting her head upon his lap. Will stiffened. 'Get off, Prue.' He went to move her head off his legs.

'I feel faint.' Her hand fluttered towards her forehead. 'Just let me rest here a moment.'

Prue's voice held that familiar lilting whine that he'd come to loath so much when she was his wife. But he couldn't bring himself to push her away. He sighed. She was a manipulative piece of work, that was for sure, but for once in her life she just *might* be telling the truth.

Nala started to growl. Trees rustled outside. Will sat up straighter, looking towards the window.

'Oh, don't worry about it, William, it's probably just a roo.'

Will mumbled a few quiet words to the dog, who whimpered then settled.

'I want something.' Prue rubbed her hand along his lower leg like a cat.

'Not much has changed, then.'

Prue pursed her blood-red lips and then thrust her blonde head further into his lap. 'I want to come back, Will. I want *you*.' Red nails came up to stroke his inner thigh.

Rearing back, Will clamped down hard on the hand. 'Years ago I might have fallen for that.'

Prue went on as if she hadn't heard him. 'I never really wanted a baby anyhow. Not now. It doesn't suit my lifestyle. But Leyton insisted and I thought, well, surely one little dabble into motherhood wouldn't affect my life too much. But . . .' Prue looked down at her rounded belly in disgust. 'It *has* and it *will* when the little brat arrives.'

She turned to look up at him and for a moment Will

thought he saw vulnerability flicker across her face. And terror. It was in that instant he actually felt pity for his ex-wife; he saw clearly that she was unable to love anything more than she loved herself.

'I've realised I was wrong to leave you. I just want to come home. To you, to the farm, to Tindarra.'

'And what about Fowler?'

'Oh him!' Prue flicked her free hand negligently. 'Don't worry about him. I'll let Leyton have the baby . . . whatever . . . I just want to come back . . .' There was a pause before she added with a doe-like look in her pale eyes, 'to you.'

Will had seen that look on her beautiful face before. When she wanted more Paspaley pearls and he needed a new tractor. When she wanted that bloody Chesterfield lounge and all the other flash furniture and he needed a new hard hose for the irrigator. He'd ended up borrowing Wes's tractor, and patched the old hose. And she *still* hadn't been satisfied. It was then he knew that whatever he did would never be good enough.

His eyes centred on the fireplace; anywhere but Prue. He was saddened by the way their relationship ended, but the feelings of revulsion he felt for her were strong. Leaving him for that bloody horse-breeder who obviously wasn't quite as flash or rich as she thought; wanting to come back to him after she'd already taken him for half of the farm, every spare cent he had; prepared to abandon a defenceless baby, just because it suited her – he was so disgusted he nearly missed her last words, '. . . in return, you can fuck whoever you like. Just don't do it under my roof.'

Nala started a low-pitched growl, directed towards Prue. His ex-wife lifted her head slightly and seemed to smile at her own reflection in the window. She obviously thought she'd won him over.

He stood up. He felt nothing as he watched Prue reel back and scramble to get to her feet, grossly inelegant – all limbs and baby. The gloves were off. He was sick to death of her manipulations. How had he been so blinded by her beauty and honeyed words all those years ago?

'Get out. Now!'

'Oh, for fuck's sake, William. I said you could fuck whoever you wanted. Don't tell me you've fallen for Bella Vermaelon again?'

'Maybe I have . . . but it sure as hell means nothing to you.'

Prue's face turned nasty. Lips pursed again, brow scrunched, eyes squinting. 'I am your *wife*!'

'Ex-wife. Get out, Prue . . . and don't come back anytime soon.' Will manoeuvred her firmly through the lounge door.

Prue baulked near the table. 'But Bella's having someone else's baby too!'

'Yes, but at least she loves and wants that baby. She's prepared to be a mother – on her own, mind you.' Will grabbed her arm in a firm clasp, pulled her across the kitchen, out the back door, down the path and all but lifted her into the Range Rover. He leaned in and checked the gear stick was in neutral and then turned the key. The diesel engine roared to life again.

'Now get out of here . . . And for fuck's sake shut the gate as you leave.'

Man and dog walked back into the house.

At the kitchen table, he glanced out through the window. The light twinkling at Maggie's was gone. Will pulled out a chair and sat down, put his head in his hands as Nala nuzzled up to his knee whimpering. Together they waited. It was a few minutes before he heard the Range Rover drive away. It paused down near the gate. She was shutting it. In the years they were together she'd never done that, not once. Then the sounds of the engine were absorbed into the bush night.

Chapter 43

Bella didn't answer the door the next morning; instead she hid deep within the bed covers, a doona over her head. Will had nearly thumped the door down, but she kept it locked.

She screened telephone calls, the exasperation evident in Will's voice by call number three. She didn't step outside all day.

Unfortunately, when only three people live in a valley they can't avoid each other for long, so it was with dread that Bella heard a set of boots clump up the steps to the screen door in the late afternoon. Steeling herself, she answered, still in her pyjamas. It was Wes.

'Mmmuph! You look terrible, girl.'

'Thanks, Wes.' Bella's voice was wry. 'If I want your opinion I'll ask for it. Do you want a cup of tea?'

'Looks like I'd better.'

Bella moved back to let him in and shuffled towards the

kitchen to put the kettle on the stove. She turned back and found Wes right behind her.

'What's up?'

'What makes you think anything's wrong?'

Wes held up a wizened hand. 'To start with, you're in your pyjamas and it's four o'clock,' he said, ticking off one finger. 'Number two, you look like shit.' Another finger went down. 'Number three, you haven't been outside today 'cause Turbo's crying on his chain and those calves are bellowing for hay. Number four, you've been crying flat-out 'cause your eyes are red slits. And number five . . .' Wes paused for effect, a thumb still in the air, 'I saw Prowsy's green Range Rover leave Will's late last night heading for Burrindal.'

Bella managed to hold it together for a few seconds more, until the compassionate look on the old man's face became her undoing. She collapsed onto a chair and started to cry all over again.

⚜

Wes stood by helplessly and watched as Bella slowly ran out of tears. He pulled a ragged and stained hanky from his pants pocket and offered it to her. She took it and blew her nose, thankfully without looking at the state of it.

'You still in love with that boy?'

'No. Maybe. Yes. Perhaps. I don't bloody well know!' Bella blew her nose again. 'Doesn't matter now anyway.'

'Mightn't be what you think, girl.'

'I know what I saw, Wes.'

What to say? Wes had no idea what Prowsy was doing at Will's that late. But it sure didn't sound good for Bella. Wes chewed the insides of his cheek, thinking. He didn't want to see Bella hurt again. Maggie would kill both Will and him if that happened. Hell, where was that cranky bloody woman when he needed her? Sailing the blasted seven seas. He kinda wished he'd gone with her. Maggie sure wasn't gunna be happy over this little hiccup. Just when things looked like they were coming together.

Bella slowly shook her head and gave a long sigh. 'Wes, if you don't mind, I might just go back to bed. I'm not feeling so crash hot.'

Wes slowly got to his feet. He hadn't felt like a cuppa anyway. He reckoned he deserved beer o'clock early today. He had some whip-making and serious thinking to do. 'You take care then, hey.'

'Yeah, Wes. I'll be fine. Give me a night's sleep, and I'll be as right as rain.' Bella tried to smile, and failed miserably.

'Righto then. I'll call in again tomorrow.' Wes moved out to the verandah and pulled on his boots.

'And Wes?' Bella called through the screen door.

'Yep?'

'Tell Will O'Hara he's a dirty, double-crossing two-timer and I never want to see his ugly mug ever again.'

'Is that so?' A new deep voice came from up along the side verandah. 'And tell me, just how do you come to *that* conclusion?'

Bella watched as Wes scrambled down the stairs and to his ute as fast as his old legs would let him. She then turned to face Will, who by this time was leaning against the verandah pole, arms folded, taking in her general state of disarray.

'Just why am I a dirty, double-crossing two-timer? And why aren't you answering my calls?'

'Fuck off, O'Hara. Go back to your darling wife.'

'Ex-wife.'

'Whatever. Just get out of my life. Now.' Bella slammed and locked the sliding door.

It took a good ten minutes before he gave up hammering on the walls, the door, the windows, yelling at her that she'd misunderstood. He begged her to open up and at least talk about it. She missed the rest as she crawled under the doona again, hands over her ears. Finally all was quiet. She peeked out from her cocoon and heard nothing but silence.

By the next morning, Bella had semi pulled it together. She locked herself away in the house again for the morning and then spent the afternoon down by the river – anything to avoid Will. She saw his ute come by a few times; each time he paused at the gate, then drove on. Her answering machine was off and there were ten missed calls on her mobile. Then, her phones finally stopped ringing.

Good, she told herself.

So why did she feel so wretched? Why did she feel like her life had just ended? The baby kicked and then seemed to do an enormous flip, causing her to momentarily lose her balance. Okay, okay, she reconsidered, maybe her life hadn't *ended*. She clutched at her belly and smoothed her hands across the surface, soothing strokes both for herself and the baby. Fucking Prowsy.

He wasn't fucking Prowsy. Hells Bells, sometimes there's more than one explanation.

Yeah? responded Bella in her head. Well, it looked pretty self-explanatory to me. Bugger off, O'Hara.

And Bella closed her mind, her heart. It was time to shut the door on love, trust, companionship, Will . . . forever. She would concentrate on her baby. *Her* baby. As soon as her parents and Aunty Maggie came home, she would be out of here and back to Merinda.

✄

Wes called in four days later, on his way past after a trip to town.

'Here's ya mail. A postcard from the travellers in there. Looks like they're in bloody Spain. Haven't ya told your folks about the baby?'

'No. I didn't want them to worry. And, before you ask, I've sworn Justin and Melanie to secrecy too.'

'They won't be happy 'bout that.'

'They'll get over it. And don't you tell them either, Wes, or I'll let Trin know about that stash of beer you've put down near the river.'

'Hmph.' Wes cleared his thick throat. 'Prowsy's gone home.'

'I don't want to hear about the O'Haras either, Wes.' Bella was curled up on the ground trying to paint an old cradle she'd found at the op shop. It was in good nick and she was mighty proud of it.

'I mean, home to that cake place she lives at.'

'Scone?'

'Yeah, cream puff . . . sponge . . . scone? Somewhere like that.'

'Hmph.' It was Bella's turn to grunt as she found a spot she'd missed with the paintbrush.

'Word at the pub is Leyton Fowler's not what Prowsy thought

he was. Tom Lukey's brother's wife comes from that cake place where they live and they're saying Fowler's up to his ears in debt. And he's been using Prowsy's money to buy his way out of trouble.' There was no response. Wes tried again. 'Called in to see Will on the way home and he says Prowsy was out here 'cause she wanted to come back to him. Abandon that baby she's having and be Mrs O'Hara again.'

It was a long bit of gossip for Wes to share, but he felt he owed it to Maggie, to try to sort these two numbskulls out. 'Will shoved her out the door.'

'She was lying in his lap, Wes.'

That shut Wes up. Will hadn't told him that! Damn the man. Surely not? Wes tried again, 'Well, Will says nothing happened, he sent Prowsy packing and for what it's worth I believe him. Will's not a liar. But ya know what a filthy little manipulator *she* is. Maybe she saw ya, or something. Will said Nala was barking.'

Bella rocked back on her heels and finally looked up at the old man. Memories of Prowsy's smile towards the window . . .

'Will's tellin' the truth, Hells Bells. He's been desperately trying to get hold of you to explain. He's real cut up about ya and you need to know it.'

'I don't know, Wes.'

'You know, my girl, you're as stubborn and pig-headed as ya bloody aunt.' He gave a gentle smile to soften the words and touched her tentatively on the shoulder. 'Just think about it, hey?' Wes started to amble off. He'd done the best he could. Maggie be damned, it was up to the two kids now. A blast of cold wind hit his face, making him look up to the sky. 'Better batten down the hatches too. See those clouds building out to the north-west?' He flung a gnarled hand towards the mountains. 'There's some bad weather coming in pretty fast. Ya can smell it. Tomorrow's gunna be a rough one, that's for sure.'

He was right. The next day was wild. Storms blew in across the ranges. Rain and sometimes hail battered the verandahs. The wind howled at the windows, making eerie whistles as it caught and sucked its way along the eaves and under the house.

Bella ran outside mid-morning, braving the driving hail, to bring a whimpering Turbo into the warmth and safety of the lounge room. She whiled away the afternoon curled up in front of the roaring fire, reading and sleeping. And thinking.

Stubborn and pig-headed, Wes had said. The old man never wasted words he didn't mean. Deep down she knew he was right. She thought back to the conversation she had with Will the night they watched satellites track across the night sky. She'd realised then she should have heard him out in Melbourne all those years ago when he wanted to bring her home. And then there was that time on Hugh's Plain – now she'd come to know Will again, she realised that his comment that had got her all fired up that day was said in jest; it was not meant to demean her. And she'd run away without giving him a chance to fix it. And she had just done the same thing to him over Prowsy. She was like Will after Patty died – but he'd only run once whereas she'd kept on doing it. What an idiot she was. What a pig-headed idiot.

Some time later, Bella was draping some baby clothes Shelley had given her, over a clotheshorse to dry in front of the roaring fire. Turbo was running around in circles at her feet whining to be let out for a toilet stop.

'Okay, okay. I get the message,' Bella muttered to the dog, as she moved towards the door. She laughed as Turbo nearly ran head-first into the glass in his haste to get outside.

Bella walked back to the clotheshorse. Reached to straighten a jumper hanging a little awry. A sudden whoosh of water made her look down. She fought back panic. Oh hell!

❧

Will was worried about Bella. She might be a stubborn fool of a girl who wouldn't listen to a thing he tried to say, but she was still pregnant and this storm was pretty bad. Then again, she obviously wanted nothing more to with him. He thumped around his kitchen and then sat roughly on his couch as he thought about going to check on her.

He was on his feet and moving out into the night before he even knew he'd made up his mind.

❧

The rain was teeming down; huge droplets bounced at least a foot back into the air after they hit the dirt. The ground around Maggie's house had turned to a quagmire.

Will stepped onto the old verandah, dodging the gushing water streaming from the holey, rusted guttering that was weaving wildly in the wind. Thunder rumbled and spat from overhead, with only seconds between the crashes and the flashes of light splitting the sky from end to end.

Will could barely hear his own laboured breathing amid all the noise. He grabbed the handle of the sliding door and wrenched it open. He was going in whether she wanted him there or not.

Bella was draped frontwards over Maggie's old leather recliner. A beanbag was jammed between her heavy belly and the seat back. She was groaning; guttural moans coming from deep within her as she laboured over the chair.

'Bella! *Bella!* Are you all right?'

She didn't answer – couldn't even look up – as she was gripped by an almighty contraction that had her fighting for breath.

Will felt panic crash in from all sides, as his thoughts collided. She was in labour. There was a wild storm raging outside. The road to Burrindal was cut off by fallen trees – he knew because he'd tried to drive it earlier in the evening.

He saw Bella groan into the beanbag again, her whole body straining. The pain looked excruciating. He needed to do something, fast.

He used his satellite phone to ring for the emergency helicopter, only to be told the storm had moved through the whole of East Gippsland, causing accidents and mayhem. The choppers were flat-out keeping up with the demand. Even the police helicopter was way out to sea helping a yacht in trouble.

'How close is she?' asked the operator.

'How the fuck do I know?' shouted Will in frustration. 'I'm not a flamin' doctor. From what I know of cows, I'd say she's got a little way to go.'

'Well, just keep in contact with us and we'll get someone there as soon as we can.'

Bella had moved further to the ground, trying to get comfortable. Lying face-down on the beanbag balanced over a broad wooden coffee table, she writhed and moaned. Will could see it was taking its toll on her.

Bella, for her part, had tuned her out from her surroundings. She knew Will was there. Was *pleased* he was there – for her. She realised now she'd made a terrible mistake. Prowsy was more than capable of twisting a situation to suit her own ends. Wes was right: it was a matter of trust, and when it came down to it, a matter of love. And love and trust Will, she did. There was no doubt about that. No one was perfect, least of all her.

Taking a torch off the mantle, Will walked into the old hallway, floorboards creaking as they took the pressure of his weight. He headed towards the old black phone table on the far wall, slid a rickety drawer out from below the tabletop and rummaged around until he finally found what he was looking for.

Running his fingers down Maggie's teledex, he found the name and then the number he was after. Lifting up the sat phone, he dialled – heard a voice on the other end and made his request.

A nod, a yes, and Will read the numbers from the emergency coordinates up on the wall in front of the phone. Another nod, a yes, and he gently pushed a button to end the call. Putting a hand to his forehead, he pinched the wrinkled skin of his frown, thinking for a moment before he turned. Hoping he'd done the right thing.

He returned to the lounge room, to wait. To try to help Bella by rubbing her lower back as the time between the contractions grew shorter and shorter.

Whup, whup, whup.

From her place leaning over the beanbag, Bella cocked her head.

Whup, whup, whup.

A leaden feeling hit her chest and travelled down into her gut; a sense of deja vu.

Whup, whup, whup.

As it got louder, Will moved to the door to watch the helicopter materialise through the night gloom. It landed in the calf paddock beside the house, powering down from full throttle but keeping its rotor blades slowly turning while a figure climbed out through the passenger door and hurried across the grass. With the lightning and thunder now gone, Will walked out into the wet blackness, ready to meet the man as he came through the garden gate.

Another contraction kicked in. She'd known she was carrying the baby posteriorly but hadn't known the labour would all be in her back; Dr Weir hadn't mentioned that. She'd been so sure the baby had moved around the right way when it did that enormous flip the other day. But if it had, her tummy would be rhythmically contorting with pain, not convulsing alongside this excruciating backache.

And then she was gone into her own insular world, totally focused on getting through the next few minutes, breathing heavily, rocking and writhing with the pain, trying to find some relief.

'Your ride's arrived, Bella.' Will's deep voice came from somewhere near her ear.

She realised he was on his knees beside her. Then she could hear him getting up and walking around gathering pillows, blankets and her suitcase, which had been sitting half-packed in the corner of her bedroom. The pain eased and she could focus once again, eyes opening to saucers when she saw who'd arrived.

Warren stood uncomfortably just outside the sliding doorway.

'Bella.' A self-conscious nod and then a flick of his eyes, focusing somewhere over her head.

She sat back on her heels, pale-faced and exhausted. She looked up at Will, a challenging question in her eyes.

Will shrugged, his eyes soft even as his face hardened in concern for her. 'It's for the best, Bella. It'd take me at least eight hours to cut us out of here and the medivac chopper will take a while, they've got a bit on and we haven't got . . . I mean *you* haven't got that long to spare.' His voice almost pleaded for her to forgive him.

She paused for a moment, stiff and restrained, as if there were a decision to be made. It only lasted moments and then she dropped all pretence of being in control. Will moved to her side and gently lifted her into his arms and carried her towards the door.

'Grab the case, Warren. And could you belt out to the shed and flick the red stop button on the generator? Here, take this so you can see what you're doing.' Will motioned with his head to a big no-nonsense Dolphin torch sitting on the kitchen table. 'I'll put her in the chopper.'

Warren grabbed the case with his pale, soft hands and stumbled towards the shed. Opening the large stable door, he clicked off the big red button on the generator and then carried the case towards the gleaming Oxford, Bride and Associates helicopter.

As he ran to the front passenger door, he could see that Bella was belted in and Will was clipping up his own seatbelt beside her. He watched as Bella reached out to grab Will's hand. Warren then wrenched open his door, jumped into his seat, clipped up his belt and then nodded to the pilot. The helicopter powered up and slowly lifted off, to spin south and fly over the mountains; to carry its passengers through the night to the regional hospital at Narree.

Chapter 44

The two men lounged on opposite sides of the waiting room, a glass-encased cubicle outside the hospital's maternity ward.

Warren sat in his Italian wool suit, knees crossed primly, head thrown back staring at the ceiling.

Will sprawled with his denim-covered legs stretched out in front, ankles crossed where his work boots met thick cotton socks. A cream battered Akubra rested at an angle from head to chest, shading his eyes from the bright fluorescent light overhead. Their clothes had dried out thanks to the warmth in the hospital.

And Will was praying hard.

※

The doctor looked all done-in as he made his way to the doorway of the glass cubicle. It had been a bloody long day and it was now chiming eleven on his Rolex wristwatch his boyfriend had given him for his last birthday. He'd wanted to go home – but now this emergency had come in. As he got to the door of the waiting room, he took in the two men sitting before him on opposing sides of the room.

'Who's the father?' asked the doctor, trying to inject the appropriate tone of concern into his voice.

Will's hat fell to the floor as both men jumped to their feet.

'He is.' Two voices rang out in unison, the men pointing directly at each other.

The doctor looked taken aback.

As did Will.

But not Warren.

He just shrugged and slowly dropped back down into his chair. He gracefully stretched his legs and lifted his head to blink at the ceiling once again.

'What did you say?' asked Will bewildered, until a vision swam before his eyes. The sun kissing the naked girl lying in the thick native grass of an open mountain plain.

Will focused and stared hard at Warren. 'What did you say?' he asked again.

Warren continued to look vacantly at the ceiling, mute.

The doctor cleared his throat. 'Ah, well . . . It appears there's a bit of confusion?' His question hung in the air before he rushed on. 'Well . . . that's something you blokes need to sort out.' He waited a moment then added, 'If you're interested, we're about to take Isabella into surgery. We're doing a Caesarean.'

'Is she all right?'

'A Caesarean?'

Will and Warren voiced their questions simultaneously – then glared each other down.

The doctor looked from one to the other and shook his head, wishing he was gone from this place, longing for his bed.

'She's doing okay, but it has to be an emergency Caesarean. Little one's stuck trying to turn around for the entry into the birth canal. Lucky you got her here, that's for sure.'

'Can I see her before she goes in?' asked Will, picking up his hat and moving it distractedly through his hands. His mind was dashing in so many directions, trying to make some sense of it all.

'Ah yes, well, once you've sorted things out . . .' The doctor's hands waved between Will and Warren '. . . you can see her.' He waited a moment then decided to say what was on his mind. What he felt, under the circumstances, he *had* to say.

'Best work out who the father is first. I don't want my patient upset. It's a major operation she's facing, you know, and she's fragile, so don't bugger her around.'

Abruptly the doctor turned, making his way back into the operating theatre. He pondered over the little ruckus. If he were a betting man he'd back the flannelette shirt and Wranglers over the Italian suit. A Wrangler-clad butt always did it for him.

Will sat down in the hard chair and glared across at Warren, who sat up and glared right back.

'The baby's yours, you know. Well, I'm guessing that's the case. You're the only other possible contender,' said Warren, finally turning his head away, back up towards the roof. But not before Will glimpsed a glassy pool of tears held firmly in check within bloodshot eyes.

'Mine?'

'Yours,' confirmed Warren. 'I can't have kids. I've had a vasectomy.' He slowly got to his feet. 'I guess that's it then. I'll be off.'

Will sat motionless. 'Mine?' he said almost to himself. 'Are you sure? Not that it matters. I love her, you know.'

'About ninety-five per cent sure, and yes, I do know,' said Warren, now standing in front of his adversary. 'Good luck.' His head dipped again as the tears threatened to spill.

Will pulled himself together and stood. 'You won't stay and see her afterwards . . . I mean *them*?' he asked.

'Well, I don't think that's really appropriate considering the circumstances.' Warren gave a half-smile and cocked his head. 'In my world it's the father's privilege to be the first to see his child . . . and its mother, of course.'

Will slowly nodded his head.

Warren turned towards the door, the lift within his sights.

'Warren? Thanks, mate. For the helicopter, for the flight, for tonight, for all this . . .' Will flailed his hands around uselessly, not really knowing what he was trying to say.

'Not a problem, old chap, and glad we could help.' The words were stilted as Warren stared straight ahead. At the lift he called back down the passage, 'Just look after them,' before turning away.

Will nodded, then watched as Warren walked into the lift and out of their lives. He paused for just a moment then headed towards the room where they were preparing Bella for the operation.

Why hadn't she told him he was the baby's father?

He swung through the doors just in time to see Bella being helped onto a gurney. Her face lit up at the sight of him.

'Will!' she called across the room.

Why *the fuck* hadn't she *told* him? He could have helped her more, been more involved.

He strode towards her, his anger compelling him on. 'Am I the baby's father, Bella?' He took hold of her arm. 'Am I?'

She nodded once. Then a contraction hit her hard. She gasped and the nurse pushed Will aside, trying to help Bella through the pain.

Another nurse came barging through the doors that led to the operating suite. 'We have to get her into theatre.'

'Bella. Bella! Why didn't you *tell* me?' Will called as the gurney started to move towards the door. He needed to know, to understand.

'You said you didn't want children,' she gasped. 'Said you didn't want to take the chance of losing someone you loved again.'

The night of their dinner together. Months ago. Probably before she even knew she was pregnant. Will groaned.

Bella closed her eyes and allowed the nurses to wheel her away.

❧

Any anger Will felt at Bella for keeping the truth from him melted away as he walked into the single hospital room a while later, the only one with the softly glowing light. Bella lay tucked into a white hospital bed, a pink nightie softly framing her face. Her hair was lank and clumped high on her forehead, her face as white as the pillow. The stunning lapis eyes were surrounded by dark purple rings. But she looked happy, content, beautiful.

Tucked into her other side was a pink flannelette bundle. A tiny, fleshy arm had found its way outside the soft rug.

Will pulled up beside the bed, looking across at his daughter. Bella glanced up at him while her baby remained attached to a bared breast, little cheeks chugging away every now and then.

'Hello,' said Will with a gentle grin.

'Hello.' Bella's return smile was dazzling. 'Isn't she beautiful?' she said, as she looked down at her daughter.

'She certainly is,' said Will with reverence, his deep voice causing a pert little rosebud mouth to pop off the nipple and turn towards her father.

'And so are you.' He leaned in and kissed the mother of his child firmly on the lips.

She looked into his eyes as he pulled away. 'And so now you know.'

'I know,' he confirmed as he sat gently on the side of the bed. 'I still can't believe you didn't tell me. I know I said I didn't want kids, but I didn't really mean it.'

'Yes, you did.'

'Well, yes, at the time, I probably did. But I've changed my mind – *you* changed my mind. Sometimes these things happen for a reason, and I guess this is one of those times. You should've told me, Hells Bells. I could have done more, helped you—'

Bella broke in. 'I didn't want you to feel trapped. And, selfishly, this was something I had to do by myself. After I left Melbourne I needed to work out who I was and what I wanted. Where I fit in. And this little one has helped me do that. And really, it was hardly your fault. I was just there, that day, waiting for you.'

'You were sure it was going to be me?'

'Yes. I knew you'd be the one. I must have unconsciously known then that things weren't over between us. There were still things to be done.'

'Things to be done, all right,' said Will as he gently took his proffered daughter into his arms. 'I'd say we've done them pretty well, too. What do you reckon, little one?'

Bella looked at the man who was so much a part of her life and wondered how they managed to waste the last eight years.

But it wasn't a waste, said the voice in her head. *You wouldn't be the people you are now unless you'd done what you did.*

Yes, but we would have been married and on our third child if we'd just got our shit together earlier, Bella replied silently. There'd have been no Warrens or Prowsys to bugger up our lives. And all our babies would have been as gorgeous as this one.

Warren didn't bugger up your life. You made choices, girlfriend, and have to take some responsibility too. And Prowsy? Well, men are men and they have an itch that needs to be scratched. Even my brother.

Bella knew Patty was right. She was as much to blame as Warren for the failure of *that* relationship. Never again would she lose touch with herself and what it meant to be surrounded by those she loved. And Prowsy? She could have a nice life far away, baking cakes in Scone.

Bella smiled as she watched her daughter cast a special kind of magic over the father who held her within his arms.

'I love you, Bella,' said Will, looking straight into her eyes. 'What you saw in that window . . . it wasn't what you thought. Nothing happened. There's no-one else I want but you. Since the day you nearly ran me down in Queensland, there's been no-one else for me but you.'

Bella was shocked at the vulnerability in his eyes. And in that moment she realised only she and their daughter were at the centre of his universe.

'I believe you, Will.'

'Thank God,' he said. He quickly looked back down at his daughter, cupping her fingers with his own. But not before Bella saw the tears come into his eyes. She reached up and wiped one away.

'I'm sorry I've been so pig-headed,' she whispered. 'Wes told me that, and he was right. I've never given you a chance to explain. Not in Melbourne, not at Hugh's Plain, not with Prowsy. I've just run a million miles in the opposite direction, assuming all kinds of things.'

Will nodded before looking up. 'Probably . . . but I'm guilty too. I just jammed my running into months rather than years. I still love you, regardless.'

'You're a bit of all right too, you know.' Bella's voice was teasing.

'Only *a bit* of all right?'

'Well, maybe a *big* bit.'

'Does that big bit have any love in it?'

'Maybe a bit.'

'Only a bit?'

'Maybe a *big bit.*'

Will leaned over his daughter's head again and stared deeply into Bella's eyes, his gaze holding a challenge.

'Okay. Okay. You win. I love you too, my darling man.' She tapped him on the nose. 'Now give me back my daughter. I'm supposed to be trying to feed her, even though my bloody milk hasn't come in.'

'What are we going to call her?' said Will, passing his little girl to her mother.

Bella paused for a minute, before lifting her hand to caress the tinge of red down on top of the baby's head.

'I was thinking Sophie. Sophie Patricia O'Hara.'

Will smiled at his tiny daughter. 'Perfect.'

Epilogue

Three years later

Will O'Hara drove the four-wheel drive through the farm gate that passed as a check-in for the Nunkeri Muster. After paying their dues and passing the time of day with the blokes manning the gate, the family wended their way along the track beside the creek.

To the right-hand side of the track, flash off-road camper trailers, caravans and horse-movers were scattered across the plain; mixed among these were utes with tarps attached and held up with anything from sawn-off tree limbs to electric fence posts. Swags littered the ground in all directions.

'I wonder who had a dawn dash this morning?' Bella's eyes twinkled at Will.

Will grinned and Bella could see that memories of another time were on his mind.

Strapped in her seat, Sophie squealed excitedly, returning them both to the moment. 'See horseys, Mummy . . . horseys!'

'Yes, sweetheart. Hang on a minute and we can go have a look.'

Sophie started to chant. 'Horseys, horseys, I see the horseys!' Her little brother Matt tried to join in, 'Ga, Ga, orss.'

Will looked at Bella, who had turned and was gazing at both her children with a mixture of exasperation and adoration. How could he have once thought he didn't want this? He loved them all, so much that he thought his heart would burst. He could hardly believe he and Bella were here, back where it all started.

Finally they found a place to park the twin-cab ute. After helping the children from the car, they walked together towards the huge crowd gathered around the marquee in the distance – Bella carrying Matt, and Will toting Sophie.

They passed the remnants of a massive bonfire lying in the middle of the plain, witness to a celebration held the night before. Country music blared from the big speakers. Horses cantered past, warming up for the Stockmen's Challenge.

They heard the distinctive sound of two whips cracking. Near the marquee a young woman stood in the middle of a circle, enthralling the audience with her whip-cracking display. Trains clacking across railway tracks, windscreen wipers, whip passes to the front and back, were all on show with breathtaking speed and style. Bella knew it took hours and hours to get that good at cracking one whip, let alone two. She was mesmerised.

Will leaned across his son's head and whispered to Bella, 'I dare you to!'

Startled, Bella shot him a look, amazed that he could read her so well.

But Sophie couldn't be held any longer. In her little brown leather elastic-sided boots, cowgirl shirt and tiny Wrangler jeans, she was having no more. Pushing her legs straight and twisting to the ground, Will was forced to put her down.

'Daddy, I want to see the horseys *now*.' A stomp of a size-six boot followed, and then a moment or two later, a very small, '*Please?*'

Bella and Will each took a hand of their gorgeous little girl. Auburn hair that twisted into corkscrew 'kissing curls' at the first touch of damp accompanied a flawless complexion and cornflower-blue eyes; a winning, toothy white smile touched by twin dimples on each side of her mouth – at three, Sophie was already breathtaking. There were those who said she resembled the late Patty O'Hara. Others said that apart from the colour of her hair, she was a dead ringer for her mother.

And then there was one-year-old Mattie, who was already showing signs of being a little devil. As he was hoisted up to his father's hip, little legs dangling, he was spellbound by all the action on the plain. His dark brown eyes never missed a trick.

The genes worked, guys! Bella could still hear Patty sometimes. Every now and then, her friend's voice rang clear and true in her head.

The loudspeakers announced it was time for the Stockman's Challenge. The four of them wandered over to the strings of flags marking the start of the course. Will kneeled down and plonked Sophie on one knee and Mattie on the other.

'Now, Sophie, you have to stay here, okay? On my lap, and then you'll see all those horseys over there come thundering down straight in front of us.'

Sophie nodded seriously, her gaze immediately taken by

the big horses lunging about the start area of the track to their left. Bella, standing behind them, was also watching the finest of bush riders prepare to start the race of the year. The horses lined up.

'But, Daddy, they're going the wrong way! Didn't you say they were going past us? Daddy?'

At that moment the loudspeaker beside them squawked, '*Go!*'

The horses and their riders spun on the spot, turning about-face and into an immediate canter then gallop. They thundered down the track towards them. Sophie shrunk back into the safe folds of her father's shirt. Mattie was oblivious to the danger, leaning as far out from his father's arms as he could.

Momentarily distracted from the showy start of the race by Sophie's piping voice, Bella gazed down at her family. She would have loved to be down there with Sophie, cuddling into the muscular, broad chest of that caring, wonderful man.

Will looked up at Bella and caught the end of her sigh into the damp mountain air. His pupils dilated, eyes darkened and he quietly groaned as he read her thoughts. He winked wickedly. 'Hold that thought for later, cowgirl.'

Bella blushed, then grinned. 'You're on a promise.'

Then the horses were upon them.

'*Go*, horseys!' Sophie was in her element.

The crowd yelled with her, cheering on the riders and their horses as they raced at breakneck speed up the hill, then down across the flat, through the creek and up out of sight. Moments later they were back, down through the creek again, another run across the scrub-laden flat, up into the surrounding bush, dodging massive gum trees strewn in their path. Disappearing again around a bend. Minutes ticked by, the crowd rumbled with anticipation and then Sophie cried, 'Daddy! Horseys again!'

The crowd went berserk. The horses thundered down the hill, slipping, sliding, riders hanging on for dear life. Scrambling to catch their feet as they hit the bottom, the horses and their riders hit the long straight for home. The moment of truth had arrived.

Who would be this year's winner of the Stockmen's Challenge?

As the horses flashed across the finish line, Isabella Vermaelon O'Hara knew she really didn't care. She was just happy to be here. She watched her little daughter going crazy in her father's arms.

'Did you see *that*, Mummy? Can we go see the horseys?' Sophie was twisting her way free of Will's arms once more in her eagerness to watch her beloved horses parade past in a winner's lap of honour.

Will took in the tears in his wife's eyes. 'Are you okay?'

Bella shook her head.

'Hmm. Now why is that?' Will queried as he put down a struggling Mattie and stood up.

Bella shook her head again.

Putting his comforting, warm arms around her, he said, 'Come on, Hells Bells, you're scaring me.' He looked apprehensive.

Bella smiled at the man who breathed joy into every day of her life. He was her lover and her best mate. They had the world in front of them. A life filled with farming, laughing, loving.

'I love you, Will. You are *so* good for me.'

'I love you too, cowgirl, but why the tears?'

'Just happy, I guess.'

'You've got a funny way of showing it.'

Bella nodded and snuggled in close. Will could barely hear her as she spoke into his chest. 'We wasted so many years. But we wouldn't have been right for each other back then. Before Patty died — before Warren and Prowsy. I think we needed to take the long way so we could become the people we are now.'

Will stared off into the distance, thinking. 'Yeah, probably.'

Bella's voice suddenly became stronger. 'You know what, though?'

'What?'

'Being back here, we've finally made it home.'

'Yep, I think you're right.' Will lowered his head and kissed his wife with love and satisfaction.

'You know, sometimes I hear her . . .' Bella said sometime later. She cleared her throat. She'd never said this aloud.

'You hear who? Sophie?'

'No. Patty. I hear her talking in my mind.'

'Yeah, I used to as well.'

Bella looked at Will in surprise.

'I mean, you know realistically it's just your imagination. Your own thoughts or conscience talking,' explained Will, looking uncomfortable. 'I don't hear her anymore, but when I did, it was comforting to have her voice in my head, second-guessing my choices. She always was a bloody know-it-all.'

Bella smiled, remembering.

'You sure you're okay?' Will raised an eyebrow.

'Yeah. I know it's my imagination, but still . . .' She trailed off, looking across the plain towards the massive mountain ranges surrounding them. Her eyes were wistful as she took in the magnificence and splendour of the place.

Imagination, my arse! Pah, what do brothers know? You're not going to be rid of me that easy, Hells Bells!

Bella smiled to herself. She didn't want to be rid of Patty. Ever.

She'll be driving six white horses when she comes . . . YEE HA!

Acknowledgements

A novel is a huge undertaking, particularly the first. I'd like to thank my agent, Sheila Drummond, for her work and support. Also, Random House Australia for making this dream a reality, particularly my publisher Beverley Cousins for her enthusiasm, guidance, expertise, and for loving *Bella's Run* as much as I do, and Claire de Medici for her incisive editorial suggestions.

Appreciation also goes to Dr Jonathon Ruddle for his persistence and care, Michelle and Rob Bradshaw for the place of inspiration and Mark Coleman for his advice. Diana Hurley – your whip-cracking skills are legendary – thank you. And for a scene or two, I raise my glass to Kevin, Sallie and family and the Bald Hills.

For their love and support over the years, a huge thank you goes to Sue and Wayne; Linda; Kaylene and Gary; Ross and Miriam; Kylie; Helen and Paul; Karen and Richard; Leonne and John; Debbi; Carol (my reader) and Barrie; Coral; Erlina;

Petra and Russell. Gratitude also to Heather and Sue for all things country; Clare for Queensland; Michelle for remembering what I forget; and Kenielle for her superb horsemanship and practicality. You are all the best mates.

Appreciation to the lovely Sara Storer, Carmel Iudica and Donna for your assistance; Rebecca Faltyn for my page in the *Gippsland Country Life*; Chris Manning for your loving care; and our marvellous Helen for making sure the house stays in some sort of order.

While it was up to me to write the novel, it takes certain wonderful friends to help anchor you. *Bella's Run* wouldn't be here without Emma and Buck Williamson (and their ute!); Jenny and Dot Green; Sandra and Doug Dekkers; Carmel Kuizenga (and my beautiful Alice); the Killeen family - darling Andrea for sharing the rollercoaster ride, thanks girl; and the Beveridge family for Christmases at Nunniong; especially to Pam for her support and love, and Mal for answering *so* many questions, brumby hunting and taking us to 'where no man has been before'.

I also offer thanks to the Victorian Writers Centre, in particular Sallie Muirden and Andrea Goldsmith for teaching me so much, and to the Little Lonsdale Writers Group – I am privileged to be among you. Credit to Kath Ledson – your passion abounds – and also to Sherree, Lisa and Jane: thank you for sharing the ride.

To my friend and critique partner Kate Rizzetti, your support in helping me get this novel over the line is much appreciated. Cheers to my long-time friend and road-trip partner Rachael Treasure, who encouraged me to 'make and shake' this dream alive. And to Fleur McDonald, who set down the challenge and held my hand while I completed it,

I thank God for bringing you into my life. Credit also to Kim Wilkins and Bronwyn Parry for their advice and Fiona Palmer for her enthusiasm.

For all things medical, thanks go to my talented sisters-in-law, Anne and Trish. To my other medico – you know who you are – I also offer my sincere appreciation. Any errors made are entirely mine.

Thanks to my great aunt, Margaret Caffrey, for her interest, friendship and love – you have taught me so much – and to my uncle, Graeme Osborn, for the serene peace of the homestead to write and for always being there.

To the rest of my family, immediate and extended, heartfelt gratitude for your love, support and for putting up with me. In particular, appreciation to Pat for helping with the children and to my sister, Kerry Wadey, for giving me feedback and advice when I needed it.

To my wonderful father, John, your love and support over the years has far exceeded anything a child should expect. Thanks, Dad, for *everything* – it's incredible how such a simple word should be expected to convey so much.

To my beautiful children: Brent, one of my biggest supporters, thank you for being a great mate, for the drives in the ute (all thousands of miles of them) and the book covers, which helped make it so real. Callan – my farming inventor – your gentle love and hugs just thrum through my heart. And to Katie – my gorgeous little princess – you are the bright, shining light in all our lives.

To my darling husband, Hugh. You are the rock amid my ocean, the calm among the storm. I couldn't have achieved this dream without your whole-hearted love and support. We've done this together. Thank you, hon.

If you enjoyed BELLA'S RUN, look out for Margareta's new novel

HOPE'S ROAD

In the rugged and beautiful high country of East Gippsland, Hope's Road connects three very different properties, and three very different lives . . .

Sixty years ago, heartbroken and betrayed, old Joe McCauley turned his back on his family and their fifth-generation farm, Montmorency Downs. He now spends his days as a recluse, spying upon the land – and the granddaughter – that should by rights have been his.

For Tammy McCauley, Montmorency Downs is the last remaining tie to her family. But land can make or break you – and, with her husband's latest treachery, how long can she hold on to it?

Wild-dog trapper, Travis Hunter, is struggling as a single dad, unable to give his son, Billy, the thing he craves most. A complete family.

Then, out of the blue, a terrible event forces the three neighbours to confront each other – and the mistakes of their past . . .

Read on for an extract . . .

MARGARETA OSBORN

THE NO.1 BESTSELLING AUTHOR

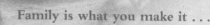

Family is what you make it . . .

Hope's Road

Hope's Road

MARGARETA OSBORN

Prologue

The girl clambered through the boundary fence. Spindly arms, matchstick legs, long brown hair flying in bits across a grubby face. Her clothes were getting caught on the razor-sharp barbed wire. He could see her little body twisting this way then that, trying to unsnag herself. She was a determined little devil. Would she be game enough to set foot on the place?

Others had come before her: sneaky little bastards trying to get the better of him. They'd come on good days and he'd only shot at the air above their heads.

Today? Well, this day was different. He was mad. Wild crazy off his head.

That morning, Mae Rouget, gliding down the main street of Narree. Immaculately dressed, beautiful as ever – every inch the princess who should've been his. The woman who had remained in his dreams for years . . .

Joe took another look in the gun scope at the boundary. The girl had made it through the wire and now was standing looking up at his hill, one hand on her dirty brow, another on a slight hip. She was dressed in buttery yellow shorts and a mud-coloured top that he guessed had once been white. The sleeves of the shirt were torn and decorated with splatters of ruby-red. The barbed wire had obviously cut a bit deep, although it hadn't stopped her from getting through. She was a McCauley: that was for sure.

Joe contemplated her a minute longer, made a decision and started to sneak down the slope through the scrub using a track barely discernable to the eye. As he snuck along the path that hugged the boundary fence, tall box and ironbark trees with their thick, crusty trunks stood sentinel in the adjoining state forest.

He swung inland, creeping past massive red gums that stretched resplendent limbs to capture air and sky. Centuries old, they had seen their fair share of hard times, just like the elderly man sidling under them. The scattered eucalypts then gave way to dense burgan and black wattle scrub, determined in its effort to claim this eastern side of the hill. The thick bushes, with their understorey of bracken fern, hid him from anyone looking up. As he rounded a blind corner he startled a grazing wallaby, sending it on an erratic escape, bounding back towards the scrub that surrounded his property on three sides – this rocky, dry hill with its miserable soil. The place he called home.

It took him a good five minutes to reach the bottom of McCauley's Hill, but there she was. She hadn't moved: still stood standing like she was contemplating what to do next. A Jack Russell ran around at her feet, nose to the ground, the scent of rabbit probably wafting from the burrows threaded through his gravelly mountain. She couldn't have been any older than five or six. It was the granddaughter.

He pulled up his gun. 'Get the hell off my farm, you land-grabbing little fucker!'

Chapter 1

The currawong's cry floated on the wisp of a breeze into the dairy. Tamara McCauley hauled down on the milking machine, urging the final milk to keep flowing into the cups attached to the cow's teats. With the new run-off property to pay for, she needed every drop she could get.

'Whoot, whoot weee-ow,' the pied currawong called again. Piercingly, this time.

It was going to rain. The bird was an infallible storm predictor. And she'd just ordered irrigation water, damn it. This would send Shon over the edge. Tammy shivered and automatically fingered her left eye. The bruise was turning a light bluish-purple colour.

The marriage was over, of that much she was sure. She was going to kick him out, however frightened she was of the confrontation.

Tammy pulled off the teat cups, let the platform of cows go

and followed them out to a nearby paddock to latch the gate. Gravel crunched on the driveway and she looked up to spy a small white car sitting beside the mail-drum at the entrance to the farm. Lucy. Just finished her night shift, no doubt. She would want a cuppa and some toast before heading home to bed. Of course that was after she'd finished rubbing the prodigious stomach of the Buddha sitting hidden in the grass beside the old gatepost. Wealth and good fortune was supposed to be the reward for such loving care and Lucy couldn't go past the old fella without stopping and giving him a tickle. Tammy wasn't sure what the forty-year-old nurse was wishing for though. To Tammy's mind her friend had it all – a lovely quaint cottage painted a delicate shade of lavender, a lazy tabby cat for company and a nice pot-belly stove to keep her warm.

Not like the homestead here, which was a cold, dark place most of the time. Heavy antique furniture guarded a century of memories and, when Shon was around, the place was filled with tension and anger. They had a cat somewhere too but it knew to stay out of the way.

Tammy started to trudge back towards the dairy, her gumboots flipping and flapping against her slim legs. She wished so hard for a life filled with love and family again. After her grandparents had died eight years earlier it had seemed like all the light and energy had disappeared. The only family she had left was her husband, a man who was currently stomping on their marriage as though it was dog shit. The only man in the family left standing.

Well – that wasn't *entirely* true. Her eyes flicked up towards the mountain partially shrouding the farm in its early-morning shadow. So deep was the cleft at the base of the mount, the sun hadn't yet penetrated that part of its eastern face. Shadows left a deep scar at the bottom of the rising bush, a black space like a roaring monster's mouth, warning all and sundry not to enter. Tammy stifled a shudder. Well, that was a pretty apt representation of old Joe McCauley, the man who owned the mountain.

A smudge of smoke wafted lazily through the crisp air, probably from Joe's chimney. Tammy squinted: if she looked hard enough there were actually two wisps of smoke up there on McCauley's Hill. The one to the south came from Travis Hunter's; he was the new wild-dog trapper, moved in six months back. The plume to the north was old Joe's, and by the size of it his fire was burning well this morning, which meant Joe himself was up and about. She really shouldn't have to tell whether her great-uncle was alive and kicking from a curl of smoke, but that was life here in the Narree Valley – life for the remaining McCauleys at least. Some disagreement between him and Tammy's grandfather had led to this point. He was her only relation but he hadn't spoken to her since she was a small kid, and that had been to swear at her for trespassing.

She was only six at the time. Had gone home repeating the word he'd used – had seemed to take such delight in. 'Fucker. Fucker.' Rolling it around her tongue until she got the inflection right. She'd sounded just like him – that crazy old man! She'd yelled it at Jack the dog, when he took off after a rabbit, and stood there, proud of herself. She hadn't known her grandfather was coming up behind her with a bowl of dog food.

The Tabasco sauce her grandparents had put on her tongue that night for saying such a word had burned like heck. They hadn't asked her where she'd heard it, which was just as well because she would have had to lie. Even back then she sensed it wasn't good to talk about the man who had a face like her grandfather's but was never mentioned by name.

As Tammy walked, she gazed out beyond her farm towards the Great Dividing Range guarding this little hamlet in Gippsland from the rest of the world. She sighed. Montmorency Downs, her family property, went back five generations. A place inexplicably linked to her by blood, dirt and, once upon a time, by love. At the moment she wished she were a long way away.

Her eyes drifted back to the gateway and the little white car. Lucy was still rubbing the old guy's tummy. Putting two fingers to the roof of her mouth, Tammy let out an ear-piercing whistle. Lucy stood up and waved, then moved towards her vehicle.

Shon had given her the concrete cast of the Buddha one Christmas a couple of years back. A backhanded slap at his wife's Catholic roots, she guessed. A wife who, he'd stated the night before, was worthless and useless.

'I feel nothing for you. Nothing, ya hear me! You're a frigid bitch of a thing; I wish I'd never laid eyes on ya.' Shon's ruddy face had pulsed with fury. Purple veins stood out on his temples as he pinned her down on the ground with his knee in her chest. 'Give me those bloody keys. I'm going.'

'You're not getting them. You can't leave for the weekend. I need you here!'

She may as well have spoken to the Buddha. Shon ignored her then just like he'd ignored everything she'd said for the last few years.

'Give me them fuckin' keys!' He was unrelenting, sitting his solid weight on her thrashing legs, pulling at her arms, ruthlessly digging the car keys out of her hand. 'Where's that big almighty God of yours now?' he taunted, with one last jab into her chest with his knee. He got up, victorious, keys dangling in his hand. 'Fuckin' pissed him off too, I'll bet.'

The disgust on his face as he looked down at her was enough.

She'd lain on the ground, trying to not show fear or how much she hurt. Trying not to give him the satisfaction. But he knew. His triumphant smile told her he had her right where he wanted her. Way down low – as low as her self-esteem could go. Oh yes, Mr Shon Murphy was all-powerful, wearing king's clothes last night. And she, Tammy McCauley Murphy, was the doormat he could wipe his boots on whenever he felt like it. Well, she'd show him. My oath she would. Enough was enough.

'Gidday!'

Tammy hadn't heard the car reach the yard.

'What's up your gander this fine morning?' asked Lucy as she emerged. 'Your face looks like it's swallowed a lemon.'

Tammy shook her head, tried to stop her hands from trembling. 'The only lemon around here is that Ford you're driving.' She dodged as her friend threw a fake punch with mittened fists.

'You better watch out, woman, or one day you'll feel the end of my glove up close and personal. I'm doing boxercise, did I tell you?'

Tammy rolled her eyes. 'Last week it was Zumba, this week it's boxing. What's next week? Pole dancing? When the hell are you going to stick to one form of exercise, Luce?'

'As soon as I get rid of this spare tyre I've been lugging around.' Lucy grabbed at her middle and pinched at a roll beneath her tasselled jumper. 'Variety is the spice of life. I can't get it from this diet I'm on or from a bloke, so I've only got exercise left. I just have to find something that suits me. That goes for both physical activity *and* men.' Lucy's smiling face suddenly turned thoughtful. She wrinkled her nose, causing the tiny stud clinging to the side of it to glint in the sun. 'Mmmm . . . pole dancing? Now why didn't I think of that?'

'Forget I said it. Boxercise sounds fine.'

'Oh, you can talk – you tiny little thing. Metabolisms like yours make me sick. I swear you could live on chips and cakes for a whole month and you wouldn't put on a kilo. Not fair, Mrs Murphy, not fair at all.'

Tammy scowled. She didn't want to hear that surname this morning. 'It's Ms McCauley to you, you insolent witch.' She tried to smile to take the sting from her words. It nearly worked. The thought of Lucy pole dancing was what did it. Those short stocky legs, entwined around a stainless-steel pole.

'C'mon, woman, you might get some toast if you're lucky. You need feeding up, with everything you've got going on in your life.'

Tammy started to turn and walk towards the house. It was right about then that Lucy noticed her limp.

Bugger.

She grabbed at Tammy's arm, spun her around. 'What happened to you?' She wasn't playing any more; the look in her eyes was serious.

'A cow kicked me this morning while I was bringing her into the cow-yard. It's nothing.'

Lucy leaned in and took a closer look at Tammy's face. 'And what about this? How'd the cow kick you up there?' A soft hand cupped Tammy's chin and turned her face into the light. 'That *fucking bastard*! He's bloody well gone and done it this time. He's hit you, hasn't he?'

'It's nothing, I said.'

'Like hell it's nothing. He can't do this to you, Tim Tam.'

The pet name her grandpa gave her when she was little.

'He can't do this,' Lucy repeated. Her fingers reached out to probe around Tammy's left eye.

Tammy quickly moved her face away. 'Let's just go and get some toast, okay?' And she turned towards the homestead, long unsteady strides covering the distance to the sprawling, mocha-coloured brick house. Moving fast. She could hear Lucy huffing and puffing behind her, and knew she should wait, or at least slow down and let her long-time friend catch up. But she also suspected that if she did – if she turned her face towards her – that would be the end. The thing that would finally break Tammy down into tiny pieces. And she couldn't afford that. Not at thirty-six. She'd already broken and repaired herself once – after her grandparents died. She was frightened she wouldn't have the energy to do it all over again.

So she put her head down and kept walking.

A BUSH CHRISTMAS
A festive novella

by Margareta Osborn

Jaime Hanrahan does not want anything to do Christmas this year.

She's just been retrenched, and if that wasn't bad enough, this is her first Christmas without her beloved father Jack, who died last Boxing Day.

Determined not to spend it with her mother, who has already remarried, and her friends, who *still* have six-figure jobs, she jumps at the chance to house-sit a mansion in rural Burdekin's Gap.

Two problems . . .

Number one, the property comes with a handsome station manager, Jase Stirling, who doesn't take kindly to a city chick destroying his peace. Especially when she needs rescuing from stampeding cattle, falling Christmas trees and town ladies wielding catering lists and tablecloths.

And two, in Burdekin's Gap there's no chance of escaping the festive season. For the town has its own unique way of celebrating Christmas – big time, BUSH style!

Available as an ebook only

Loved the book?